Pride and Joy: Book 2

Books by Robert Winter

Pride and Joy series

September

Asylum

Nights at Mata Hari series

Every Breath You Take

Lying Eyes

Vampire Claus

Discover more about the author online:

Robert Winter

Pride and Joy: Book 2

BY ROBERT WINTER

Best wishes!
Robert Winter

A Publication from Robert Winter Books
www.robertwinterauthor.com

First Publication March 2018 v. 1.0
Print Edition

ISBN-13: 978-1948883016 (Robert Winter Books)
Printed in the United States of America

Author's Note

By some estimates, the United States hosts more than eleven million men, women and children who entered the country without authorization, or remained once their authorization expired. The reasons they come and stay are individual and complex, but I believe there are common threads. They come to escape violence, persecution, poverty or hopelessness; their journeys are perilous; they live under a perpetual threat of discovery and deportation; and they would become citizens if they could.

I based Hernán's past on the specific experiences of two young men who came to the United States without visas, and the things they endured. Certain details and locations have been altered or fictionalized, but the core of their journeys—as related by Hernán—is a combination of two true stories.

Most of Hernán's journey to the U.S.—except for what happens to him in chapters 16 and 19—comes from the experiences of my friend Elías. He spent hours with me to explain what it was like to grow up in El Salvador, knowing he was gay but unable to tell anyone. He feared he was targeted by a gang, was actually stabbed, and ran for his life. Ultimately, he achieved asylum, and now he is a citizen of the United States with aspirations of some day running for office.

If Hernán's story—so much of which is Elías' story—illuminates what might drive a person to risk everything to come to a country where he or she will be treated like a criminal just because of a lack of a proper visa, then I have succeeded. I may upset people by writing a main character who is a person of color. To that, I plead only that I made every effort to strike a balance between respect of Latin culture and Elías' experiences. Sensitivity readers have pointed out where I was blind to my own privilege, and I've made adjustments where I could while remaining true to the essence of Elías' journey.

In the end, if I've caused offense, all I can do is apologize and hope for your forgiveness

Two notes about the text. First, several of my characters speak

Spanish. Because Hernán is from El Salvador, I've tried to give him regionally-appropriate phrases to speak, such as "bicha" instead of "chica". My beta readers have helped my Spanish where they could; any remaining errors are entirely mine.

Second, conventional style manuals usually dictate that non-English words should be italicized, at least at their first use. One of my sensitivity readers persuaded me that italicizing a word just because it is not in English emphasizes its otherness. For that reason, I chose to italicize words in Spanish only for emphasis, that same way I would for English words. Where a character has dialogue in Spanish, I chose to signal that by surrounding the words with double chevrons rather than quotation marks.

Dedication

To Elías Flamenco,
whose courage and willingness to share his story inspired
Hernán's journey.

Chapter 1

A MAN SILHOUETTED in moonlight teetered drunkenly at the end of the pier. Crying out, his legs flew up, and his body disappeared from sight. Hernán was running toward the water's edge before he even heard the splash. Rejecting thoughts about how cold the water would be, he threw himself into Provincetown Harbor.

Even though the mid-September weather was mild, his hands and face numbed quickly in the chilly water. He thrust himself to the surface.

"¡Mierda!" he shouted, tossing hair out of his eyes as he sought out the man who had fallen.

There he was. About ten feet away, the man thrashed and then went down. Hernán swam over with strong strokes, dove under and wrapped his arms around from behind. He tugged the flailing man to the surface, nearly receiving a black eye for his troubles.

"Cálmese," he shouted, and then added in English, "I've got you. Stop hitting!"

The man went limp. Hernán hooked his waist more securely with one arm, and with the other swam them both toward the boat launch ramp about twenty yards away. The weight of their waterlogged clothes threatened to drag them down. The stranger gasped, but Hernán kept paddling with one hand, kicking hard, drawing closer to the ramp. Water slapping against the seawall shoved back on Hernán, swirling around his jeans and sweatshirt as it tried to pull away the man he held.

He tightened his grip and maneuvered them both through the water until he found the concrete of the ramp. Once his feet were underneath him, he heaved the man forward and to safety. They collapsed on the wet slope. The man ended up on his ass with his hands across his chest while Hernán rested on hands and knees, panting as water splashed over his ankles. When he had his breath again, he shuffled further up the ramp and away from the harbor.

"What happened?" the man slurred. He looked up at the night sky, and then rolled his head toward Hernán, shadowed eyes difficult to read. In the uncertain glow from a few light poles, it was impossible to be certain of age, but the man didn't look more than a few years older than Hernán. He wore leather shoes, khaki pants, a blue woolen sweater over a white button-down shirt, and a yellow bowtie. Seawater dripped from his dark hair and across his pale face, catching the moon and shining silver light around his head.

"You fell, hombre," Hernán told him. "Didn't look like you meant to go for a swim."

The man blinked dazedly as he processed the words. Finally he shook his head. "Nope. Din't wanna swim." Shivering a little, he suddenly levered himself to a sitting position. He craned his head around, clearly confused.

Hernán climbed to his feet and held out a hand. "We need to get dry," he said. "It's not too cold tonight but this isn't exactly comforta-ble."

The man focused on Hernán then. Some awareness returned to his face, yet he made no move to take the proffered hand. "I fell in the water?" he asked.

"Sí. Well, fell or jumped. ¡Dios mío!" Hernán exclaimed. "You didn't jump, did you?"

The man tilted his head back to look at the moon, weight on his arms, hands propped behind him. A definitive shake of the head, and he spoke again. "No, I din't jump. Too much to drink, so I think I took a walk t' sober up."

Despite his heavy, dripping clothes and the slight quaking in his limbs from the combination of adrenalin and effort, Hernán had to laugh. "I bet you're getting sober now. And colder. Come on, stand up." He again held out his hand, his tennis shoes squelching as he braced himself. This time the wet stranger took it, his grip stronger than Hernán would have expected as he rose.

He was slender, and stood a few inches taller than Hernán once on his feet. Clean cut, with brown hair that would probably be short and straight when it dried. Almost the stereotypical tourist Hernán had become used to in Provincetown, but surprisingly handsome in a way he associated with American life.

Water streaming from their clothes ran down the rar
river. The stranger patted his shirt pocket inside his swea
relief as he pulled out a pair of glasses. Putting them on, he
I put these away 'fore my walk." His voice sounded steadier as the nigh
air seemed to counteract his inebriation.

"Maybe you should have kept them on, hombre. You know, to see how close you were to the edge." Hernán's voice was teasing, and the man's lips quirked up a bit.

"Thank you. Seriously. My fall could have turned into something a lot worse." The man looked down at the concrete of the boat launch. Hernán would bet he was blushing, though the moon and lamplight cast too many shadows to be sure.

In a soft tone, Hernán said, "Don't worry. Everybody's been trashed at least once, right?"

The man shrugged and turned self-consciously to frown at ripples of white and silver and black in the harbor. The Long Point lighthouse rotated its beam through the night, and beyond, distant lights sparkled along the opposite shore of Cape Cod as it arced back toward the mainland. He muttered, "I don't remember getting so drunk before. And I guess I know why." He was starting to look ill. Even in the near-dark, Hernán could tell what was about to happen. "Y' know, I don' feel so good..."

"Over here, chero," Hernán said as he pulled the man over to some bushes, just before he fell to his knees and vomited up a lot of liquid. Hernán rubbed his shoulder and tried not to lose his own dinner at the sight. He swallowed hard, and then said, "Get it out. I know it isn't pleasant but you'll feel better."

The man heaved twice more before collapsing back on his heels and hanging his wet head. "Shit," he sighed forlornly. "Now I'm even more embarrassed."

"Hey. No one saw but me, and I'm probably just a figment of your imagination anyway."

The stranger looked up at Hernán as he swiped awkwardly at the corner of his mouth. Through his glasses, blue eyes glittered in the light of a streetlamp. He muttered, "I don't have that good an imagination."

Hernán surveyed the parking lot. "Stay put," he instructed, and then jogged over to a pole holding a roll of plastic bags for dog walkers to clean up after their pets. He ripped off a bag and came back to the man, whose head once again hung down.

"This isn't much, but it's clean. You can wipe your mouth at least," Hernán said as he offered the bag. The man accepted it mutely and swabbed at his face. Hernán took an arm to get him on his feet. "I think you'll feel better if we walk. We both need to get out of these clothes."

"Please remind me never to drink so much again," the man muttered as he began to walk beside Hernán.

"Well, I would, but remember—I'm just a figment."

Moonlight glinted off the man's glasses as he turned to look Hernán full in the face. "You're not a figment. Maybe an angel."

"Hah! Tell my cousin that."

"Who's your cousin?"

"Never mind."

They crossed the parking lot, their shoes sloshing with each step. Hernán was dreading his own walk home in wet clothes. The man had begun to shiver slightly, and glanced back at the harbor. In a low voice, he said, "I remember I was looking out at the water and just feeling sad. Then I was wet."

They reached the top of the lot, and he looked left and right along Commercial Street. "Hell. I have no idea where I am."

Hernán shook his head and laughed. "When you decide to get drunk, you don't go halfway. Where are you staying?"

"I'm at The Brass Key. Do you know where it is?"

"Sure. That's a nice place." Nice, and very, very expensive. If the guy was staying there, he had some money. "I can walk you to the Key, if you want."

"I shouldn't be any more trouble," the man protested. "You're already wet because of me and my midnight swim."

"It's all part of an angel's duties, chero. Besides," Hernán lied, "I don't live far from there." He actually lived about a twenty-minute soggy walk in a different direction, but he felt sorry for the blanquito and wanted to make sure he got dry and safe. "Come on. It's this way."

The pair headed east on Commercial, shoes slapping the asphalt as they walked. Two elderly women passed by with a small dog on a leash. When they looked slightly scandalized at the dripping men, Hernán called out, "We lost a bet!" One of the women laughed but the other scooped up her dog.

The stranger gave a soft chuckle, but otherwise remained silent, his head down. Perhaps he needed to talk about how he ended up in such a state. "Why were you sad, when you were looking at the harbor?" Hernán risked.

The man sighed. "My best friend got married today. I thought I was in love with him, but he loved somebody else."

Hernán wasn't surprised at the pronouns. It was Provincetown, after all, where the size of the gay population almost matched the straight. "That must have hurt. Did you tell him how you feel?"

"Sort of. He and the guy who's now his husband broke up for a while, and I thought maybe I had a shot. I asked him out on a few dates, but nothing clicked. He wasn't over David. Then some bad shit happened and it brought them back together again. Now they're married." The man shook his head ruefully and muttered, "Come to think, it's my fault. I'm the one who called David when Brandon was in the hospital."

"Okay, this sounds interesting. Do you want to tell me about it while we walk?"

Hernán caught the slightest curve of the hapless man's mouth as he said, "The thing is, I had a crush on Brandon from the minute I met him. But I tried to play it cool. To wait him out, see? We hung out as friends, but I was waiting for the right time to ask him to dinner or something. I waited too long, though. The first time Brandon told me about David, I knew what he felt was real. Even Brandon didn't seem to catch on for a while, but I could tell he was a dead duck. All David had to do was reel him in." He frowned. "What a terrible metaphor. I'm ashamed."

Hernán chuckled softly, even as he wondered, *What would it feel like, to find someone so perfect for you even your friends could see it? What would it be like to be so exposed?* All he said was, "So-so metaphor, sad story for you. I'm sorry."

"It's a love story, just for someone else. Thanks though." The stranger was quiet for another block, but then he said, "You called me 'chero' twice."

"Uh, it's just a term," Hernán temporized. "Doesn't mean anything."

"You think I'm a friend?"

Oh shit. He knows some Spanish. "Hey, I'm not real, right? I'm just an angel you dreamed up to get you out of the water so of course I'm going to be sweet to you."

The man chuckled. "I'm going to be mad if this does turn out to be a dream. So far this is the most adventure I've ever had in my life."

Hernán grunted. "Lucky you." Unbidden, memories of the dilapidated house in the border town surfaced. *Huddled in a corner, next to the girl he'd been told to pretend was his sister in case Immigration caught them, he watched as the handlers looked over their chickens with hungry eyes. Even though he'd failed Albert and Andrea, he was glad they weren't there to see. The girl next to him tried to make herself as small as possible, but one of the handlers looked their way…*

"Where'd you go?" the man asked, and Hernán shook his head to refocus.

"Sorry. Is this your first time in Provincetown?"

The man nodded. "Yes but I should have come before. I spent time in Nantucket growing up, but I never made it here. It's an amazing place. How about you? Where are you visiting from?"

"I live here." *For now.* "I'm staying with my cousin until I get set."

"Oh."

They walked quietly for a few more blocks. Since it was mid-September, the tourist crowds had thinned to a fraction of what they were in July and August. Some of the restaurants and shops lining Commercial Street had already closed for the season and their owners were off to warmer environments.

Hernán didn't miss the crowds but he missed summer. On a humid day, certain parts of Provincetown reminded him of home. With the autumn chill coming in, though, he had a harder and harder time pretending he was anywhere familiar.

Provincetown remained a mystery to him, even after nearly five months of working there. The restaurant where he washed dishes every afternoon and evening would soon be cutting its staff. Even the house cleaning service where he worked some mornings would need him less as the stream of renters and non-resident homeowners trickled off. He didn't know what he and Rudy would do then. Maybe it was time to think of heading to Boston, to see if they could get work in a restaurant there.

When they reached Carver Street, Hernán led them up a hill. "Oh, I see it now," the man said as they neared The Brass Key Guesthouse. A bell tolled on a nearby church, its sonorous tone stirring Hernán's heart with a longing for home. He was suddenly lonely and reluctant to let the luckless stranger go. *Stupid, stupid. You know how this plays out.*

Hernán squared his shoulders. "Okay. You've got your key?" he asked, and the man nodded.

"Yes, key's still in my pocket." He blushed and said awkwardly, "Um—can I offer you a towel? Or buy you a drink to say thank you?"

Hernán froze. Of course he knew the man was gay, and he'd sort of expected a come-on for blocks. He even wanted to accept the offer, to get dry and continue the conversation.

But no. No way was he going into a stranger's room for a towel. His chest tightened. The chill spreading through him had little to do with his damp clothes.

The man looked embarrassed again, probably at the alarm on Hernán's face. "I'm sorry. I don't mean to… I shouldn't have assumed you were… Oh shit."

"It's fine." Hernán tried to calm himself. He gave a smile that felt artificial, focusing on even breaths until his shoulders relaxed. "*I'm* fine. I'll be home soon to get dry."

"Okay. Well, um, thank you again. For saving me." The streetlights near the inn showed his face more clearly. Humiliation was plain to read there, and Hernán felt bad. The guy was having a shitty night already, and he'd just been shot down.

"I'm glad to help. Now, back to my imaginary status. An angel's time is never his own." Hernán tried for a laugh to make the man feel better; at least he drew a small smile. He held out his hand. "Go get dry. It would be a shame if I saved you from drowning and you died of pneumonia."

The man huffed out a chuckle as he shook hands, turned, and walked through the front door of the inn. Hernán waited to make sure he could get inside. The stranger paused at the threshold to look back at him for a long moment, light glinting off his glasses.

Seconds ticked by, and Hernán had the sudden urge to change his mind. To take up the offer of a towel, or a drink. Instead, he waved and turned away to begin the long walk back to his tiny shared apartment.

Chapter 2

COLIN WOKE WITH a throbbing headache, a terrible taste in his mouth, and a sense of half-remembered shame. It took him several minutes to figure out he was in his room in the Brass Key guesthouse in Provincetown. Light streamed in through French doors leading to his private balcony; he'd neglected to draw the curtains when he stumbled in. Spotting his soggy clothes where he'd dropped them on the bathroom floor, he cringed as the evening started to come back to him.

THE WEDDING ITSELF had been lovely and serene. Brandon Smith and David James both looked handsome and right together, standing on the beach to exchange their vows. Colin was dying a bit inside, yet he was happy and proud for his friend. Brandon had been through so much the prior year. After a hit-and-run driver left him for dead, a month in the hospital threatened financial ruin, and then doctors had to amputate his leg. David cared for him in every way possible through his recovery. Colin couldn't say he was surprised when Brandon called him on Christmas morning to say David and he would marry on David's fiftieth birthday.

Months of preparation culminated in a small but beautiful celebration on Herring Cove Beach in Provincetown, and Colin was honored to be a part of it. He couldn't imagine a more perfect evening, as if someone up there had arranged flawless weather and a perfect sunset just for David and Brandon.

After the ceremony, a waiting motor coach took the wedding party to The Red Inn for the reception. The small, historic inn had a lovely garden festooned with little white lights woven into and around the charming garden and shrubs. A deck outfitted with Adirondack chairs faced the Provincetown Harbor. The reception guests sipped cocktails and champagne on the deck under a thrilling twilight sky of deep purple and burnt orange.

That cocktail hour was Colin's first mistake—he started with a manhattan, straight up. The bourbon went right to his head, but he welcomed the fuzziness. The liquor muffled the throb of his bruised heart. By the time the party went inside to sit for dinner, Colin was on his second manhattan. David outdid himself with the wine selection. It started with a rich, white burgundy to accompany the appetizer and then moved to bottles of a California cabernet from Chateau Montelena to pair with the main course.

About then, Colin's evening started to grow hazy.

He didn't think he'd done anything *too* embarrassing, like dance on a table. Or dance at all, for that matter. But then David's brother Matt gave a toast; Colin drank with everyone else to David and Brandon's happiness. Brandon's sister Jo-Lynn told a funny story about Brandon, and everyone drank. David's friend Terry tried successfully to embarrass David, and everyone drank. Their friends Jane and Sara rose to offer a prayer in memory of David's deceased lover Kyle. When Brandon raised his glass into the respectful silence to honor the man David had lost, Colin drank too.

Perhaps that heartfelt but melancholy moment did him in. Colin was suddenly, profoundly, alone in a crowd of kind, well-meaning people. David and Brandon's happiness was palpable. He *yearned* to have someone gaze at him in total adoration, the way Brandon looked up into David's eyes. But he hadn't dated a man steadily since Pranav in college, let alone had one he could call "boyfriend."

Maybe it was Colin's own fault, for keeping himself so guarded, so walled-off. On one of his rare dates, at any question that strayed close to his family or his upbringing, he'd find a way to change the subject. He chose topics so carefully, worded his answers so closely, that he probably came off as evasive. But he'd seen the other side of things as well, when he revealed too much about himself and watched the change come over someone's face.

Gazing at David and Brandon through bleary eyes, he started when Joe Mulholland sat down next to him. Joe was in his sixties. He had white hair and bright blue eyes, and wore a loose-fitting blue silk shirt and pale green trousers for the celebration. Although he stood no more than five and a half feet tall, his charisma filled the room.

They'd met a few times while Brandon was still in the hospital, and then at occasional dinners and cocktail parties organized by Brandon and David. Joe was a former monk, a fact delighting Colin to no end. He ran a shelter for homeless LGBTI teenagers with the help of his husband Terry.

For the preceding few months, Colin, David and Joe had all worked together to protect a thirteen-year-old girl with no immigration papers whose parents had been deported to Honduras. Her foster family threw her out when she admitted she was a lesbian. Colin's work at the not-for-profit association Immigration Initiative in Washington, DC, gave him access to valuable resources to help David, a lawyer, prepare the necessary papers for the Customs and Immigration Service.

Joe rested a hand on Colin's. In his raspy Boston tones, he asked brightly, "Dear heart, are you enjoying the party?"

Colin nodded and answered, careful to enunciate around his thick tongue. "I am. Enjoying it, I mean. How're you doing, Joe?"

"Marvelous, my dear," he enthused. "What a celebration! What joy! I'm simply ecstatic when two people find their way together like this." Colin smiled and said something polite in response.

Joe crooked his head. His blue eyes gazed at Colin penetratingly. Joe patted his hand, leaned slightly forward, and dropped his voice as he murmured, "Your time will come."

Colin blinked rapidly. "Thanks, Joe. I hope so."

"Trust Mother Joe. When you least expect it, love will find you." Joe patted his arm again, rose, and moved off to chat with David's brother.

Colin watched the festivities for a few moments longer, but his head began to spin. Brandon caught his eye as he stood, wavering slightly on his feet. Colin mouthed to his friend, "I need to walk." Brandon smiled and nodded back.

COLIN RECALLED STEPPING out into the crisp fall evening and then swaying a bit as he tried to pick a direction. He more or less put his head down and started to walk, unsure of the location of his inn or even the center of Provincetown. His shoes scuffed along the asphalt. Left right left right.

When he looked up again, he found himself in a parking lot, mostly empty, abutting the harbor. He staggered over to the raised concrete edge to look across the water. By that point the alcohol had him firmly in its grip. He remembered looking down and noticing water lapped near the top of the embankment. The moon reflected on the surface of the rippling water and maybe he bent over to take a closer look. Then he was wet and cold and thrashing around, until a strong arm gripped his waist and a deep voice told him, first in Spanish then in English, to stop struggling. He instinctively relaxed into the man's hold.

And then Colin had proceeded to humiliate himself over and over.

His face burned at the recollection. When the shame grew strong enough, he forced himself out of bed to shut the curtains and get a glass of water. Looking through his shaving kit, he fortunately found some Tylenol. A glance at his phone showed it was still early in the morning. *Good thing I left it in the room. Otherwise I'd be looking for a bowl of rice to dry it out too.*

He climbed under the covers and tried to go back to sleep, but it was too late. His brain filled again with memories of talking to the stranger who'd rescued him, and of every inane thing he'd said.

Oh fuck, I threw up too. Colin burrowed under the covers as he remembered the man handing him a plastic bag to wipe his mouth. *A bag for dog crap. How appropriate.* He could almost hear his sister Katherine berating him for his foolishness. In getting so drunk. In falling into the water. In making an idiot of himself in front of a handsome stranger.

Well, his sister probably wouldn't have commented on the stranger's looks, but from what Colin recalled, he'd been striking. Almost beautiful, in fact. Tawny, smooth-looking skin. Dark eyes that seemed almost obsidian. Thick black hair, and a neatly-trimmed beard and mustache. Lithe body clad in jeans and a wet sweatshirt hinting at a well-shaped chest and broad shoulders.

Chero, Colin recalled. The stranger had called him "friend" in Spanish that sounded, to Colin's experienced ear, more Central American than Mexican. *I should have spoken to him in Spanish. Maybe it would have gone better.*

On the other hand, his rescuer's English had seemed strong, even idiomatic. Many of the people from Latin America who Colin encountered in his work struggled with the oddities of the English language. Not the prior night's angel of Colin's imagination however. Colin chuckled briefly at the memory of light banter as the man guided him to his inn.

Then he groaned as he recalled his inept attempt to make the guy stick around. *A towel or a drink. Jesus. I might as well have offered him a condom and begged him to fuck me.*

Drunk or sober, he seemed to have a knack for misreading cues. It was why he dug in his heels when his boss Maryanne tried to make him take on a prominent role at the Immigration Imitative. She kept telling him he could accomplish more if he got out of his office, but it was where he felt safe. He liked working behind the scenes, preparing those better suited for lobbying lawmakers on Capitol Hill. If he went along to a meeting, he'd probably garble the script or accidentally insult an important staffer.

Fatigue and a hangover fueled his self-flagellation until he slipped back into a doze. Waking for the second time when his phone chirped, he squinted at the display before snagging his glasses off the nightstand to read the message from Brandon:

Lost you last night. Everything OK?

He positioned himself against the soft pillows and typed back:

Yes, just over-imbibed and am paying the price.

Brandon sent a sad-face emoji with a message:

You up for lunch with me today?

Aren't you and David leaving for honeymoon?

We head to Boston in AM to get flight to London.

Oh right. David and Brandon would spend some time in London first, and then head to France for ten days. It would be Brandon's first trip outside the United States and he was incredibly excited.

A second message from Brandon flashed up:

David is taking Matt and my sisters sailing today but I don't feel steady enough on my prosthesis. So let's have lunch!

Done. Where and when?

Haven't been to Veranda all summer. Meet me there.

Two hours later, Colin slid into an outdoor booth at a restaurant called Veranda. The September weather was beautiful. A strong sun shone down brightly on the tourists strolling Commercial Street to enjoy the tail end of summer. A series of blue and yellow umbrellas sheltered Veranda's outdoor space. Its white wooden benches were strewn with yellow and blue pillows in a variety of patterns and sizes.

"Two for lunch, sir?" asked a dark-haired waiter in white shorts and a white polo shirt. "Can I get you anything to drink besides water?"

Colin tilted his head. Something about the waiter seemed familiar, though he was sure they'd never met before. Perhaps it was just the waiter's slight Central American accent. He debated ordering a cocktail as hair of the dog, but ruled it out as memories of his embarrassing night crashed back into his head. "Just an iced tea, please. And yes, there will be two of us."

"Of course. I'll leave these menus and I'll be right back with your tea."

Colin was still trying to figure out why the waiter seemed familiar when Brandon walked up to the restaurant and, catching Colin's eye, gave a quick nod. Brandon moved effortlessly on flat ground, despite the artificial leg beginning below his left knee. He wore shorts and made no effort to disguise his prosthesis. In fact, he'd added racing stickers to the metal post that ran down to the sandal covering his carbon-fiber foot. He'd trimmed his blond hair and beard recently for the wedding, and the light in his blue eyes radiated his joy.

"Well, afternoon, sunshine," Brandon said with a big grin as he slid into the booth across from Colin. "I've seen you look better," he drawled. His Texan accent always struck Colin as exotic, and so much more interesting than the way people talked in New Jersey.

Colin groaned. "Don't remind me. I got completely carried away last night."

"I worried when you didn't come back to the reception, but I figured this is P-town. How much trouble could you land in?"

"What about a late-night swim?" Colin began to tell Brandon about his drunken adventure when the waiter returned.

"Oh my God!" the waiter exclaimed. "It's Brandon, isn't it?"

Brandon looked up at the waiter and blinked before recognition dawned. "Rudy! How are you?"

Rudy leaned down for a hug, while Brandon awkwardly patted his back. "It's so nice to see you again," Rudy cooed. The reserved waiter who seated Colin was gone, and an effusive and happy boy began to gab with Brandon like they were old friends. "Do you come up to Provincetown a lot? I haven't seen you since last summer. I think it was Memorial Day. Are you seeing that handsome man from last year or is this your boyfriend?" Without taking breath, Rudy turned and thrust a hand out to Colin. "Hi, I'm Rudy."

Colin shook it, bemused by the man's enthusiasm. "I'm Colin. And no, I'm not his boyfriend."

Brandon said, "I'm still with David. We just got married yesterday at Herring Cove."

"Married!" Rudy sighed dramatically. "So exciting. Oh, that David was just dreamy. I'm so happy for you."

"Thanks, Rudy. Do you work here now?" Brandon asked cautiously.

"Yes. I've been here all summer. Gerald kicked me out last fall when we were back in Boston, and I tried a few different jobs there. Nothing panned out, though, so I decided to come back to P-town in May. At least I know the place."

"I'm sorry to hear it didn't work out with Gerald," Brandon offered.

Rudy flipped his hand dismissively. "He was a pig in the end, but I can't say I was surprised. He had another boy in place before he told me to pack a bag."

Colin sipped nervously at his tea. He didn't know who they were talking about, but the gist of Rudy's comments was clear.

An older man walked by the table then and gave a very pointed cough that made Rudy jump to attention. "Let me get your order, boys. Maybe we can chat again before you go." He jotted down their requests and scurried off.

Brandon shook his head as Rudy left. "I only met him once before, but he was just the same then. Chatterin' like we'd been friends forever."

"I think you told me about him, when we talked about that party you and David went to," Colin said carefully. The party had led to Brandon and David breaking up, until Brandon's hit-and-run accident brought them together again. He didn't know if Brandon would want the reminder.

His friend seemed unfazed however, and they resumed their discussion of Colin's adventures. When he described his ineptitude in asking his savior in for a towel or a drink, his head sagged. Brandon reached across the table and gripped Colin's wrist.

"Hey, buddy. Maybe he had a boyfriend or girlfriend. Maybe it was just bad timin'. But it's good you put yourself out there. You need to do more a' that."

"Easy for you to say, with your looks." Brandon's heavily-muscled chest and arms made Colin feel underdeveloped. No matter how much time he put in at the gym, he couldn't seem to add any bulk.

"You're good lookin', Colin. You'll find the right guy."

Rudy returned then with their plates on his arm. "Here we go, boys. Fish and chips for the bride, and a Cobb salad for the bridesmaid."

Colin had to laugh. "What, I don't get to be a groomsman at least?"

"Bridesmaid is a much more important role." Rudy winked at him and started to turn away, but the color left his face as he stared hard at a man walking into the restaurant. "Every damn day," he muttered.

Brandon noticed as well and turned to follow Rudy's gaze. He sighed. "Gerald. Of course. David 'n I managed to avoid him all summer. Guess my luck ran out."

The newcomer was not as tall as David, but probably broke six feet. His silvering hair swept back dramatically, and he wore a fisherman's sweater and jeans that looked too tight. His face was a bit jowly; Colin would place him around fifty-five or so. He had presence, though. He surveyed the restaurant like he owned the place, spotted Rudy, and walked over.

"I assume he's working today," Gerald said to Rudy, oblivious to the presence of customers.

Rudy flushed. "Yes, working. As in busy. Just like every time you come in here."

Gerald looked down his nose at Colin, and then did a double-take when he focused on Brandon. "Oh. We've met." His gray eyes narrowed in concentration. "Bradley, wasn't it?"

Rudy said, "It's Brandon. He came to the party you had last year, with David Something-or-other." A glint of malice twinkled in Rudy's eye as he added, "I remember how often you talked about David after that. Too bad he's off the market. He and Brandon just got married yesterday."

Gerald's eyebrow twitched. "Married?" A flash of regret, confusion and longing crossed his face. Blankness covered it all quickly as Gerald turned to sneer at Rudy. "Well, I guess Brandon here knew how to play the game better than you."

Rudy flushed and Brandon turned red. Colin saw he was about to do something rash. He picked up his fork and said loudly without looking at the asshole, "Thank you for stopping by, but we're just about to eat. Rudy, could I get another tea?"

Gerald was clearly unused to being dismissed. Before he could say anything, Colin focused on Brandon. "So, David is off sailing with your sisters?" Rudy tittered and disappeared, and Brandon's color returned to normal. Gerald stood there a few seconds longer before stomping off to a table in the corner of the restaurant.

"Nicely done," Brandon said. "I almost lost it, but you kept cool."

"Hey, I learned how to cut from the best hostess in Bergen County, New Jersey. You should see my mother working the room at a charity event. Icicles trail in her wake if anyone displeases her."

"Charity events?" Brandon asked curiously. Colin realized his slip. He usually tried very hard not to mention his parents or anything about his family, so it was no wonder Brandon would take the opportunity to ask.

"Sometimes. Anyway, sailing?"

Brandon waited a moment, but then nodded. "David rented a boat to take Jo-Lynn, Suzanne and Matt out on the bay. I think Terry was goin' with 'em too." He chuckled. "Joe says the Lord may have walked on water but *he* prefers dry land."

As they chatted, Colin noticed Gerald wave Rudy over to him. Rudy looked around the restaurant, but apparently could find no way to refuse without Gerald causing a scene. The restaurant was quiet enough he heard Gerald order Rudy in a peremptory tone, "Tell him to come out and talk to me."

Rudy shook his head. "He's working. He can't take a break."

Gerald snorted and gazed over the menu. "I could always have a chat with Claude. You know Claude, don't you, Rudy? The owner of this restaurant? I think he might be shocked to find out what's going on in his kitchen."

Rudy flushed and pursed his lips. He looked around nervously, and then disappeared to the interior of the restaurant. A few moments later, he returned, accompanied by another man. He was slightly shorter than Rudy, and looked a few years younger, but the family resemblance between the two was strong.

That was why Rudy had looked familiar to Colin—he was clearly related to the man he led out. The man who had saved Colin the previous night.

The angel of his imagination.

Chapter 3

HERNÁN'S STOMACH CHURNED as Rudy led him out to the front of the restaurant. In Spanish, Rudy whispered, <<I'm sorry, Nán. Just talk to him. Maybe that's all he wants.>>

Hernán shook his head tightly. Rudy of all people should know this Gerald Nimble pendejo wanted more than conversation, and wouldn't take no for an answer. It was all happening again. He was being dragged before a man who wanted to make Hernán his property. Just like in the dilapidated way-house, when the thugs had reached out, not for the girl pretending to be his sister, but for him.

Rough hands wrapped in his shirt as they dragged him up. The other chickens huddled on their beds in the dormitory and looked away, relieved the handlers hadn't come for them or their loved ones. Only for Hernán, who meant nothing to any of them. Even his "sister" dropped her head forward and rocked her thin body to avoid his eyes. The thugs led him out and up the stairs to the room with double doors. Inside, he *was waiting for Hernán...*

"It'll be fine," Rudy said uncertainly in a low voice as he slung an arm across Hernán's shoulders. Hernán shuddered and fought the urge to run as Nimble watched them approach. The predatory look in his flinty gray eyes was one Hernán had seen too many times in his young life, from men who coveted Hernán for themselves. Nimble ignored, or perhaps thrived, on Hernán's humiliation as Rudy dragged him out to parade like a piece of meat.

That's not fair. Rudy doesn't want to do this.

He knew, but it didn't help. Despair threatened to swallow him. No matter how hard he fought to survive, someone always waited to pull him down into inky black depths. Even when he resisted, he failed, like he'd failed Albert, Andrea, and even Isela. Nausea roiled his belly but he kept his gaze squarely on Nimble's face. He tried to blot out everyone else in the restaurant. He wanted to look away, but that sign of weakness would make him appear even more vulnerable.

"Hernán, how delightful you look today," Nimble said in a voice oozing with oil and possessiveness. "Though you should keep your hair short and let people see your lovely eyes. Thank you for coming out to say hello."

Hernán refused to answer, but Rudy spoke. "He came out like you wanted. Now he needs to get back to the kitchen."

Nimble sighed theatrically. "Hernán, I don't know why you insist on wasting your time here. I have a big, beautiful kitchen. I've told you, come cook for me. You'd be so much more comfortable living in my house than wherever it is Rudy is staying these days."

Rudy snapped, "I'm where I landed when you threw me away."

Nimble rolled his eyes. "You were always so dramatic. Our affair had simply run its course and you needed to move on."

"I did move on, when you brought in that Troy person."

"Ah, Troy. So willing to learn. I miss him still."

Rudy nodded furiously. "Yes, I heard about it. You caught him with another man and had him arrested for stealing."

"Troy did steal from me. The police still haven't found the antique cufflink set he took."

"I suppose I'm lucky you spared me that humiliation."

"All in all, you were quite reasonable, Rudy. Now, piss off, would you? I'd like to talk with Hernán and you're giving him a bad impression of me."

Hernán spoke for the first time. "Believe me, I don't need Rudy's help to see what kind of man you are."

Nimble's mouth tightened. "That's unjust. I can be a very good friend. I was generous with Rudy, after all. Clothes. Vacations. The finest restaurants. I seem to recall a Rolex watch when I was swept up in romance at the beginning."

With a grunt, Rudy said, "Sure. Generous. As long as I wore exactly what you wanted me to wear, said what you wanted me to say, had sex with you the way you wanted to be—"

Nimble cut him off with a hand gesture. "Now, now. No disclosure of pillow talk. That was quite clearly a stipulation in our agreement when I let you keep that very same Rolex."

Rudy flushed but said no more. Hernán shook his head slowly.

"You're wasting your time. I don't sleep with men."

Nimble tilted his head. "Then you simply haven't had the right incentives. In the end, flesh is flesh. You'll find there's more to me than a large bank account and a large house." He leered at Hernán. "Have dinner with me and we'll discuss what might entice you into my bed."

"No. Are we done here? I have to get back to work."

Nimble's face hardened. "A quick refusal to a business proposition is tiresome. It simply indicates the other party fails to understand what he might gain…or what he might lose." Hernán's jaw ached because he clenched it so tightly. When he flicked a glance at Rudy, his cousin was pale.

"Claude is coming to dinner at my house Sunday evening," Nimble continued, and his thin lips curled at either side. "I can imagine at least two ways our dinner conversation might trend. Hernán, if you were there with me, and consented to stay afterwards for a deeper discussion, we'd have a lovely chat about books or art or whatever local gossip Claude is interested in. On the other hand, if I'm alone, I could see a warning about hiring practices. Perhaps the advisability of Claude taking a fresh look at those he employs."

Hernán felt his cheeks burn, and Rudy was chewing the corner of his mouth. Nimble could cause great difficulty for both him and Rudy; losing their jobs at Veranda would be the least of it.

Hernán couldn't do what Gerald wanted. He could *not* submit to this man. But if he didn't…

Nimble seemed to like the expression he found in Hernán's face. He said, "Well, I've kept you long enough today. I'll expect you at eight-thirty Sunday evening. Rudy can give you the address."

Dismissed, Hernán turned to walk back to the kitchen. Only then did he spot the handsome man he had pulled from the harbor the night before, sitting with a blond guy.

In the daylight, his skin looked like porcelain. The afternoon sun brought out rosy undertones in his cheeks and glints of copper in his hair. They were close enough to Nimble's table they might have heard the entire exchange. The stranger's blue eyes burned into Hernán's, full of what looked like anger and concern and some other emotions Hernán didn't recognize. He blushed even more, focused on the ground and slunk to the kitchen.

COLIN WATCHED HIS savior retreat to the back of the restaurant. His head was down, shoulders slumped, and shame radiated from him as he walked away.

He'd heard Gerald call the man "Hernán." Colin picked up enough of the conversation to give him a pretty good idea what was going on. It was something he encountered constantly in his work. The situation made him furious at this Gerald prick.

Brandon had sat quietly when he realized how intent Colin was on the exchange with Gerald. Finally he leaned forward and asked in a low voice, "Hey. What's up?"

Colin didn't answer him directly, but caught Rudy's eye and raised a finger. Rudy hurried up as a flighty mask slid across his pale and drawn features. "Gentlemen, so sorry I was distracted." He was breathless as before but his eyes betrayed his nervousness. "Are you through with your plates? Can I get you more water, or tea?"

In a quiet voice that wouldn't carry, Colin asked Rudy, "Is he blackmailing you?"

Rudy started and flushed, but wouldn't look directly at Colin. "I'm not sure what you mean. Are you ready for the check, Brandon?"

Colin tried again. "Rudy, I work with a nonprofit association that helps immigrants. Legal and otherwise. I know someone without proper papers may be vulnerable. Can I help?"

Rudy met his eyes briefly, but then looked away and began to gather their lunch plates. Brandon caught on, and he said to Rudy, "Colin's a good guy. If you need help, talk to him. Or to my David. He's a lawyer, and he's done some immigration work too."

Rudy chewed on the corner of his mouth as he finished stacking their plates and silverware. Colin thought he would leave without speaking, but at the last second, he flicked a glance at Colin. "If I knew someone who wanted to talk to you, how would they find you?"

"I'm staying at the Brass Key. My name is Colin Felton. Someone could ask for me at the desk, or leave a note about how to get in touch. I'm not leaving Provincetown until tomorrow afternoon."

Rudy nodded slightly, and then said in a bright voice, "I hope you enjoyed your lunch, gentlemen. I'll be right back with the check."

As he scurried away, Brandon leaned in toward Colin. "I picked some a' that up, but what's goin' on?"

Colin inclined his head subtly in Gerald's direction. "I think your friend there is blackmailing one or both of those guys over their immigration status. Likely to force them into sex."

"Gerald is no friend a' mine. And it's gotta be the guy who came out from the back. Gerald and Rudy were together for at least two years, so I can't see why he'd blackmail Rudy back into bed."

Colin looked toward the interior of the restaurant, where Hernán had disappeared. "He's the man who helped me last night when I fell in the water. Maybe I can do something for him." He noticed Brandon's look of concern then. "What?"

Brandon frowned. "He's really good lookin' 'n all. The guy who pulled you out a' the water."

"I heard Gerald call him 'Hernán.'"

Brandon nodded. "OK. *I* heard Hernán say he doesn't sleep with men."

Colin flushed. "That isn't what this is about. I just can't stand someone like that asshole using the immigration laws as a weapon. I've seen that movie too many times, and it's evil and dirty."

"I think I get it. But y'know, Gerald's a big hedge fund manager or somethin'. He has lots a' money, probably lots a' connections. Maybe you want to tread carefully there."

Colin almost bared his teeth as he sat straighter in the booth. "My friend, I have connections too. Fund managers are a dime a dozen, believe me. If Hernán wants my help, I'm not worried in the slightest about Gerald."

RUDY BUSTLED BACK to the kitchen, excited and fluttery. Hernán tried to ignore him as he stuck his elbows deep in the sink to scrub a stubborn pot. His skin crawled at the thought of Gerald putting hands on him.

Rudy said to him, <<Nán, I'm sorry I got you into this.>>

<<Not here, Rudy,>> Hernán answered as he scrubbed harder. Lips pursed, he worked with a scouring pad to rub the bottom and eradicate any trace of grime.

<<I know, but those customers at table fourteen. They may be able to help.>>

Hernán shook his head furiously. <<You think some random gay guys in a restaurant are going to help me out of the goodness of their hearts? Even if they could help, they'll just want the same thing as your

ex.>>

<<I don’t think they’d do that.>> Rudy chewed his lip. <<At least not Brandon. I met him a while back, when I was with Gerald. He’s not like what you’re saying. But anyway, Nán, what have you got to lose to just talk to them?>>

Hernán glanced up at him and shook his head. <<You’re so naïve. I love that about you, but it’s too risky.>>

<<The other one, he says he works with people who are undocumented. I think he was serious. He wants to help.>>

Hernán’s face burned as he thought about the intense eyes of the man he had pulled out of the harbor and guided to his guesthouse. That same man looked ferocious when he caught Hernán’s eye after the nastiness with Nimble. There was a warrior inside his lean body. The drunken, sad man from the previous night had been replaced by someone full of righteous determination. A fire burned within, making him shine with innocence and resolve.

Rudy took his silence for encouragement. <<Just go by his hotel, Nán. His name is Colin something…Colin Felton.>>

Colin. A nice name to go with a strong face.

No. Hernán wouldn’t consider it. The risks were too great. <<Rudy, what if it’s a trick? Maybe he’s really with ICE.>> But even as he said it, Hernán knew he didn’t believe Colin worked for Immigration and Customs Enforcement. He had a sincerity about him Hernán sensed when they’d walked through town the previous night. But the risk wasn’t just his to take. <<Suppose Gerald does turn us in to Claude. No way he doesn’t fire us both at a minimum. It doesn’t matter you’ve got your green card. He’ll shit-can you for covering for me.>>

Rudy looked shaken, but Hernán pressed on. <<And what if Claude calls ICE? Or your shitbag ex does? Sure you’ve got your green card, but it can probably be revoked. We could both find ourselves on a plane back to El Salvador.>>

His cousin retreated as the implications began to sink in. Hernán continued ruthlessly to make sure Rudy didn’t do something stupid, like go talk to that *Colin* on his own. <<Can you imagine being back in San Marcos, Rudy? It was hard enough when we were kids. You think you could make it as a straight man there? Or do you think Cuernos would come for you like they came for me?>>

"Stop it, Hernán," Rudy whispered in English. "You don't want to talk to the guy. I get it. But what are we going to do about Gerald?" He was pale, and Hernán felt ill for terrorizing his cousin and best friend.

"I don't know, Rudy. Let me just…think about it. Okay? We'll talk tonight. At home."

Rudy nodded and went back to work, as Hernán returned to scrubbing the rest of the dirty pans.

Chapter 4

AFTER LUNCH, COLIN walked with Brandon down Commercial and stopped in a few shops. Colin's favorite was called Hook. It sold t-shirts, sweats and other clothing with fascinating, original nautical images and themes. Laughing over them with Brandon, he bought several of the less-suggestive items for his niece and nephews. Christmas was months away but it was hard to shop for kids who literally had everything, so he usually opted for unique and quirky.

Eventually they strolled slowly back to the captain's cottage on Pleasant Street David had purchased several years earlier. It was a small but charming house, painted a buttery yellow. Brandon had planted chrysanthemums and replaced summer annuals, beginning the transition to autumn. The couple had spent most of their summer weekends in Provincetown, in part to prepare for their wedding, but mainly because it was a perfect place for two men to be in love.

And they were very much in love, Colin knew. One could hardly pass the other without reaching out a hand to touch. Whatever Colin's one-time crush for Brandon might have become had circumstances been different, he had no doubt Brandon and David belonged together.

Seeing them reminded him of how little affection he found in his own adult life. Hookups happened now and then, if he could overcome his nerves and get out of his own way. Even when he did hook up, though, the other guy never invited him to stick around for breakfast. Maybe he just wasn't good at sex, or perhaps it was the nature of his own upbringing.

As an introverted middle child to Type A parents, the well-intentioned pressure Margaret and Jim Felton had poured on Colin's shoulders sometimes felt as if it would crush him. As far back as he could recall, the parents shuttled him from enrichment activity to play date to guided mindfulness as they searched for the thing at which he could be a prodigy.

His sister Katherine excelled at everything—gymnastics, math, flute. Griffin, younger than Colin by three years, was born to play soccer and football. He was even elected prom king, for Christ's sake.

But Colin? Nothing seemed to come naturally to him. Piano lessons, soccer, swimming, even singing—his parents sent him to class after class. If he didn't triumph in the first day (and he never did), they yanked him, afraid to scar his psyche. They would blame the inadequate teachers and move on to the next attempt.

By the time Colin was ten, he thought he had tried every peewee sport, every musical instrument, and every form of art. In the name of encouraging his freedom, his parents let him spend no time on anything at which he was merely mediocre. As a result, he entered junior high with the firm conviction there was nothing in the world he was good at.

At least academics came more easily to him than art or sports. His parents pushed the administrators of the elite prep school he attended with his siblings to enroll Colin in the most advanced classes available.

He was barely able to keep his head above water. It meant endless nights and weekends of studying. He discovered, though, being alone in his dorm room or the library was preferable to the longing he felt when he watched a group of schoolmates head to the pep rallies or athletic fields for a game.

If there weren't already enough walls between him and his classmates, the chauffeur made it worse. His parents insisted on sending Watkins to pick up Katherine, Griffin and him on weekends or at holidays. He'd be waiting by the black town car to drive them from their school in New Hampshire to their ostentatious house in Saddle River, New Jersey. They were far from the only rich kids at school, but none of the others seemed to flash it about the way his parents did.

Colin tried to get them to stop but his mother just laughed. "Oh Colin. You don't want to be crammed into a train or a bus for hours. Trust me. This is better for you."

Katherine pouted, "I'm not sitting on a bus because you feel guilty or something." Griffin just shrugged; it made no difference to him.

With no support, Colin backed down.

It wasn't until his senior year he found the strength to resist the plans his parents made for him. They wanted him to go to Yale, as

Katherine, their father and their grandfather had, to study actuarial science and business. Quietly, Colin applied for and got into the University of California Berkeley to pursue international studies. He didn't know exactly what he wanted to do with that degree. What he did know, however, was working with Katherine and their father in the family's insurance business would not be his future.

He weathered the storm of parental disapproval and of threats to refuse tuition, and finally—for perhaps the first time in his life—he won. The helicopter parents who had second-guessed every decision he ever made caved and let him go to California.

Getting away helped. He missed his well-meaning, smothering parents. Being on his own, though, gave him the courage to step out into the sunshine. He would never be as natural and easy-going as his brother Griffin, or as take-charge and dynamic as Katherine, but he found groups to join. He slowly started to make some friends.

The Queer Student Union was perfect for him. The LGBTQIA group was active in addressing issues of gender and orientation identity, and it organized events around campus. Colin discovered he was good enough at graphic design to work with some marketing students on posters and flyers for their various events. The first time he opened a box from the printer to find posters with *his* design made him ridiculously proud.

An unexpected skill he found was the ability to solicit other student groups to pair for special events. One of his early successes was a combined effort of students from the Black and the Queer student unions to celebrate Black History Month. He got so involved in finding performance space, obtaining concession permits, and recruiting presenters he barely slept for a week. The evening came off without a hitch, and the student union made him special events coordinator in his sophomore year.

It was at a joint fundraiser between his union and the immigration alliance that he met Pranav Banerjee. Pranav was a law student, a few years older than Colin, and active in rounding up speakers to address the student body about issues of immigration. After a panel discussion on the impact of immigration policy on families, at a small reception, Pranav drew Colin aside.

What started as a conversation in a darkened corner turned to a light touch here, and quick caress there. Suddenly Colin found himself making out with funny, passionate, handsome Pranav. That night Colin finally lost his virginity. When he woke up in the morning, sticky and pleasantly sore, to find warm brown eyes and a wide grin facing him, his heart flipped.

Pranav kept it casual between them, though. He must have known how Colin felt, but he was careful about the amount of time they spent together. Maybe once a week he'd call Colin over to his place, or agree to see a movie. It didn't matter. Colin waited patiently for each call. He tried to be satisfied with the time Pranav gave him because when they were together, it was glorious.

Pranav liked to cook and he started coming over to Colin's apartment once in a while to assemble fantastic dishes from Southern India. Sometimes other students would join them. When Colin looked around his small dining room to see men and women chattering away as they enjoyed Pranav's cooking, his heart would fill to bursting.

It lasted for three months, until Colin got a phone call from Pranav. He'd been picked up by immigration officials for overstaying his visa by several years. Colin was shocked. He had no idea Pranav was in the country illegally, or what to do about it. The authorities began deportation proceedings.

"Can you help me?" Pranav asked, and Colin didn't know what to say. He'd had no occasion to brush against the law, ever. The idea of being detained, even deported, was completely foreign to his consciousness. And his parents would never give him money to help Pranav get a lawyer.

Trapped in his own consternation, he must have hesitated too long because Pranav said, "It's okay. I get it. Take care of yourself, Colin." He disconnected.

A few weeks later, Colin heard Pranav had been deported to India. They never spoke again.

So many questions ate at Colin as he tried to understand what had happened. How had Pranav managed to stay past his visa? How did he enroll, and work, and find a place to rent? How much fear had he lived with, that immigration officials would one day catch up with him? Had he made some mistake that led to the unraveling of everything he worked for? What would happen to him, back in India?

What, if anything, had Colin meant to him? What more could Colin have done?

The lack of answers drove him to become increasingly involved in the immigration alliance. By the time he graduated, he knew what he wanted to do with his life. His trust fund gave him plenty of freedom to take an unpaid internship in Washington with the non-profit center called the Immigration Initiative. Once a low-salaried position opened up, he took the job. He'd been there ever since.

The work was rewarding, and worth the aggravation when his father tried to get him to come join the family firm instead. His mother, at least, seemed to accept his choice. She'd even held some fundraisers for his organization, drawing big money for their little non-profit. Detente seemed to be the word of the day with his family. He'd take it.

But he wondered, often, what became of Pranav and whether he blamed Colin for his weakness. In quiet moments, the shame of it rolled through Colin like a wave crashing on the shore, leaving him cold and breathless.

It hit him again, as he walked the quiet streets of Provincetown. Maybe Hernán didn't want his help at all, and maybe he was right to reject Colin the night before. Maybe he could tell Colin wasn't strong enough to see it through, to work with Hernán and help him to stay safe.

He didn't even know why he'd made the offer of help to Rudy in the first place. Surely it wasn't just Hernán's dark eyes stirring something inside Colin. The quiet confidence Hernán had in himself, the humor and warmth he'd shown, even the way he stood up to Gerald… All of that spoke of a strength Colin envied and, truth be told, found attractive.

He'd heard Hernán clearly tell Gerald he didn't sleep with men, so at best Colin was setting himself up for more heartache. Even if he persuaded Hernán of his sincere desire to help, even if they became allies, Hernán would be able to give him nothing more than friendship.

Well, so be it. Colin would keep the attraction he felt to himself, and focus on helping Hernán because it was the right thing to do. To say thanks for pulling him from the harbor and getting him to safety, and because he'd been unable to help Pranav when he needed it. Then, once he'd given whatever aid he could to Hernán, they would inevitably go their separate ways.

Yet Colin was unable to kill completely a spark of hope.

HERNÁN STOOD ON aching feet, scrubbing the seemingly endless stack of pans, pots and plates. The humiliation of the encounter with Gerald burned in his stomach and had him grinding his teeth.

Rudy shot anguished looks in his direction every time he came through the kitchen. It wasn't Rudy's fault, no matter what he thought. Gerald Nimble singled Hernán out for no better reason than he sensed his helplessness. He was just the latest in a string of people who saw something they wanted in Hernán's face there for the taking.

He'd been told since childhood he was beautiful. Sometimes it was an old woman, stroking his cheek or running her hands through his thick hair as she exclaimed at how pretty he was. Sometimes it was a girl at school, looking up at him from under dark eyelashes and offering a shy compliment.

One terrible time, when he was very young, it was a worker delivering sodas to his tío's grocery.

Hernán's immediate family was mostly gone by then, either to the United States or to heaven. His father made the border crossing when Hernán was an infant; he'd never known the man except from letters and phone calls on scattered holidays. His mother left El Salvador when he was five and took his older brother, putting him and his younger sister in the care of his father's mother.

Abuela was a stern and unloving woman who narrowed her eyes when Hernán was too effusive or happy. "Pedro left me with two useless girls," she'd say to him. "What will you do when you start bleeding like a woman—stick a tampon up your ass?"

He asked her once for a princess Barbie for his birthday. She beat him. "Boys don't play with dolls or they turn into homosexuals. If you turn out to be a fag, I'm throwing your useless ass onto the street. I'm not raising Pedro's faggot son."

His hand still ached from the day he told Abuela about the man in the grocery store. She hit it again and again to make sure he told no one else. Lesson learned, he kept it from everyone—even Rudy—in case they thought he wanted what the man had done to him. He learned to keep quiet, and to avoid attention. He grew his hair longer and let it fall in his face, even though that too angered his grandmother.

Being away from her was one of the few good things about where he found himself. He missed his home terribly sometimes, because apart from Abuela, he'd managed to have a happy childhood. He could still call up that sense of safety, of security, he'd known playing soccer in the street and other games after school with kids who were his friends and neighbors.

Even more than his friends, though, he missed school. Hernán wanted an education more than anything, and as he grew older, he had dreams of becoming a teacher. In his little school in the Las Margaritas neighborhood of San Marcos, he sat straight in his desk each day, and felt polished and bright. His homework was always completed, always neatly organized, and almost always correct.

His teachers adored him, for the most part, because they could see his hunger. At the end of the school year, his teacher Mrs. Alvarado would give him a first place present. Miss Cruz got him to read poetry, though he knew to keep those books in school and far away from his grandmother's sharp eyes. Miss Cruz also encouraged his writing, and entered one of his essays on the history of El Salvador in a competition. He won.

That feeling of pride, at being the smartest kid in his class and having the best grades, made up so much for the biting sarcasm from Abuela. His other family and neighbors, at least, would be proud of him. They gave him respect for his drive, and would tell him about their expectations.

Languages were his best subject of all. He studied English avidly, and practiced with the few American tourists he encountered or who wandered into his uncle's grocery store. He'd spend hours flipping through his textbooks with their made-up dialogues and their cultural discussions.

One of his teachers loved to play old black-and-white American films when she hadn't prepared a lesson, and those got him into reading books in English like *Wuthering Heights*, *Great Expectations*, and *To Kill a Mockingbird.* Enchanted by the indigenous people he saw and their brightly-colored clothes, he learned Nahuatl. After that, he managed to pick up a smattering of some of the other languages including Quiche, Mixteco and Zapoteco.

When he was older, he moved on to French. A teacher in his college encouraged his natural linguistics skills, and even got him started with Arabic.

For all his facility with language, though, mathematics escaped him. His sixth-grade teacher was Mr. Muñoz, from Colombia. Mr.

Muñoz tried every technique he could think of to make Hernán understand. He even offered to tutor Hernán at his house. They picked a Saturday afternoon, but his grandmother heard about it first.

"You aren't going there," she decreed. "He lives alone. A real man shouldn't be a teacher anyway," she said as she threw a dark look in Hernán's direction. She muttered "maricón" as she turned away, and he didn't dare ask if she meant Mr. Muñoz or Hernán.

He was afraid to tell Mr. Muñoz, too, because he didn't want to say why he couldn't go to the teacher's house. Instead, he just didn't show up. Mr. Muñoz was polite to him after, but didn't try so hard to break through Hernán's difficulties.

Even with his poor grades in math, though, Hernán thrived. He talked to his mother and father three or four times a year. He did what Abuela told him to do around the house, and otherwise stayed out of her way.

He spent as much time as he could with his favorite tío, Juan, helping him in his grocery store. Oh, and the trips to the countryside to visit family for holidays. His aunts and uncles had places with creeks, mango trees, jocote trees. He and his cousins all raced to climb to the best branch with the best view. Christmas Eve and New Year's Eve were exciting because he got to wear new clothes. Even as tight-fisted as Abuela could be, she bought Hernán and his sister Brijith new outfits for the family gatherings. They would sit among their family and watch fireworks launched to celebrate the New Year.

He saw how everyone mocked his older cousin Rudy, of course, until Rudy's father took him away to the United States. He learned from that to hide many things about himself—many desires—from his family. Still, his life was mostly good.

Until the Cuernos del Diablo. Until they picked him, and stalked, and stabbed. Until he ran, and fell prey to Lonnie, who dragged him…

No. That's done.

He had to find a way to escape from Gerald's demands without putting Rudy's job in danger. But he had no clue how to accomplish that. Reluctantly, he thought about Rudy's words. The man Hernán had pulled from the harbor said he could help. *What if he can? What is there to lose?*

Stupid thought. Despite the small favor Hernán had rendered, the stranger would no doubt demand payment for any help. And what could that young, soft, kind but transparent *Colin* do against a vile bastard like Gerald anyway? Hernán was grasping at clouds to even consider talking to him like Rudy wanted.

The problem was his. He had a little more than a day to come up with a way to neutralize Gerald, or he would have to submit.

Chapter 5

AS COLIN WALKED back into the lobby of The Brass Key with his shopping bags, Rudy jumped up from a chair. The man behind the registration desk said, "Mr. Felton, this gentleman has been waiting for you."

"Thanks, Ken." To Rudy, Colin said, "I'm glad you came by. Let's go talk in my room so I can drop off these bags." He gestured with his head for Rudy to follow him up the stairs and through the corridors.

"Make yourself comfortable," he said when they entered his room. He tossed his bags on the bed and then came over to the sitting area. Rudy fidgeted as he looked out the French doors to the courtyard of the guesthouse. He couldn't seem to hold his hands still, one fluttering up to touch the drapes, the other alternating between his front and back pockets.

Colin sat down in a comfortable chair and waited. Rudy gnawed on his lower lip like a piece of chewing gum. Finally, he huffed, "I hope this is right." He sank down into a chair next to Colin's, both seats angled to look out the French doors.

Leaning forward, Colin met Rudy's nervous gaze. "I won't repeat anything you tell me. I want to help if I can. I've heard many stories of undocumented people being pressured into something terrible. I don't want that to happen to you or to Hernán. That's his name, right?"

Rudy sighed and crossed his legs, hands folded on his knee as he rocked slightly. "Okay. Hernán would think I'm crazy but I feel like I can trust you. This…it's hard to talk about."

<<Would you rather discuss it in Spanish?>> Colin asked in that language, and smiled when Rudy's mouth opened in an O of surprise. <<I'm pretty fluent. Maybe you'd be more comfortable.>>

Rudy gave a small grin but shook his head. "Thank you, but I try hard to stick to English. Other than a little bit of sexy talk, most of the men I meet don't want to be reminded I'm not from the States."

"Where are you from?" Colin asked to break the ice.

"We—both Nán and me—we're originally from San Marcos, in El Salvador. My father got his green card a long time ago. He was able to bring my mother and me in about nine years ago. I'm here legally. But Nán's father... He got in trouble, was deported, came back. He couldn't get any kind of immigration permit. Something bad happened to Hernán last year, though, and he couldn't wait anymore. He, you know..." Rudy swallowed hard. "He came across the border."

Colin nodded. From his conversations with clients at the Immigration Initiative center, he knew a little about the journey people undertook when they were desperate to come to the United States. No one made that expensive and hazardous trek lightly.

"Can you tell me what happened to Hernán?" he asked.

Rudy shook his head. "He wouldn't like that. He's very private."

"Okay. Tell me what I can do to help."

Rudy collapsed back into his chair and waved his arms wide. He sounded close to tears. "I don't know. Hernán shouldn't have to do this. Go with Gerald, I mean. But Gerald can make things very bad for both of us."

He fell silent and then brushed away a tear from his cheek. "I used to think I loved Gerald. Isn't that pathetic? I was with him for more than two years and I really believed for a long time that it meant something to him. That I was more than his kept boy. Then he made me leave and he got lawyers involved and I was so embarrassed. I thought that was as low as he could go. But now... Now he's trying to make my cousin go to bed with him. Hernán can't do that."

Can't? To Colin, that seemed a curious word to use, but it was beside the immediate point. "Have you or Hernán talked to a lawyer about whether any immigration options are open to him?"

Rudy wiped his eyes with the back of his hand and shook his head. He mumbled, "We can't afford it."

"That's where we need to start then. I know good lawyers who handle some matters like this pro bono, so you might be able to get help without paying. We need to get Hernán to tell someone his story. Since you've got a green card, maybe we can use that to have you sponsor him. Or another relative, if he has one in the States legally." Colin sat back with a whoosh as he ran through options in his head.

"What else could work? Maybe asylum."

"What's that?" Rudy asked.

"Asylum is a special path to get permission to stay in the U.S. for someone who's likely to be persecuted in his or her home country because of religion or membership in a political group. Or certain social groups, for that matter, like being gay or transgendered."

Rudy sat up straight. "You can stay here just for being gay?"

Colin shook his head. "It's not quite that simple. You have to prove that you have a well-founded belief you've been targeted for harm specifically for your sexual orientation or identity, and that the circumstances in your home country are such that you couldn't get protection anywhere."

Rudy muttered, "El Salvador is terrible that way. My friend Linda was transgender. She was murdered in San Marcos and the police wouldn't do anything even though they knew who did it. The man who killed her was in church the next week. Everyone knew and no one said anything."

"That's so sad. I'm sorry about your friend," Colin said, leaning forward to meet Rudy's eyes. After a respectful pause, he continued, "We'd have to study that avenue more. Is Hernán part of some group where he was being persecuted? Maybe a political group?"

Rudy turned red and rocked back and forth. "I can't… He'll be so mad at me."

Colin tapped his fingers on the arm of his chair. "Can you get him to talk to me? Maybe if he trusts me, he'll tell me. Or let you talk about it."

Rudy jumped to his feet as he all but wailed, "He won't come. I begged him." He paced around the sitting room, stopping to look out at the courtyard. Finally he asked, "What if you come to the restaurant? At closing time. He's usually done and ready to head home about eleven. That's late, I know, but if you're there and I get you two talking…"

Colin stood and put a hand on Rudy's shoulder to calm him. "I'll be in front of Veranda at eleven."

AT THE APPOINTED time, Colin stood shivering on Commercial Street. The damp ocean air had morphed into a low-hanging fog that shrouded the street lamps in gauze. The top of the Pilgrim Tower, a huge granite monolith looming over the town, was completely lost from sight.

For a Saturday night, the street seemed fairly quiet. People huddled into their jackets as they passed by. The clothes Colin had brought for the trip weren't really warm enough. He wore a light sweater under his mid-weight jacket, his hands were stuffed into his jeans, but the chilly night air felt much colder than the temperature indicated on his smartphone. If the fog didn't lift, he mused, he was going to have trouble getting out of Provincetown the next day.

Finally he heard two voices speaking low in Spanish, and Rudy and Hernán materialized through the fog. Rudy sounded desperate when he switched to English and hissed, "Just talk to him. Please. This is my fault and I can't let you just give in to Gerald."

Colin stepped forward and offered his hand to Hernán. He said, "We meet again. I think I was warmer last night when I was wet." Hernán looked up at him from under his bangs, his eyes showing only suspicion.

Rudy looked back and forth between the two of them. "Wait, you've met?"

Colin nodded. "Your cousin threw a line into the harbor and fished me out." He smiled, and Hernán finally softened his glare. A slight twitch at the corner of his mouth gave Colin hope.

Hernán said in a rough voice, "I was hoping for some tuna but I think I pulled up a dolphin."

Colin barked out a short laugh. "I may not look like it, but I can be a shark when necessary."

Hernán studied him for a long moment, and then looked at Rudy. He stuffed his hands in his pockets. "I think the expression is, 'It's colder than a witch's tit.'"

It sounded like an opening, so Colin said, "Let's get out of this fog. Where can we talk?"

Rudy piped up. "Not your inn. Gerald sometimes likes to go to the bar there. We don't want to run into him."

"The Little Bar is probably quiet enough to talk," Hernán offered.

"Lead the way."

The three walked along Commercial until Hernán turned into a small street and led them to an old building. Further down the block was the dance club Atlantic House. A steady beat of Saturday night house music pumped against Colin's ears but when they left the street the pulse became more muted.

The Little Bar was just that—a small, narrow room that ended in a stone fireplace where a good blaze crackled. The bar that lined the left side of the space was old, its wooden counter scarred. A man with a thick gray mustache and beard served drinks behind it. Only a few patrons claimed seats at the bar or stood around.

Rudy said, "Get me something fabulous. I'll go save those chairs near the fire."

"Hey George," Hernán called out with a broad smile as they stepped up to the bar, and Colin had time to wish that smile was for him. The bartender tipped his head in greeting. "Let's get a cosmopolitan for Rudy, and I'll take a Sam Adams. You?" he asked Colin.

"I'm buying these, to say thank you for last night. I'll take a Coke." George pulled a beer bottle out of his bar fridge, filled a cup with soda, and then started to assemble Rudy's drink. Colin pulled some twenties out of his pocket.

"You don't have to do that," Hernán said, a slight edge harshening his tone. "I can buy my own drink."

"I'm sure you can, but I was raised to show thanks when someone does something nice. You got wet last night. Let me buy," Colin all but pleaded.

Hernán glared at the counter until George came back with Rudy's pink cosmo, a plastic mermaid dangling from the rim of the glass. Colin laughed at that and Hernán looked quickly at him. He gave a small, reluctant grin himself. He didn't protest again when Colin slid money across the bar to George.

Rudy had arranged three wooden chairs in a way that maximized their privacy while giving him a chance to look over all the men in the bar. Hernán shook his head as he handed over the cocktail. "You looking to pick up some company tonight, primo?"

"I don't want to be a waiter forever," Rudy answered with a dismissive wave of his free hand before he sipped delicately at his cosmo. "I need to find a man to keep me warm."

Colin settled in with his soda, to the right of Hernán's chair. "It must get lonely in Provincetown over the winter, when all the tourists go home."

Rudy said, "I guess we'll find out, if we don't get good jobs in

Boston. There are a few restaurants here that stay open year round, and a couple of the shops and galleries. We'd probably find something."

Hernán grimaced. "You can wait tables anywhere. I don't think there are enough dishwasher or cleaning jobs to keep me going." He glanced at Colin, and frown lines appeared on his forehead. "Enough of that. Why are we here?"

Rudy leaned forward and said in a low voice, "Colin has some ideas for ways you could get documents and stay here. Then Gerald wouldn't be able to threaten you. *Either* of us."

Hernán turned red and growled, <<Dammit, Rudy. I told you I'd handle this.>>

Colin interjected. <<I heard what that Nimble asshole wants you to do, Hernán. It's terrible and you shouldn't have to put up with that kind of harassment.>>

Hernán stared at him blankly for a moment. Then he muttered, "I forgot you speak Spanish." Silence stretched between them. Colin gazed back into Hernán's obsidian eyes, trying to make the stubborn man see that he genuinely wanted to help.

Rudy said softly, "Nán, we don't have anyone else to turn to. Just hear him out."

Hernán grunted and inclined his head. Grudgingly, he asked Colin, "And why is it that you have ideas about this? Are you a lawyer?"

Colin shook his head. "No, I work for a non-profit that helps immigrants get acclimated to life in the States. I meet a lot of people there who got their green cards or work permits in different ways. We help with jobs training, language classes, all kinds of things like that. Also some lobbying on Capitol Hill about immigration issues, particularly the ones that keep families apart. We need to get you together with an immigration lawyer who can really explore the options. I have a lot of contacts who might be willing to help."

Rudy interrupted eagerly, "Nán, he says there's a thing called asylum. For people who've been persecuted and can't be protected by the police where they come from."

Colin nodded. "It's a little more complicated than that, but maybe that's a possibility. You have to show that you've been persecuted because you're in a special group. Like a religious or political organization—"

"Or gay," Rudy interrupted.

Hernán shot him a hard look and Rudy shut up. To Colin, he said, "I can't afford a lawyer. Even if I could, that takes a lot of time, right? Gerald is a problem right now."

Colin set his cup on a table and rubbed his palms against his jeans. "I, uh, I thought about that today. After Rudy and I talked." He felt his ears beginning to burn. "You could, uh, leave P-town while the process happens." Hernán frowned, Rudy looked puzzled, and Colin blurted out, "You can come to DC and stay with me."

Hernán's jaw dropped and a peculiar combination of emotions flared in his eyes. The only one Colin was sure he could read was fear. Even Rudy looked suspicious. *Shit, I'm making a mess again.*

Hernán opened his mouth to dismiss the offer but Colin jumped in. "Look, I'm sure it sounds ridiculous. But hear me out. I have plenty of space, and you'd have your own room. If you're in DC, I can get you together with people who may be able to help."

He glanced at Rudy, trying to get support. "David, the man Brandon married. He's a very good lawyer with several immigration wins. Or he can help us find someone else. But he lives in DC as well, so everything will just be so much easier if you're there too."

Cautiously, Rudy added, "Brandon says Colin is a good man..."

The fear on Hernán's face gave way to anger. His eyes narrowed and his brows furrowed. He barked out, "And just what would I have to do, to pay for my room and this legal help? You going to make me suck your dick every night? Let you fuck me?" He surged to his feet. "I might as well let Gerald do what he wants. What difference does it make who turns me into a puto?"

Slamming his bottle on the table, Hernán stormed out of the bar.

Colin looked at Rudy with wide eyes. "I don't want anything from him. I feel like I owe him for rescuing me. I want to help."

Rudy bit his lip, trembling so much he sloshed his cosmo. "It's complicated. I believe you mean to be nice, but... It's bad for Hernán. Worse than it ever was for me." He looked ready to cry again. "I guess he's right. Anything you can do is going to take time. We don't have time."

Colin could hear his mother's voice in his head. *Well, you tried your best. That's my brave boy. Sometimes you can't help, no matter how much you want to. Trust me. You have nothing to blame yourself for. You offered help and he didn't take it. Just go back home and keep working at your little charity. That's enough. It makes you feel good.*

The memory of Pranav's voice on the phone clawed at his stomach. *Can you help me?* Colin had done nothing, and then Pranav was gone.

No.

This time Colin wasn't going to give up after one try. He wasn't going to slink away. What Gerald demanded was *wrong*. Hernán needed help and that meant Colin had to find a way to convince him he would be safe in Washington.

He said to Rudy, "I'm going after him."

"He'll be heading right, when he gets to Commercial Street."

Chapter 6

HERNÁN STRODE ALONG the sidewalk, teeth grinding, fists shoved into the pockets of his hooded jacket. He was freezing and his muscles quivered. Damn Rudy for stirring up this shit. Now *another* person knew he was in the country illegally. He could almost feel ICE officers breathing down his neck already.

Colin's not like that. He won't expose us.

It was a stupid thought. He didn't know this Colin person. Neither did Rudy. So how could they know what Colin would and wouldn't do? Find him a lawyer, give him a place to stay, all out of the goodness of his heart. Yeah, right. Everybody wanted the same thing from Hernán, and when he tried to say no they *took* it. They took it no matter how he twisted and tried to get away…

Lost in bad memories, he didn't register the sound of footsteps running along the pavement until a hand touched his shoulder. He whirled with a cry, hands up before him automatically to push, but Colin grabbed his fingers first.

"It's just me. Colin. I'm sorry I scared you."

His grip was icy cold but surprisingly strong. Hernán jerked his hands away and said angrily, "What do you want, pendejo?"

"I want to help." Colin's glasses reflected the glare of the streetlamp. He lowered his head minutely and Hernán could see his eyes clearly, flashing blue. There was sincerity in them. He really seemed to mean what he said, but Hernán resisted the impulse to trust.

"You can't help," he growled, but it was softer than he meant it to be. More anguish showed in his voice than he intended to share and he cleared his throat awkwardly.

Colin didn't move away. "I can," he argued gently. "You don't know me. I get that. But you saw me at my absolute worst last night. You took care of me, and you got me to safety. Did I seem to you like the kind of person who would abuse your trust?"

Reluctantly, Hernán shook his head.

Colin sighed in relief. "Good. Because I'm not. I owe you a debt. When I offer you a place to stay, it's with no strings attached. I don't need money, and I know you aren't gay." He didn't seem to notice when Hernán shuffled his feet awkwardly. "I despise people like Gerald Nimble who try to twist the law to serve their petty little vices. I'm offering this because you're a good man, he's a bastard, and you don't deserve to be forced into anything."

The look in Colin's eyes was fierce and determined. The warrior shone out again, and Hernán felt himself yielding to it. He wanted to trust *someone*. Rudy was his best friend and had done all that he could, but he wasn't able to get Hernán out of the mess Gerald threw his way. Maybe, just maybe, this Colin meant it. Maybe he could help without expecting Hernán to...*do* anything.

No. No one helped out of the goodness of his heart. Everyone wanted something. In Hernán's experience, usually the *same* thing. His voice rasped in his throat as he said reluctantly, "I believe you mean well. But no way am I going to leave town with you. I'll figure something out, or I'll just..." He gestured awkwardly and flushed.

"Don't do it, Hernán," Colin urged gruffly. "Don't give in to Nimble."

Hernán's eyes burned and his throat tightened. He imagined that terrible man's hands on his shoulders, pressing him to his knees. He shook his head fiercely to clear the image, and his words sounded harsh on the darkened street. "I have to. It's about Rudy's safety too."

He turned and started to walk away, to leave behind Colin and the impossible lifeline he offered. At least he knew enough about Gerald to understand it would only be about sex. Gerald was an asshole to Rudy but he'd never physically hurt him. Compared to the things that had happened to Hernán, a night with Gerald would be...well, not easy but survivable.

Colin called after him. "Hernán, I'm not giving up that quickly. You have until tomorrow evening, right? I'm going to stay in Provincetown another day. Please. Talk to me before you go to his house."

Hernán stopped where he stood, but he didn't turn back. Pride and fear battled in his gut. If there was a chance Colin could help, he'd be a fool not to accept. He squared his shoulders. Without turning his head, he said, "I finish my cleaning job at eleven in the morning and I don't go to the restaurant until two."

Colin's voice when he answered was strong and determined. Warm. "I'll do everything in my power to help you get this resolved."

Hernán let the words wrap around him like a blanket. For a moment, he wished it were Colin's arms, not his voice. He jerked his head awkwardly and resumed his walk home.

Colin called out before he'd made it ten yards. "Will you have lunch with me tomorrow? So I can tell you what I've been able to do by then?"

He stopped again but still didn't turn around. He couldn't. "I'll be at Chach at noon. It's a restaurant. Anyone can tell you where that is."

"Thank you. I'll be there." Colin didn't say anything more as Hernán resumed his long, lonely walk home.

COLIN HURRIED BACK through the fog to The Brass Key. Ken was still on duty when he stopped at the front desk.

"Good evening, Mr. Felton. Can I do anything for you?" There was a flirtatious tone to his voice but Colin assumed that was for every customer.

"Two things, actually. I'm supposed to check out tomorrow but I'd like to stay another night if the room is still available." Ken checked his computer. He clicked a few keys, and then nodded.

"It is, actually. Someone was booked in but I can easily move him to a comparable room that'll be empty."

"Excellent. Also, can you tell me how to get to a restaurant called Chach?"

In his room a few minutes later, Colin fired up his laptop. He sent a quick email to his colleagues to let them know he was taking an additional vacation day. It was unprofessional of him but, hell, he rarely took vacation at all. He'd deliberately kept his work schedule light, figuring he'd probably be slightly depressed after the wedding.

Next he began to run Google searches. After typing in *Gerald Nimble hedge fund* he scoured the results. Quickly he located the name of the fund that Nimble managed, along with his professional biography. It was the typical puff piece, next to a photo of Nimble leaning earnestly toward the camera and radiating trustworthiness.

"Dickwad," Colin muttered, and kept clicking through to the links for the fund. He read through its prospectus and press releases, but found nothing useful. Following links to the fund's umbrella investment organization, he read a variety of materials on its goals, strategies and analysis of market trends. Still nothing. Two hours in, he began to despair.

Then he got to the page for the board of directors.

He sat back and smiled. "Gotcha."

COLIN TRIED TO sleep in the next morning to make up for his awful, drunken Friday night, but it was no use. He waited until he was sure his parents would be awake but before his father would have headed out for his usual Sunday round of golf.

His mother answered on the second ring. "Colin, dear. How was the wedding?" she asked brightly.

"Hi Mom. It was really nice. They held it on the beach at sunset."

"How lovely. We had gorgeous weather in Nantucket so I hope you had the same."

"We did. Listen, I'm sorry to be abrupt but is Dad still there?"

"Yes, he's just coming downstairs now. Would you like to speak with him?"

"Thanks, Mom. I promise I'll chat more soon." His mother called to his father, and then a warm baritone laced with surprise filled his ear.

"Well, good morning, Son. You never ask to talk to me. Is everything all right?"

"I know, Dad. I need to check in more often."

"You should fly yourself up to Saddle River soon. Your mother misses you."

"That'd be great. Right now I'm still in Provincetown. Listen, I kind of need a favor."

HERNÁN PACED AROUND his apartment Sunday morning after his shift cleaning houses, his nerves like razor blades. He had to face Gerald that night. Even though he wanted to spit in the man's face, he couldn't take the risk to Rudy.

It's sex, he tried to tell himself. *Everybody does it. Do what he wants, get it over with, and get out of there.*

Another part of his brain chimed in. *What if he wants me to do it again? He'll still have the same leverage.* Hernán groaned at the thought.

Making things worse was the lunch with Colin. He didn't know why he'd agreed to meet, except that he was desperate. Colin seemed honest and well-intentioned, and maybe he did have a backbone in that tall, sleek body. But what good would any of that do against someone rich and powerful like Gerald?

Maybe he'd just forget about showing up to lunch. A sleepless night had given way to a rough three hours of scrubbing toilets and changing beds. Grimy and sweaty despite the mid-September chill, he'd come home just long enough to put on the clothes he wore to wash dishes at the restaurant.

Then why am I wet? Hernán was shocked to realize that, as he fretted, he'd unconsciously jumped into the shower to clean off the residue of his morning job. He never did that before heading to Veranda because he'd be a sweaty mess again inside an hour of the start of his shift. Almost angrily, he toweled himself dry. Thank god Rudy wasn't there to make fun of him. He hadn't come home the night before, so apparently he'd picked up a trick after Hernán stormed out.

Shortly before noon, he walked along Shank Painter Road toward Chach, hands shoved into his pockets and head down. The whole way he continued to argue with himself. Life was complicated enough. He had no intention of accepting Colin's invitation. Colin could do nothing anyway.

And even if Hernán did accept help about Gerald, it was so much worse than Colin knew. He'd inevitably have to talk about *that* too. Hernán shivered as Lonnie's leering face flashed into his mind. Better if he just kept going right past the restaurant and went straight to Veranda.

His hand was on the glass door, pushing his way into Chach, before he consciously made the decision to show up. The bell over the door rang. *Dammit.* Shelly, a waitress with spiky blue hair and tattoos up both arms, called out a greeting.

"Hey Hernán. Table for one? You want to just sit at the counter?"

"Uh, thanks, but I'm meeting someone."

"Tall guy, glasses, brown hair? I think he's already here in the main dining room." Hernán took a peek and sure enough, Colin sat in a booth looking out the window. He hadn't yet noticed Hernán. There was still time to get away.

"Hernán! How are you?" Sara's voice calling across the dining room stopped his escape. Sara was from Jamaica, and she hadn't lost her accent. Dreads of black hair laced through with gray dripped down to her shoulders. Her wife Jane—white-haired, lightly tanned, poised and regal in a fuchsia blouse—sat across from her and waved hello as well. The women were just two booths down from Colin, and his head whipped around at Hernán's name.

Hernán sighed. *Nothing for it now but to go over.* Stopping at the women's booth, he bent to kiss Sara's cheek. She was an editor with the local paper, and Jane was a realtor in town. They'd met when he and Rudy took a gig as cater-waiters for their anniversary party at the beginning of summer. Since then, he frequently ran into one or both of them around town. As far as he could tell, Jane and Sara knew everyone.

"Hi sweetie," Jane said when he'd kissed her cheek as well. "Are you keeping out of trouble?"

"As much as I can. You know what Rudy's like."

"Will you join us?" Sara asked, starting to shift over in her booth.

"Thank you, but I'm meeting someone." He gestured vaguely in Colin's direction and both ladies turned to see. Colin's face lit up and he hurried out of his booth to come over.

"Jane! Sara! I didn't see you there," he exclaimed. They both got up to hug Colin hello. To Hernán's no-doubt perplexed expression, Colin said, "Jane and Sara were at the wedding I'm here for." They chatted for a few moments, asking questions about whether Colin was enjoying Provincetown, had Brandon and David gotten away for their honeymoon, and how did Hernán and Colin meet?

Fortunately, Shelly appeared with plates of food for the women. Hernán and Colin excused themselves to return to their booth. Sara gave a small smile as she looked back and forth between the two of them. Hernán felt his face flush but Colin didn't seem to notice.

Ensconced in the booth across from Colin, Hernán gulped water to steady his nerves. Colin's gaze was intense.

"How do you know Jane and Sara?" Colin asked, at the same time Hernán began, "Have you come up with any way—?"

They both stopped and laughed slightly. Colin nodded. "You're right, that's the most important thing." He leaned closer and spoke in a low voice so as not to be overheard. "Yes. I think I've found a way to stop Nimble from extorting you. We'll know soon if it worked."

Hernán blinked several times. He had expected lunch to be a complete waste of time. No way this nice man could go up against that cabrón Gerald Nimble, and certainly not overnight.

"Wh-what do you mean?" The anxiety and desperation he heard in his own voice alarmed him. Lowering his eyes to the tabletop, Hernán wrestled with a surge of hope. He folded his hands on the Formica, squeezing them together tightly.

"Okay so, Nimble is a manager of a hedge fund, right? And that fund is part of a larger family of funds," Colin began. Hernán shrugged; he didn't know much about finance. "Anyway, a company at the top of the pyramid makes all the big decisions for the various funds. That company has a lot of money under management, invested in many, many different mutual funds. The single fund Nimble manages is just one of those. That parent company is governed by a board of directors."

He sat back in the booth and gave Hernán a sheepish smile. "My father is one of the directors."

Hernán stared at him. "That… What?"

Colin nodded. "I know. Weird coincidence, right? Except it isn't really. The investment family that includes Nimble's fund is one of the largest, and my father has deep connections."

Hernán recalled Colin's comment about spending summers in Nantucket, and the penny dropped. "You're rich," he said to Colin, stunned.

Colin blushed. He nodded, and then said in a low voice, "Brandon doesn't know. Very few people do, so I'd appreciate if you kept it to yourself."

"How do you keep something like that private?" Hernán asked.

"It's easy to overlook me," Colin said with a shrug. "No, I mean that in a good way. The paparazzi used to run stuff on me years ago, but I was just too boring to make it worth their time. My brother still gets followed every time he starts dating a new girl because he gives them a lot more shit to work with. My father's in the news a lot too. He used to be on an economic council for the White House under the last president, stuff like that."

Colin leaned in again. "Look, that isn't important now. What matters is that I asked my father to pull some strings to rein in Nimble."

Colin's phone vibrated on the tabletop just then. He glanced at the display and smiled. "There it is. Dad talked to Uncle Samuel, who said he would speak to Nimble today."

Hernán felt frozen in place. None of this made any sense to him. He managed to ask, "Uncle Samuel?"

"Sam Roberson. He's the chief investment officer for the family of funds, and, um, my godfather." With a nervous chuckle, Colin added, "He's not really related, but we always called him uncle. My brother Griff calls him Uncle Sam but I think that's a little much."

"Your godfather," Hernán said flatly. He'd thought Colin a straightforward, uncomplicated, well-intentioned *guy*. Instead, he was wealthy, connected, and related to a financial wizard of some kind.

"It's good news, right?" Colin's nerves gave his voice an edge. He all but pleaded for a response, but Hernán suspected the question was not just about Gerald.

He swallowed hard. "I'm sorry to be stupid, but even with your uncle calling Gerald, how does that help me?"

"Well, see, I told Dad that the manager of one of the funds is extorting sexual favors. That's the kind of thing that, if it got out, would create instability in Nimble's fund. From there, it could potentially spread and create bad publicity for the entire family of investments. So as a director, Dad felt it was his responsibility to let the CIO know. Uncle Samuel's a good man. Now that he knows what Nimble is doing in his personal life, he'll make Nimble stop or fire him from the fund."

It started to sink through. Hernán didn't understand the financial stakes at play, but he got enough to know that Gerald was unlikely to risk his professional standing just to force a man into his bed.

He licked his lip carefully. "How will I know if, um, if it worked?"

Colin nodded. "I thought about that. I'd just as soon Nimble doesn't know who my family is, or I'd confront him directly. I think the best thing is for you to text him. Rudy must have his cell number, right? Then you or Rudy should send something like, what time do I have to be there. If Uncle Samuel has torn Nimble a new and sufficiently painful asshole, I'm guessing he'll respond right away and say not to come."

Hernán released a whoosh of air. It started to sink in, what Colin had done for him. He didn't want to get his hopes up, but he did feel a calm begin to spread in the center of the storm. His eyes burned. "This is… I don't know what to say."

Colin blushed. "Don't say anything until we know it worked. Give it an hour or so. Send the text then and we'll find out."

We. The simple word reverberated like a caress in Hernán's anguished head. For whatever reason, Colin had made Hernán's terrible problem his own. He had done it despite Hernán's protest, despite his rudeness.

Some small part still worried what Colin might expect in return, but he crushed it viciously. *No.* He knew next to nothing about Colin except that he was apparently fucking rich. That he kept his money a secret. That the man he loved had married someone else. That he was laid low by too much to drink. That he went out of his way to repay the small kindness Hernán had shown when he fished him from the harbor…

Huh. It turned out he knew a lot about Colin after all. And one of the things that he *knew* was that Colin truly expected nothing in return.

Shelly bustled over. "Are you boys ready to order?"

The interruption gave Hernán time to get his head under some kind of control. He hurriedly ordered an omelet topped with pork and green chili.

Colin said, "That sounds good. Same for me please, and some more coffee." He too sounded relieved at the chance to shift the focus. Shelly brought his coffee and then Sara stopped by their booth.

She rested a hand on Hernán's shoulder. "I don't know if either of you is free tonight, but Jane and I are hosting a potluck dinner. We'd love it if you could join us."

Colin smiled up at her. "That's really kind. I was originally heading back home today but I decided to stay another night. I'd love to come."

Hernán had a feeling Sara and Jane read something into his lunch with Colin. Hernán never dated at all since he got to town, but they certainly knew Rudy and his reputation. They also knew Colin somewhat, apparently, and that he was gay. It wasn't a huge stretch for them to think there might be something going on between Colin and Hernán.

He was certain, though, that they didn't know Colin's real secret. Sudden pride bloomed in his heart. Colin had trusted him with something he hadn't even told Brandon, the man he was in love with.

Maybe...maybe Hernán could trust him too, with his terrible secrets.

Sara still looked at him expectantly. *Oh right. The dinner.* "I'd really like to join you, but I'm working at Veranda until eight."

"Just come by after," she insisted. "There'll be plenty of food." Colin looked hopeful as well. Against his better judgment, Hernán heard himself agreeing to go. Sara gave Colin the address, kissed Hernán's cheek, and hurried off with Jane.

The two of them were quiet through the rest of their lunch. Hernán didn't really know what to say, and Colin also seemed to struggle. He made a few noises about the food, asked for coffee, blushed as he looked at Hernán. When Shelly brought the check, they both reached for it.

A wordless argument took place across their faces:

Let me get this. You know I can afford it.

I don't care. I owe you.

You saved me at the harbor.

You protected me from a monster.

Colin relented and dropped his fingers from the check. Hernán smiled at his small victory.

Chapter 7

THAT EVENING, COLIN took a circuitous route from his inn to Sara and Jane's address so he could spend more time exploring Commercial Street. Since it was a Sunday, many of the weekend tourists had gone. The town seemed quieter than on the day before, or even that morning.

Reaching a gap between shingled houses, he spotted a sign indicating a public path and followed it to the beach. The tide was in and so he stood for a while next to a row of small houses lining a pier and watched a few boats bob at anchor.

The water was glycerin-clear at the shore, deepening to azure as his gaze tracked to the Long Point lighthouse in the middle distance. Brandon had pointed it out to him as they walked through town on Saturday. Beyond the spit of land on which the lighthouse rested, a distant blur that was more of Cape Cod curled around the bay.

His phone trilled, making him jump. He hauled it out of his pocket quickly, hoping for a text from Hernán. His father'd confirmed earlier Uncle Samuel had a frank and unpleasant telephone call with Gerald Nimble, and he believed the message had been received. Still, Hernán hadn't contacted him about whether Nimble did indeed drop his extortion.

The incoming text read, "First stop!" It was from Brandon, attaching a picture of David and him mugging at Nelson's Column in London. In the picture, David's lips were pressed to Brandon's blond hair. The huge grin on Brandon's face brought out one on Colin's. It was sweet and Colin typed a short reply, with a recommendation for one of his favorite restaurants in London.

Only when he put his phone away did he notice the usual regret he felt upon seeing Brandon and David happy together was missing. In some ways the absence of emotion alarmed him, but in others it was a relief.

He had long tried to accept Brandon and David belonged together. Even so, he couldn't quite let go of his own fantasies of what might have been, if he'd had the balls to ask Brandon on a date before he ever met David. Of course they might not have worked out at all, but it would have been nice to *know.* Instead, for months he'd pined for Brandon from a distance at their various group gatherings, playing soccer or kickball, or meeting at a bar for trivia night.

Another member of their group, Ethan Schinderman, similarly had eyes for Brandon. Ethan was always loud and dramatic and the center of attention. Colin realized early on that was Ethan's way to deal with the fact he was overweight and the least athletic man in their group.

It didn't help that Ethan had bushy hair and his ill-fitting glasses often slipped down his nose. He was funny, though, and Colin used to think he was kind. That was probably why he agreed to go on a date with Ethan.

It'd been a disaster. Ethan brought up Brandon constantly, poking at Colin with remarks about their friend, trying to get a confession about how Colin felt. Wary, Colin had avoided revealing anything, and just remarked on general qualities like Brandon's endless knowledge of trivia.

Ethan had gotten drunk as the date went on, sharing more about how he crushed on Brandon than he managed to elicit from Colin. It seemed to be a defense thing, as if an agreement they both longed for the same man would be a shared interest on which to build another date or a relationship.

At some point, the level of detail Ethan knew about Brandon's life became slightly alarming. Colin pleaded an eight a.m. work meeting and ended the date early. He and Ethan stayed cordial in a group setting, but were often awkward around each other. When Ethan asked Colin on another date, he turned it down.

Then Brandon brought David to one of their kickball games. Ethan went out of his way to make David feel ashamed he was twenty-two years older than Brandon. He even managed to suck Colin into his spiteful whirlpool.

Things had never been easy between Brandon and Ethan afterwards, or between Colin and Ethan for that matter. They all stayed members of the same sports group, but the damage Ethan had done was too deliberate to allow friendship. Still, Colin often noticed Ethan's eyes tracking Brandon across the kickball field or wherever they met. Yet Brandon said Ethan made no attempt to apologize for his malice with David.

Colin frowned at the harbor. Why was he thinking about Ethan so many months later? Perhaps it was the realization that, for a long time, he'd been as guilty as Ethan of carrying a torch. When Brandon and David broke up over the summer, seemingly for good, Colin genuinely sorrowed for Brandon's heartbreak.

It hadn't stopped him from taking advantage of the split, though, had it? He asked Brandon out and they went on two dates, but it became clear instantly to Colin that Brandon was nowhere near over David. Then Brandon was injured a few weeks later, in the hit-and-run incident that ultimately cost him his leg. Colin had been in the emergency ward when he heard a groggy and injured Brandon call out for David.

Colin wished he could say he hadn't hesitated to make the call. At least no more than a few minutes passed before he searched for David's number on Brandon's phone to let him know Brandon was in the hospital. It was the right thing to do. When he overheard Brandon admit to David he still loved him, he tried hard to let his joy for his friend be enough. That tragedy brought David and Brandon back together and a few months later they were engaged.

Colin was weak, he knew. It had taken time to move on from his selfish regret. But looking at the picture of Brandon and David in London, he felt nothing but contentment. That surprised him at some level. Even a few days earlier, his pining for Brandon had ended with a surprise dunking in the same harbor he now regarded.

So what had changed? He tried hard not to think of his stupid, useless attraction to a straight man that had apparently taken over the space where his crush on Brandon had resided.

He sighed as a breeze rippled the water before him, rushed onshore and blew his hair into his eyes. Someday, maybe he would finally meet someone who was actually available to him.

ABOUT FIFTEEN PEOPLE had already gathered in Jane and Sara's dining room when Colin entered. He set down the dessert he had purchased earlier from Connie's Bakery, and then let Sara introduce him around.

That night, she wore her dreads gathered and tied with a black, green and yellow cloth. The guests were mostly townies who lived year-round in Provincetown, though one lesbian couple lived in New Hampshire. Jane pressed a drink on him, so he nursed a vodka tonic as he chatted.

Eventually, Sara separated him from the small throng and asked for his help in the kitchen. A gleam in her eye alerted Colin, so he was ready. When she passed him a hot casserole dish from the oven, she said casually, "By the way, I'm curious. How do you know Hernán?"

He certainly wasn't about to discuss the situation with Nimble, so he went with the truth he felt able to share, embarrassing though it was. "I don't know how obvious it was, but I got pretty wasted at the reception Friday night." The twitch of Sara's lips told him it had probably been obvious indeed. He groaned.

"Anyway, I went staggering along Commercial Street to get sober, and ended up falling into the water, drunk off my ass. Hernán was passing by, saw me fall and dragged me out. I wanted to take him to lunch to say thanks, though he wouldn't let me pay."

Sara's evaluating gaze reminded Colin she was a journalist by training, and probably sensed there was more to the story. When she just smiled, he relaxed slightly. She said, "That Hernán, and his cousin Rudy. They're some of the nicest workers in town this summer. Rudy flirts with everyone." Sara rolled her eyes comically, and then sharpened her gaze. "Come to think of it, though, I've never seen Hernán flirt. Or go out to lunch with anyone, woman or man."

Colin blushed as she came at him from a different angle. It was as if Sara could see right through him, and figured out how to pry information loose. Or perhaps she read his growing attraction and wanted to warn him off.

He cleared his throat. "That's surprising. I mean, given how good-looking he is."

"There's a story there but I haven't been able to get it out of them." Colin might have looked nervous because she leaned in close. "Don't mind me. I can't help being nosy. I actually aspire to know less than people think I should." Colin chuckled appreciatively, and Sara continued, "I promise, even if I knew the story, I wouldn't do anything to hurt those nice men."

Jane joined them in the kitchen and lightly rested a hand on her wife's waist. "Colin, has she extracted your life story yet?"

Sara answered for him. "Oh, we were chatting about Hernán and Rudy, ooman. We haven't even gotten to Colin yet."

Jane laughed. "This is one of the hazards of being a townie. After the tourists leave for the season, there's not much to do besides gossip." At Sara's squawk of protest, Jane grinned and changed the subject. "Have you heard from David and Brandon?"

Colin showed them pictures Brandon had sent of the trip so far. They chatted for a few minutes longer before they returned to their party.

He became aware he had an eye on the clock as it approached eight. Hernán had said he'd be off work then. Colin replayed the ugly conversation with Nimble he'd overheard, when the dick had told Hernán to come to his house that very evening at eight-thirty along with Hernán's boss. If Hernán wasn't confident Uncle Samuel's message had gotten through Nimble's egotistical skull, he might feel like he had to go along with the extortion.

Colin's stomach churned as he imagined that handsome man walking into Nimble's bedroom, walls closing around him like a Venus flytrap. He pictured Nimble from the day at Veranda, with his sagging jowl, plastic looks, and obvious attempts to conceal his age. Pasty hands holding his glass. The idea of those hands grasping at Hernán was infuriating, and he set aside his paper plate of food half-uneaten.

His mother had raised him to glide smoothly through social events, though. He wandered around the house, mingling, but he itched to know what was happening with Hernán. The clock he could see inched slowly closer to eight. He couldn't think of a good way to find out what was going on. They had exchanged cell numbers, but texting didn't feel right. It might imply he didn't think Hernán could handle himself.

When Hernán called out a hello to Jane and Sara at five minutes after eight, Colin nearly went slack with relief.

He watched from the dining room as Hernán kissed the hostesses on the cheek and greeted many of the other locals. He seemed distracted, though, and his head craned around the room. Sara whispered something in his ear and his gaze shot to where Colin stood. A smile lit up his features.

Colin's heart skipped a beat. *Stop it. He's straight. There's nothing for you there besides friendship.*

He resisted the urge to rush over to Hernán, partly because he was aware of Sara's all-too-knowing eyes on him. Shortly, Hernán joined him in the dining room and gave a quick sideways jerk of his head.

Colin followed him to the currently empty kitchen. Hernán turned to face him, smiling more naturally than Colin had yet seen. In a low voice, he said, "It worked. I had Rudy text Gerald and he sent back, 'Tell him I changed my mind.'"

"I'm so glad," Colin exclaimed. "It's probably the first time anyone has refused that prick."

Hernán's arms twitched, like he wanted to hug Colin. Instead, he blushed but stuck out his hand. "Thank you," Hernán said fervently as Colin shook with him. "You don't know what it would have cost me, to go there."

Softly, Colin said, "I'd like to know. If you'll tell me."

Hernán blinked at him a few times. He wetted his lips as if preparing to speak, but suddenly dropped Colin's hand instead and looked away. "Not yet," he said toward the floor.

'Not yet' means sometime he might. Colin contented himself with the thought. Aloud, he asked, "Are you hungry? Someone brought a fantastic mac and cheese with lobster."

Hernán gave him a crooked grin. "Tourist," he teased. "After just one summer here I'm sick of lobster."

"How can anyone get sick of lobster?" Colin acted scandalized to play along with the change of subject. "It's got to be the most decadent seafood there is."

"I'll take a good sopa de siete mares anytime."

"Soup of the seven seas," Colin translated. "Let me guess. It's got fish in it?"

"Fish, crab, squid. All kinds of good stuff." He gave Colin a shy smile. "Maybe I can make it for you some day."

Colin swallowed hard and was about to answer when Jane buzzed into the kitchen with a beer for Hernán. He left the two of them to talk, and rejoined the party in the living room. Now his fears for Hernán were gone, he found he could engage more naturally.

Rudy had come in while they were in the kitchen, and he was already ensconced in a corner chair. Martini in one hand, he regaled a few admiring men with tales of the sexiest tourists he'd seen over the weekend. When he noticed Colin watching he mouthed "thank you" before taking a sip of his cocktail.

Colin felt warm inside. He was glad he'd been able to do something helpful, and his father's connections had been so useful. An instinct warned him Nimble wouldn't take such an attack lightly, though. Whatever Uncle Samuel had said, it surely indicated he was aware Nimble's actions could bring legal and PR troubles upon the family of funds. Nimble would suspect Hernán had an ally, someone able to put a word in Samuel's ear. Colin had to assume Nimble was spiteful and vindictive, and would watch for an opportunity to take revenge.

After another half-hour, he was sitting in a chair on the back porch, talking to a man and woman, when Hernán joined the small group. The couple, owners of a small sandwich shop in town, greeted Hernán warmly. He smiled at them but leaned close to Colin's ear. "Would you like to get out of here?"

The words tickled the small hairs on Colin's neck and he shivered involuntarily. He nodded, and then excused himself to the shop owners. As he followed Hernán to the front door, he caught Sara's eye. She smiled at him and indicated Hernán's back. He flushed, shook his head slightly and waved goodbye.

The evening had grown chilly. Colin was grateful for the warm hoodie he'd purchased at Hook as he wandered through town.

"May I buy you a drink to celebrate?" Hernán asked. "We're not far from The Red Inn and they have a nice bar."

"That's where my Friday night binge started. Do you think I'd be welcomed back to the scene of my crime?" Colin asked.

Hernán chuffed a laugh. "I doubt anyone who even noticed you there on Friday hasn't been drunk himself."

"Fair enough. But I'm buying this time since you got lunch."

Hernán's eyes clouded with concern for a moment, but he gave a quick nod. They walked quietly through the dark and mostly empty streets to the historic red building, its garden glistening in fairy lights again. Hernán led them through the picket fence and inside, where he nodded to the host and kept going into the bar area. There were empty stools, but Hernán selected a small table away from the few patrons.

A big, burly man with a fierce black beard came up to them. "Hey, Hernán. What'll it be?"

Hernán gestured for Colin to order first. "A, uh, a Grey Goose on the rocks please."

"I'll take a pint of whatever ale's on tap," Hernán said. "Zeke, this is Colin." The waiter inclined his head in greeting before heading off to get their drinks.

"I love how you know everyone," Colin said.

"It's a small town really, when you get past the tourists. It doesn't take long to meet everyone working here, or people like Jane and Sara who go out of their way to make people feel welcome."

"It must be nice. I've never lived in a small town like this. Well, I spent my summers in Nantucket, but I don't think that really qualifies." *Not with my parents' big house, the servants, the yacht club…*

When Zeke returned with Hernán's beer and Colin's vodka, Hernán took the opportunity to ask a few questions. Colin talked a little about his brother and sister, his boarding school days, even his nanny. Normally he kept those things private because he didn't want his friends to think differently of him, once they knew his upbringing.

A part of him squirmed as he worried what Hernán would think. *Am I showing off? Will he see me as some over-entitled rich boy?* Hernán's opinion of him mattered deeply to Colin, for no good reason.

Not true. I want him to trust me so I can really help him.

As Hernán drained the last of his beer, Colin decided the time was right to bring it up again. He turned his nearly-full glass in his hands and focused on the table as he said, "I'm glad Nimble will leave you alone now, but he's just one asshole. There will be others, and your…" he looked around the bar but no one was near, "immigration status will always be an issue."

He glanced up to see Hernán staring into the bottom of his glass, cheeks red. Quickly, Colin said, "I don't mean to embarrass you. I just… I want to help. I really do know lawyers in DC who handle immigration cases all the time."

He caught Hernán's eyes and said firmly, "I don't want anything in return. But please. Meet me halfway here."

Hernán rolled the edge of his empty glass on the tabletop. Finally he inhaled deeply through his nose, set the glass aside and leaned forward. Hands folded on the bar table, he met Colin's gaze. "I believe you. And I…trust you. But I need to tell you something first, so you know what you're getting in to."

Colin waited, racking his brain to guess what Hernán was worried about. He kept silent and eventually Hernán continued. "It's not just about Gerald. I mean, why I tried to keep a low profile here, and worked in the kitchen instead of taking a better job as a waiter."

"What do you mean?"

"I guess Rudy didn't tell you. I'm, well, the reason I left San Marcos, is…I was targeted by Cuernos del Diablo."

"The gang?" Colin's jaw dropped.

Cuernos del Diablo was an infamously vicious group of thugs. Its members were linked to drugs, child prostitution, sex trafficking, and brutal murders. People who threatened to inform against them had been beheaded. Prosecutors who tried to bring cases against its members were killed horribly, along with their families. The gang was terrifying. It had formed originally in the States, and then took hold as well in El Salvador and other Latin American countries when a large number of its members were deported years earlier. The current administration nevertheless used the specter of such gangs who were found in large cities like L.A. and New York to justify its draconian efforts to change the immigration laws.

"Were you mixed up with them?" Colin asked, shocked.

Hernán shook his head desperately. "No. Never. About eleven months ago, though, some of them started following me around every day. Three men, mainly. I knew what they were because of the face tattoos. There's a gang symbol a lot of them use, of the horns of the devil."

Colin nodded; he'd seen pictures.

"I don't know why they chose me at first," Hernán continued. "If it was an initiation thing or what. But every day, they'd call out things they wanted me to do, or were going to do to me." He closed his eyes and all but whispered, "Sex things. They waited near my college or my house.

"One day…," he swallowed hard. "One day they stabbed me. I ran to jump on a bus and got away, but I nearly died."

"The police?" Colin asked.

"One officer tried," Hernán said sadly. "The police were usually just as scared to mess with Cuernos as I was. This guy, though, Martín Alba…he told me we had to stop them. I knew two of the men who attacked me, from school." Hernán brushed the heel of his hand over a cheek. "I gave him the names, and they were picked up and put in jail. Two weeks later, Alba was killed. Word came I'd be next."

He shivered and closed his eyes. "My uncle Juan told me I needed to get out of El Salvador or I'd be murdered. He helped set everything up, and I ran." He looked intently at Colin, and his voice shaded with fear. "But you have Cuernos in the States too. More so than in my country."

He sighed. "Juan warned me to stay hidden always, keep out of sight. Who knows how far they'd go? It isn't like I can ask anyone, hey, are you looking for me? But if they are, if you get mixed up in this, if Cuernos finds out where I am..."

Colin didn't waver. "I understand. Thank you for explaining but I'm willing to take the risk. I've been in a few situations that would surprise you, and I can get us protection if we ever need it."

Hernán gave him a small smile. "Shark, not dolphin?" He looked down at the tabletop again but Colin waited him out. Finally, Hernán asked, "If...if I came to DC, how would this work?"

Colin exhaled a sigh of relief. "Okay. We'd leave tomorrow, without telling anyone at your job, just to make sure Nimble doesn't have another change of heart. He won't know where you've gone. Once he accepts that, hopefully he'll drop this all for good and leave Rudy alone. You'll stay in my guest room as long as you need, and we'll try to get some time with David James or another lawyer to begin talking about immigration options for you."

"How would I get to DC? I mean, it's got to be expensive and I don't have much money saved yet."

Colin grinned widely. "Airfare is the least of our troubles, I promise. How do you feel about small planes?"

Chapter 8

RUDY WAS TEARFUL and dramatic as Hernán finished packing the last of his clothes into a large knapsack. "What if I never see you again?" he wailed.

"Rudy, it's only DC. It's maybe a few hundred miles. You have the address and Colin's phone number so you'll be able to find me."

"I'll be so lonely without you, Nán."

The stranger snoring away in Rudy's bed in their small studio apartment grunted and rolled over then. Hernán smiled. "I don't think you'll be so lonely as all that."

Rudy looked over his shoulder. "Oh. Vinnie? It's just a comfort thing. He doesn't have any money."

"Well, you'll have more room to entertain without me here. Maybe snag that rich guy you dream about," Hernán teased.

"I'd rather have you," Rudy said and hugged Hernán.

"Me too, primo. I know how much you've done for me. Without the money you came up with, I'd still be—"

"Don't talk about it. It was just a watch."

"Your Rolex."

Rudy sighed. "The only thing I got out of the relationship with Gerald. But it went for a good cause." He released his hold on Hernán and stepped back to wipe his eyes. "Are you sure about this, Nán?"

Hernán shook his head. "No, I'm not sure. But I think I trust Colin. You and I were probably going to have to leave Provincetown anyway for the winter. If it turns out Colin's not all he says, at least I can look for work around DC. Maybe I'll find jobs for both of us."

"You should tell him," Rudy said, a bit reproachfully.

"Maybe. But I don't want him thinking I'd...you know."

"Something tells me he'd understand, and he wouldn't push."

A horn beeped outside. "That's my cab. I'm meeting Colin at the airport."

"Did he buy you a plane ticket?" Rudy asked.

"Not exactly. Apparently he's a pilot and he has his own plane."

"Marry him, Nán," Rudy declared. "Or I will."

Vinnie-in-the-bed called out for him just then and Hernán laughed. He hadn't mentioned Colin's revelation about his wealth, though the plane thing was certainly a hint. Cousin or not, Rudy might cut him for a chance at a rich, good-looking, sweet man with a heart of... *Shit. Stop thinking about him that way.*

"You've already got a man," he snorted at Rudy. "Go take care of him."

HERNÁN BROODED ABOUT Rudy's advice all the way to the airport. *You should tell him.* The taxi wove through scrub pines and dunes, offering periodic glimpses of the beach and Atlantic Ocean to one side and Provincetown spread out on the other. The sky was a crystalline blue. A few cyclists passed in a line, apparently returning from an early morning trip to Race Point beach where Hernán often went in the morning when he wanted to be alone. If he wasn't working, the apartment he shared with Rudy was too small to think, so he'd pedal Rudy's old bike along the dune trails and then walk on the shore with his pants legs rolled up. The cries of the gulls, the roar of the surf, and the sand under his feet were his companions as he tried to understand how his life had led him to a place so far from home.

Hernán shook his head as the taxi pulled into the Provincetown airport's small parking lot. His palms were sweaty on the door handle. What was he doing, preparing to climb into a plane with a man he'd only met two days earlier? Was he putting himself in the same danger again?

He was tempted to tell the driver to turn around and take him back to Rudy's place. Then he spotted Colin waiting outside the terminal building, a bag at his feet. A tan jacket, belted at the waist and falling just to his thighs, draped Colin's tall, lean form elegantly. His short, brown hair was combed neatly to the side, and his glasses flashed as he looked up. A big smile lit his face when he spotted Hernán in the back of the arriving taxi.

It's okay. He's *okay. I can do this.*

Hernán paid and got his knapsack from the back. Colin reached to take it from his hand but he resisted. "I've got it."

"I wasn't entirely sure you'd come," Colin said.

"Neither was I," Hernán admitted shyly, turning his head to watch the cab pull away. His memories tormented him. *Can I do this? Colin trusted me with a big secret. I can trust him. I need to trust him.*

He lowered his bag to the pavement and looked up at Colin. "Before we go, I think there's something else I should tell you." Colin nodded and tilted his head expectantly. Hernán's breath came faster and the back of his knuckles ached with memories of his Abuela's punishment. He flexed his fingers and almost dropped his bag. "I'm, uh..." he tried. Bile rose in his throat.

I can't say it.

I will.

Hernán tried again. "What you said before, about my not being gay." *Oh Jesus, I'm going to throw up.* "The thing is..." His chest heaving, he couldn't get a decent breath. Colin stayed still and kept his hands in his pockets, his eyes intent on Hernán's.

"I am. I'm gay." *Aaaah I said it. I said it out loud.* Hernán almost collapsed but suddenly he could breathe again. He took great gulps of air.

Colin's eyes went wide and his mouth dropped open in surprise. "I heard you say to Gerald you don't sleep with men."

"I don't. I mean, I want to but I can't. I was...when I was little. And then when I came here—"

Colin pulled him into a hug. Hernán started to resist but then he just didn't. He sagged in Colin's arms. Even though the man was thin, he held Hernán firmly, taking his weight easily.

"Rudy knows," Hernán whispered against Colin's jacket. "No one else."

"I'm glad you told me."

"I'm not sure why I did." Hernán stiffened slightly. Colin released him immediately, but the loss of his warmth made Hernán sad. "I guess I thought you should know. Before you take me on your plane. I don't know why you're doing all this but you need to know I'm really screwed up."

"Nah. It just gives us more to talk about," Colin said softly. "Come on. It's a beautiful day for flying."

Colin led him to a security gate, which he opened with an electronic code, and then guided Hernán out to the tarmac. Ten or fifteen planes were lined up. It looked like each of them would hold maybe four people at most. He began to feel anxious. The planes were a lot smaller than he'd ever realized. Were they actually safe? Did they ever collide in the air?

"It's called a tie-down," Colin explained as they walked, indicating ropes on the tarmac. "Here we are," he said as they stopped at a blue-and-silver plane with indigo details painted on the body, "N7AV" appearing near the tail.

Hernán took unsteady breaths as he looked up at the machine. It was like a car with wings. His palms began to sweat.

Oblivious, Colin said, "You just wait here for a minute and I'll get her ready." He walked around the plane, apparently inspecting its surface as he stopped to untie a rope beneath each of the wings and the tail. He pulled some kind of plugs out of the front, just behind the propeller, and then removed a small sock of some kind from a tube beneath the left wing. He stowed those in a luggage compartment and performed several more mysterious tasks quickly and efficiently.

Hernán watched Colin's assured movements with an increasing sense of confidence, yet he couldn't help a small tremble. He told himself Colin clearly knew what he was doing. After all, he'd flown himself up to Provincetown. *Lots* of people flew in small planes. But Hernán had never been on any kind of plane at all before. Colin's seemed very small, compared to the images he'd seen in movies and in his books.

Eventually, Colin declared in a bright voice, "We're good to go." At that point he seemed to notice Hernán's trepidation, because he stopped what he was doing and came closer.

"I know it can be scary when you go up the first time. I've been flying for nearly ten years, and I've logged over three thousand flight hours. I fly a Cirrus SR 22. It's arguably the safest single-engine aircraft available, and it even has a full-plane parachute." He gestured to the tail assemblage. "If there's ever an emergency, I can pull a lever inside the cockpit and a little rocket shoots through the skin of the plane to deploy the chute. We'd drift to the ground like a feather."

"I never heard of anything like that."

"It's one of the reasons I fly a Cirrus. Safety always."

Colin said the flight would take less than three hours. He waited, probably hoping for a sign he'd eased Hernán's nerves. His kindness in explaining, not mocking Hernán but calming him, meant everything. Hernán's fists unclenched and he rolled his shoulders to loosen them. Colin wasn't the type of man to take unnecessary risks, he could tell. If Colin said the plane was safe, it was.

Determinedly, he said, "Let's fly, Maverick."

Colin laughed loudly. "A *Top Gun* reference? I assure you, this is nothing like the flying in that movie."

"No dogfights with other planes?" Hernán managed a grin. "Maybe I'm a little disappointed."

"We'll save a dogfight for your second flight. Okay?" Still chuckling, Colin stowed Hernán's knapsack in the luggage compartment with his own suitcase and closed it up. He helped Hernán climb into the cockpit and get situated on the passenger side.

The bucket seat was surprisingly comfortable. Colin clasped the seatbelt harness across Hernán's chest and got it adjusted, and then handed him a headset with a microphone attached. "It's really noisy when the engine is going so we'll talk to each other through these mics. You'll hear me talking to the air traffic controllers as well."

Colin made sure the gull-wing passenger door closed securely, and then came around the plane to climb into his seat. He began running through a checklist, flicking buttons and switches and performing little tasks that meant nothing to Hernán. Colin looked around to make sure no one was on the tarmac nearby and then started the engine. It roared to life, the propeller whirling so fast Hernán could see right through it. Colin continued his checks, programmed a flight plan into his navigation system, and started a dialogue over the radio.

"Cape Clearance, Cirrus November Seven Alpha Victor, at Papa Victor Charlie." The radio crackled back as Colin got the information and approval he needed. He checked one more time that Hernán was doing all right, and then gave the engine enough power to get them rolling. After steering the plane toward a narrow strip of tarmac parallel to the runway itself, he said to Hernán through his mic, "We'll do our final checks just before we take off."

A few minutes later, Colin toggled his radio and said, "Provincetown traffic, November Seven Alpha Victor departing runway two-five to the west." He grinned at Hernán and asked, "Ready?"

Hernán gave him a thumbs-up and tried not to hyperventilate.

Colin added power steadily and the plane began to roll down the runway, picking up speed. The dunes flashed by as Colin intoned, "Air speed is live, instruments are in the green." He pulled smoothly back on the stick and the plane left the ground.

Hernán's heart hammered in his chest as Provincetown fell away beneath them. Colin took them in a gentle turn as they climbed higher. It brought the plane right over the town. Through the headset, Colin said, "It looks amazing from the air, right?"

Hernán nodded. There it was, spread out below him. The sight was so beautiful his breathing returned to normal and he forgot to be scared. He put his fingers up to the window. "I never realized how narrow the inhabited portion of Provincetown is."

Colin responded, "David told me it's because most of the end of Cape Cod was federally protected from development. That keeps the number of houses low."

"Look, there's the monument," Hernán said excitedly. "And the library. Town Hall. I guess that's The Boatslip."

He fell silent while Colin made some more radio calls and adjusted their flight path to take them away from Provincetown and across Cape Cod Bay. The dark blue water below them was flecked with white, and a few fishing boats bobbed near shore. A large white ship left a huge wake and Hernán commented, "I think that's the ferry to Boston." He turned and grinned at Colin. "This is wonderful."

"I'm glad you like it. It's a different way to see the world, for sure."

"Have you been flying long? Oh, you said earlier. Ten years."

"Yeah. My grandfather was a private pilot too. He used to take me up. My parents *hated* when I started flying lessons but they finally gave in, thanks to Gramps." A soft smile appeared on Colin's lips. "He even bought me this plane. Before he died two years ago, he had to give up flying, but he'd still get me to bring him. We flew together the week before he died. We were out all afternoon and there was this incredible sunset as we headed home. Reds and oranges and everything in between. It was a great day."

Hernán felt his throat get tight as he watched Colin's face. The serene expression he wore drew Hernán. It was as if Colin had no darkness in him, just happy, easy memories floating on the surface like rose petals. He had money, family, a job he apparently loved, even a plane.

Hernán had no memory of his own grandfathers, and his grandmother had never shared anything remotely special with him. Nothing floated on his mind but a dark slick of shame. He tried hard to keep it at bay but it was always there, giving every good moment a bitter aftertaste. Even tainting the thrill of seeing Cape Cod spread out below him. *It won't last. Not for you, little maricón.*

"You're very lucky," he said hoarsely.

Colin glanced at him. "I am. I know."

They flew over Massachusetts, and then Rhode Island. Colin pointed out landmarks but the names meant little to Hernán until they crossed to Long Island. "Can we see New York City from the air?" he asked breathlessly.

"It's a really clear day so yes, I think you'll get a good look at the skyline when we fly over JFK."

Hernán kept his eyes glued to the horizon in the direction Colin indicated, scanning back and forth until...

"There it is. Right? The tall tower there, and the buildings around it?" The edifices and manmade canyons of Manhattan clustered in the distance, strong sunlight gleaming off windows and chrome. Hernán sighed happily.

"Yep," Colin confirmed. "That's the Freedom Tower, and the other buildings down there are all lower Manhattan. See, further up to your right? The Empire State Building."

"And the open green space north of that. Central Park?"

"Right. You know a lot about New York," Colin observed.

"I took many English classes in school and there were often lessons about American culture. New York City always seemed to be the main focus."

"Maybe, uh..." Colin stopped talking, but Hernán prompted him. "Maybe one weekend we can take the train up to New York. So you can see it from the ground."

Hernán blinked. It sounded wonderful, except it wasn't. "You know I don't have any money, and I'm not letting you pay for me. You're already doing too much."

Colin let it go, but the comment had started a chain of thought in Hernán. He gnawed on his lower lip and tugged idly on his harness until Colin said, "Something's on your mind. Do you want to talk about it?"

Hernán stopped chewing and looked at the land passing below them. "Is this New Jersey?" he asked.

"Yes."

Colin announced they had crossed into Delaware before Hernán finally answered his earlier question. "I'm going to need to find work," he said. "Even if I'm staying with you, I've got to make money."

"Hernán, I'll cover everything. I assumed I would, when I asked you to come stay with me."

"I can't take so much from you. A spare room is one thing. Food? Other stuff? No."

"But what can you do? You don't have a work permit." Hernán gave him a long look, and Colin sighed. "I'm being naïve. I know. You didn't have a permit to work in Provincetown either."

"I'll find something off the books, or…" Hernán let it hang. If Colin worked with immigrants then he no doubt understood how they had to go around the system.

"I'm worried you could hurt your chances, if you get caught doing something illegal," Colin said.

Hernán turned away to stare out the window again. His jaw hurt until he realized he was grinding his teeth.

Hurt my chances by surviving? Was he different somehow than the hundreds of thousands of people who came to the States and did what they had to in order to feed and clothe themselves and their families? What did this rich prick know about the things he and people like him did to get by? No, he didn't want to use a false social security number or scrounge for jobs paying strictly in cash. But those were far better than the alternatives he could think of, or had heard about.

Colin finally said into his mic, "Look. I'm sorry. That sounded judgmental, and that's not what I mean. I'd just rather keep you well on the side of the law as much as we can."

Silence weighed between them until Colin announced, "And there's my home airport." He brought the plane down onto the runway in a small valley and taxied to a gas pump refuel. Then he moved the Cirrus to his hangar, where he had Hernán stand aside while he got it stored away.

In less than twenty minutes, they loaded their bags into Colin's Audi and drove the final miles from the Maryland airfield to Washington, DC.

The discussion in the plane apparently made them both nervous. It exposed how little they actually knew about each other, and how many adjustments they might both have to make if Hernán had a prayer of getting permission to remain legally.

But in the heavy silence of the car, Hernán realized something else. If he worked off the books and got caught, there could be repercussions for Colin too. The oily, black slick of his life would begin to taint Colin, and ruin the innocence and happiness radiating from him.

Whatever else happened, Hernán could not permit that. If his own darkness threatened Colin's light, he would go.

Chapter 9

COLIN PULLED HIS car into a parking garage underneath his condo building and turned into his assigned space. The silence during the drive was nerve-wracking so as soon as he turned off the engine, he pivoted in his seat to catch Hernán's eyes.

"You've been through terrible things. I get it. I want you to feel safe here and that means I won't ask questions. Even when we start working with an immigration attorney. If you want to be alone to talk with him or her, just say so. Okay?"

Hernán nodded slowly. The pinched expression on his face started to relax and Colin gave a sigh of relief. "Good. Let's get you settled." He led the way to the elevators and up to the top floor, and then into an apartment. He dropped his bag and waved his arms generally. "This is it."

Hernán looked around with wide eyes and a slack jaw as Colin showed him the place. The main room was actually two stories tall; a chimney faced in rock ran all the way up the twenty feet to the ceiling. The living room, dining room and kitchen were all in an open plan. Oriental rugs covered the hardwood floors.

Full-length windows and sliding glass doors faced west and let in the early afternoon light. Beyond the doors was a good-sized balcony on which Colin had a teak table set as well as two arm chairs, angled to catch the view. An overhang formed by the patio immediately above, also Colin's, sheltered the seating area.

Next to the dining room was a bedroom Colin used as an office-slash-den. Two deep, upholstered chairs with ottomans flanked the walls, and books filled three tall cases. He led Hernán in. "This is where I work when I'm at home and I like to come in here sometimes to read. You can use the computer any time you want. There's a full bathroom down the hall there," he gestured.

Hernán trailed behind, seemingly dazed. Colin brought him up a staircase to the second floor. Immediately to the right he opened the door to his guest bedroom and gestured for Hernán to enter. Because of the unusual height of Colin's living room, the bedroom had a window that opened to the living room below rather than directly to the outside. A queen-size bed and a wardrobe were the biggest items of furniture, while a flatscreen TV sat on a low-slung entertainment center.

"This is where you'll sleep. I have some clothes in here but it'll be easy to make room for whatever you brought." He indicated a closet. "The bed's recently been changed but there are spare sheets and towels in here for you."

Across the hall was a bathroom with a tub. "Sorry it isn't en suite," Colin apologized, "but at least it's just a few steps away." He continued down the hallway which, to the right, overlooked the living room, and to the left opened into a bedroom.

"This is mine," he said. "My bathroom is through there so you don't have to share with me." A small balcony was accessible by doors from Colin's bedroom or from the hallway. "Sometimes I'll sit out there in the morning, or on the balcony below, with a cup of coffee. If you want to go out, don't worry about disturbing me."

A spiral staircase from the second floor took them up to a small triangular room with its own sliding glass door to a large rooftop terrace. The afternoon sky was blue and streaked with high clouds. Decorative planters filled with shrubs created the sense of an outdoor room. A big wrought-iron set of furniture provided seating space. Outside, the noise of the city could be overwhelming, but the day was relatively quiet.

Colin gestured to the south. "Over there is the George Washington University medical center, so we often hear a lot of sirens, I'm afraid. It isn't bad inside, but it can get pretty loud sometimes out here."

Hernán leaned against the railing of the deck and gripped it hard. "This place…it's amazing." He turned dazzled eyes on Colin, who had to look away from the intensity of his gaze.

How would it feel for him see me like that? Colin repressed the thought. The spark of hope he already nurtured flared when Hernán said he was gay, but Hernán had obviously suffered trauma. What it meant for his homosexuality was unknown. Colin couldn't risk pushing

Hernán away, so he had to keep his distance and treat him as a roommate.

"I really like this unit," Colin said. "I bought it a few years ago, before the DC housing market went crazy."

"You *own* this? ¡Hijo de puta!"

"Um, yeah. I think I'm pretty lucky because I don't know of any other buildings where the units get three outdoor spaces like this."

Hernán gave him a stare. "That's why you're lucky," he said flatly. "Because of your outdoor space."

Colin flushed, squirmed, and looked away. "Sorry. Dumb comment. Anyway, do you want to get settled?" He led Hernán back down to what would be his room and moved a few things around in the wardrobe. "There. Let me know if you need more storage."

"Uh, is it okay if I leave my toothbrush and things in the bathroom?" Hernán asked hesitantly. "Or do you want to keep it clean for guests?"

"Oh no, don't worry about that," Colin exclaimed. "Leave your things in there. It's your bathroom. I never have guests anyway." He flushed again as he saw a pitying expression cross Hernán's face. "My family's up in New Jersey and we get together there for holidays." Hernán turned away to look around the room. "I'll give you some privacy," Colin said, stepping out and starting to pull the door closed behind him.

Hernán grabbed the edge. "No. Please." He looked down at the floor and mumbled. "I'd like to leave it open."

"Oh. Sure. I'll probably be downstairs in the library unless I run out to the grocery store, so just relax and get settled."

LEFT ALONE, HERNÁN dropped onto the bed, stunned. He'd never had so much space to himself in his entire life. The bed! He flopped backward and sank into the thick comforter. So soft. And who would need so many pillows?

A princess is who. Filthy little boy.

He cringed at the voice cackling in his head. Thousands of miles he'd traveled and still Abuela haunted him. What would she say if she knew he was staying under the roof of a homosexual? Her words would be vile, for sure.

He rolled over and buried his face in one of the many soft pillows covering the bed. *I said it out loud and the world didn't end. Colin hugged me and he didn't push or ask for more.* Other than hugs from his sister or cousins, he couldn't remember the last time he'd been touched with simple affection. He wasn't blind—Colin would like more. But he seemed strong enough to control his desires, and just be a friend to Hernán.

A friend. Is that what Colin is? They'd only known each other for a few days. Yet Hernán had left his job and Rudy to fly hundreds of miles to a strange city on Colin's say-so. He'd done it because he trusted the warrior he spied, and felt safe with him. Colin was bright and shining, an open book left to warm its pages in the sunlight. Hernán wanted that warmth, that light, to help him find his way through the darkness.

I might want to be more than his friend.

The revelation made Hernán sit up in alarm. He didn't even know Colin.

Yes I do. I know everything important about the kind of man he is. The rest is details.

He shook his head angrily. Regardless of what his brain was telling him, the truth was Hernán brought out the worst in the people around him, like the Cuernos gang members. Or he failed them, as he did Albert and Andrea. He poisoned their lives somehow and he could not—*would* not—let that happen to a man as good as Colin.

If he could just hug me and have it be enough. If Colin would do that… No. It wasn't fair to ask of him. Colin deserved a man who could touch him, who could give him his body, yet Hernán's flesh simultaneously hungered for and crawled at the thought of hands on him in lust. Hands that were demanding, forcing, taking.

Unable to imagine a time when he would be able to permit such intimacy, a lonely ache settled into his bones.

WHEN COLIN HEARD the shower running upstairs an hour or so later, he set aside his book. He needed to see what food he had available. Given how Hernán reacted in the plane, it seemed unlikely he'd let Colin take him out to dinner.

He found green and red lentils in the pantry, onions and some chicken breasts in the fridge. Perfect. He'd make an Indian dal and serve it with grilled chicken.

After grabbing cumin, turmeric and deggi mirch out of his spice cabinet, he heated some oil in a pot and tossed in the spices to roast for a few seconds. When the aroma of toasted cumin hit his nose, he added a mix of dried lentils and let that roast for a minute to bring out extra flavor. Then he poured in some water and brought the mix to a boil before covering the pot and reducing the heat to a slow simmer. The chicken breasts went into a simple marinade of yogurt, lemon, grapeseed oil and a few spices. He checked on his dal before starting to slice onions thinly.

Perhaps drawn by the aromas, Hernán came down the stairs. Instead of the baggy clothes Colin had usually seen him in, Hernán wore a pair of jeans and a tight Henley pushed up at the sleeves. The shirt revealed a well-muscled chest and great biceps. His thick, corded forearms looked hairless. Longish hair was damp and hung forward, but Hernán's head was up for a change.

Even with the bangs and loose hair, Colin had his best sight yet of Hernán's face. His heart beat faster. He'd known Hernán was handsome, but wasn't prepared for the impact of piercing eyes under black eyebrows, sharp cheekbones, full lips tinged with pink, and a cleft chin under his glossy beard.

"Oh my God, you're gorgeous." It burst out before Colin could censor himself and he felt his face flood with heat. "I'm sorry. You probably get sick of hearing that. I just didn't…um. Anyway, sorry."

Hernán winced and looked down at the carpet. "It's okay." He glanced at Colin from under his long black lashes. "It's not like you haven't seen me before."

Colin's ears burned as he concentrated on the onion he was slicing. He mumbled, "I guess I really hadn't, until now. You don't meet anyone's eyes for long. And you usually keep your head down so your hair falls in your face."

"Do I? I guess I forgot."

Silence reigned for a few moments before Hernán leaned against the counter near where Colin was prepping. "What are you making?"

"I hope you like Indian. It's a dal, a kind of lentil dish. I'm going to grill chicken to go with it."

"I don't think I've ever eaten Indian food but it smells great. Can I help?"

Colin looked around the kitchen. "Well, how are your knife skills?"

Hernán smiled shyly at him. His teeth were dazzling. "Try me."

"I need some ginger and garlic minced up." He grabbed the items from a basket and set Hernán up with a knife and his own cutting board. Hernán efficiently peeled back the skin from the knob of ginger and diced it up finely with smooth, efficient motions of his knife.

He grinned at Colin, more naturally that time, before moving on to the garlic cloves. "What do you think? Do I pass?"

"With flying colors. I wish I had skills like yours," Colin said. "I love to cook, but I'm not the fastest. I tend to take my time, which is why I have to start hours before I'm hungry enough to eat."

"I could show you some tricks. I've done a lot of prep work the past few months." They chopped side by side. Sharing his kitchen was a novel experience for Colin. It was nice, he decided. After finishing his onions he started a pot of basmati rice going on the stove.

"Okay, these are ready. What else can I do?" Hernán offered.

"Are you as good on a grill as a cutting board?"

"As a matter of fact, I am."

"Ooh, cocky. I like that," Colin teased. "Bring it on."

Hernán gave him a smirk but didn't respond. Colin pulled the marinated chicken from the fridge, grabbed a plate and some utensils, and led Hernán to the balcony where his grill was set up. Leaving Hernán to it, he went back to fry up his onions, ginger, garlic, cumin seeds, some whole dried red chilies and a little cayenne. By the time Hernán returned with the beautifully grilled chicken breasts, the dal was just about ready to assemble. Hernán set the table with the plates and silverware Colin pointed out.

"What would you like to drink?" Colin asked. He added the fried onion mixture to the lentils and transferred the finished dal to a serving bowl. "I'm having a glass of white wine."

"Oh. That sounds nice."

Colin poured them each a glass of a dry Riesling he liked with Indian food and brought those to the table with the dal and rice. Hernán looked a little uncertain so Colin started by helping himself to a chicken breast. Then he scooped a mound of rice and a big portion of dal onto his plate.

Hernán followed his lead, humming appreciatively when he tasted the dal. "That's fantastic. Caliente. Nice heat level."

Colin ducked his head and his face grew warm again, which seemed to happen far too often around Hernán. "I'm glad you like it," he said, grinning. "In India we'd be eating the rice and dal with our hands and maybe a piece of naan, but I'm too Western to do that in my own home."

Hernán winked at him. "I won't tell." He sipped his wine and nodded appreciatively. "Nice."

"This chicken is grilled perfectly," Colin said around a forkful. "I sometimes dry it out but you got it off the fire at the right time."

"We have a mutual admiration society going on here," Hernán teased. "Seriously though. You're a good cook, Colin. I can show you some shortcuts if you want, but you have a great hand with spices."

"Do you like to cook too? Or is it just a job you've had?" Colin asked.

Hernán wagged his hand in the air back and forth. "I'm an okay cook. My grandmother wouldn't let me in the kitchen at home, but when I stayed with my uncle or other relatives, I'd make different dishes."

"Sounds like a match made in heaven then. We can try to get better together." Colin raised his wine glass to clink against Hernán's as they shared a small grin.

When dinner was done and the kitchen cleaned, Colin poured them each more wine. They moved to the living room, where Hernán sat rather stiffly in a side chair and looked around.

"Would you like to watch TV?" Colin asked. "Or a movie? I have video games too."

"Anything is fine." Hernán fidgeted. "Sorry. I think I'm nervous."

Colin set his glass down on the coffee table and leaned forward. "Tell me what I can do to help you relax. It will take a few months to get through the immigration process even in the best of circumstances. We're going to be living together, so I want you to be comfortable here."

Hernán sipped his wine. "I know. It's just, everything you have is so nice. I feel like I'm going to get it all dirty."

"What? Please, don't worry about that. Look," Colin paused to put his feet up on the coffee table, "I'm a bachelor slob. If everything looks nice and clean, it's because I have a cleaning service in a few times each week." He snapped his fingers. "I'll have to introduce you to them on Tuesday. Oh, that's tomorrow. I also need to give you a set of keys, and let the doormen know you'll be living here too."

Hernán gave a whoosh of breath and shook his head. "This is so different from my life with Rudy. Or back in San Marcos. You can't imagine."

"Are you ready to tell me about it?" Colin asked softly. Hernán met his gaze and this time it held. He gnawed on his lower lip as he thought, and Colin watched wariness and fear flicker across his face. "I'm sorry. You don't have to talk about it with me. Ever."

Hernán nodded and gratitude replaced the concern he'd showed. Still his gaze stayed fixed. The hairs on Colin's arm and neck stood up, and his breath grew rough. The dark eyes in Hernán's beautiful face, the raw emotion he was letting through, worked on Colin like a drug.

He hadn't even finished his second glass of wine but he felt happily drunk. He was in the perfect state where the world was soft, his nerves were calm, and he was in complete control. It was as far from his sorry-ass state Friday night as he could imagine. He never wanted to look away.

Then he recalled Hernán's confession. Hernán was gay but he didn't want to act on it. Bad things had happened to him; things Colin didn't want to imagine. No matter his own fantasies, Hernán was not interested in starting anything up, and Colin would respect that. He needed Hernán's trust if he was going to help, so his attraction would have to stay unvoiced. He liked Hernán too much to risk driving him away.

In an artificially bright voice, Colin said, "I'm wiped from flying. Let's just watch a movie, okay?" He picked up the remote and started searching his Netflix queue for something to distract them. "What kind of movies do you like?"

Hernán stared at him silently for a few more moments. It seemed as if there might be something he wanted to say. Finally he shook his head and moved to the other end of the sofa where he would see the screen better. "Something light. A comedy maybe?"

"Hey, do you like *Doctor Who*?"

"What's that?"

Colin's jaw dropped exaggeratedly. "You've never heard of *Doctor Who*? Oh my God, you have to give it a try." Hernán chuckled at his enthusiasm, even though it was slightly forced, and sat back while Colin searched for the perfect episode.

"Which companion?" he muttered to himself. "Donna's the best.

Oh I know." He flashed through various screens until he landed on an episode. "'Partners in Crime'. This one is really funny. All you need to know is The Doctor is a Time Lord and he travels through space and time in a blue box."

He pressed play and sat back to let the magic pairing of David Tennant and Catherine Tate unravel while he prayed Hernán would enjoy it.

Soon Hernán was chuckling next to him. When the episode ended he smiled at Colin. "I like it. I don't get everything going on but Donna's funny. She's going to travel with Doctor Who?"

"Just The Doctor. He's never called Doctor Who," Colin corrected. "But I'm glad you like it. I knew you had good taste!"

"The two of them are like Spencer Tracy and Katherine Hepburn, with the bickering."

Colin gasped. "You like old movies?"

"I do," Hernán said with a nod. "I had a teacher who liked to run American films, and I got hooked."

"Where have you been all my life?" Colin gushed. "I see a movie marathon in our near future." Hernán reddened and looked away, though, and Colin cursed himself. *Too much. Pull it back.* He clicked on to the next episode, "The Fires of Pompeii", and Hernán was soon smiling again.

When it ended, Colin asked, "Another one?"

Hernán gave him a rueful look and shook his head. "I didn't get much sleep last night, thinking about your plane and coming here. Plus that wine kind of went to my head. I think I'd like to go to bed."

"Oh, sure." Colin jumped to his feet and turned off the television. "I'm sorry I kept you up. I think I'll turn in too." He showed Hernán where the coffee maker was in case he woke up first, shut off all the downstairs lights and followed Hernán to the second floor. He was about to brush past but Hernán hovered in the door to the guest room.

"Uh, Colin, I wonder..."

Colin waited with his head tilted. When Hernán blushed and looked over his shoulder, Colin finally prompted, "Do you need anything? Another blanket?"

Hernán pressed his lips together and shook his head slightly. "Can I...can I have another hug?" Colin knew his eyes must have been as big as saucers. Hernán hurriedly added, "Just a hug. I'm sorry that's all I can do but...yeah. It was really nice when you hugged me at the airport. So." He dropped his gaze to the ground again and stuck his hands in his pockets.

Oh yes. Colin could give him a hug. He stepped closer and breathed in the scent of wine mixed with the Indian spices they'd consumed, the herbal body wash and shampoo from Hernán's shower, and a warm underlying note of Hernán's natural smell.

Hernán quivered lightly as Colin slid his arms around, careful to keep his hips away. Hernán wouldn't like feeling the instant erection that sprang up at the contact, he was sure. He rested his chin on Hernán's shoulder and just held on with his arms wrapped tight. The body under Hernán's shirt rippled with muscle, and the warmth rising from his skin felt like homecoming.

The tremors quieted as Hernán wrapped his own arms around Colin and hugged him back, their chests pressed together. They stood there for a full minute, just breathing. Colin thought he might be in heaven.

When Hernán gave a contented sigh and pulled away, Colin released the hug immediately and stepped back.

"Thank you," Hernán said quietly. "I really needed that."

"Any time." Colin gave him a small smile. "Good night, Hernán."

As he headed toward his bedroom, he heard a soft "Good night, Colin."

Chapter 10

HERNÁN WOKE FROM a nightmare, sweating and tangled in soft sheets. Blood pounding in his ears, he looked around the dark room frantically, trying to remember where he was. Then he connected the soft pillow beneath him with the day before.

Colin's apartment.

He lay awake for a time, thinking about his dream. In it, Albert had been crying, and Andrea asked, "Why did you let them do that to us?" As he stared at the ceiling, tears leaked down the sides of his face. The creaks inside the apartment and the occasional street noise from outside were unnerving. He couldn't help but listen for the scrape of a foot along the hall carpet, a sign that Colin had come for him after all.

Eventually, exhaustion won out and Hernán slipped back into fitful sleep.

He woke again on the second night, still straining in the darkness to hear a footfall. As unjust as that fear seemed in the daylight, he couldn't keep from tensing in his borrowed bed at every strange sound.

By the third night, though, his unconscious began to accept what his conscious mind had decided when he agreed to come to Washington with Colin. He slept that night through, and the next.

Colin and Hernán worked out their roommate arrangements within the next few days. Gradually, Hernán relaxed and felt more natural in the apartment. Colin showed him a gym in the basement, where Hernán hit the weights and ran on the treadmill daily. The equipment wasn't as extensive as at the P-town gym where he worked out his frustrations all summer, but it gave him a good workout.

He wished Rudy could see where he'd landed. He'd send pictures but his phone was so cheap it didn't have a camera. Anyway, Rudy had lived with Gerald in some big houses. He wouldn't be as impressed by Colin's apartment as Hernán was.

A few days after Hernán arrived in DC, over dinner Colin showed him some materials to help him prepare for the immigration process.

"I'm checking with my resources to get a good lawyer, but there are a lot of steps you can get started now," Colin said. He gave Hernán samples of some personal statements that had been filed in support of asylum applications, with names blacked out for privacy.

"See, these will give you an idea of the level of detail you need to provide. You've been reluctant to talk, but I think you need to get an idea of how much you're going to have to disclose eventually. Maybe you could start roughing out notes for when we get you in front of a lawyer."

Hernán nodded nervously. "That's fine." He looked over the array of personal statements with growing trepidation. "These seem really, uh, thorough. I guess I didn't understand how much I'm going to have to say."

Colin gave him a sympathetic look. "I'm sure it seems intrusive. And it is. But the immigration officers are just people. They need to hear a good story so they get on your side and *want* you to be able to stay. And frankly some of them are bigoted jerks. I know one man who got all these rude questions about what bars he went to, how many men he'd had sex with and things like that, because the asylum officer didn't believe he was really gay. That's why it's better to disclose too much upfront, so those kinds of questions don't even arise in the interview."

Hernán set aside the materials to study further. "Thanks, Colin. I think I get it. I'll start working on this."

Between forkfuls of dinner, Colin said, "We also need to get you a physical because one of the forms that you have to file is a medical examination and vaccination record. If it's okay, I'll make an appointment for you to go see my regular doctor." Hernán nodded his acceptance.

HE CALLED RUDY the next day to report how things were going.

"Was Claude mad when I quit that way?" he asked.

"Of course. You know what a big drama queen he can be, but what could he do?" Rudy giggled. "Gerald came by again yesterday and he was furious when he found out you'd gone. He didn't believe me but Claude started bitching up a storm about it too."

"Did he make trouble for you?"

Rudy paused for a moment, but then said, "No. At least, as far as I know he didn't say anything to Claude. He's an asshole and a user but I don't think he wants to hurt me. Not really."

"Rudy, he threw you out."

"I know. I'm not defending him. I just mean that I don't think he'll try to get me fired. Anyway, tell me how it's going with Colin."

"What do you mean? I told you, he's being really nice."

"He was obviously smitten with you or I would have gone after that tall, thin mister man. Has he made a move?"

"You know I don't do that. No, he hasn't made a move."

Hernán didn't mention the hugs, which had been repeated each night at bedtime. In some ways, it was the best part of his day and he found himself looking forward to bedtime just so he could feel arms around him. He hadn't realized how starved for touch he was until Colin gave it to him unconditionally. Part of him wanted to talk to Rudy about it, but the more sensible part knew his cousin would make him crazy if he tried.

"I know, Nán. I just thought maybe if you were together for a while you might start to feel more safe."

"I, uh, I do feel safe. With him, I mean." Hernán felt his cheeks heating even though he was alone in the apartment and no one could see him. "He's this nice guy who has everything but he doesn't really know how lucky he is. That's good though. I mean, he doesn't show off or try to impress me. He's just a happy, bright man who wants to do good things for people."

"Oh Nán," Rudy sighed heavily. "You've got it bad."

Hernán snorted. "Don't be silly. We're friends. That's it."

"For now."

Hernán thought about what Rudy had said all afternoon. He didn't know exactly what drove Colin to give so much to him with no expectation that his generosity would be returned. He was different from the other men Hernán had known. Innocent maybe, but not entirely naïve. And those blue eyes… Hernán shivered.

Something Hernán had noticed was that Colin didn't know how strong he was. For whatever reason, he perceived himself as weak, not at all the warrior Hernán glimpsed from time to time. He needed to do something nice for Colin, to show his gratitude. That evening, instead of just chopping vegetables for Colin to cook, he went further and prepared one of the dishes he used to make for his uncle when he visited, pollo encebollado.

When Colin entered the apartment that evening, he sniffed loudly. "What's cooking? It smells great."

Hernán called from upstairs where he was folding laundry. "It's a dish from my country. Chicken and onions, basically. It'll be ready in about twenty minutes."

"Perfect. Would you like a drink before dinner?" Colin called back. Hernán grunted acceptance. When he came downstairs a few minutes later Colin had mixed them each a vodka tonic.

"The weather's really nice for late September," Colin said. "Let's sit on the balcony and enjoy it."

Hernán followed him out and they sat side by side in armchairs that faced west. The sun was low though it was not yet full sunset. Thin white clouds streaked the sky, which began to take on a pink tinge.

Colin's apartment looked out on the Reagan International Airport flight path for planes landing or taking off, depending on the winds. That night the jets crossed from right to left across their view as they descended toward the airport.

Hernán sipped his drink. "Did you pick this apartment because you could watch the planes?" he asked.

Colin grinned sheepishly. "That was a big draw, yes. I've thought sometimes about giving up the nonprofit work and becoming a commercial pilot for one of the airlines. Although I really love what I do."

Hernán watched Colin's face as he talked. The flash of his glasses as he craned his head excitedly to explain aviation, the color rising in his cheeks, produced a curious sensation in Hernán's chest. It was like a tickle around his heart. He'd never felt that before and had no idea what it meant, but he kept asking Colin about planes until dinner was ready. Just so he could keep the glow in Colin's eyes.

After dinner, Colin thanked Hernán for cooking but said he had to make a phone call. "We have this new lady from Martinique who was referred to us for help, but she can't come to the office during the day. Plus she only speaks a little English. I offered to call but I'm not sure how my Spanish will get through to her French."

"I speak French fluently," Hernán said. "Can I help?"

Colin's face lit up. "Really? I didn't know that. Yes, please. I'll put the call on speaker and maybe you can translate as needed." They left the dinner dishes and moved into Colin's home office, where Hernán pulled up a chair as Colin dialed. The woman who answered spoke with a heavy French accent.

"Is this Simone Barnet?" Colin asked. "I'm Colin Felton, from the Immigration Initiative. My colleague is going to translate as needed."

Silence came back over the line, so Hernán repeated the introduction in French.

Immediately, the woman began to speak excitedly. With Hernán's assistance, she explained she was in the country on a visa but her job was ending. She needed help to understand what options she might have or how to look for more work. Hernán conveyed some ideas from Colin to get her started, and set up an appointment for her to come to the Initiative on her day off for more direct guidance.

The call ended with profound expressions of thanks and relief from Simone.

When Colin disconnected, he grinned proudly at Hernán. "You're full of surprises. Mad cooking skills, loves old movies, and now fluent in French. Any other ways to amaze me?"

Hernán blushed. "I also speak Nahuatl, if you ever need that one. I started Arabic, but I'm not fluent."

"Nahuatl," Colin said, inclining his head. "That's used in Central America, right?"

Hernán nodded. "Yes. Well, Mexico and Central America. It evolved from the language originally spoken by the Aztecs. A number of indigenous cultures still use it exclusively among themselves, and only speak Spanish when they deal with outsiders."

Colin's grin only got wider. "So Spanish, English, French, Nahuatl and some Arabic. That's amazing."

"Languages always have come easy to me for some reason," Hernán muttered.

"It's a real gift. I do pretty well with Spanish because our cook taught me when I was little, but I don't really have the knack for picking up other languages. I'm kind of jealous."

Colin's praise embarrassed him but, he had to admit, pleased him as well. "I'd like to meet the lady who taught you Spanish," Hernán teased gently. "She let you get away with bad habits in your pronunciation. Anyway, let me know if I can be of any more help."

AS THE DAYS passed, to keep busy Hernán walked all over Washington, or used the gym in the basement of Colin's building. Colin usually got home from his job around six, so Hernán made sure he had food ingredients prepared and ready for Colin to work his magic. The weather was turning colder as October loomed.

A little more than a week after Hernán arrived in Washington, he strolled the city as he imagined Provincetown. Would it look like the pictures he'd seen of New England in the fall?

Musing about it reminded him to check in with Rudy again. He decided he had time to catch his cousin before he headed to work, so he made a cup of tea and went out on the porch with his phone.

"Nán!" Rudy exclaimed. "You don't call enough."

Hernán chuckled. "Sorry, mom. I'll do better."

"I don't mean it like that. I just miss you."

"I miss you too, cousin. What's happening in Provincetown? Are you staying busy?"

Rudy said something noncommittal and then launched into chatter about a man he'd met. "He came to town to act in one of the plays for the Tennessee Williams festival. We started talking when he came by Veranda after his performance. He was staying in some people's house so we couldn't go back there. I thought he seemed too classy to bring here. Guess what we did?"

"Please don't say you went to the Dick Dock." The area underneath the Boatslip Resort, at the edge of Provincetown Harbor, had a long history of attracting men for public, usually anonymous, sex.

"We did!" Rudy squealed. "It was cold down there but ooh he kept me warm. It was kind of romantic with the water and the moonlight, except for this other guy who was looking for company. He kept coming close and trying to join us, but August was a gentleman and he didn't let the man touch."

"Classy. And what kind of name is August?"

"He's a drama teacher at a school somewhere. Vermont, I think. Anyway, he's coming back to P-town next week to see me. I think this could really be it. Can't you just picture me on a college campus?"

"Maybe." Hernán shrugged even though Rudy couldn't see him. He'd learned not to bother holding his cousin's feet to the ground. "You changed the subject before, though. What's going on at Veranda?"

Rudy sighed. "It's the end of the season. Claude will shut Veranda down next week and I haven't been able to line anything else up yet."

"Didn't Claude put in a good word for you?" The pause was pronounced, so he prompted, "Rudy?"

"I think Gerald got Claude to spread the word I'm not reliable."

"That's bullshit!" Hernán exploded. "You never missed a day of work."

"There aren't that many jobs anyway. Most restaurants close for the season. Unless August sweeps me off to Vermont, I've been thinking it's time to go back to Boston and see what I can find there for the winter."

Hernán wished he had money to help Rudy out, but the small cash reserve he'd built up over the summer was going quickly to cover the groceries he and Colin ate. Colin resisted taking anything in payment but Hernán needed to believe he wasn't wholly dependent on Colin's generosity. He didn't know what he'd do when the last of his money ran out, and he didn't know how Rudy was going to make it without Hernán to split the bills.

The situation made him realize all over again what a vulnerable position he'd allowed himself to fall into. And how selfish he'd been. Rudy had given up his Rolex watch to get Hernán away from Lonnie, and his job situation was precarious because he tried to cover Hernán's immigration status. Yet Hernán let Colin whisk him away to Washington and left Rudy to fend for himself.

"I can hear you beating yourself up, Nán," Rudy said in his ear. "Don't. I've got rent covered through November and that leaves me time to take the ferry to Boston a few times and look for a job. I'll be fine."

"I wish there was some way I could help you." He heard the desperate edge to his own voice.

"You're helping me by getting permission to stay here legally. That way I won't have to worry about you. How are things going with that mister man?"

"Um, it's good," Hernán temporized. "Colin's doing a lot for me."

"I had a good feeling about him, but you stay smart. Don't get mixed up about why you're there. Hey, I need to get to Veranda while I still have a job. Love you, primo!"

"I love you too, Rudy. Call me soon and let me know what happens in Boston."

After the call, Hernán stayed out on the porch and watched planes in their landing pattern. The irony of Rudy warning him to be careful would have made him laugh if he weren't afraid that Rudy was right. He was foolish to become so dependent on a man, even one as kind as Colin.

As he fretted, the housecleaning service team arrived and began to clean inside. It shamed him to sit on his ass while they worked. The first time they'd come after Hernán's arrival, he'd tried to help but the man in charge of the team chattered at him to stay away and let them do their job.

What does he think I'm doing here? Does he think that Colin and I... That we...? Shit, he couldn't even say it to himself. He looked down into the depths of his cup and slowly enunciated the thought: *Does he think that we have sex together?*

The idea was terrifying and yet...maybe less overwhelming than it had been. Colin's respectful distance meant so much to Hernán. His initial fears that Colin would be like everyone else who looked at him *that way* eased day by day. They would say good night, hug tightly for a long moment, and then Colin would head down the hallway to his bedroom.

His own terrors and inexperience kept him from seeking more than their daily hug, but Hernán's body was hungry. Rudy had sometimes brought men back to their apartment in Boston, and then in Provincetown. From Hernán's narrow bed, he'd peer into the darkness, watching Rudy and his companion. He'd hear the slide of skin on skin, or the wet suckling as Rudy took a man into his mouth. With a hand on his own hard cock, he'd inhale sharply when he heard Rudy's slight gasp and the bedsprings began to squeak.

He burned to experience for himself so many things Rudy did, or told him about. Was Colin the one with whom Hernán could finally move beyond his fear?

Maybe.

But after his call with Rudy, and the judgmental looks he imagined from the cleaners, and his awareness of dwindling funds, he found his leg moving jerkily up and down on the porch. Desire was one thing. He couldn't allow himself to depend so much on Colin that he became trapped again.

He kept thinking about it even as he went inside and turned to his immigration papers. The forms reminded him yet again how precarious his place in the United States was, and how few options were open to him. He understood Colin's worries about him seeking work under the table, and he didn't want to believe it had anything to do with keeping Hernán vulnerable and penniless.

Yet that was the end result, wasn't it? If he couldn't work, he'd have to rely on Colin for not only his shelter but his food, his clothes, every necessity. His gut clenched and rebelled at the thought.

That was probably why, when Colin walked through the door that evening, the first thing Hernán blurted was, "I need to get a job."

Colin blinked at him and slowly set his satchel on the floor. After a moment, he asked, "Can we talk about it, or are you telling me what's going to happen?"

Hernán flushed. "I didn't mean it to sound like that. I just, uh…¡mierda!" He stood from the dining room table where he'd been drafting out a letter to the hospital in San Marcos to obtain his medical records. "Let me try that again. Colin, I really think I need to get some work and I'd like to talk with you about it."

Colin smiled. "Sure. How about you give me a few minutes to change my clothes and then we'll sit down and discuss it?"

Hernán nodded. "Would you like some tea? I can make it while you change."

"Perfect. Be right back."

Hernán fixed mugs of herbal tea and carried them out to the balcony. The late September evening was brisk but not really cold. Sunset over Washington painted high clouds in orange and purple, while the contrail of a jet traced a white line toward the riot of color.

Hernán breathed deeply, trying to let the wonder of that sky lift him away from his nerves. He was so small in the scheme of things. His troubles seemed enormous, but every person he could see on the sidewalk below probably carried burdens that felt just as heavy.

He had a tremendous advantage over those men and women, though. He had Colin, offering him a helping hand, if only Hernán could accept that help.

The sliding door opened and closed again, and Colin sank into the chair next to him. He picked up his mug and tipped the edge of it against Hernán's before inhaling deeply. "Jasmine. Very nice." They watched a plane grow larger as it cut across their view on a descent to the Washington airport. Hernán breathed easier, with Colin there next to him.

After a few minutes of quiet companionship, Colin spoke. "I haven't taken my plane up since we came home and I'm getting itchy. Do you think you might like to fly with me this weekend?"

"Sure. Flying was pretty amazing. Where do you like to go?"

"Well…" Colin trailed off and stared into his tea. "I haven't been to see my folks in a while. Maybe we could go up to New Jersey, spend the night and come back on Sunday." He looked earnestly at Hernán, a hopeful expression visible in his eyes even through the glasses.

Hernán still knew little of Colin's family except that they were rich. What would they think if Colin showed up with a strange man? His clothes were shabby and he needed a haircut. He felt his cheeks color at the thought of meeting Colin's parents in his needy state.

"We can do something else if you want," Colin said quickly. "Maybe fly over the Shenandoah to see the foliage changing colors. Anyway, I derailed us. There's something you want to talk about."

Hernán nodded. "I'm, uh… This is difficult." He leaned forward in his chair and set his mug on a small wooden cocktail table between them. "I'm almost out of funds, Colin. You're generous with letting me stay here and everything. I can take it from you if I'm able to give something back, but that's about to end. I'd really like to get a job so I can pay my share."

Colin focused on his mug and took a sip. Carefully, he said, "You know I don't need the money—"

"You don't need *anything*," Hernán interrupted. "But I do. I need to do something so I'm not just letting you take care of me."

Colin's glasses flashed when he looked up quickly. "You're wrong, Nán, when you say I don't need anything." Just what he needed remained unspoken. Colin flushed slightly and continued. "But you said 'take care of you'. Is this about that Nimble guy in Provincetown?"

"No. Yes." Hernán shook his head. "I don't know. Right now everything is coming from you and it scares me."

"I would never cut you off or throw you out."

"I guess." Hernán squirmed. "No, I trust you or I wouldn't be here. But I have to be able to contribute something."

They sat in silence for a few minutes. Colin's voice sounded tight when he spoke again. "I'm worried if you get a job off the books. Like I said when we flew back to DC, if you're caught it could be the end of your attempt to get documents. Tell me something. Is it really about earning money, or more that you don't feel useful?"

Hernán had to think about that one. Realistically, he knew what he'd been putting toward groceries was a drop in the bucket compared to everything Colin did for him. So what was it that really mattered?

Standing on my own feet. Feeling like I'm someone Colin wouldn't be ashamed to be seen with in public, or introduce to his family.

Hernán scratched above his eyebrow. Sheepishly, he admitted, "I guess it isn't the money as much as wanting to be proud of myself."

"I get that. I don't have to work but I *do*, if you know what I mean. If you'd take it, I'd just give you—Hey!" Colin's head snapped up. "Here's an idea. We always need translators and tutors at the immigration center. Spanish speakers from all over need help acclimating. French, too. Courses in English as a second language are in big demand, but we don't have enough teachers. We try to help non-English speakers with other things, like how to open a bank account or apply for a job. Some people need a translator so they can talk with a lawyer.

"So hear me out. I make a, uh, sizable contribution every year to the Initiative, anonymously. I also give for special projects or activities when I see the need. In fact, I've been doing some research lately into what it would cost to hire a dedicated English teacher. In DC, a tutor can typically command around thirty dollars an hour. At thirty hours a week, then, that's a little over a thousand. A DC pubic school teacher is going to earn on average around sixty thousand a year, not including benefits."

Colin leaned toward Hernán. "Your language skills would be really valuable to the center. It can't pay you, though, since you don't have an Employment Authorization Document. But let's say I give you the amount of money that I otherwise planned to donate to pay an English teacher full time. In exchange, you volunteer at the center as an ESL tutor and translator for thirty hours a week."

Hernán frowned. "Is that legal? I can't get you sucked into my trouble."

"It's fine. In a few states that really fight to limit immigration, they might say I'm harboring a fugitive." Colin snorted and shook his head disgustedly. "But in most places, including here, this would just be considered a gift. My accountant will figure out how to report it."

"When, uh, when would this begin?" Hernán asked cautiously.

"I feel like we should get further in your immigration process so the work doesn't distract you. That's still the most important thing, right? We'll have you start when we're sure working at the center won't interfere. To tide you over, I'd like to give you an advance of, oh, two thousand dollars, and then a thousand a week."

Hernán sputtered. "That's too much!" he protested. "Two or three hundred is more than enough for me."

"Seven-fifty a week, fifteen hundred upfront, and that's my final offer," Colin said with a grin, "And this is the strangest negotiation I've ever had."

Sipping his tea to buy time, Hernán thought about what Colin offered. It was more than generous. It went beyond kind. Colin understood what was really bothering Hernán and offered a solution to let him keep his pride. The salary fiction was a fig leaf for Colin putting money in his pocket, but Hernán was prepared to work very hard at the center in return.

The idea of teaching English to others began to excite him. He'd dreamt of becoming a teacher, back when his world seemed bounded by San Marcos. With the role Colin offered, he could do something meaningful for others and find out if he was any good as an educator, all while bringing in money that he could share with Rudy as well.

Hernán's heart thumped and his eyes burned as he nodded his acceptance.

Over dinner later that evening, Colin said, "So speaking of your immigration process, I talked to David James today. That's Brandon's boyfriend. I mean husband." He squinted at the ceiling for a moment. "Huh. Still not used to that."

At his pause, the warmth in Hernán's chest ran cold. Recalling Colin's past with Brandon, he berated himself for selfishness. Colin clearly wasn't entirely over it and, given the quick look he'd had of Brandon back at Veranda that one time, he could understand. Brandon was vibrant and handsome. No wonder Colin still had feelings for him.

He gave his friend what he hoped was a sympathetic look, even as he ignored a sharp pang in his gut.

Colin shook his head clear and continued. "Anyway, David called me from Paris. He's set us up to meet with a colleague of his tomorrow so we can start developing a plan to get you a work permit or other permission to stay. When David returns from the honeymoon, he'll be more involved personally."

"That's great," Hernán said, unconvincingly. He tried to be more enthusiastic when he added, "I was wondering when I'd have to start telling my story."

Staring at the ice cubes melting in his glass of water, Colin quietly asked, "You know you're going to have to be really honest with the lawyers, right?"

Hernán's guard immediately went up. "What do you mean? I've always told you the truth."

"I know that," Colin protested quickly. "I wasn't implying anything. What I mean is, you're going to have to tell them everything if they're going to be able to help you. Including the things you don't want to talk to me about."

Hernán's heart began to race. He'd known that was coming, but not that it would be tomorrow. *Exposure. And in front of strangers.* He muttered something about seconds and hurried to the kitchen with their plates. Retrieving a platter from the warming oven, he fought to control the quivering in his stomach. *I have to talk about Lonnie.*

"Breathe," Colin said behind him, and only then did Hernán realize he'd been holding his breath. When he tried to serve a piece of chicken, his hand trembled so badly he couldn't hold the tongs. Instead, he rested his palms on the kitchen counter.

Colin's brow furrowed deeply. "I know this will be very difficult. Can you do it, or do you need more time to prepare?"

Hernán's head shot up. *Could I put it off? Another week—surely I'd be ready then.* He'd work up to it, maybe try revealing little pieces to Colin. To practice.

No. Every day he delayed meant more time that he was sponging. Every day meant he was risking Colin's happiness. Sooner or later, the darkness that followed Hernán would begin to seep into Colin too.

He cleared his throat and said roughly, "I'm ready." He carried the refilled plates back to the dining table.

Colin beamed as he sat down again. "That's great. I know you can do it. What do you think, though? Would you want me to be there when you talk to the lawyers, or should I keep out of the way?"

"Please be there," Hernán said immediately, almost gasping. Then he regretted his neediness. He stuttered. "If...if you want to be there. I mean, it's rough to hear. I'm, uh, I'm afraid..." He stopped talking and almost ran from the table again, but Colin's steady gaze held him in place. Colin had given so much that the least he could do was be honest about his craziness.

His eyes blurred and he looked down at his food. "I'm afraid you'll think less of me when you know."

A soft noise of protest brought his gaze back to Colin. "Never, Hernán. I think you're brave, coming to the States. People I've worked with at the center have sometimes told me their stories. Horrific accounts of why they left their home countries and what happened to them on the journey. I can imagine how hard that crossing would be."

Hernán bristled. "Can you? What exactly is it in your life that lets you imagine the choice between staying where you are and being murdered, or coming to a country where you'll be a criminal? When has your family had to scrape together every penny it had to pay smugglers to take you on a journey so terrible that you sometimes wished you could just die?"

His voice had grown strident, and Colin blinked at him nervously. He held up a palm. "Point taken. I didn't mean to be patronizing. And you're right. I can't really imagine what you've been through. But I'm here to learn, if you'll teach me. Besides, you put your trust in me and came to Washington. That took courage. There's nothing you could tell me that would make me think less of you."

He sounded so certain that Hernán let himself believe it might be true. Sincerity shone in Colin's blue eyes, and Hernán drew strength from it. His heart still thumped painfully, but it grew less erratic. And gradually, he realized, he *was* less afraid.

Then why was his face still warm? Why did the blood rush in his ears? His stomach was in knots too, and his hands shook slightly. But...he almost liked it.

Hernán slid back, stood, and came around the table to crouch before Colin, who turned in his chair. Hernán looked up at his blue eyes. He gently pulled Colin's glasses off, a slight quiver in his hands making the frames rattle as he set them on the table. Colin hardly breathed as Hernán studied him.

So handsome. Can I do this? A lock of Colin's brown hair fell forward and Hernán automatically stretched to brush it back. The soft feel of it under his fingers seemed to quiet his tremors. He rose to his feet and grasped Colin's hands to tug him up too. They stood so close together Hernán could see Colin's pupils dilate.

Want and *need* called on him to move the final two inches keeping them apart. Colin's tongue darted over his own lower lip and Hernán had to know what that lip tasted like. He put his hands to either side of Colin's face and pulled him down to join their mouths in a kiss.

The pressure was feather-light at first, but Colin's lips felt warm and soft. Their velvet touch was something Hernán had never before known but didn't think he could continue to live without. He drew Colin to him more forcefully, slanting his head instinctively to deepen the kiss, tangling his fingers in Colin's soft hair as their lips slid together. At the brush of Colin's tongue against his mouth, he opened for it. The sensation of a tongue meeting his own electrified him. Colin tasted of the jasmine tea he'd been drinking earlier, and the food Hernán had prepared for him. A fire began to burn in his belly at the overwhelming intimacy, and he wanted more.

A moan reached Hernán's ears but Colin kept his arms loose at his side. Hernán released Colin's hair so he could tug Colin's arms around him, showing him that he need not fear. And there it was—the safety and security of Colin hugging him tightly, making him feel protected. Desired.

Loved? he wondered.

No, of course not. Colin was still in love with Brandon. But he liked Hernán enough to share his home. That was enough. Colin held him carefully as if afraid Hernán would bolt at any moment until Hernán too wrapped his arms around Colin's back and pulled him in hard. Their tongues danced, not thrusting but simply caressing.

Kissing was far, far better than Hernán had ever had reason to suspect, but eventually it had to end. He leaned back but made no move to break the hug. He kept his arms around Colin's waist and asked uncertainly, "Was that okay?"

Colin sighed happily. "More than okay. That was maybe the best kiss of my life."

Hernán grinned shyly. "Hey, not bad for my first time at bat."

Colin's eyes widened in surprise before he nodded his understanding. "I'm deeply honored, to be your first kiss."

Hernán let his head fall onto Colin's chest. He mumbled, "I want to do more but…"

Colin kissed the top of his head. "Shh. You don't have to do anything you aren't ready for. Just holding you is like a dream."

"I think I'd like to try kissing again," Hernán said with his red face buried in Colin's shirt. He felt a rumble as Colin gave a small, happy laugh.

"I'd like that too. What would you think about laying with me on the sofa?" Hernán nodded so they left their dinner and moved to the living room.

Colin kicked off his shoes and stretched along the cushions of the sofa. Hernán removed his sneakers and lay down, snaking his arms under and over as Colin wrapped him up as well.

"Much better," Colin said softly. "You feel really good."

"I like it too," Hernán answered before stretching his neck to find another kiss. The second time was even better. Hernán grew bolder with his tongue and Colin permitted him to explore his mouth, to run his tongue over Colin's teeth and along his lips.

It went on and on until Colin shifted them into a different position. Suddenly Hernán could feel the erection pressing into his side.

His stomach hurt suddenly. Sweat dampened his pits.

Colin kissed him back and gently licked at Hernán's lips. Hernán's breath came faster and his hands trembled. The upholstery of Colin's sofa grated against his skin.

He fought not to push away.

Colin broke the kiss and leaned back. He took one look at Hernán's face and struggled up off the sofa. "Jesus, I'm sorry. I went too far, didn't I? I didn't mean to scare you." His voice implored Hernán for forgiveness.

"No, it's all right. Honestly. I just got a little… You didn't do anything wrong."

"Are you sure?"

Hernán stood to take Colin's hands. "We're good," he said shakily. "But is it okay if we leave it there for now?"

Cleaning up after they finished their dinner, Hernán could tell Colin was still upset and worried about having crossed a line. He berated himself for making Colin unhappy. As he put away the last of their dishes, he asked, "Have you ever seen a juicy show called *Club de Cuervos?* Rudy and I watch sometimes. It's campy and great. I think you'd like it."

Colin bobbed his head eagerly, as if desperate to restore Hernán's level of comfort. "You queue it up. I'll get us some vanilla."

Their ritual of TV and ice cream seemed to be what was needed. By the time Colin came in, Hernán had his feet up and grinned like a schoolboy at getting to share one of his favorite secret pleasures. Colin sat down at the other end of the sofa as usual. Hernán accepted his bowl, paused a moment, and then shifted down to sit right next to Colin.

He might not be Colin's first choice, but he could give him companionship. Comfort. Remind him that he wasn't alone.

Colin flashed a smile as he leaned slightly until their shoulders met. All that light Hernán craved was there again, pouring out of Colin's eyes. He prayed he'd still see it once Colin knew everything. His cowardice. What he let happen to Albert and Andrea. What he allowed to happen to himself.

Tomorrow I have to tell it. All of it.

He shivered, and Colin said in an undertone, "It'll be fine. I'll be right there for you."

Hernán put his head on Colin's shoulder and sighed when an arm wrapped around him. They stayed that way through two episodes of *Club de Cuervos.*

Chapter 11

THE NEXT MORNING found Colin gazing out of his office window. He couldn't get that first kiss out of his mind. The vulnerability in Hernán's eyes, the tenderness with which he'd removed Colin's glasses, the heat when he'd brought their lips together… Colin shivered.

Yes, he'd screwed up by taking things too far. Yes, he wanted more than Hernán seemed ready or able to give. Yes, he was taking a risk with his crush on a man who had deep scars etched on his soul.

Yes, he was falling in love.

His boss Maryanne bustled into his office with a set of materials. Tiny and dynamic with black hair pulled into a bun, her bespectacled eyes stayed on the folders in her hand. She said without preamble, "This is the shit for the lobbying group next week that I want you to handle. We've got confirmations for two representatives and two senators, the draft agenda, bios for the group you'll be escorting through and—What the fuck is the matter with you?"

Colin started, heat immediately rising in his cheeks. Maryanne had finally looked up from her notes and focused on his face. She frowned, and so he was sure he looked guilty or…something.

"Oh, just wool gathering I guess," he answered, trying awkwardly for a nonchalant tone. He failed.

"Did you get laid? I haven't seen a shit-eating grin that big since the day my brother discovered the bathhouse."

Colin's ears burned but he couldn't stop the smile that stretched his mouth. "Nothing like that. Not that it's any of your business. Gimme," he said as he made grabby hands at the folders she held.

She passed him the folders but shook her head. "Deny all you want. I'm taking it as confirmation. Fuck, if you get married and run off I'm gonna be so screwed. You do so well with the lobbying teams."

"Calm down, Drama Debbie. It's not like that and I'm not going anywhere."

She threw herself into one of his visitor chairs. "What's his name, how did you meet, when are you bringing him by, does he have money we can get him to donate, and Nigel the student intern is gonna be really disappointed because I've seen him scope out your ass."

"Um, what? Nigel?" Colin furrowed his brow. He tried to think of who Maryanne meant. "The skinny guy from Harvard?"

"Yup. He's wanted to have your babies since the second day he showed up. Is it within my power as your boss to order you to put out for Nigel before you get too committed in this new thing? I want him to move to DC and join us when he graduates next summer."

"I'm trying to decide which questions to answer and which ones to file away as potential grounds for a sexual harassment lawsuit." He tapped his desk when a distracted Maryanne glanced at her vibrating cell phone. As she looked up again, he announced, "I'm not doing Nigel, it's new but I really think it's going to work, and we met in Provincetown. That's all you're getting."

Maryanne snorted. "So cliché. Go to a gay wedding, end up married yourself a few months later. It's like a social disease with you guys."

"Whereas you ladies so sensibly show up for the second date with a moving van and two cats."

"Hah. That one was old when I was still in the test tube."

"Your moms must have gotten a mix of sperm from Ken Jeong and Chris Rock to end up with you," Colin teased.

"Don't forget Lea DeLaria."

"Do we have to have the talk again about how boys are different than girls?"

Maryanne shot him a middle finger. "You're just jealous because Lea probably has bigger balls than you and your new boyfriend combined. And I'm way funnier than Chris Rock."

Boyfriend? Do I have a boyfriend? Colin was too distracted to come up with a response and Maryanne snorted.

"Oh for Christ's sake. You're ass over tits about whoever."

He didn't bother to deny it, but fiddled with the stack of folders to change the topic. "Are you sure you want me to take this group? It's an important piece of legislation we're fighting. Maybe Leslie—"

"I want you to do it," Maryanne declared forcefully. "You are more than capable of taking the lead. You've always been good behind the scenes and I think you need a bigger role." Colin bobbed his head nervously. "Anyway, I'm worried about Sabeen Hassani pulling out. She's got a great story but freaks at the idea of public speaking. I've done my best to explain that she'll only be talking to a few people at a time but we could lose her before the Hill visits begin."

Colin opened the top folder and scanned the list of attendees on his lobbying team. "We'd still have three constituents who can talk from personal experience if we lose Hassani."

"Yah, yah, but then we have no 'in' to talk to Gerragos from Maryland. I'd really like all four constituents so we don't lose one of the slots. See what you can do with calming her down, okay?"

He set aside the files and his discomfort. He knew he should be able to handle what Maryanne asked, but he didn't like taking on a public role any more than Sabeen Hassani, apparently. "Okay. I'll study these materials and we can talk again. Any more harassment, or can I get to work?"

"Oh, you're *working* today," Maryanne said with exaggerated emphasis. "The way you've been looking at puppies and children in the park there made me think you're just mentally choreographing your flashmob proposal."

"And that's why I'll never let you meet Hernán."

"Hernán!" she crowed. "So we have the first name. Soon all your secrets will be mine."

Shit. He didn't mean to give the name. Especially as Colin was going to bring Hernán to the center soon to start volunteering. He'd already decided there was no reason to explain his agreement with Hernán to Maryanne since it didn't affect the Immigration Initiative's finances. Still, he had a feeling she'd remember Colin's slip.

Aloud, he said, "Out, please, or I'll remember that I really don't need this job."

"Okay, okay. Normally getting laid makes people happy but you're just touchy." She said it with a smile, though, so Colin knew she was goading him.

Not that she was off-base about his distractedness. He wanted to send Hernán flowers and goopy text messages. He wanted to take the rest of the day off, go home and take Hernán for a lunch or picnic or something. Was the DC zoo open? Gah, he wanted to take the *week* off and fly Hernán to New Jersey to meet his parents.

Oh fuck me. What would his parents think? How would they act? It was fifty-fifty whether they'd embrace Hernán right away or hire a private investigator to make sure of his motives.

Okay, so no trips to New Jersey yet. He needed to talk to someone, though. Maryanne couldn't keep her fucking mouth shut, so she was out. Brandon wasn't due back from his honeymoon for a few more days. He could probably wait that long, but just to make sure he was on Brandon's schedule he grabbed his phone and sent a text:

Hey B. Hope you're loving Paris still. When you get back can we grab lunch? All good but I need advice.

He jumped in surprise when his phone chirped with a reply a few minutes later.

David's taking me to opera house in an hour. Do you need to talk now?

It can wait but thanks. You'll have great time at opera. Gorgeous building.

Brandon returned a thumb-up symbol. Colin set his phone aside to get some work done until he picked up Hernán for their appointment with the immigration lawyer.

HERNÁN PACED AROUND the conference room while Colin fixed himself a cup of coffee from the setup on a credenza. A few minutes later, a woman in a suit joined them. She was a young Latina with long, black hair, perhaps in her mid-twenties, and carried herself with assurance.

"Colin, hi," she said and held a hand out to Hernán. "I'm Sofia Mosquera. I work with David James."

"Hernán Portillo," he responded, shaking with her. "Is it all right if Colin sits in with us for this?"

Sofia took a conference room chair. "It's fine. One thing I need to caution you about, though, is that with a non-lawyer present the attorney-client privilege won't apply. While I'm just getting to know you and your story, that isn't a problem at all. If it gets to the point we're discussing legal strategy, we may want to revisit."

Colin spoke up. "I don't want to jeopardize anything. Hernán, maybe I should take off?"

Sofia apparently noticed the panicked expression in Hernán's eyes, though, because she said quickly, "No, stay. What Hernán's going to tell me will ultimately make its way into a public document, so I'm less worried about the privilege not attaching. It's just something for us to be mindful of going forward."

Hernán pulled out a chair next to his own. "Please stay," he begged softly. The vulnerability tore at Colin's heart.

"Of course."

Sofia started them off. "Hernán, I want you to know that I've handled several immigration and asylum cases successfully. I'll be taking the lead on preparing your application. When David returns he'll work closely with us too."

Colin spoke up. "I've worked with Sofia before. She handled the asylum hearing for a woman who came to the center, Aamiina Nuur."

"I was glad that worked out so well for her." Sofia returned her attention to Hernán. "What I'd like to do today is hear your story before we figure out the best avenue for you to immigrate legally. From the little David passed along to me by email, we already have some ideas but we don't want to prejudge the right approach. Once you and I have talked, I'll do some strategizing with David. We'll all get back together afterward to talk through next steps. How does that sound?"

Hernán nodded slowly. "I think I understand."

"Good. I'm going to take a lot of notes as we talk." Sofia opened a notebook she'd brought in with her and picked up her pen. "Let's start with your background, Hernán. Where exactly are you from?"

"I lived in San Marcos, in El Salvador."

"Do you have family there still?"

"Yes, my grandmother and my younger sister Brijith. I also have an uncle who lives just outside San Marcos. Some cousins and aunts, too. Everyone else is in the States."

Colin appreciated the way Sofia eased Hernán into the interview. She got him talking about easy things to establish a rapport. Gradually she elicited details of Hernán's father coming to the U.S. and his mother following three years later with Hernán's older brother.

Colin noticed that Hernán steered away from any discussion of his grandmother, other than to say it wasn't a close relationship. They talked about Hernán's love of school. When the conversation began to touch on why he hadn't finished college, he again redirected to talk about how great his favorite teachers had been.

It was all interesting to Colin, but not germane to the work at hand. Hernán carefully avoided any mention of the things that he had hinted to Colin, or that he was gay.

Sofia seemed to recognize as well that she wasn't getting the full story she needed. After an hour of the dance, she suggested they all take a break. She caught Colin's gaze as she left the room and, frowning slightly, tilted her head almost imperceptibly toward Hernán.

Colin got it. Sofia needed him to step in.

When they were alone in the conference room, Colin crouched before Hernán in his leather chair. Hernán flushed and tried to swivel away, but Colin put a hand on his knee to keep him from hiding.

"You know what I'm going to say, don't you?" Colin asked. "Hernán, you have to go deeper. I get that you've kept being gay deeply hidden from almost everybody, but this is a safe space. David's gay, and Sofia has dealt with several LGBTI cases. I doubt there's anything you could say that would shock her."

Hernán slid his gaze nervously around the room. "I understand." He looked out the window and said, "It's got to be weird for you, working with this David guy. I mean, he married that man you have a crush on. Brandon."

Colin frowned as he pushed himself to his feet. Hernán was trying to deflect him as well, but he'd dealt with that often enough in his lobbying activities. He said calmly, "David's a great lawyer and he can help if you'll be open with him and Sofia."

He belatedly registered the tense Hernán had used about Brandon. *The man you* have *a crush on.* Did he think Colin was still in love with Brandon?

Perhaps a little honesty on his part would make things easier for Hernán.

"By the way," Colin added casually, "the Brandon thing is really old news. I thought you understood that but I should be more clear." Meeting Hernán's eyes, he said softly, "He's my friend, and that's it. There's someone else I have a crush on now." It went deeper than a crush but Colin didn't want to scare Hernán more than he already was.

Hernán blushed but he didn't look away. His eyes danced back and forth on Colin's face like there was something he wanted to say. He wet his lips and opened his mouth.

Just then the door opened and Sofia returned. "Ready to keep going?" she asked.

Hernán blinked several times but he kept looking at Colin, standing next to him. Finally he said, "I'm ready."

He turned to face Sofia squarely. "Colin says I'm not giving you what you really need. I'm trying but this is very hard for me." He swallowed hard and squeezed the hand that Colin rested on his shoulder. He stammered out, "I…I'm gay."

Colin beamed at him and Sofia said solemnly, "Thank you for telling me, Hernán. It goes no further than this room until you're ready. David and I have worked with several people from Latin America who experienced great difficulty in telling their families about being gay or transgender. I'm third generation but my great-grandfather was born in Ecuador and he still says shocking things. Will you talk to me about that?"

Hernán sighed but he nodded again as they all resumed their seats. It went much better the second time.

In a halting voice, he talked about his grandmother and the things she had said to him. He talked about his cousin Rudy and the times he was beaten up for being swishy. How glad he was that Rudy's father Elías had been able to bring him legally to the States before Rudy could be seriously hurt. He talked about things his father had said in their few conversations over the years so that he knew he'd never be able to come out to his parents.

And finally…

Finally he was ready. He reached out blindly to grab Colin's hand, and he talked about being a little boy alone in his uncle's store.

Chapter 12

Fourteen years ago…

HERNÁN LAY SPRAWLED on the floor of the store, flipping through a Richie Rich comic book. He was seven.

The door jingled, but he ignored it. A man called out for Juan. Hernán knew his tío had gone to the outhouse with a magazine under his arm, and would be gone a while. He kept turning pages while the man walked the few aisles, calling again for Juan.

"I got your cases of soda here," he yelled out.

And then the man stood there above Hernán. He seemed huge. He was thick-bodied, with a stained white t-shirt and dirty jeans.

"Where's Juan?" the man asked through yellow teeth. The smell of beer and cigarettes came off his unwashed body. Hernán just pointed to the back and looked down at his comic book.

The man didn't move. and Hernán knew there was something very bad about that.

"Pretty like a girl," the man drawled. "You here alone?" He looked around quickly, leered, and dropped one hand to squeeze his crotch as he reached for Hernán.

COLIN TOOK HERNÁN'S trembling hand in both of his own and kissed the joined fingers. "We know," he said. "You don't have to tell us the details."

Hernán shuddered but sent a questioning look across the table. Sofia nodded her agreement with Colin. "Okay." He exhaled raggedly.

LATER, THE MAN told Hernán, "Shut up with that crying. You say anything, and I'll tell 'em you begged me for a lick. Everyone will know you're a fag." The outhouse door banged shut just then. The delivery-man turned and walked out the front door of the store.

Hernán didn't know what to do, but he found a rag and wiped off his face. Even at seven, he was sure being a fag was a very bad thing. Abuela told him all the time.

Still scared and shaking when he got to the house in the Las Margaritas neighborhood, he stood in the kitchen door, trembling. Abuela looked up from the pot she stirred and gave a snort when she saw Hernán. "You're crying again? Weak little boy. Men don't cry."

He should have known better, but it came out then, about the man in uncle's store. Her eyes just got meaner and meaner. She beckoned Hernán closer and he went to her. She was his grandmother, after all. He was supposed to mind her.

She made him hold out his hand, and then grabbed it in her own. Right into his face, she said, "I knew you were a fag," and rapped his knuckles hard with the spoon, hot from her cooking. Hernán tried to pull away, but she was too strong. "Just shut up about it." *Rap.* "You weren't hurt, not really." *Rap.* "Talk about it and everyone will know I've got a fag-boy here." *Rap.* "I'm not living with that shit. You hear me?" *RAP.*

AFTER, HERNÁN DID everything he could to hide *whatever* it was about him that told the man and his grandmother he was a maricón. But he didn't really understand how they could tell. He walked stiff-legged. He stared at the ground. He smiled when the boys around him talked about girls.

For years, he hid behind carefully constructed walls and he thought he had succeeded.

Eleven months ago…

TO THAT DAY, Hernán didn't know what he'd done to attract the attention of the Cuernos del Diablo gang. He was twenty and walking home from college one afternoon in San Marcos when he spotted the group of young men lounging near a bus stop. He didn't even need to see their tattoos to know who and what they were.

Two of them had been in high school with him, though a year behind. Both were skinny and wore sleeveless shirts with tight jeans ripped at the knees. The biggest of the idlers was older, maybe as much as twenty-five, and a stranger to Hernán. His red t-shirt looked like a sausage casing around his thick belly, chest and arms. He had on black jeans and white sneakers, and lounged against a wall with one leg propped on the bricks behind him, smoking a cigarette.

Hernán looked at the three of them, and then quickly down and away.

The leader laughed crudely and called out "bicha." The other two picked up the taunt. Hernán ignored them, but it only seemed to inflame the hoods. "Hey, pretty girl, gonna suck my big dick?" the large one shouted. Hernán's knuckles suddenly ached, and he could smell again the dirty thing that man in the store had rubbed on his face.

He ran. His weakness was apparently a red flag to madden the bull, and the gangbangers gave chase.

He sprinted for nearly fifteen blocks, dodging through crowds, turning corners so fast he almost fell into traffic. Behind him, he could hear the Cuernos closing in. His throat hurt and his pulse raced faster even than his feet. Someone on the street cursed as Hernán shoved him out of the way, the gangbangers nearly on him. Any second, one of them would grab his backpack and jerk him to the ground.

He tried to stay on the busiest streets because he knew—he just *knew*—if he were trapped in an alley, what would happen to him would be so much worse than that day in his uncle's shop.

Before him a bus stood at the corner, its door open. The driver reached for the lever to close up, and Hernán cried out, "Wait! Please!" He stumbled up the metal steps of the bus, scraping his shin badly. His heartbeat thrashed in his ears and his lungs heaved as he saw over his shoulder the door close in the face of the Cuernos chasing him.

The bus quickly pulled away from the curb. He looked up at the driver, barely able to stand on his quivering legs. Quietly, the driver said, "Calm yourself. Then you can come up and pay me."

Hernán muttered "gracias" and slid into a seat. The bus headed in a different direction than Abuela's house, but that was okay. He was safe.

Except the initial chase turned out to be just a beginning. The next day as he left college, he saw a Cuernos leaning against a light pole. It was one of the kids who used to go to his high school; no doubt he'd recognized Hernán as well. Hernán joined a group of teenagers walking down the sidewalk. Though they looked at him strangely, they didn't abandon him.

Then it was the leader of the little group of hoods. He sat on a bench at the bus stop across the street. When he caught Hernán's eye, he spread his legs wide and slid to thrust his groin forward. Hernán turned around and went back into the school. He ended up sitting in the gymnasium while cheerleaders practiced, so he couldn't be caught alone.

Day after day it continued, and Hernán ran out of ways to hide. Finally he told Abuela he was sick and couldn't go to school. She snorted and said, "What do I care? You're too old for school anyway. Get out there and find a job to pay me back for the food you eat."

He stayed home that day and the next, until it had stretched to three weeks of hiding. Abuela complained loudly and often he was a lazy ass. He should get out of her way and either go to school or go to work.

Unwilling to abandon college yet, he finally dared to venture back. Two more weeks passed when he saw no Cuernos. He began to breathe more easily. Perhaps it was finally over.

He was wrong.

One evening, having grown complacent, Hernán stayed late after class to catch up with work he'd missed. He talked to a teacher for a while, and then went to the library until the librarian told him she was closing up.

He looked through the front doors of the school, and realized his mistake. There were no other students or adults around he could trail behind for protection. Still, he saw no trace of the gangbangers. It had been weeks since he last spotted them. Maybe he was safe.

He walked down the street toward his bus stop, pivoting his head left and right warily. His bus pulled to the curb a block away and he began to hurry.

"Maricón," he heard in his ear. Before he could turn to see who said it, he felt the most surprising pressure in his side. It was like he'd been punched, though that didn't seem quite right. He gasped and stumbled into a run that carried him right up the steps of the bus.

The driver's eyes widened strangely as Hernán flashed his pass and swung toward an empty seat. The bus pulled away very fast and he fell back against the plastic-covered cushion.

A woman across the aisle from him had a hand to her mouth as she stared at his waist. Hernán looked down and tried to remember when he'd changed shirts. He was sure he had just been wearing white, but now he could see only red. It looked wet, and he suddenly grew nauseous.

Pulling the shirt out of the way, he saw blood pulsing out of a hole in his side. He put his hand over it to stop the bleeding. A jet of warmth spurted against his fingers, just as the pain set in.

The bus driver apparently pulled over at some point and got the attention of the police. A policeman applied pressure to the wound until they got him to a hospital, where doctors rushed him into surgery.

He woke up when he heard his sister praying. The ache in his side was terrible. He could see a few other beds lined up near his.

"Is this a hospital?" he asked, and his voice sounded like gravel. His throat was sore.

Brijith looked up from her rosary when he spoke and jumped to her feet. She leaned over him. "Yes, Nán. You're in the hospital. You were brought in yesterday."

"What happened? Was I in an accident?"

"You were stabbed. The bus driver saw the whole thing. A Cuernos did it." Hernán was silent, but Brijith continued, "You had two surgeries already, and they have to do another one later today." Her fifteen-year old eyes widened with concern. "You nearly died, Nán."

"Does Abuela know?" he croaked, and Brijith nodded.

"She was here last night for a while, and told the doctors to call her if they need her."

Hernán rolled his head away and passed out again.

RECUPERATION TOOK A very long time. He ended up having four surgeries and even then, the doctors couldn't save more than half of his left kidney. In between operations, the police came for a statement. Abuela stood in the room like an iron pillar, arms crossed, glaring at him.

He knew what she was thinking, because he was thinking it too. If he told the police about the gangbangers and the way they had been taunting him, they would ask why Cuernos thought he was a homosexual. The *police* then would know about him. And he read enough news to understand a fag was not someone the police would waste their time protecting.

"I don't know why they attacked me," he said. Abuela nodded grimly behind the backs of the policemen as he added, "No, I don't know who they were. I didn't get a look before I was on the bus."

The police snapped their notebooks closed, seemingly disgusted by the whole thing. A lone stabbing on the streets of San Marcos was not unusual or even interesting. The older of the two policemen was fat, sweaty and smelled of onions.

"Probably another initiation," he said. It was the same tone in which another man might have said, "Boys will be boys."

The younger officer, Martín Alba, was slender and handsome, and had kind eyes. He glanced at Abuela and his partner before saying to Hernán, "We'll file the report and see what turns up. The driver gave a good description of the attacker."

Later, Officer Alba came back to Hernán's room alone. He pulled a chair next to Hernán's bed. "Look, I get you're scared of Cuernos. Everyone is. But that's why we have to do more. Do you see? Every time they get away with hurting someone like you, it just encourages them to do more. If you know anything, *anything* that could help, please. Tell me."

The expression in his eyes was earnest and hopeful. Maybe it was the painkillers in his system, or Alba's handsome face. Maybe it was because he wanted Alba to be right, that if people fought back enough Cuernos could be curbed.

"I went to school with two of the men who have been following me." He gave Alba their names.

THE HOSPITAL DISCHARGED Hernán far sooner than his doctors advised because Abuela refused to keep paying. "He's just laying there on his ass," she screeched. "He can do that at home and won't cost me so much money."

Back in his own bed after weeks of the hospital, Hernán lay carefully to protect his sutures from the most recent operation. He stared out the window. He could hear Abuela on the phone, yelling at his father to send money for his goddamn son's surgeries because she wasn't going to pay it all. He closed his eyes.

His uncle Juan came to see him, bringing comic books even though Hernán had outgrown them. His aunt came with three of his cousins. When he had healed enough to move around, his sister asked in a whisper when he was going back to school.

"I don't know. I might not," he told her, and it felt like getting stabbed again. He didn't know if Cuernos would still be watching for him. Maybe they thought he was dead, but maybe not. He secretly hoped he'd learn Officer Alba had found a way to stop them.

Instead, Juan came into the house one night, highly agitated. He ignored his mother and went right to where Hernán sat on the sofa.

"What did you do?" he asked gruffly. "Yesterday I heard Officer Alba and his partner picked up two guys and charged them with the assault on you. This morning, they found Alba's body. They blinded him, and then…"

Juan shook his head, unable to continue. Abuela narrowed her glare at Hernán. "His partner hasn't been seen all day. Nobody knows if he ran or if they got him too. Did you talk to the police, Nán? Is that how they made the arrest?"

Hernán looked back and forth between his uncle and his grandmother. "I…he asked for the names. Alba. He said we had to fight back."

With a disgusted snort, Abuela returned to the kitchen and began to slam drawers. Brijith huddled in the doorway to the living room, her face pale and eyes round.

Juan sank down next to Hernán, shaking his head. "No one can fight. Don't you know that? Cuernos are into everything these days. They have people who work for them in the police and other places. They can't let anyone oppose them. You see? If they had Alba's name, it's only a matter of time until they know you talked. They're going to come for you, too."

Brijith began to cry. Hernán's side ached and his head swam. Maybe the gang didn't know yet exactly which house he lived in, but it was only a matter of time. He wasn't safe there. Maybe *Brijith* wasn't safe. They would come in and they would finish what they started with the stabbing.

Even if he went to his uncle's place, or any of his cousins', it wouldn't be hard to track him down. Cuernos del Diablo were everywhere. Gay people disappeared every day, and no one cared. There was no place he could go in San Marcos to stay safe.

"Wh-what do I do?"

Juan looked out the window and tapped his fingers against his thigh frantically. "I don't know. Anywhere in El Salvador, they'd probably find you." He returned his gaze to Hernán, eyes sad. "Maybe…"

"What?" Hernán prompted after the silence stretched.

Juan stood and paced the living room. "I don't know if it would be enough, but I can think of only one place to go where Cuernos might, just *might*, leave you alone. The United States."

Chapter 13

ABUELA STORMED BACK into the living room.

"You can't stay in this house," she declared. "They'll track you here soon enough. You caused this, with your school and your hair and the way you walk." Her voice grew uglier and more strident. "Just get out. Tonight."

Hernán's eyes filled with tears, and Brijith began to sob. As horrible as Abuela had been to him, her house was the only home he knew.

Juan turned on his mother, eyes narrowed. "Selfish bitch," he barked at her.

She grabbed Brijith's shoulder. "I've got to worry about this one too." She shook Brijith hard and said to her, "Stop crying, right now. It's driving me crazy."

Juan turned back to Hernán. "Grab a bag. You can come with me until we figure out what to do."

Hernán ran up the stairs and threw a few handfuls of clothes wildly into his school backpack. When he came down, Abuela was in the kitchen again with Brijith, ranting. Juan gestured him out the front door, and they left without another word.

They drove to Juan's store; he lived on the second floor of the building. Hernán had felt safe there the times he got to stay with his uncle. He'd begged in the past to come live above his store. Juan had shaken his head, but regretfully.

"I can barely keep myself fed," he'd said. "And my place is just too small for more than a weekend." Hernán had understood, though it nearly killed him to return to Abuela's house.

That night, as he entered the store behind Juan, it seemed to him a terrible way to get his childhood wish.

"I've got to think," Juan muttered as he paced. "I don't see how anyone would find you here." He caught sight of Hernán's face. "You look like crap. I guess you haven't been sleeping." He gestured with his head. "Get some rest and we'll talk in the morning."

Hernán nodded and slunk up to the small, cramped living space over the store. It consisted of two messy rooms, and the narrow bed in the back part hadn't been made. Juan wasn't married and apparently saw no reason to straighten up for himself. Hernán crawled into sheets smelling slightly of mold, and lay staring at the ceiling. Surprisingly, he did sleep.

When he woke up in the morning, Juan had apparently already eaten. He'd left an old Mister Coffee machine on and dripping. After it finished, Hernán poured two mugs, added sugar and milk to his uncle's, and went downstairs.

Juan was stocking shelves. Hernán handed him his coffee, which Juan took with a grunt and a quick nod. They faced each other over their steaming mugs, without speaking. Juan finally sighed. Turning back to his shelves, he said, "Grab a carton there and help me. We can talk while we work."

Hernán obediently scooted a box of dry goods along the floor and began to transfer items to the racks. Minutes passed, and the words built in Hernán's chest until he wanted to burst with them—about what he knew of the Cuernos members who'd come after him, what they said, what they seemed to want from him.

He couldn't do it, though, without admitting he was like Rudy. Juan was the kindest and most loving of his relatives still in San Marcos, but he didn't know if even his closest uncle would help if he knew Hernán's secret.

After Juan finished emptying a box, he picked up his coffee again and took a long drink. Setting it down once more, he asked, "You talked to Pedro about all this shit with Cuernos?"

"No," Hernán said, shaking his head as he worked on his shelf. "He only calls a few times a year."

Silence reigned as Juan returned to loading dry goods, his brow furrowed. Finally, he flicked a glance at the screen door to make sure no customer approached. "I know a coyote," he said cautiously.

"Coyote?" Hernán asked.

"A smuggler. He has the connections to get someone across the border. It's expensive though. Have you got any money?"

"I've saved up a few hundred dollars. Is that enough?"

Juan shook his head. "I hear it costs six thousand dollars."

Hernán gasped. *Six thousand dollars.* He dropped the bag of flour he'd picked up back into the carton and doubled over. *I won't cry. I won't cry.*

Juan dropped a hand on the middle of Hernán's back and rubbed a little. "I've got about a thousand. My mother won't help, but I'll see if any of the family will contribute. Well, let's try Pedro. See if my worthless brother will step up to help his son."

He glanced at a clock loosely mounted on one wall opposite the register. "I might be able to reach him now. You keep stocking the shelves and I'll call."

Hernán made his way through the boxes, listening intently as Juan spoke into the phone in his office. He could only catch parts of the conversation but Juan got louder and more strident.

"… Going to get himself killed if he doesn't get out of here… No, of course Mamá isn't going to give him any money… Well, find it or I'm going to call Immigration myself and give them your fucking address and number, you piece of shit. He's your *son.*"

Juan slammed down the receiver and stormed back into the aisles, his face red. "We'll see," he said, trying for calm as he ran his eyes over Hernán's face. "Go upstairs. I'll finish this."

As Hernán made a simple breakfast for himself, he thought about Juan raising his voice to Hernán's father. It might have been the first time he'd heard someone fight for him.

Juan let him stay that day and the next while they waited to hear from Hernán's father. To pay him back, Hernán took shifts in the store and cleaned the upstairs rooms. No Cuernos turned up at the store that they noticed. Even though he had only a pallet at Juan's, he slept better than he had in weeks.

Brijith came by after school, when she could avoid Abuela. She told Hernán their aunt had agreed Brijith could live with her; she was waiting for a chance to slip her clothes out of Abuela's house.

Juan also quietly asked their relatives for money to help Hernán, and scraped together several hundred dollars more. Finally, on the third day, Pedro called. Elías, their other brother and the father of Hernán's cousin Rudy, was going to help with the rest of the funds. Relief almost brought Hernán to his knees.

Elías sent money to Juan's bank in San Marcos to bring the total to three thousand dollars. "We pay half up front," Juan told Hernán, "and then the family pays the rest right before the coyotes turn you over in the States."

JUAN AND HERNÁN met with a smuggler a few days later. The coyote had wrinkled skin and small eyes. No names were exchanged, but they made a deal. A few anxious days later, Hernán was ready to go. As instructed, he wore clothes—smuggled to him by Brijith—to look like he was going to a club. The unnamed coyote had told Juan and Hernán in his cigarette-rasped voice to dress that way. "If you're caught, it looks like you're out to have fun. Got it?"

At five in the morning, Juan and Brijith waited with Hernán in the predawn chill for the coyote to pick him up. A few other relatives arrived with a thermos of coffee and pastries. His aunt said a loud prayer for Hernán, and many of the cousins joined in.

Brijith hugged him close and whispered in his ear, "If you make it, please try to send for me. I want out too."

A very dusty and ancient car turned a corner and headed their way. Juan picked up Hernán's backpack for him. It contained a toothbrush, toothpaste, deodorant, three pairs of pants and three shirts; nothing more. Resting a hand on Hernán's shoulder, he whispered a blessing.

"Uncle...," he began, but his throat constricted and he couldn't finish.

Juan nodded at him. "Be careful, Nán," he said.

Brijith burst into tears then, and ran to be comforted by her cousins. If Hernán hadn't felt so scared, he would have laughed at her theatrics.

The two-door car pulled to a stop. Its windows were tinted. No one climbed out so Hernán opened the passenger side door. The unnamed coyote was at the wheel, and hiked a thumb at the back so Hernán pulled the seat forward and climbed in.

A little boy and girl sat there already, their matching, wide eyes meeting his. They were probably around eight or nine years old, but dressed as if going to their first communion. Each held a small plastic backpack decorated with Disney characters.

Hernán squeezed in next to them. Coyote leaned across the passenger seat and pulled the door shut. "These are your cousins," he rasped at Hernán. "If anyone asks."

The girl looked intently at Hernán, curiosity and even excitement showing in her face. The boy stared at his knees and sniffled. Hernán wanted to comfort him but he didn't dare open his mouth in front of Coyote. The car pulled away and Hernán turned his head to watch his uncle, sister and other relatives disappear behind him in the dust.

A part of him was relieved, and maybe a bit eager. He had no idea what the journey would entail, but he was heading away from Cuernos. Away from Abuela. That had to mean hope.

Coyote drove a little slow, Hernán noticed, probably to avoid attention. After twenty minutes he came to another stop. A woman opened the passenger door and this time Coyote indicated she should take the front seat. She was pretty, probably in her early thirties. Hernán saw the leer on Coyote's face as she climbed in, and his stomach tightened nervously.

They drove on, Coyote steering with just his left hand. After a mile or so, he started to slide his right hand along the back of the seat. The woman shifted as close to the door as she could get, and Coyote gave a nasty, low laugh.

In another half-hour, Coyote pulled over on a deserted strip of road. "Gotta piss," he muttered, climbing out. He left the door open; Hernán heard the pull of his zipper and then the splash of urine.

He whispered to the little boy and girl, "Do you need to go pee?" The girl nodded. The boy just kept staring at his knees. When Hernán touched the woman's shoulder to get her attention, she jumped, but then opened the passenger door so they could climb out.

Hernán led the children further away from the road, and the woman followed. Possibly she just wanted to stay close, and away from Coyote. She took the little girl's hand and led her out of sight, while Hernán helped the little boy.

He crouched to deal with the boy's stuck zipper. "I'm Hernán," he said in a low voice. What's your name?"

After a pause, the boy whispered, "Albert."

"Is that girl your sister?"

Albert nodded and volunteered, "Andrea."

When they returned to the car, Coyote had a cigarette on his lip as he stood by his open door. He ran his eyes up and down the woman's body and then tilted back his head to blow away a plume of smoke. She kept her gaze on the road. Once Albert and Andrea were in the back,

Hernán pushed the woman to join them and took the front seat.

Coyote scowled and spat out the window. When the car stopped again, he ordered, "Out. Wait for the bus."

They found themselves in front of a church Hernán thought was north of San Marcos. Five other people of various ages, each dressed in nice clothes and carrying a single pack, stood in a loose cluster near the steps.

Hernán shouldered his pack. He took Andrea's hand, her head craning around to take in everything, while the woman guided Albert. Coyote peeled away in a cloud of dust.

While they waited, Hernán whispered their names to the young woman. She nodded. "I'm Isela," she finally said.

Nobody else spoke to them. Nobody had to. It was clear what they all were there for, and no one knew what would happen next.

The silence was heavy, pressing them down as hours passed. Scary.

Hernán's earlier elation at getting away from Cuernos gradually faded to dread. He couldn't imagine opening his mouth to make conversation. What would he say? Everyone with him knew the danger they were in. Probably even his "cousins" understood. He wanted to know why the children were alone, where they were going, and yet...he couldn't ask.

Better if everyone kept their privacy. That way, if picked up, they didn't have enough information to implicate others.

The men and women exchanged nervous glances. Had they been duped? Did they pay so much money only to be abandoned at the very beginning of their journey? Albert started to cry again, softly. When Hernán picked him up, he clung to his shoulders.

Andrea took that as permission to wrap her arms around Hernán's leg. Isela crouched to pat her back and shared a shy smile with Hernán, gone in a second.

The bells of the church tolled four in the afternoon before a woman emerged. She looked indigenous, in her bright orange dress embroidered with flowers, and a multihued shawl wrapped over her head. Its ends trailed down her shoulder. The group looked at her expectantly, until the rumble of an approaching bus drew their attention.

It pulled to a stop in front of the church. When the door opened, the woman clad in orange ushered them together and up the stairs. Hernán asked her in Spanish if she knew where they were going. When she didn't answer, he asked again in Nahuatl. She looked surprised, but answered, "Toward Guatemala."

Everyone settled on the bus quickly. Albert wouldn't let go of Hernán and so he took a padded bench with the boy. Isela sat with Andrea one row forward. The driver turned to look over his cargo.

When his eyes settled on Isela too long, Hernán clenched his fists. He was still recovering from his wound. Albert and Andrea had attached themselves to Hernán. If it came to a fight to protect Isela, how would he choose who needed him more?

"Okay, chickens," the driver said. Juan had told Hernán the smugglers called their cargo pollos or chickens. "We'll be on the road about three hours. I'm not stopping so if you have to go to the bathroom, do it now." He fixed Hernán with a stare and jerk of his head that took in Albert, Andrea and Isela. "Any trouble, those brats are your children. She's your sister. Got it?" Hernán nodded.

The bus pulled away to make its journey along a rough highway. The shocks were bad. It squeaked and bounced as the miles melted away, but as long as it was moving, Hernán's unease about the driver lessened. The rocking gradually lulled him down into a fitful half-sleep.

He stirred when the bus shuddered to a stop, to find it had grown dark outside. The door hissed as the driver operated the mechanism to open it. He gestured and cursed until all the passengers had climbed off.

Three handlers or coyotes waited for them. One aimed a flashlight at the ground and guided them to a concrete warehouse of some kind. Inside was cold and stark, but food and water were available. Isela darted forward and claimed as much as she could while Hernán found them a place against a wall.

The coyote with the flashlight waved it to get everyone's attention. "You're here for the day. When it's dark again, we leave."

One of the pollos asked querulously about bathrooms, showers. The smuggler laughed at her. "Piss outside but stay hidden. Patrols sometimes come through here. No showers."

They all slept badly, stiff and cold on the concrete floor, and woke in heavy silence as they waited for orders, or at least some information. None of the handlers told them anything more. Andrea wandered around the room, trying to talk to other travelers with mixed success. Albert wouldn't leave Hernán's side.

Both children grew listless as the day dragged on, and drank or ate only when Hernán or Isela made them. The small amounts left for them by the handlers went quickly anyway. Hernán knew he should be hungry, but the oppressive dankness of their quarters drained any appetite.

In the afternoon, as Albert and Andrea slept, one of the coyotes sauntered in their direction. He was scrawny, and his jeans and shirt didn't look like they'd been washed in a long time. He held a bottle of water, its sides dripping with condensation. He stopped near Isela and wiggled the bottle.

"You want some cold water to drink, bonita?" he asked in a reedy voice. He stuck one hand in his jeans pocket and made a show of adjusting himself. "I got better food too."

She shook her head and looked away. Hernán tensed. What would he do if the smuggler grabbed her? After just two days he was already exhausted, hungry, and dehydrated. The smuggler looked much tougher than him. If he got hurt or killed trying to help Isela, what would happen to Albert and Andrea? Nobody else had shown the slightest interest in protecting the children.

The guy crouched on his heels and reached out to push Isela's hair off her face. "I got a big one, girl. You'll like me."

She shrugged off his hand and burrowed further down. A flash of annoyance crossed the coyote's face and he raised his hand again. Hernán freed himself from Albert's sleeping head on his lap and the smuggler shot him a glare. "Stay outta this, faggot," he rasped.

Hernán stood anyway, trying to lock his legs to conceal their trembling. The smuggler narrowed his gaze and rose slowly, menacingly, to his feet.

"What the fuck are you doing?" barked another coyote who suddenly loomed behind the first and cuffed his head. "Rules are simple. You stay away from the chickens. We got to keep a clean shop or the chickens stop coming."

He cuffed the smuggler again. "Get the fuck out of here and go check the schedule." The boss glanced at Isela and Hernán as the aggressive smuggler slunk away, but he didn't say anything. He just turned and left.

Isela's head bowed but Hernán saw tears slip down her nose. Andrea patted her cheek and tried to comfort her. Isela pulled the girl into her lap and they rocked together.

Finally the handlers got everyone to their feet and led them out of the warehouse. A rusty car pulled up and the driver yelled through the open window at the nearest pollos to get inside. Four squeezed into the car and it pulled away.

Isela sidled closer to Hernán as he rose from the bench, and the children each clutched at one of his hands. He understood. They had begun their journey together; he didn't want them to get separated either.

When a van pulled up that looked big enough, he rushed forward, almost pulling the children. Isela followed. They were rude and aggressive but they pushed through other pollos and secured the back seat. Albert sat on his lap while Andrea wiggled down beside Isela. A pollo with very dark eyes glared at them as he climbed in, hauling up a woman who was possibly his wife, but Hernán gave him back a level stare. The man dropped his gaze first.

With six travelers piled in, the van driver pulled away. He was a stick-thin teenager with stringy black hair. In the rear-view mirror, Hernán watched the driver's eyes flicker between the side mirrors and out the front. He tapped his hand incessantly on the steering wheel as if urging it for more speed.

Ten minutes later, flashing lights appeared behind the van.

Chapter 14

"SHIT!" YELPED THE driver. Hernán looked out the back and saw two police cars gaining on them. The pollo Hernán had jostled earlier leaned over the driver's shoulder and yelled at him to go faster. The van lurched, gears ground, but it burst ahead.

The driver took a sharp turn, causing Hernán to smash up against Isela and Andrea. Albert began to cry and Hernán held onto him as best he could with the van careening down a dark road. The police lights were still behind them, though the van had gained some distance.

The driver yelled, "Hold on!" and took another sharp turn, and then a third. Through the windshield Hernán could see a dirt road stretching straight ahead until the headlights switched off.

The teenager drove in darkness for another few minutes, leaning so far forward his head almost touched the glass. Abruptly he slowed and turned off the dirt road. The van bounced along a rutted path for another hundred yards and came to a stop. A smallish house with a fenced garden stood in the middle of a moonlit field, soft lights glowing through its curtains.

"Go," their driver barked. "Get inside. Now."

Everyone scrambled out of the van. No sooner had Hernán closed the sliding door than the driver took off again. He made a wide circle to get back to the rutted path, flicked on his headlights, and screeched away in a cloud of dust and exhaust. When he rejoined the dirt road, he turned back the way they had come. His shrinking taillights still glowed red when two police cars flashed by in the same direction.

The convoy disappeared into the darkness.

Hernán turned around again to see a woman ushering the pollos inside. A man waited there, maybe her husband, and guided them all to place their bags in a corner. After showing them the outhouse and a water pump, he turned to a large pot simmering over the fire.

Hernán took Albert with him to the outhouse, and when they returned Isela took Andrea. Shortly, they sat cross-legged as the woman passed out bowls of chicken soup. The homey smell awakened his appetite and he finished two helpings.

Their hostess seemed quite taken with Albert and Andrea as they ate. She kept offering the children bread and fruit to go with their soup. Albert shied away from her, but Andrea happily took the proffered plum. "Thank you," she said seriously to the woman, who stroked a hand down Andrea's black hair.

"Two hours you sleep," the man croaked, so the travelers found places against the wall to settle down. The children drifted off immediately and Hernán followed right behind.

All too soon, the woman shook the travelers awake, gathered them and led the way outside. The man who had been their host held up a lantern and strode away through the near-darkness, further from the dirt road.

When Albert stumbled, Hernán picked him up. His head fell against Hernán's shoulder as they walked; eventually he fell asleep again. Andrea kept up, little legs marching steadily, her hand in Isela's.

They had probably walked for thirty minutes when the man brought them to a halt. Silver glinted at his back; Hernán realized it was moonlight reflecting on a river.

"I hope you can all swim," the man said with a chuckle, but it sounded kindly. He took off his clothes down to his underwear and stuffed them in a plastic sack. He passed out more bags.

Shyness be damned, apparently. Hernán stripped to his jockey shorts, bagged the clothes, and then helped Albert take off his shoes, pants and shirt. When everyone was ready, packs on their backs, bagged clothes in their hands, the man led them down the riverbank.

Hernán couldn't tell how deep the water was or how strong its current, but it looked wide. How would Albert and Andrea manage? How would he hold on to all their clothes and keep them afloat if they had to swim?

The man walked right into the water, and then Hernán breathed easier. The eddies around his legs were gentle when he followed. Even ten yards out the water wasn't as high as his knees. Isela held Albert's hand and he took Andrea's as they waded forward. Silt squelched under their bare feet as they moved deeper, but the water wasn't cold.

Perhaps thirty yards from shore, the man held up a hand in warning. "You have to swim a little here. Not far." He kept going, his plastic bag held over his head, and in a few more feet the water was to his waist, and then his chest. With his bag aloft in one hand, he paddled with the other. After a few yards, he seemed to have his feet on the bottom again and he walked until the water came no higher than his knees.

Hernán said to Isela, "You take the four bags of clothes. I'll get the children across." She nodded, gathered the bags, and soon was across the deep spot. Hernán took Andrea first and told Albert, "I'll be back in a few minutes. You don't move until I'm back. Okay?"

The little boy nodded, eyes shimmering in the moonlight, but he didn't cry again. Hernán felt Albert's gaze on him as he waded deeper with Andrea. She clutched his neck tightly as the water rose over her legs. He leveled them out and dog-paddled with one arm. Andrea began to stroke too, helping to pull them across.

When the river was shallow enough for Andrea to stand, he said to her, "You're so brave. I'm very proud of you."

Leaving her with Isela, he hurried back for Albert. He peered across the water, but his stomach gave a lurch He couldn't see the little boy. Craning his neck left and right, he sucked in a trembling breath. He wasn't sure it was safe to call out.

Where *was* he?

Finally he hissed, "Albert." Some reeds moved to his left, parted, and the boy stepped into view. Only then did Hernán realize a slight current had pushed him a short way downstream as he crossed and so he was looking in the wrong place.

With a great sigh of relief, he paddled over. Albert splashed forward to meet him and gave a yelp as the water closed over his head. Hernán was there in an instant and pulled him up. Albert hugged his neck so hard Hernán was afraid he would choke. He shuddered in Hernán's arms but he still didn't cry.

"Good boy," he whispered. "Let's go find your sister."

ACROSS THE RIVER, the guide gave them a little time to rest. They had no way to get dry and it was unpleasant putting on the clothes from their bags. Albert and Andrea were dead on their feet when Isela asked the guide, "How much longer?"

He shrugged. "Two hours."

"The children will never make it," she protested but he shrugged again and turned away. Isela stalked back over to their little group, fuming but helpless.

"Can you manage all the packs?" Hernán asked her. "I'll carry them both."

After just ten paces, his arms ached from the weight of the two sleeping children. The trip became a walking nightmare. Isela stayed slightly ahead, glancing back often with a worried expression. Blisters formed and broke on Hernán's feet. His arms and shoulders burned and throbbed.

He tried to recite poetry in his head. He prayed. Anything, to keep his mind off his body.

His only break came when the guide called a halt so everyone could step into bushes to relieve themselves. Andrea tried to stretch out on the grass to sleep and Hernán had to scoop her up.

"I can walk," Albert said sleepily. He stuck close to Isela as they resumed the march, Andrea asleep in Hernán's arms. Albert made it almost twenty minutes before he grew too tired to continue. He sank down, his face crumpled and forlorn in the scant moonlight.

Hernán had to wake Andrea and put her down. "I'm sorry, little one, but you need to walk for a while on your own. Okay? Hold on to Isela." He shook out his arms, desperate for a rest, but the guide and the rest of the pollos already moved on, the distance between them growing. Hernán scooped Albert onto his shoulders and held his wrists for security as they tried to catch up.

Finally the guide brought them to a ramshackle building surrounded by weeds, where he opened a door and ushered everyone in. The shed stank terribly, like something had died there and been left to rot.

"Sleep," the guide said. "A car will pick you up in a few hours."

"Where are we now?" Isela asked.

The guide answered, "Guatemala."

Hernán talked quietly with Isela as they arranged their packs. "I think that's why we used the river," Isela guessed. "So we wouldn't go through a checkpoint as we crossed the border from El Salvador." Hernán nodded.

The group huddled together. For warmth, for comfort—he didn't even know.

A pickup pulled to the door of the shack a few hours later. The burly man who entered the shack was gruff as he rousted everyone and pushed and cajoled them toward the truck bed. Hernán got the children situated on either side of Isela, with their backs to the cab of the truck. He climbed in himself with the other two travelers in their party.

Albert said plaintively, "I'm hungry."

The burly man took in Albert and Andrea. He made a face and disappeared, but returned in a few moments with some pieces of fruit, a bottle of water and a few corn tortillas for the children.

The man traveling with them looked greedily at the food. Ignoring his own thirst and empty belly, Hernán positioned himself so he was between the man and the children, and gave his flattest, most dead-eyed stare. The pollo shifted around and muttered to the woman with him.

A THREE-HOUR DRIVE brought them into the capitol of Guatemala. The pickup stopped at a house where an old woman who reminded Hernán of Abuela herded them inside. She had two pails of water and cups; everyone jostled to drink. A table was strewn with simple food but it looked like a feast by that point.

"You buy from me. What you don't eat you can take with you," the old woman said. The pollo with them pulled out a twenty-dollar bill and swept a big pile of tortillas into a plastic bag, his eyes daring Hernán to stop him.

He was too tired to fight, though. He pooled money with Isela, and helped her bag up what remained. Isela made sure the children drank but they had nothing they could use to take water with them.

Hernán asked the old woman, "Can we get some bottles?" She stared at him, her cold gaze chilling him to the bone. He could almost hear his own grandmother's voice telling everyone what a disappointment he was. The woman snorted and left, returning with four empty plastic bottles. "Thank you," he muttered.

Soon they were directed onto a very old bus, joining perhaps thirty other people. Many of the seats were already claimed, and over half of the riders looked to be indigenous. They found no seats together so Albert sat on Isela's lap and Hernán took Andrea a few rows back.

The bus creaked and tilted to the side as an extremely fat man, mustache covering his mouth, climbed to the driver's seat.

They drove for hours, stopping only when the driver needed to relieve himself. The woman who shared a seat with Hernán and Andrea kept looking obsessively at a piece of paper on which Hernán could see a name and address. When she wasn't looking at the paper, her lips moved as if she were reciting the words over and over, a magic spell to get her out of Hell.

The rattling bus, the smell of so many bodies in a cramped space, and the lack of enough food and water gave Hernán a terrible headache. Andrea seemed to sense it and patted his cheek sweetly. He gave her a wan smile.

More hours passed, and a stupor came over Hernán he couldn't shake. His arms and legs hurt from the long trek the night before. He began to wonder whether he had made a terrible mistake, starting this journey.

He lost track of the times they stopped, the places their handlers hustled them in and out of. Somehow he remained mindful of his little group, always with an eye on Albert and Andrea, and a helping hand for Isela. The responsibility he felt for them was loaded with fear, but, he thought, perhaps it gave him a reason to keep moving as well.

He ate or drank when he could, and ignored his empty belly and dry mouth otherwise. Albert replaced Andrea and huddled as close as he could every time they stopped, clearly worried. Isela gave him some of her food at one of the driver's piss stops. He tried to push it back but she said, "We need you. Please, Hernán."

He ate the food.

The driver finally left them huddled in a bus station with as many as fifty people milling around. The place stank of urine and feces. An underfed dog trotted around outside and collapsed in the sun, panting.

Two prostitutes worked their way around the station; occasionally one would go off with a man around a corner. The sounds of grunting and flesh slapping on flesh filled the air. Isela tried to cover Andrea's ears as she hunched over the girl.

A man with a glass eye shambled by, muttering a list of drugs. He leered at Albert and caught Hernán's eyes. "I'll give you a dime bag for that one."

Hernán shook his head fiercely and tried to marshal his strength in case it came to that. "Go away," he croaked out. "Just go away."

The drug peddler laughed and shuffled on.

They moved again, ten or twelve of the travelers flocking onto another bus. Hernán remembered a man with a wooden leg holding up the line as he tried to climb in. The handlers muttered curses and threatened to leave his ass behind. Isela helped the man up the stairs finally.

The bus carried them through what looked like a banana plantation. That night they slept in a barn, in hammocks hung from the rafters. The slings were big and sturdy, and the four managed to claim one hammock for themselves.

Isela and Hernán lay with their heads at opposite ends, Albert and Andrea between them. Albert had grown hollow-eyed and quiet, but Andrea scooted up toward Hernán's head.

"Is this what camping is like?" she whispered, sounding more excited than at any point in their journey.

Hernán managed to return a small smile. "Sort of. I went camping with my uncle and my cousin Rudy once. We had to sleep in bags on the ground and I told my cousin to watch out for snakes. He screamed and couldn't rest all night." Andrea giggled and snuggled in against Hernán's chest.

THEY WOKE TO growling stomachs and parched mouths. Albert stayed close to Isela wherever the young woman went, and sat at her feet when Isela was still. Andrea explored a little more, but never wandered far from Hernán's sight.

Around midmorning, a woman entered the barn with a tray in her hands and a plastic bag over her shoulder. The tray held packets wrapped in foil, which she offered around for a dollar each. Bottles of water were also a dollar. Hernán pulled some of his carefully hidden money out of his underwear and bought four packets and two waters.

Peeling open the foil, he found a tamale filled with a little shredded chicken. He ate it quickly, and then helped Albert and Andrea get theirs open. Isela split her tamale in half, and divided one portion between the children. Hernán immediately felt guilty, but he was still hungry. He turned to ask the woman if there was more food, but she set aside her empty tray.

The day dragged slowly, listlessly. The four sipped carefully from one of the bottles of water, unsure when they would find more.

The barn erupted into unexpected movement around midafternoon. Suddenly handlers began jostling and herding a group of about fifteen passengers—including their little family—onto a boat. It sat low in the water as they climbed on, one at a time.

Hernán was last. When he stepped from the dock to the stairs, water sloshed over the edge. The boat had a small pilothouse and a single cabin below deck, which the coyotes claimed for themselves. Hernán told the children to stay close and maneuvered his brood to the stern, where a few ragged life preservers hung.

One of the handlers passed around damp blankets that smelled of mold, and they managed to claim two. Isela tucked the children between Hernán and herself, blankets around them.

The boat roared away from shore and cut into the night. Hernán had only been on a few boats in his life, and this one seemed to him to be going too fast. It was so dark he couldn't imagine how the captain knew where he was going. He began to wonder what would happen to them all if the boat were to capsize far from shore. He looked around for more life vests or preservers but spotted nothing.

It began to rain, and Isela tugged one blanket up over their heads to try to keep them dry. Hernán muttered thanks and she nodded. The boat roared on and on through the dark and the rain. It began to feel like a terrible dream from which he couldn't wake.

By the time the rain ended, Albert was asleep but Andrea sat rigidly against him, trembling. He put an arm around her, trying to convey calm he didn't feel.

It had to have been midnight when the engine cut low and motored to a small dock. They seemed to be in a desolate stretch of jungle, with no sign of habitations around them. One of the coyotes began to refuel the boat from canisters lodged in the sand, while another led the pollos in among the dark and menacing trees. They didn't go very far, however, before their path opened into a clearing and a small house.

The handler ushered them all inside and gestured at jugs of water and bags containing rice, beans and a few vegetables. "Cook outside only," he growled before returning to the boat.

One of the women strode over to the supplies and hefted a bag. She gave the few other women, including Isela, a challenging glare. Obeying her silent command, they scurried over to gather the remaining supplies, and then followed the natural leader outside. The men shifted around bags and blankets, making nests. Hernán took Albert and

Andrea a few steps into the jungle to use the bathroom.

Later, the women served up small plates of rice and beans. It wasn't much food, but Hernán was grateful to have it. Isela sat next to Albert with her own little plate.

"Thank you," he whispered to her.

She gave him a little smile. "It's nice to do something normal like cook." She tilted her head at the woman who had chivvied the others into helping her prepare food. "That one reminds me of my aunt. Bossy but usually right."

MORNING BROUGHT STRANGE birdcalls and slight rustlings in the brush near the clearing. No animals appeared though. The pollos wordlessly prepared themselves for a departure. They waited. And waited. Once again they were subject to the handlers' pleasure, with no clues or explanation. Hernán took the children into the jungle to explore and keep them busy, while Isela tended to their meager belongings and prepared more food with the other women.

The morning gave way to stifling heat, with their group napping fitfully. The jungle had begun to darken around them once more when the handlers stirred everyone up. "Let's go, let's go," they said loudly, tugging and pulling until everyone reloaded the boat. The engine fired up and they roared off again.

Isela had managed to fill their water bottles from the jugs in the little house, so the second trip was a little less miserable. They roared over the waves, hour after hour.

Hernán somehow slept. He woke when the pitch of the engine dropped, to find the handlers guiding the boat toward a dock lined with warehouses. Wherever they were, it seemed more industrial than other places they had stopped.

The boat veered off and puttered toward a dark shore instead of the dock, away from lights and, presumably, naval checks or a coast guard patrol. When the hull scraped on sand, the coyotes emerged from below deck and started pushing the passengers off.

"Where are we?" Hernán asked one.

"Oaxaca" was all the answer he got.

Their shoes and pantlegs got wet because the boat was still several yards from shore. A coyote led the way from the water and to a street, where a series of taxicabs pulled up to take small groups. Another handler herding pollos into cabs grabbed Isela and Andrea, trying to shove them into a back seat.

"No!" Andrea screamed, kicking and writhing. She got away from the smuggler and ran to Hernán, but the door slammed and the cab pulled away with Isela inside. He saw her pale face looking back at them through the rear window, mouth open, tears on her cheeks. Andrea sobbed against his leg.

He had no time to react.

He looked around wildly for someone to help, but the next cab pulled up and the smuggler angrily waved Hernán and the children into it. Guilt choked him. Hernán tried to ask for Isela but the smuggler shoved him down and into the back seat, and then slammed the door.

The taxi drove through the night and eventually pulled up to a small house at the edge of a field. A votive candle glowed and flickered on a low table near the door. A small statue of a human skeleton, draped in a red cloth, stood propped next to the candle.

Hernán stiffened. Even from outside, he read the signs.

This was a house where Santa Muerte was worshipped.

Chapter 15

STORIES HERNÁN HAD heard about the worship of Our Lady of the Holy Death ran through his mind. The priest in his grandmother's church complained of the practice, calling it a form of devil worship. But people there in his church also lit candles and made offerings as if Santa Muerte were just another saint. He had no way of knowing which stories of her worship were true.

The door opened and a woman beckoned them inside. She was small and plump, with iron-gray hair pulled back tightly. Her skin was thickly wrinkled but her eyes glinted. Hernán kept a firm hand on Albert and Andrea's shoulders. He looked around but they were far from any other shelter. The woman beckoned again, impatiently this time.

There was no choice. He whispered, "Stay close to me," and guided the children inside.

The interior boasted a large shrine on the wall opposite the door. More statues of Santa Muerte lined the shelf; all were skeletons in various degrees of craft.

The largest stood at least a foot tall and wore cloths of many colors. Real and plastic flowers protruded from the folds of cloth draping it, and a shiny plastic crown perched on her head. She held a scythe and a globe. Next to the statue burned a tall candle with rings of gold, silver, copper, blue, purple, red, and green.

The woman who had summoned them inside tracked his gaze to the shrine. She cackled. "Scared of the Lady of the Shadows? How about you, little ones?" She crouched down. Albert pulled back to hide against Hernán's leg but Andrea faced her bravely. She shook her head defiantly. "Good, good. The Lady brings gifts and protection. If you ask Her for help, She will give it."

Standing again, she brought them to a table on which sat a stack of bowls, and then ladled soup into three of them. It smelled delicious and Hernán's stomach rumbled. He felt immediate guilt for thinking about food when Isela had been separated and he had no way to know if they would ever see her again.

He didn't even know her full name, or where she hoped to go if she made the crossing.

The statue on the shrine drew his eyes. He couldn't help thinking, *Take care of her, please.*

As if he'd read Hernán's mind, Albert asked plaintively, "Where did Isela go?"

"I don't know. Probably to a house like this one." More confidently than he felt, he added, "We'll see her again tomorrow, I think."

It seemed to be enough reassurance because the children tucked into their soup. After a moment he did as well.

"This is very good," Andrea said seriously to the lady. Albert nodded as well.

"I'm happy you like it," she said with a broad smile that stretched her wrinkles alarmingly. "Have more if you want."

Hernán dished them each some more soup. He'd learned to take as much food as possible when offered, because they couldn't be sure when the next meal would come.

Their clothes were stained from travel. Since the woman seemed kind despite the signs of a religion foreign to him, he took a chance.

"Is there a place we could wash up, or maybe clean our clothes?"

"The Lady gives protection to outcasts and brings safe passage. Ask Her," she chortled, angling her head toward the tallest statue.

Hernán swallowed hard and tried to think of appropriate words. He crossed the small room, knelt before the shrine, and lit a small candle there. Bowing his head and folding his hands as if in church, he said, "Santa Muerte, please help us. We are weary travelers who need your intervention." He looked over his shoulder at the woman to see if it was enough.

She nodded as if satisfied. "Come with me," she said, rising. Hernán and the children followed her to a small bathroom that had a shower. "No washing machine or dryer here. You can rinse out things and set them to dry but they might be wet when the car comes for you tomorrow morning."

"Thank you," he said fervently. A shower sounded like heaven. "Do you know where we go next?"

She shook her head and left, but returned in a moment with some thin towels. Hernán hesitated with the children but decided it wasn't the time to be modest. He hustled them out of their clothes and put them both in the shower, helping them to wash their hair and making sure they used soap. He dried them both off roughly and said, "Stay in here but face the door. Understand?"

They nodded and sat down, still wrapped in the thin toweling. He stripped quickly and took his turn in the shower.

The pressure was low, the water lukewarm, but it felt wonderful to clean himself. After he dried off and wrapped a towel around his waist, he crouched and did what he could to rinse their underwear and socks. He decided against washing their shirts. After draping wet items along the shower rod to dry as best they could, he accompanied the children back into the main room.

The woman gestured a casual arm toward the wall where a small stack of blankets and pillows rested. "Get some sleep now. The car comes early." She went off to bed, leaving them alone.

Hernán made a nest for each of them, wishing it was out of sight of the shrine. The flickering candle seemed likely to make it hard for him to rest. Hernán kept his eyes on the skeleton statue. Shadows cast by the candle flame flickered along the white bone, swaths of cloth and golden crown.

It didn't seem to bother Albert and Andrea nearly as much as it did him. Perhaps the children's calm spread to him because he found himself comforted. His eyes remained on the statue until they drifted shut.

He nearly jumped when the woman shook his shoulder. "Time to get up," she said. "I have some tortillas and beans for you."

Their underclothes had dried enough in the night that it wasn't uncomfortable getting dressed again. Refreshed by the best night's sleep he'd had since setting out from San Marcos, Hernán sat at the rough-hewn table with the children and joined their scant breakfast.

If they weren't reunited with Isela immediately, he resolved to make a fuss with the coyotes.

A car pulled up the dirt road soon after that, and the woman gathered them together. With a glance at her, he made a bow to the statue of Santa Muerte. She nodded approvingly.

"The Lady watch over you," she intoned seriously.

THERE WAS NO sign of Isela or anyone to ask about her when the latest anonymous driver left them in the middle of a dusty town. At least no one attempted to separate Hernán from the children, so perhaps the Lady did help them, a little.

A nice woman at the way-station wandered over carrying a tray. With hand signs she offered to sell them water and snacks. Hernán spoke to her in Nahuatl and she smiled at him, delighted. She praised his beautiful children; Hernán didn't correct her. Before she left, she reached into a pocket of her skirts and produced some small sweets for Albert and Andrea. Hernán thanked her fervently, hoping the treat might keep their thoughts away from Isela.

They waited with five or six other pollos. A few of them looked familiar by then, though others were strangers. A Corolla pulled to the curb and its trunk popped open. A fat man with a sweat-stained shirt and a big mustache bustled out of the way-station and swept Albert up in his arms. Hernán started to protest but the man already waved him over with Andrea.

"In, in," he ordered as he deposited Albert into the trunk of the car. Dread crawled up Hernán's spine. He could see air holes, a few bottles of water, a blanket. Three adults had already climbed into the trunk of a second car. At least with Albert and Andrea, they wouldn't be quite so crowded.

Santa Muerte, if you are *there, please protect these children.*

Hernán settled Andrea and climbed in beside her. When they'd lain down as best they could, the fat man closed the trunk on them. A scent of mold, urine and wet blankets immediately cloyed at him. A little light came through the air holes. If he moved his head, he could see glimpses of the road behind them.

Andrea started to sniffle, and then Albert. "Where is Isela?" she asked in a small voice.

"She's safe, in another car," Hernán said with surety he didn't feel.

The vehicle rattled over a bad road, jolting them where they lay pressed together. Tight space and poor air soon gave him a throbbing headache. He roused Albert and Andrea every so often to make sure they drank a little water.

When Albert complained he needed to pee, Hernán told him to use one of the empty water bottles. The car stopped after a few hours; the driver let them out by a deserted stretch of road before he went into the brush with a roll of toilet paper. The three of them managed as well as they could before the driver returned to reload them into the truck once more.

AFTER WHAT HERNÁN realized later was about a nine-hour trip in total, he came out of a stupor when the trunk opened again. A tall, thin man with a lazy eye and a friendly smile hiked Andrea out of the back and set her on her feet. He waited to make sure she could stand on her own, and then turned for Albert.

Hernán's legs were asleep when he tried to move, but the man placed a hand on his shoulder to lever him up. He nearly fell but the handler kept him steady.

Hernán looked around. They were in a parking lot, closed in on three sides by tall warehouses. Over those, he saw buildings rise to the sky. The noise of traffic penetrated to the parking lot.

"Where are we now?" he croaked.

The thin man passed him a bottle of cold water and then handed one each to Albert and Andrea. He ruffled Albert's hair before turning back to Hernán. "This is Mexico City. I'm supposed to drop you at a bus station where you'll spend the night."

He looked at the hollow eyes on the children, and their travel-stained clothes. His gaze ran over Hernán just as his empty belly rumbled.

The man shook his head. "Fuck that. You and your kids stay with me and my wife tonight. Tomorrow I'll take you to join the others. Come on."

With a hand on the backs of Albert and Andrea, he guided them all into a small car. He drove to a little apartment where a woman cooed and fussed over Albert and Andrea.

A wall covered with pictures of men, women, and children drew Hernán's attention. The images of loved ones, of happy celebrations, brought him a surge of homesickness. Silently, he asked his deceased relatives for guidance.

The host couple had a washing machine and a shower; the woman took all their clothes while they cleaned up. Hernán felt he was in a strange sort of dream, to be grateful for such things. Again they followed the same pattern of the children waiting on the floor together while Hernán washed himself.

Two showers in two days—he nearly teared up with gratitude but didn't know who to thank.

Maybe Santa Muerte.

A dinner of beans, rice and chicken seemed like a feast. The woman asked questions about their journey. Hernán had already warned the children again to tell anyone who asked that he was their father, so he relayed their story as if they were a single family. He didn't mention Isela, though he wondered what had happened to her. He hoped she'd found kind people like the couple housing them for the night.

The next day, the woman made them a good breakfast and helped repack their cleaned belongings into their battered and stained packs. She uttered a prayer out loud to more traditional Catholic figures, and the thin man bowed his head.

Hernán followed suit. It couldn't hurt to have more saints watching out for them.

His brief touch of optimism flared brighter when they were dropped at a bus station, because Isela stood among a group of women. When Andrea spotted her and called out, Isela started like a bird. She ran toward them and went to her knees; Albert and Andrea nearly choked her with hugs. She didn't seem to want to look at Hernán, though.

He thought she must be mad at him. "I'm sorry we got separated," he said immediately. "It happened so fast."

She nodded but kept her head down. Her blouse was torn at the shoulder.

The brief hope he had felt turned to queasiness. "Are you all right?" he asked cautiously.

Isela shot a quick glance at him and looked away again. She gave a small shake of her head. *Oh no.*

He wanted to ask more, or scream, or hug her. He had no idea what to do. When Isela stood, one child holding on to each of her knees, he offered his hand. She took it and squeezed.

"Right," a coyote called as he gestured for everyone to crowd closer. "In twenty minutes you're getting on buses. You'll be on for about sixteen hours. Use the bathroom and remember it will be a long time before you have another chance."

Peddlers wandered around the station with trays of food and bottles of water. "Stay with Albert and Andrea," Hernán said to Isela. "Take them to the bathroom and I'll get food." Isela produced some money and slipped it into Hernán's hand. He managed to buy them fruit, water, tortillas and a packet of wet wipes.

When buses began to pull up, instead of allowing the pollos into the coaches, the handlers directed them to luggage compartments underneath. One space was just large enough for the four of them. Hernán and Isela crowded in quickly with the children before they could be separated again. The coyotes laughed amongst themselves as they lowered the metal door to their compartment, closing them in with a clang.

THE TRIP SEEMED endless and terrible. At first Andrea chatted away at Isela, telling her of Santa Muerte and the nice people in Mexico City. Isela offered nothing of her own journey, and Hernán was afraid he knew why.

All talk died away as the constant rumble of the road under the bus and the heat of the storage compartment became overwhelming. They had no room to move; both Albert and Andrea wet themselves, adding to the funk of their confinement. Hernán finally did too, grateful the dark interior hid his burning face.

Their food and water were long gone by the time the bus finally came to a halt after fourteen hours. The luggage compartment doors opened and the driver waved everyone out.

"We're through the checkpoint," he said. "You can ride up top now. There's a toilet."

Hernán unfolded himself stiffly and helped Albert climb out, and then Andrea. Isela handed over their packs as the other pollos emerged as well. The driver gave everyone a few minutes to change to dry clothes and clean themselves as best they could.

The last two hours of the bus ride seemed to pass in comparative luxury, after the journey in the luggage compartment. When the bus stopped again, Hernán peered curiously out the window. They seemed to be in a village. Signs read in both Spanish and English, so he guessed they might be near the U.S. border.

Everyone got off the bus and waited for the next instructions. Eventually a second bus pulled in to the same area, which he realized was a motel parking lot. The drivers and handlers talked animatedly amongst themselves; one of the coyotes spoke into a cell phone as he gestured wildly.

Hernán heard enough to understand that there had been a third bus, but it was caught by a patrol.

A van pulled up to the motel eventually, and fifteen or sixteen pollos were pushed and jostled until they climbed in.

THEY RODE FOR another half-hour until discharged in the drive before a very large but rundown house. Its walls were dingy white, and the red clay tiles of its roof showed large gaps in places. Three coyotes stood in a line at the bottom of the steps leading to the house's porch.

The smuggler who had driven the van cajoled the pollos into a loose group facing the row of large, forbidding men. Other people peeked at them from the porch or out of windows. Stillness gradually settled over the group, and yet the men in line said nothing.

The front door opened, letting out a shaft of light. A shadow moved and resolved into the silhouette of a man. Hernán could make out none of his features for the glare, but something about the shape terrified him.

The man walked forward slowly, his boots thudding on the wooden porch with each step. He came down a few stairs and stopped three risers above the line of coyotes. Hernán could see him finally, and regretted it.

He was not tall, but very thick and muscular. A black wife-beater shirt exposed pale white arms covered in a fever-dream of tattoos—skulls, birds, flowers, crosses. The thick belt running through his jeans had a skull for a buckle. His red hair was closely cropped all over, giving his skull an appearance of being coated in blood. A reddish mustache curved down on either side of his cruel-looking mouth.

"Listen up," the man said in a loud, rough voice. His accent didn't sound Mexican. American, Hernán guessed. "I'm Lonnie Heath. This is my house. You made it this far. Not too long to go now."

He pointed with one hand across the desert. "That's Texas, a few kilometers away. Before we take you there, the other half of your fee is due. Tomorrow, you call whoever is paying and make arrangements to get the rest of the money to us. When that happens, you finish your trip and we drop you in Houston."

He swept his gaze over the assembled pollos, stopping when he saw Hernán. His eyes narrowed, and the tip of his tongue ran along his lower lip. Hernán felt his balls shrivel in fear. He knew that look.

Lonnie spoke again, but kept his focus on Hernán. "You get water and lodging while you're here, but every day we have to feed you gets added to your bill. Understand? The longer your family takes to get us money, the more it's going to cost them. You've got three ways out of here." He held up the fingers of his left hand to make his point. "One, your family pays in full and we take you the rest of the way. Two, you turn yourself in to the Immigration authorities and take what comes. Three, you head into the desert and take your chances alone. Carlos," he barked.

"Yes, Lonnie," one of the muscled coyotes answered.

"How many bodies did we find in the desert this past year?"

"Fifteen, last count."

Lonnie shook his head. "Fifteen." He scanned the pollos again, gave a snort, and turned to walk back up the stairs and into the house.

The three large coyotes went into action, barking instructions and herding them all inside. Hernán and his little family stuck close together until they were in a dormitory of sorts on the second floor. It took time, but finally they found three beds together. That would have to do.

Isela stayed with their belongings while Hernán took the children to the bathroom, and then she went herself. There were showers at least, and toilets. Things that he took for granted all his life were luxuries by then.

An elderly woman one bed over introduced herself as Violeta as she fussed over Albert and Andrea. "Such beautiful children," she praised. "My granddaughter is in California. I'll be with her soon. You want to see a picture?"

Isela nodded and made appropriate noises at the photo of a little girl in a yellow dress. "How long have you been here?" she asked Violeta.

"Four weeks. But my son is getting the money. He'll have it soon."

Hernán asked, "What do we do with our things? I mean, is it safe to leave them here?"

Violeta shrugged. "Usually, but things go missing. I don't think any of the pollos steal, but the people that run this place..." She shuddered.

"This Lonnie is in charge?" Hernán probed.

"Yes. Well, he has bosses but they don't come that often." Violeta lowered her voice to a near-whisper. "I heard he used to be with the American border patrol. He was fired or arrested or something for things he did to people they caught crossing. Then the bosses hired him to work here."

Hernán shivered.

"What do we do about food?" Isela put in, changing the subject.

"Two meals a day, breakfast and dinner. It's run like a cafeteria. You can take on other jobs to earn more food, like cleaning the bathrooms or washing dishes."

Hernán sat beside Albert and Andrea on the single bed he'd been able to find for them. He'd avoided asking many questions so far, but the time had come. "Is there someone to call to get money for you?"

Andrea looked at Albert, bit her lip, and then emptied her pack. Inside, under a torn flap of plastic, a phone number had been written in permanent ink with a name: Miranda López. Hernán nodded. "Good. I'll help you call." He looked at Isela. "How about you?"

"My sister," she said shyly. "She has a good job in San Antonio."

They sat at dinner with Violeta. The mood was somber anyway, but suddenly the room became entirely silent. Hernán looked around and saw Lonnie walking the perimeter of the dining hall, his hands clasped behind his back. Two of the big coyotes accompanied him. Lonnie's eyes surveyed his kingdom with a smirk curling the corner of his mouth.

His green, glittering eyes lifted and speared Hernán with his gaze. Hernán's stomach churned and he fought the urge to flee. The reptilian look from Lonnie scared him like nothing else on the trip.

The next morning, after breakfast, handlers came around to take people, one family at a time, into a room with a phone. Hernán took Albert and Andrea in and dialed the number from Andrea's pack. After several clicks, the phone connected.

"Hello," he heard a woman say in English.

"Is this Miranda López?" he asked in Spanish.

"Yes," she answered, also switching to Spanish. "Who is this?"

"My name is Hernán Portillo. I'm with Albert and Andrea."

She gave a sharp gasp. "Are they all right? Where are you?"

"They're scared but they're okay. I've been with them from El Salvador. We're close to the U.S. border so now you have to get the other half of the fee before the handlers let them move on."

"You're sure they're well?"

"Yes. They're great kids."

She sobbed. "My babies. I was so scared but there was no one to bring them to us in Corpus Christi. Javier tried and tried. No one would come. But I need them here."

Hernán wanted to rage at Miranda. How could she let two little children make that terrible journey alone? What if it hadn't been Hernán and Isela who got in the car with them?

He kept still though. None of that mattered anymore. He let Albert and Andrea have the phone, and they chattered at their mother, happier than he'd seen them since the trip began. The hardships of the journey already seemed to fade in their minds. Trusting them to strangers and possible saints seemed cavalier to Hernán, but it had worked.

After a minute, though, the coyote snarled, "Enough," and held out his big paw for the receiver. Albert handed it over, his eyes wide.

The coyote spoke to Miranda in a compassionate tone that nonetheless raised the hair on Hernán's neck. "These children are small. The way we cross requires long, long walking. I'm not sure they can make it."

The tone became wheedling. "For an extra fee, we have a different way. We give them American passports for children of about the same age and looks. We put them in a car and drive them over the border. It's another two thousand dollars each, but much safer for them.

"Of course, we can't risk them getting nervous at the checkpoint so we have to give them something so they sleep through it."

Hernán gasped and pulled Albert and Andrea closer to him. Surely their own *mother* wouldn't...

The coyote smiled triumphantly at Hernán, dark eyes glittering, as he said, "Good choice." He gave her the instructions and amount for the money order. "Once we confirm receipt, your children will be on their way."

Shaken, Hernán took his turn next and called the number he had memorized for his father. It rang.

And rang.

He disconnected and tried again. Still no answer. His heart began to race.

"I must have the number wrong," he said to the coyote and heard pleading in his own voice.

"Try again tomorrow. Other people are waiting."

Chapter 16

HERNÁN BARELY REGISTERED what he was doing until he sank heavily onto his own bed. Albert and Andrea excitedly told Isela they had talked to their mother, but she kept her eye on Hernán.

Softly, she asked, "Is there a problem?"

Hernán didn't want to discuss the new plan for the children in front of Albert and Andrea. Instead, he swallowed hard and said, "There was no answer at my father's number. I don't know anyone else to call."

She moved over to his bed and put a hand on his. "What about back home? Can you call where you came from and get help?"

The words penetrated his fog. "Maybe," he said, after some thought. "My uncle. He can tell me if I got the phone number wrong. Or maybe he can find out why no one is answering."

He focused on Albert and Andrea, their shining faces excited and troubled at the same time. He had no right to interfere though, and no alternative plan, for that matter. They had struggled through long walks already, and barely made it. If the coyote was telling the truth about the last stage, Albert and Andrea might be left behind, abandoned by the other pollos.

The children glanced back and forth between Isela and Hernán, and it seemed to dawn on them things were about to change. Albert started to whimper.

"None of that," Hernán said kindly, standing so he could scoop the boy up. He pushed away his own worries to give his attention to the children. "You get to see your mother soon. You and Andrea are going to start a new life." Albert tightened his arms around Hernán's neck.

"Can you come live with us?" Andrea asked plaintively. "Mamá and Papá will let you."

Hernán smiled at her. "We'll see." He glanced at Isela. "I forgot to ask you. Did you get your sister?"

Isela looked down at the bed and brushed a hand over the thin blanket. "She doesn't have all the money yet. But soon, she said."

"Well, we'll at least keep each other company for a while," he said with forced brightness, meeting her eye and tilting his head at Albert and Andrea. She nodded. They kept the conversation light, chattering about things that had happened on their journey. Violeta joined in.

It wasn't long before Albert and Andrea fell asleep. Hernán's throat felt tight as he tucked them under the blanket, maybe for the last time. Only then did he tell Isela in a low voice what the children's mother had decided to do.

Looking at the backs of her hands in her lap, Isela said softly, "So much money. But if I had it, I'd try the new route too. Even if they had to drug me to get me over the border."

Hernán didn't know what to say. He'd cared for Albert and Andrea for nine days. Still, that gave him no right to dictate how they should cross.

He muttered a prayer that night to Santa Muerte. She'd been good to them all so far. Well, for the most part.

THE NEXT DAY, when he was summoned to the phone room, he tried his father's number again. Still no answer. Then he called his uncle Juan.

When the call connected, he almost sobbed in relief. "Tío," he said. "It's Hernán."

"Where are you? Did you make it?"

"I'm in Mexico, at a way-station. I can't go on until the handlers have the rest of the money but I didn't get an answer when I called the number you gave me for my father." He repeated the digits to make sure he had them right.

Juan blew out air in frustration. "Pedro probably fucked up. Look, I'll start calling. Track him down or...something. I don't know. Can I call you back?"

Hernán checked but had to tell his uncle no. "They'll let me call you once a day."

"Okay. Call tomorrow and I'll try to have some answers."

That afternoon, he sat outside with Isela, Violeta and the children when one of the smugglers came to find them. "The money order for the new route came through." He smiled at Albert and Andrea, though it looked more like a rictus than a grin. "You're a lucky boy and girl. Tonight you will go to sleep, and when you wake up you will be with your mamá."

Hernán helped them pack their bags. Isela dropped to her knees to kiss them goodbye. Hernán picked them up, first Andrea then Albert, for a last hug. Then it was time for Albert and Andrea to leave for the brazen route through the checkpoint. Two coyotes would drive them across the border and into the States, to deliver to their mother's house.

If they made it.

The handler from earlier in the day brought water and some pills. Albert didn't want to take them, and the man grew angry.

Before it got to the point he forced the capsules down Albert's throat, Hernán realized what he had to do. Guilt and shame churned in his belly, sickening him, as he crouched to hug the children and kiss their brows.

"Be careful," he whispered, hearing the quaver in his voice. "You're almost there. Your mother wants you to take this medicine, okay? It'll help you rest for the long ride. Don't you wish we had something like this when we were on the bus before?"

He hated himself when Albert took the pills and swallowed them down with some water. Andrea complied as well, her wide, trusting eyes on Hernán's as she held her glass with two little hands. He wanted to weep at his betrayal.

The children looked back once more as they climbed into the van with the smugglers. The door slid closed, and it took off in a cloud of dust.

And then Albert and Andrea were gone.

HERNÁN CALLED HIS uncle Juan every day but he had no news. Isela kept checking as well, but her sister said it was going to take a few more weeks to raise the funds.

The coyotes kept looking at pretty Isela. She huddled as much into herself as possible, and kept her hair forward to hide as best she could, but Hernán knew she felt the weight of the stares.

He knew, because he felt the same thing when Lonnie patrolled the dining room each morning and each night. And when Hernán spotted him during the day, as he went about the chores he'd taken on to get more food for himself, Isela and Violeta.

On the third day after the children left, he was working outside when he heard two of the handlers arguing with a much older man who looked indigenous. Their voices rose louder and louder, but it seemed clear the man didn't understand. He cried out something in words that sounded to Hernán like Zapoteco.

One of the handlers shoved him, and Hernán dropped his rake to run over.

"I can try to talk to him for you, I think," he said, desperate to end the fight before it began. In halting Zapoteco, he said to the elderly man, "Can I help?"

The man gaped at him as his wide eyes ran back and forth over the two taller smugglers. Eventually Hernán pieced together that the man was trying to explain one of the Mexican border patrol groups had changed its route, bringing it too close to the stopover point where the man was in charge.

Hernán translated to Spanish. One of the smugglers nodded and then jogged up to the house, returning with the big coyote named Carlos. He listened to Hernán, arms folded across his huge chest. Then he gave a series of instructions, which Hernán managed to translate to Zapoteco. Eventually the man left with his new orders.

Carlos gestured with his chin at Hernán and said to one of the smugglers, "Give him an extra portion tonight for his help."

Afterward, they used Hernán a few more times to translate instructions and convey information, either in person or over the phone.

AFTER A WEEK, Juan finally had some news to share. "Pedro was picked up by ICE and he's going to be deported, the asshole. He's in detention, apparently. Elías is trying to raise the rest of what we need."

"What about my mother?"

Juan sounded embarrassed. "She won't send any money. She says with Pedro gone, she can't afford anything."

Rage and grief surged through Hernán. His parents had abandoned him to his bitter old grandmother, they'd barely contacted him, and when he truly needed them…

He sagged in the chair where he sat in the phone room. Why should he be surprised? The only one who had ever seemed to want to help him was Juan. Maybe Abuela was right. He was just a worthless fag.

"Look, Hernán. Hold on. We're doing everything we can. Okay?"

"Okay. Thanks, Tío."

TWO NIGHTS LATER, the coyotes came. They wandered into the dormitory where he and Isela had beds. A quiet man had claimed the bed Albert and Andrea used to share.

Isela saw the handlers first, and went very still. Hernán looked up too. His heart thudded painfully as he watched the men circle the edges but come closer and closer toward their corner of the room.

He sat next to Isela, their thighs pressed together. She clutched his hand and kept her eyes on the blanket. He saw her lips moving in prayer.

The men were so much bigger than him. If he tried to stop them from taking Isela, they'd beat him and still do what they wanted.

Then the coyotes halted by the bed where they sat together. The bigger of the two reached out and grabbed Hernán by the shoulder. His blood turned to ice, his bowels to water.

Isela looked on, mouth open wide, as the handler pulled Hernán to his feet. Violeta said a prayer aloud to Mother Mary until the second handler shot her a glare. She shut up.

They pulled Hernán roughly out of the dormitory and up the staircase to the third floor. Down a corridor to a set of double doors. They knocked.

Hernán heard Lonnie's voice call, "Enter." The sound chilled him to the bone. The coyotes opened the doors, brought him inside, and closed the doors behind themselves again.

Lonnie lay sprawled on a leather sofa, patched in places with duct tape. A big bed stood against one wall. Hernán tried very hard not to look at it. A desk, bookcases, other furniture… It didn't matter. Lonnie stood and came closer.

He looked up and down Hernán's body and nodded slowly. "That steak for dinner was good. Wasn't it, boys?"

The handler to his left chuckled and said, "Yeah. Good steak." Hernán and the others had eaten beans and rice.

Lonnie cupped his own package with two hands and squeezed. "Sometimes, boys…sometimes I still want chicken." He reached for Hernán's shirt while the men on either side held him motionless—

"HERNÁN, YOU DON'T have to go on." Colin's voice broke through his story.

Hernán blinked and looked around. He'd gotten through by detaching so thoroughly from himself he couldn't recall where he was for a moment.

Sofia had a stricken look on her face and a sheen in her eyes. Colin was on his knees by Hernán's chair, holding both hands in his own.

"I'm so sorry," Colin said.

Hernán's throat was tight. He tried to speak but he'd lost his momentum. The memory of hands forcing him down, holding him spread for Lonnie, made him shudder. He pulled his hands free of Colin's and dropped his head into them.

"Just give me a minute," he croaked out.

"We can stop there if you need to," Sofia said, her own voice riven with emotion and distress.

After a moment, Hernán pulled himself together. "I'd rather finish."

Colin stood and stroked Hernán's hair. "Whatever you want. But we understand what happened. You don't have to give us the details."

He nodded and drank the glass of water Sofia set before him. Colin took his seat again, and Hernán made himself tell the rest.

ISELA COULDN'T LOOK at him when they brought him back to the dormitory, afterward. It went on every night for a week. Hernán thought it was a week; he lost the ability to separate the time. During the day they used him to translate. At night they brought him to the third floor.

Maybe eight days after the first time in Lonnie's room, when Hernán called Juan, his uncle sounded excited. Elías had enough money to get him out. Hernán felt tears begin. He made Juan repeat the news because he couldn't believe it was almost over.

He told the coyote, who left the room and came back with Lonnie. The thick, red-headed man just stared at Hernán with burning eyes when he said his family had the money. Hernán's stomach seethed with acid, and he clutched the phone receiver so hard it made his knuckles hurt. *Please let me go, please let me go…*

Lonnie scratched his ear and sneered. "You've been here so long, the price doubled."

Hernán felt a sick certainty move through him, right then, like raw sewage. He was never going to get away from Lonnie. Somehow he managed to whisper to Juan about the price, and his uncle started to scream and yell.

Lonnie took the phone away from Hernán, dropped it in the cradle, and walked out.

He thought about killing himself that night. Or getting away and finding the immigration checkpoint to turn himself in. He'd be sent back to El Salvador. Deportation might lead to the same thing when Cuernos came for him, but at least it wouldn't be suicide.

The next morning, as Hernán worked outside by himself, a big, black car pulled up to the house. The driver came around and opened the door; a man in a fine suit and holding a walking stick or cane climbed out. Lonnie came down the stairs to shake hands.

The man said something harsh-sounding and Lonnie glanced over at Hernán. Those eyes that haunted Hernán's dreams glittered, and made his stomach roil in fear. The big coyote Carlos gestured to summon Hernán, and they all went into the phone room.

The man in the suit took a chair, but Lonnie remained standing, looking nervous. Silence weighed down on Hernán's head, the pressure making his ears want to pop, as the man stared steadily up at the light fixture. Finally he spoke in a voice heavy with contempt and exasperation.

"Heath, we are business people. Yes?"

Lonnie nodded sullenly.

"And we offer a service. A service that is valuable to our customers and lucrative to us. You understand, right?"

Lonnie started to turn red.

"So what do you think happens when word gets out our handlers cannot be trusted with the pollos? What happens when a family is told a price, and meets the price, and then is told it has *doubled*." With the last word he rapped his cane hard on the floor, making Lonnie jump. "Answer me!"

Lonnie cleared his throat and said defensively, "We always charge more when the family doesn't pay."

"A reasonable surcharge, yes. Double the fee? No. And you're avoiding the question."

The seated man shot a look at Carlos, who nodded and punched Lonnie in the gut. Lonnie doubled over, retching. As if nothing had occurred, he kept talking.

"I'll tell you what happens. Our customers look for more reliable alternatives. Others can establish a network and follow the routes and make the connections. They can even use our same contractors.

"This is a straightforward business. And we placed you here because of your knowledge of the American border patrol. We trusted you to run this important aspect of the business. Then I get word a customer is extremely and vocally unhappy. One of the men who finds us chickens is therefore also very unhappy, because a chicken is kept in the coop even when his money is ready."

Lonnie was purple in the face and wheezing. He tried to straighten but Carlos put a heavy hand on his shoulder to keep him bent. Lonnie glared at him with malice but the big coyote seemed unfazed.

The man in the suit continued. "Now, Heath. You have created a problem for our business. I'm here to find out why." The man looked at Hernán for the first time. His eyes traveled dismissively up and down.

"Why did you make me come all this way to this disgusting house for this…" He gestured vaguely at Hernán, the unspoken word nevertheless hanging in the air.

Lonnie licked his lips and hesitated. "He's useful for translating with some of the contractors who don't speak Spanish. We could use him to expand—"

"He's fucking him," Carlos volunteered. Lonnie gave him a look of pure loathing.

The man sighed. "Of course you are. Weak, Heath. A businessman controls his appetites. You can get what you need for a few pesos on any corner in this shithole of a town, but instead you pollute our reputation.

"So. I have received the original, agreed upon payment and I have assured—*personally* assured—this boy's family he will leave today. I want extra precautions taken to make sure he isn't picked up by Immigration. If this"—he waved again at Hernán—"Portillo boy arrives in Houston safely and his family is satisfied, you may keep your position here."

The man went silent and stood, apparently seeing no need to explain the implied *or else.* He left without another word.

Lonnie glared at Carlos, still standing too close to him. Teeth gritted, he said to Hernán, "Get your shit ready. You leave in one hour." He stalked out.

Hernán found Isela in the dormitory. They couldn't meet each other's eye—hadn't been able to since Lonnie started up with him—but he opened his pack and said, "I'm leaving today." When his few belongings were stored away, he zipped it up and risked a glance. Isela finally looked at him, tears streaming down her face.

"I'm glad you're getting away." She wiped her cheeks with the back of her hand. "And I'm sorry I didn't know what to say to you."

"It happened to you too. Didn't it?" Hernán wasn't surprised when she nodded sharply. He sat on the bed next to her, hands folded in his lap. "I hope your sister gets the money together soon."

"Me too."

There didn't seem to be anything else to say. Finally he stood and gripped his backpack.

She rose as well. "My name is Isela Vargas. When I get across, I'm going to live in San Antonio, in Texas. Maybe you can write to me, when you write to the children."

Hernán nodded. "I'm Hernán Portillo. I think I'm going to Maryland where my uncle Elías lives, but I'm not positive."

Isela gave him a quick hug, and then dropped her arms. He said goodbye to Violeta and went outside to join one other man, a pollo who was crossing that afternoon. Three coyotes were to accompany them, which was more than he'd seen leave with other groups.

They drove to a river; from Hernán's studies he guessed it was the Rio Bravo. A boat waited for them. After a short trip across, as they neared the opposite shore one of the handlers said, "We have a short window during the guard change. As soon as we stop, we run. Keep close to me. If I drop, you do too. If you hear gunfire, cover yourself any way you can. Keep running in the same direction and we'll try to meet up afterward."

The boat ground against dirt. The handlers leapt over the side, followed by Hernán and the other man. They ran away from the water, across a field. Hernán's heart was in his throat as he listened for sounds of a patrol, for gunfire. He had a stitch in his side, the backpack banged against his neck and shoulder, but he kept going.

Eventually they slowed to a jog, then to a walk, then to a short halt to drink some water. After just minutes, they moved on.

It seemed they walked forever but, in hindsight, it was about six hours. They went under fences, and around small, lighted towns. Hernán wondered if Albert and Andrea would have made it, or if the walk would have proved too much for their little legs. He wondered if Isela would make the same journey soon, and Violeta.

Finally they reached a house on the outskirts of what seemed to be a larger town. When the lead coyote knocked rapidly on a back door, an elderly man opened it. He peered out through a screen door and said something softly in Spanish to the handler, who answered. The man nodded, opened the screen door, and came outside.

He quickly led them to a shed. Inside, the coyotes helped raise some floorboards and then the group climbed down into the darkness. The dirt floor beneath Hernán's feet smelled of urine. The elderly man replaced the boards and they heard him leave.

Time passed. Hernán and the others sat on their heels or on their backpacks, waiting. A scuff of noise turned all their heads upward. Through the slatted boards, they could see a flashlight beam raking across the interior of the shed. Voices in English sounded, and one said, "All clear." The flashlight beam vanished.

After another twenty minutes, the elderly man came back. He helped them up into the shed and gave them each water and a bag of food. They slept for a few hours, and then the elderly man rousted them up. "Quickly, before the patrol comes again," he said querulously as he gestured for them all to be gone.

The handlers led the way out of the shed and into the early morning light, down to a country road, at the side of which a flatbed truck sat parked. The lead handler gestured for them to wait before jogging over to talk to the driver. He opened the bed of the truck and got them all lying down, alternating head to feet, before closing the tailgate again.

They drove for a long time, and Hernán watched the sky lighten overhead.

He had made it. He was in the United States. The relief he should have felt was muffled in such exhaustion and shame, it might all be a dream.

After a few hours they stopped and had to walk again. A youngish coyote, more talkative than the others, told Hernán they had to get around a U.S. checkpoint. Eventually they rejoined the road where the same truck waited for them.

A few hours after stretching out on the pickup bed again, Hernán could tell they drove into a city. The tops of buildings became visible where he looked skyward. The truck eventually came to a stop and the driver let them out.

Hernán looked around to find himself amid a series of dilapidated buildings. All the signs he could see were in English. Above the crumbling and peeling walls, the tops of skyscrapers glittered.

The lead handler brought everyone inside. Bathrooms, food, water, and then they were guided to an open space, where a woman with a clipboard bustled over. The coyote said something to her and she handed him a cell phone.

He beckoned Hernán closer and held out a piece of paper with a phone number on it. "Call this. Tell them you're in Houston and find out where you should go next."

Hernán took the phone and pressed the buttons with shaking fingers. The call connected almost immediately.

"Hello?" he heard a shaky voice ask.

"Rudy? Is it you?"

"Hernán! Are you okay? Where are you?"

"I'm in Houston. In Texas. They said I should ask you where to come next."

"Dad and I talked about it. We think it makes most sense for you to come to Boston, where I live. That's in Massachusetts. I'll meet you at the bus station."

"Um, okay." To the handler, he said, "Boston." He said goodbye to Rudy, pocketed the phone number, and the next thing he knew he was being loaded onto one of many large buses. From hurried conversations and calls across the floor, he learned the buses carried the immigrants to different destinations around the country.

The coyote who had escorted him gave him one hundred dollars. "This has to cover you until you get to Boston. Everything is expensive here so be careful with it."

"I will. Um. Thank you." He held out his hand to the coyote, who looked at it, shook his head, and walked away.

THE BUS TOOK Hernán from Houston through Atlanta, up through the mid-Atlantic region, to Connecticut, and finally Boston, a journey of several days. He called Rudy from a rest stop when the bus got to Massachusetts, and he was at the bus station when Hernán stepped off.

They lived in Rudy's apartment for a few months. That was where Hernán discovered Rudy sold a Rolex watch he'd received as a gift to help raise the money to get Hernán out of Mexico.

Funds started to get low. Hernán called his mother to ask for help once, but she said no. He'd never spoken to his parents since, though he called Juan sometimes to check in on him and Brijith.

Rudy and Hernán grew more and more nervous about being in Boston, even though it publicly declared itself a sanctuary city. They decided to seek work in Provincetown, where Hernán could be more confident about staying clear of ICE. He kept as far out of sight as possible, worked what jobs he could find without proper documentation, and prayed that his new life would be enough to keep him far away from the eyes of Cuernos.

Chapter 17

SILENCE REIGNED IN the conference room when Hernán finished his story. He realized he had unconsciously shredded a pad of paper, and immediately started to sweep the pile into his hands.

"Leave the paper," Sofia said softly. "Do you know what happened to the others? To Isela, Albert and Andrea?"

Hernán blinked away his memories, trying to refocus on her. "I managed to find Isela's sister in San Antonio. She got her money a week or so after I did, but her group was caught. Isela was sent back to El Salvador. I don't know if she tried again."

His vision blurred, and his voice when he could speak again sounded hoarse. "I was never able to find Albert and Andrea's family. I don't know what happened to them."

Sofia nodded. As she stood and pulled herself together, she said, "I think I should give you two time alone. Hernán, I know that was difficult. Why don't we leave it for today? I have enough to begin developing the narrative and evaluate strategies. When David returns we'll call you to discuss our next steps."

She came around the table to rest a hand on Hernán's shoulder, and then shook with Colin. "The conference room is yours for as long as you want it."

After she left, Hernán turned to face Colin for the first time since he'd stopped speaking. He didn't know what to expect, but probably disgust. Certainly pity. Embarrassment, maybe, that Colin had gotten himself involved with someone as weak as Hernán.

He didn't expect the glow of pride shining from blue eyes. Colin said fiercely, "I'm so grateful you're in my life."

The cold shell Hernán had wrapped around himself to get through the story began to fracture. "You don't hate me?" His lower lip started to tremble. The room blurred. "But I was so weak. I helped those animals drug Albert and Andrea. I didn't know how to help Isela. I couldn't escape Lonnie."

Colin took both of Hernán's hands in his. "How could I hate you?" he asked incredulously. "I'm *amazed* by you. The courage you have." Shaking his head, he said, "I wouldn't have even begun the journey."

"It wasn't courage. It was fear. That's all it was. I was terrified to stay in San Marcos and then I was afraid to run away from the way-station."

"Oh no, Hernán." Colin stood and pulled him into a hug. "Don't you know how brave you are? Those children never would have made it so far without you. Even Isela. You did everything in your power to help. You've been abused in so many ways but just look. You set your mind to escaping El Salvador and you did it. You're in the States. You're safe and you made it."

Colin pulled back just enough that Hernán could see tears shining in his eyes but also a determined set to his jaw. He glimpsed the warrior in Colin, and it recognized him.

It said, *you are a warrior too.*

The shell splintered completely and he couldn't hold back any more. He began to sob in Colin's arms, wracked with everything he'd kept inside for so long. He clutched at Colin's shirt and hid his face against the smooth fabric. Colin was an anchor for him and Hernán kept hold when his terror and the darkness threatened to pull him under.

Hernán didn't know how long he cried. It seemed as if every time the tears stopped, a fresh wave of grief and remembered fear washed over him. His throat was sore and raw, and he realized he'd been moaning. Colin held him and there was no place Hernán wanted to be except in his arms.

There came a massive shift inside, like a stone tilting ponderously away from the front of a cave in which he had been trapped. His stagnant grief and self-loathing drained away in his tears.

Gradually he realized he was just absorbing Colin's warmth. His tears had stopped, and he'd become more aware of Colin's trim body than ever before. Their proximity made him nervous, not because he had the slightest fear of Colin, but because he didn't know *what* he was feeling.

He tensed slightly and Colin released the hug. Hernán missed his arms keenly, but only then noticed what he'd done to Colin's shirt. As he ran his hands over the wrinkles and the wet patches, he muttered, "I'm sorry."

Colin smiled gently at him. "Don't worry about it for one second. Do you need a napkin or a tissue?"

Hernán couldn't look at him directly but he said, "I think I'll go to the men's room and clean myself up. Okay?"

"I'll be here," Colin said firmly. Hernán no longer doubted it.

THE DRIVE BACK to the condo building was quiet, but it didn't feel heavy to Colin. Hernán looked out the window as they made their way through traffic but when a current pop song came on the radio, he tapped his finger against his leg in time with the beat. He noticed Colin watching him and gave a slight smile that lifted Colin's heart. When they got home, Hernán excused himself to take a nap.

Colin settled in to his home office to catch up on some work he'd neglected while accompanying Hernán. He found it difficult to concentrate though.

His thoughts kept taking him back to the blank look on Hernán's face as he described the things he'd been through and what had been done to him. It was almost like he spoke on autopilot, describing events he'd seen in a movie rather than things he'd experienced. Telling it all out loud seemed to mortify Hernán; hopefully it was also—possibly—liberating.

The story he told was sadly similar to accounts Colin had learned from clients of the Immigration Initiative. So many people, desperate for the promise that the United States held itself out to be, risked everything. Hernán was far from the first person who told stories of sexual abuse during the journey. In truth, Hernán was one of the lucky ones; many, many others disappeared on their journeys, sometimes into sexual slavery or unmarked graves.

The injustice of Hernán's grandmother, the torment of the gang members, the cruelty of Lonnie, all felt like wounds on Colin's own body. He'd wanted to stop Hernán several times but realized—once begun—the tale had to come out. All he could do then was hope Hernán drew security and strength from his presence.

By the time Hernán had finished, Colin was nearly blind with his own rage, yet bursting with pride at Hernán's victory. Sofia's eyes were glassy and her face was a mask of pain and sorrow. Strangely, Hernán had seemed the calmest person in the room.

A few hours later, alone and with time to process, the horrors Hernán described began to enrage Colin again. Colin wasn't a violent person but if he could find that Lonnie hijo de puta and make him pay, he would.

Even Hernán's grandmother. What kind of woman could be so cold and cruel to her own flesh and blood?

So many things made more sense to Colin. The way Hernán tried to hide by keeping his hair long and drawn forward over his face. The bleakness Colin could see creep into his eyes at times. The way he seemed to welcome Colin's hugs, yet could allow no more.

Since he wasn't getting work done anyway, Colin began to research. The internet drew him into an ocean of pain and healing as he tried to educate himself about sexual abuse and rape.

He had no illusions that he'd be able to lessen Hernán's trauma—indeed, one thing he quickly realized as he read through innumerable stories of survivors was that Hernán needed professional therapy. But he hoped to learn from the stories of the loved ones of survivors, so he wouldn't again stupidly trigger a response in Hernán like he had when they kissed.

Eventually Colin realized it was dinnertime so he shut down his search engine and hurried to fix something simple. It didn't seem like an evening for an elaborate meal, but he hoped Hernán would feel like talking more about the things he'd revealed. When Hernán came downstairs for dinner, Colin glanced up at him from the kitchen and then did a double-take.

Hernán's hair was pulled back into a ponytail, exposing his face in a way Colin had rarely seen before. He even looked bigger, as if he'd been so oppressed by the burden of secrets they'd kept him in a slouch. With his pain out in the open, Hernán stood taller.

He met Colin's stare and blushed, but didn't look away as he walked into the kitchen. Coming right up to Colin, he pulled him into a rough hug. Colin couldn't help but close his eyes with a soft sigh as Hernán tucked his head under Colin's chin, the clean scent of Hernán's body surrounding him.

"Thank you." Hernán spoke in a low voice Colin almost couldn't hear. "For being there today."

"I'm very proud of you," Colin said and squeezed tightly.

Without releasing the hug, Hernán leaned back slightly and then pressed his lips to Colin's. Hernán's mouth was warm and lush, and Colin's pulse pounded when he slanted his head to deepen the kiss. Hernán's tongue lightly stroked the seam of Colin's mouth. Colin opened but didn't try for more. Whatever Hernán wanted was his to take, but Colin wouldn't push.

Yet he couldn't entirely repress the moan that rose from his heart. Hernán in his arms, kissing him and tasting of sunshine… He'd dreamt of it since their first walk through Provincetown.

Hernán's lips curled slightly against his before he broke the kiss. "That was nice," Hernán said, smiling. "Even better than the other night. I'll want to do it again."

Colin released him with difficulty, regretting it the moment his arms were free and Hernán stepped back. "You can kiss me all you want." He grinned shyly. "That was hella good."

Hernán laughed gently. "Look at you, talking like a cool kid."

"Hey, I'm not a complete nerd, you know."

"Says the *Doctor Who* fanatic."

"We're called Whovians, and don't think I missed it when you teared up at that last episode."

"It was dust in my eye." Hernán looked around the kitchen. "What can I do?"

"Just set the table. It's nothing fancy tonight, a little stir fry."

"Well, it smells good. I woke up hungry."

Colin watched with one eye as Hernán lay out plates and silverware, seeming lighter somehow. He moved easily, and his laugh sounded more natural. "I'm glad you got in a nap," Colin said cautiously. "It was an emotional day."

Hernán turned to face him, leaning back against a dining chair with his hands resting behind him on the top rung. He nodded and said, "But you know? Somehow talking about it made it, not okay but maybe…" He frowned slightly. "Over?"

"I get that."

"I mean, I know it's going to come up again and again as we go through this process." Hernán shivered slightly.

Colin dished up the sliced pork and mixed vegetables into a serving bowl. He brought it to the table while Hernán poured them each a glass of water. "Speaking of talking it out, how would you feel about seeing someone over what happened to you? A therapist." He cringed even as he asked, afraid he was overstepping.

Hernán frowned but he seemed thoughtful, not angry, when he responded. "A therapist? I don't know. Now it's all out, I can deal with it."

"It's your choice, but someone trained in this may be able to come up with ways to handle things you wouldn't otherwise know. Like, how to get calm if something triggers a bad memory."

Hernán considered as he chewed. "Let me think about it. This food is good, by the way."

Colin accepted the change of subject and the rest of the dinner passed comfortably. They cleaned the kitchen in an easy dance around each other.

When Colin started for the living room and their usual ritual of watching some television together, Hernán put out a hand to stop him. He curled his fingers into Colin's and looked up at him from under his lashes.

The warmth of the hand in his did funny things to Colin's stomach. The feeling grew more frantic when Hernán took a step closer to him, cleared his throat, and said, "What would you think…?" He stopped, blushing.

Colin waited before prompting him. "About?"

Hernán licked his lips nervously, and then stepped even closer, heat rising off his body. Colin's dick began to swell from the proximity.

Oh no, don't look down. Please.

"Colin, I like you more than I've ever liked any other man, and I trust you. Talking about what Lonnie did… It lanced something inside me. I think I can make new memories now. So, I want to try something different tonight."

Colin's heart beat faster. "I think you know how I feel about you, Nán. Anything you want to do, I'm up for."

Hernán flicked his glance down to Colin's crotch and gave a small grin. "So I see."

Colin's cheeks burned. He tried to pull away but Hernán held tight to his hand as he continued. "When I was lying there upstairs on the bed, I thought about you." He bit his lip and hesitated, but then he swallowed. He looked squarely at Colin, resolve shining in his eyes.

"I suppose I've always known I'm gay, but I'm twenty-one and I've never really touched a man. A man's body, I mean. We hug but that's different, and what Lonnie did—that wasn't touching. I—I want to touch you. I don't know how far I can go but I'd like to try."

Colin fought to control his breathing as hope flared in his belly like a star going nova. He brought Hernán's fingers to his lips and kissed them. "You set the pace, Nán. You're in control."

Hernán led him up the stairs by the hand and drew him into the guest room. He'd left the small lamp on the side table burning, making the room seem intimate and cloistered. Colin waited to be told what to do.

Hernán leaned against the wardrobe, eyes holding Colin's gaze. He blushed fiercely before he finally asked, "Can I see your body?"

Colin hesitated only a moment. He hadn't been naked in front of another man in quite a while. He didn't have the muscles of his friend Brandon, or a physique like he'd glimpsed on Hernán through his clothes. But he kept active and watched his diet. He felt good enough about himself to give Hernán what he wanted. What he needed.

He toed off his shoes, removed his socks and then pulled his sweater over his head, leaving him in a white T-shirt and khakis. Hernán studied him avidly. Something exciting burned in his dark eyes. It gave Colin the courage he needed to lift the hem of his tee, pull it off and toss it aside. The slight chill of the room made his nipples pebble as he stood there under Hernán's gaze.

Colin tugged his belt loose, unfastened his pants, and slowly lowered the zipper. Hernán tracked the movement of his hand as the pants fell open to reveal his white jockey shorts. His erection pressed against his hip to the left, a damp patch spreading where precome had begun to leak. He let the khakis drop to the floor and stepped out of them, leaving him in his shorts.

He hesitated until he saw the gleam in Hernán's eyes and the flare of his nostrils. Hernán breathed heavily, but in excitement, not fear. His own pants had tented—Colin seemed to be turning him on. That gave the last push he needed to hook his thumbs into his shorts and shove them to the ground. He kicked them away and then stood straight, arms loose and shoulders back, to await Hernán's next step.

His erection throbbed when Hernán came closer. He put a trembling hand on Colin's chest and slowly dragged his fingers across the smooth skin there and toward his right nipple. He just brushed over it but Colin released a small gasp and shivered.

Hernán smiled as he continued his exploration, sliding over Colin's ribs and down to his belly. "You're so lean," he murmured. "Your skin feels like silk stretched over stone. I can see every single muscle shift underneath."

Instead of moving further south, Hernán trailed up Colin's arm instead. He gripped the bicep and ran his thumb over it before stroking Colin's shoulder and running up his neck. Colin inclined his head toward the roving hand as it glided over his cheek and up to his brow. Hernán's smoldering eyes followed his fingers, but Colin couldn't look away from Hernán's intent expression and full, reddened lips.

His breath hitched when Hernán slid his other arm around Colin's waist, put his hand on Colin's back, and pulled him into an embrace. Standing completely nude and hard against Hernán, still dressed, seemed surreal and erotic at the same time.

Carefully he raised his own arms to return the hug, sensitive to any resistance or fear from Hernán. When he wound them around, though, Hernán just pulled him in tighter and sighed. The sound was content-ed. Happy.

Hernán rested his cheek against Colin's chest. "Your heart is pounding. Mine too." After a few moments, he said, "I'd like you to lie on the bed now."

Colin stretched out with his head on the pillow. His erection stood tall and firm, its head glistening from his excitement. He fought the urge to grasp himself, because he was close to coming. Just from the light touches of Hernán's hands and eyes.

Hernán kicked off his own shoes. When he pulled off his shirt, Colin inhaled sharply at the slabs of muscle exposed. Hernán's quarter-sized nipples accentuated the curve of his pectorals. Rippling abs ran down his stomach and disappeared into his pants, like something out of Colin's most fevered fantasies.

The ragged scar from Hernán's stabbing and surgeries carved a lightning stroke over his side. Colin wanted to touch and kiss the mangled skin, but he didn't dare move until Hernán was ready. Still, he couldn't help saying, "You're beautiful."

Hernán blushed and seemed uncertain for a moment until Colin's dick flexed. That seemed to help him decide his next command. "I want to see you touch yourself," Hernán rasped.

Colin nearly cringed with embarrassment. He'd never done that with anyone present, not even a mutual j-o session with a boyfriend or hookup before—but he was being stupid. He did it alone every night, and lately it had always been to images his brain conjured of the man watching him avidly. The fact Hernán wanted to see him stroke off was a compliment.

I can do this.

He ran his gaze over Hernán's body as he licked his left palm and reached for his dick, wrapping his fingers around the warm shaft. The silky skin slid up and down as he moved his hand slowly. Hernán inhaled sharply when he paused to swipe his thumb over the slit. Hernán's eyes grew hot and his cheeks flushed. It gave Colin the impulse to raise his thumb to his mouth and suck off the precome coating it.

Hernán's mouth opened slightly as he tracked that thumb, as if he were the one loving it with his tongue and lips.

Colin returned to stroking his shaft, dragging his fingertips lightly along the skin. Electric shocks lit up his body from the self-torture, and he raised his free hand to tug on his right nipple.

Hernán lay down on the bed next to him, still wearing his pants but visibly hard and excited. Colin rolled his head to smile at him as he kept gliding his hand up and down his dick. Hernán shifted closer so his smooth, bare chest pressed against Colin's arm. The warmth of his body, the firm muscle there, drew out a happy sigh from Colin that stuttered to a ragged gasp when Hernán covered Colin's moving hand with his own. Their fingers twined together as they pulled and tugged and twisted on Colin's cock.

His balls pulled up tightly. "I'm going to come," he choked out. Hernán tightened his grip and helped to draw the orgasm from the depth of Colin's soul. He pressed his lips to Colin's neck while Colin shot warm come all over his belly and chest, and kept stroking until Colin's tremors stopped.

"Ah God, that was good," Colin gasped when his chest stopped heaving. He nuzzled Hernán's cheek and murmured, "Oh, my angel. Mi ángel." Hernán burrowed more deeply into his neck and rested his hand on Colin's softening cock.

Colin turned his head until he could run his eyes over Hernán's handsome face, unable to hide any more what he felt. Hernán looked nervously back. He tensed, but when Colin made no move toward him, the tight lines around his eyes smoothed out. He leaned forward into a kiss.

Colin relaxed his jaw slightly and was rewarded when Hernán slipped his tongue tentatively over his lips before pressing a little way into Colin's mouth. He couldn't help but stroke Hernán's tongue with his own.

Hernán pulled back, but not out of fear. Colin found heat and excitement in Hernán's flushed face, and then Hernán unbuttoned his own pants and shoved them down with his underwear. He kicked them to the floor and lay again so their naked bodies pressed together.

Heedless of the come cooling on Colin, he tugged their bodies around until they were chest-to-chest, thigh-to-thigh. Hernán's thick erection pressed against Colin's stomach and Hernán kissed him again with his own gasp.

When Colin's tongue invaded his mouth, Hernán whimpered. Suddenly he rolled onto his back and grabbed his hard dick, stroking it furiously as Colin watched. His meaty cock had the most perfectly shaped head Colin had ever seen, appearing and disappearing as Hernán drew the foreskin up over it and back.

It took no more than ten strokes before Hernán's muscles all went taut. He growled as he arched his back and shot rope after rope of gleaming white come up to his chest and neck. Spasms wracked his body.

He sagged onto the bed as his strokes grew lazier. Colin fought against the temptation to lick his chest and neck clean; as much as he wanted to do so, it felt like a step too far. Instead he got up long enough to grab his T-shirt and wipe Hernán down before swabbing his own sticky stomach and chest.

Standing over Hernán, breathing in the scent of sex, he was taken by indecision. He knew what he wanted—to climb back into bed, wrap Hernán in his arms and sleep beside him all night—but he had no idea what Hernán was ready for.

Hernán smiled up at him, a relaxed and genuine grin, warmer than any Colin had yet seen on him. "Your shirt didn't do much," Hernán said. "Maybe we need to take a shower." He rolled off the bed, took Colin's hand, and led him toward the guest bathroom.

Colin's body flooded with warmth, and he felt his own grin stretch his face ridiculously. Emboldened, he said, "We should use my shower. It's a lot bigger." Hernán glanced back at him and changed course to lead them through Colin's bedroom and into the bathroom.

He waited while Colin got the water started from three different shower heads and finally declared it warm enough, and then stepped into the spacious tiled chamber.

Colin adjusted the water so both of them stood in warm spray before he reached for body wash. Pouring some green liquid that smelled of pine trees into his palm, he looked at Hernán for permission. At the small nod, he began working up a lather to run hands over Hernán's broad shoulders, muscled chest and sinewy arms. Hernán's firm body responding to his touch was nothing short of a miracle, one he drew out as long as he could.

He had Hernán raise his arms alternately so he could admire the stretch of his bicep and lats while he washed his pits. He pulled suds along Hernán's arms and to his fingertips. Crouching, he worked down Hernán's leanly muscled thighs and legs, his dick hanging thick and heavy mere inches from Colin's face. So tempting to open his mouth and draw it in, but he wasn't sure Hernán could take that much intimacy so soon.

With a glance up to make sure it was all right, he worked lather through Hernán's pubic hair and then stroked his hooded cock and washed his balls. He tugged on Hernán's hip lightly until he turned around to permit Colin to wash his ass as well. Colin stood to finish washing Hernán's back, rotating his pliant body in the spray to rinse off all the soap.

Hernán was smiling at him when he finished, so Colin reached for the shampoo and washed Hernán's hair as well. Hernán tilted his head left and right to rinse while Colin quickly scrubbed himself clean. The water had started to cool by the time he shut the faucets off and grabbed two towels.

When they were dry, Hernán wrapped a towel around his waist before he pulled Colin into another hug. The woodsy scent rising from Hernán's body was fresh and clean, his skin warm, when he leaned against Colin's body. "Thank you," he sighed. "For being so patient. For washing me. All of it."

Colin kissed the top of his head. "That was hot, Nán. I've never done anything like it before. I mean, just lie there together and, um, jack. It somehow seemed even more intimate than other things I've done."

Hernán tensed slightly. "I don't know when I'll be able to do those other things—"

"It doesn't matter if we never do them," Colin cut him off. "Being with you this way feels so good. I can tell you trust me, and that makes me very happy."

"I do trust you," Hernán said. He angled his head to catch Colin's gaze. "You heard my story today and you didn't run away. I didn't know if you'd be able to handle it."

"To tell you the truth, it made me furious anyone could treat you so badly."

Hernán nodded and smiled. "I know. I could see the warrior coming out in your eyes. It made me brave too."

"Warrior? Me?" Colin scoffed but Hernán pulled him in tighter.

"Yes, you. I saw it first when we were in Provincetown and you got mad about Gerald. You have a warrior inside you who will take no shit. It's why I feel safe with you. I know you'll protect me if you can."

Colin's ears burned and he mumbled, "Of course I will. But I don't... I mean, I've never even been in a fight."

"I don't mean that kind of protection. I can't explain it any better."

"Okay." Colin hesitated. He wanted to ask Hernán to spend the night with him but indecision paralyzed him again. Was that going too far? Would Hernán feel Colin was pressuring him?

They walked out of the bathroom and into Colin's bedroom. Hernán turned to look up at him.

Ask him to stay.

But he couldn't. The risk of shattering their fragile beginning was too great. After a moment, Hernán gave him another kiss. He said, "I'll see you in the morning," before returning to his own room.

Colin sighed as he pulled back his comforter and climbed into cold sheets. He began to replay how much they had done, and pictured Hernán's beautiful body.

That night was just a start, he hoped. He could wait for more, no matter how long it took. Even if they never went further than they had, touching and stroking and showering together, it would be enough. Hernán was worth it.

Chapter 18

HERNÁN WOKE ABRUPTLY in his darkened room with the sense he'd shouted. Sheets twisted around his waist, the Henley and flannel pants he slept in were soaked with sweat, and his skin was clammy and cold. He didn't know why.

A dream. It had to have been.

Vague recollection settled in. Lonnie again, like always, coming closer and closer. There had been a locked door, right? He had been very afraid, and terribly alone.

He closed his eyes and tried to recall the rest. Like pressing his tongue against a sore tooth, he didn't want to remember but couldn't help trying.

A gentle rap on the open door to his room startled him. Colin stood in the hallway, respectfully keeping his distance. "Hernán? Are you all right? I heard you shout something." The concern in his voice reached into Hernán's quivering heart, and brought with it calm.

"You can come in," he said softly. Both had spoken in low tones, even with no one else in the apartment to disturb.

Colin padded toward the bed, his bare feet rasping quietly on the carpet. Even two weeks before, Hernán had lain sleepless for fear he would hear that sound, but tonight it meant someone cared.

In the dim light Hernán could tell Colin wore sleep pants and a T-shirt. He shifted up in the bed until he was propped by the pillows, and he untangled the sheets and blanket as best he could. Colin sank cautiously onto the edge of the bed, as if afraid to get too close. One hand began to reach for Hernán but then pulled back abruptly.

Hernán took the wandering hand and twined his fingers through it. Colin squeezed back.

"I'm fine. Just a bad dream," Hernán said.

"Do you want to talk about it? Sometimes that helps."

"I really don't even remember what it was about. It was probably nothing."

Colin let it go, but he raised Hernán's hand and kissed his knuckles. It was such a casual gesture that Colin no doubt thought nothing of it. Hernán, though... He recalled his grandmother rapping his hand over and over with a hot spoon. The brush of Colin's lips against his knuckles suddenly felt more real to him than the remembered cruelty. Softer, kinder, more...

Colin said, "Okay. Let me know if you need anything." He began to rise but Hernán held onto his hand tightly. His heart fluttered again, but for a different reason than his fading nightmare. It wasn't fear, but anticipation.

"Stay," he said softly. When Colin hesitated, Hernán moved over on the bed to make room. With his free hand, he threw back the blanket and sheet. Colin made a pleased little sound that brought a smile to Hernán's face. He hesitated for a moment longer, and then climbed into the bed.

They lay facing each other in the darkened room, still joined by one hand. "I'm sorry I woke you up," Hernán whispered.

"Don't be sorry," Colin answered. Cautiously he leaned forward to give Hernán a chaste kiss on the lips.

The kind warmth Colin offered was exactly what he'd craved. After their explorations the week before, and the intimacy of the shower, he hadn't been sure what to make of Colin not asking him to share his bed.

Rationally, he supposed it was Colin's way to avoid pressuring him, and for that he was grateful. They'd hugged often in the days after, and even made out like teenagers lying on the sofa. When Hernán felt Colin's hardness through his clothes, he no longer shied away. He replayed their night together often when he was alone, grasping his dick as he remembered the feel of Colin's hands on him. Yet they had not been so intimate again in reality.

The raw, exposed part of him, though—the part that had relived his most horrific memories not only in front of Colin but a stranger as well—wanted more. He needed to be wrapped up and sheltered and comforted, but he was incapable of asking. Instead he just hoped irrationally Colin could divine his distress.

Shyness might have defeated Colin the week before, but he came immediately when Hernán needed him. His presence began to make Hernán relax, but the clamminess of his pajamas was embarrassing. It would keep him from falling asleep.

"Hold on," he muttered, and then jumped out of bed for a moment. He yanked off his shirt and his pants, but hesitated in the slight chill of the apartment. *Put on another set of clothes?* he wondered. Nerves twanged in his chest.

Or lie there exposed, like a slut for the taking... His grandmother's mocking voice in his head nearly made him scramble for the clothes chest.

Then he saw Colin's eyes shining in a small sliver of light. Admiration, longing and desire danced there, but none of the arrogant possessiveness with which Lonnie had glared at him. They had already seen each other naked. Colin had respected his limitations and hadn't pressured Hernán for more than he could give.

He suddenly ached to feel Colin's skin against his own all over again, and with that he forced away the hateful voice of a hard, old woman.

I will do this. I'm strong enough.

He climbed back into bed naked and tugged on the hem of Colin's t-shirt. Colin nodded and shucked his pajamas, tossing them into the corner of the room and waiting to follow Hernán's lead. Hernán rolled over to face the same direction as Colin and shimmied until the length of Colin's body pressed along his back and legs.

Colin's arm came over his body and under his arm to hold him around the waist, loosely enough Hernán didn't feel trapped, securely enough he felt safe.

The remaining tension drained from his body and he sighed contentedly. Colin kissed the back of his head and settled down himself. In moments Hernán fell asleep again, and that time it was dreamless.

WHEN HE WOKE a few hours later, the warmth against his nude back and the weight of an arm on his chest were momentarily alarming. He stiffened in fear until he heard a soft snuffle. *Colin.* There was no reason he should recognize that sleep sound, yet he did.

Hernán also realized two more things: he badly needed to pee, and he was rock hard. A slight, exploratory twitch of his hips against Colin's sleeping body disclosed he wasn't alone in the morning wood dilemma.

Consternation made his muscles tense. He'd never been in such a situation before, and he cursed himself as an idiot for sleeping naked. What had he been thinking? He didn't want to lead Colin on. God knew the pleasure of a warm body wrapped with his gave him the most peaceful night he could recall in a year but… What would Colin think of him? Would he expect Hernán to go all the way? And if he didn't, would he think Hernán was just a cruel tease?

The insistent pressures on his bladder and on his brain warred. "Hernán, relax," he heard Colin mutter sleepily into his ear. "I don't expect anything."

How did he know what was bothering me?

"I, uh, I kind of have to pee."

Colin kissed his hair and muttered, "Go pee then. Imma sleep some more." And he was out again.

Hernán envied his easy slumber, as he climbed gingerly out of the bed. What kind of privileged life did it take for a man to enjoy such untroubled rest?

Crossing the hall to his bathroom, he stood over the bowl. He had to press down on his hard dick to angle it properly. Normally a good piss was enough to relieve his erection in the morning, but he remained conscious there was a man in his bed. *In Colin's spare bed? In the bed he was using?* With a snort of disgust at himself, he flushed and then washed his hands quickly.

A glance in the mirror surprised him. His eyes were brighter than normal; the dark circles greeting him were less pronounced. And was that a smirk?

"Do it, Hernán," he said sternly to his reflection.

After what Colin had said about Brandon and his crush on Hernán, the way they'd been together the week before, his respect in the nights after… He realized he'd already known. Colin had shown him every day since they met how important Hernán was to him. Once he'd let go of his lingering jealousy for Brandon, it seemed obvious.

"Colin thinks he's in love with you," the man in the mirror told him. "Show him how you feel."

His stomach churned and his balls tightened. He wasn't sure whether the reaction was fear, or the memory of spying on Rudy as he moved in the near-dark with some random partner, both moaning softly with pleasure. Mirror-Hernán was having no part of his confusion. "No one is *taking* anything. If you give it freely, it's still yours."

He rinsed out his mouth, splashed water in his face, and tried to regulate his breathing. "Okay, okay, okay," he chanted quietly.

After turning off the light he returned to the bedroom. Colin lay askew, blanket up almost to his nose, hair sticking out in every direction. He gave the slightest snore and Hernán's heart turned over. The adorably awkward man currently sleeping in his bed was prepared to do anything in his power for Hernán. So Hernán had to be brave as well.

He slid back under the blanket, took a deep breath, and shifted over until he found Colin's warm body. His shins fit against Colin's calves. His thighs touched the back of Colin's legs. His chest met the middle of Colin's ribcage, and his belly fitted into the small of Colin's back, right where it curved down to the top of his ass.

Colin gave out the sweetest, most contended sigh Hernán had ever heard, and practically melted back against Hernán's body.

The last place they were separated vanished as Colin's butt pressed against Hernán's groin. His dick, which had never gone down completely despite the piss, surged to life. It involuntarily flexed along the warm crevice between Colin's cheeks.

The snoring stopped entirely and Hernán felt the tension rise beneath Colin's skin. *Now. Show him.* He wrapped his arm around Colin's chest and pressed lips to the spikes of hair standing up from his scalp, and then he rocked his hips so his cock slid along the smooth flesh of Colin's ass.

Colin clutched Hernán's arm enclosing him and released a shuddering breath. He pressed back until Hernán's hard shaft nestled securely against him. Without turning his head, Colin said in a husky voice, "Whatever you want, Nán. I swear. Anything."

Hernán slid his arm down over Colin's tight stomach and found his hard shaft, already damp at the tip when his fingers traced lightly around the head of it. The sensation of Colin's dick in his palm, the heat and weight and smoothness of it, fired something in Hernán's belly. Something like desire. No, more than that. A burning *need* rose in Hernán's chest, to connect with Colin as he'd never wanted with any other person.

"I'd like…" He paused, licked his lips and tried again. "Colin, may

I make love to you?"

Colin rolled over abruptly to face him. His eyes were bright and shiny and his cheeks were pink as he held Hernán's gaze. He nodded and then clutched Hernán's hand in his as they kissed. Hernán let himself become more aggressive, using his tongue to nudge open Colin's mouth before he plunged in.

It was nothing like the terrible room with Lonnie, where every shred of his dignity was ripped away by a cruel, grasping man. Instead, it was shared pleasure. Colin offered everything but demanded nothing.

With each stroke of his hand, with each thrust of cock against cock, Hernán let himself yield and take in equal measure. So much fire burned between their tongues, their lips, their clasped hands, that Hernán whimpered. Tears formed in the corner of his eyes.

He broke off and bent his neck to control his emotions, until Colin's lips pressed against his forehead. Suddenly Rudy's chatter about his favorite lube or brand of condoms ghosted through his head.

"Do you have...stuff?" he asked Colin shyly, hearing the eagerness and embarrassment at war in his tone.

Colin kissed his hair and said, "I'll be right back." He hurried away to his own room and returned in moments with a small box of condoms and a black plastic tube. Tossing them onto the bedside table, he climbed under the blanket and pulled Hernán to him.

They kissed more and Hernán stroked along Colin's back, his neck, down his arms with increasingly sure hands while their erections rubbed against each other.

Colin broke away to meet Hernán's eye. Hesitantly, he asked, "Have you done this before?" Hernán bit his lower lip and shook his head slightly. "Is it okay if I show you what I need?"

Hernán whispered, "Teach me. Please."

On his back again, Colin retrieved the black tube, popped it open, and then drizzled clear liquid into Hernán's palm and over his fingertips. "You're really thick, and I haven't done this in a long time. It'll feel better if you use your fingers to, um, help me open up."

Light dawned. "You want me to put my fingers in your ass?" he asked. Colin blushed as he nodded. Hernán said softly, "I'm sorry if that's crude. I don't know how else to ask."

They shifted around until Hernán could easily reach between Colin's legs, one raised and bent. He ran his slick palm over Colin's hard shaft, down to his silky-smooth scrotum, along the taut skin between his legs, and then up along his crease. He found the pucker and immediately began to circle that little furled muscle with the pads of two fingers.

Colin moaned slightly and pressed back against his hand. His eyes grew fevered and he lunged to capture Hernán's mouth just as Hernán pressed inward with the tip of his index finger. The heat fascinated him, as did the way Colin began to rut.

A part of my body is inside his. The revelation of how soft and warm Colin felt around his finger made his erection iron-hard. Soon he would be encased in that warmth. The yearning in his belly, the dryness in his mouth, made it difficult to wait, though the way Colin gripped his finger made him wonder how he would ever fit inside.

"Slide it in and out," Colin said breathlessly, and he clenched around the intrusion. His lean body, naked and smooth on the white sheets, writhed and shuddered. His blue eyes caught a glimmer of light, flashing sapphire as he gazed up adoringly. Hernán had never seen anyone more handsome.

Hernán claimed a kiss as he began to piston his finger, each time going slightly deeper, until Colin gasped and pressed their bodies together. "Two now," he instructed hoarsely, but Hernán was getting the hang of it. He felt Colin relaxing, taking more and more of him inside. He pulled out, waited for Colin's small noise of protest, and then slid back into Colin's hole.

Colin grasped Hernán's dick and just held it in his fist while Hernán began to fuck digits more quickly in and out of his ass. Since he was supposed to be stretching Colin, he spread his fingers and pressed outward against the ring of muscle, coaxing it to open further and further.

Colin mewled and pushed back until Hernán's fingers were so far inside that Colin's sac rested against his palm. Unbidden, he pulled out long enough to roll and tug on Colin's balls, and then plunged three fingers up Colin's ass.

"Move them around," Colin moaned. "You're right there at my prostate."

Hernán curled his fingers over a spot inside that felt different, and Colin shivered as he rhythmically pulsed his grip on Hernán's dick in his hand. The sensation of being milked was exotic, novel and the best thing Hernán had ever felt down there. He whispered, "Careful, or this will be over too soon."

With a small groan of protest, Colin relaxed his grip but his eyes on Hernán's were fierce. "I'm ready, Nán. I need you inside me."

Hernán disengaged his fingers so Colin could retrieve the condoms. He pulled one out of the almost-full carton. Hernán didn't know whether that meant it was a new box, or Colin didn't have much call to use them up. Selfishly, he hoped for the latter.

Colin tore open the foil, extracted the rubber ring, and rolled it down Hernán's shaft. He squeezed hard around the root of Hernán's fully-sheathed erection. "This is going inside me," he panted. "I want to see your face as you slide it up my ass."

The eagerness and passion in Colin's voice were exhilarating. The shy young man, uncertain of himself and of how fast to drive Hernán, had become one who knew what he wanted and asked for it. Hernán found he liked that Colin every bit as much as the version who rapped politely on his door.

He drew strength and heat from the more elemental Colin, flexing his dick in the man's grasp as he said in a low voice, "Show it to me, bello. Show me where my dick's going to go." He didn't know where the sexy talk was coming from, but it was clear Colin liked it.

With a sharp inhalation of breath, Colin threw off the remaining covers, rolled onto his back and put his hands under his legs to pull them up. Hernán shifted around on his knees until he was between Colin's thighs, staring intently at the asshole on display for him. He ran a lubed finger around the puffy edge of it and met Colin's eyes.

"Is this where you want me to put my cock?" he asked in an innocent voice.

Colin groaned. "Goddammit, Nán. Quit teasing and just fuck me."

He huffed a soft laugh though his heart was pounding with excitement. Uncertain of whether more lubricant was needed, he retrieved the black tube and drizzled more of the silky liquid along his sheathed length. Positioning the shiny, encased head of it right at Colin's opening, he moved his hips slightly. He began to press against the rim and retreat, before coming forward to press again in a slightly different spot.

He kept it up for another minute until Colin gasped out, "You're driving me crazy. Are you sure you've never done this before?"

Hernán stilled and waited until Colin's eyes met his. Serious again, he said, "You are the first man I've kissed. The first man I've stroked. And..." his breath hitched as the head of his cock parted the lips of Colin's ass and slid into warmth, "you are now the first man I've fucked."

Colin threw his head against his pillow and gasped, which Hernán took as an invitation. He pressed his hips forward, slowly and steadily. The sense of sliding down into Colin's body, of being gripped all along his length, of Colin's thighs cradling him as he reached his full depth, was stunning. Life-changing.

Ignorant jokes he'd heard all his life hadn't prepared him for the sensation, the beauty, of joining his body with another man. He and Colin were as close as two people could possibly be. His orgasm was right there, waiting to be triggered, but he didn't want anything to ever bring this union to an end.

He trembled when his balls came to rest against Colin's ass. Colin's sac pressing warmly between their bellies, Hernán leaned forward to seek another kiss. He clenched his teeth to try to hold off as the electric thrill in his balls and cock threatened an abrupt climax. He worried he would disgrace himself because stimulation threatened to overwhelm his control.

Colin wrapped his ankles around Hernán's back as they stayed immobile, mouths locked together but otherwise still. The inner core of him pulsed around Hernán's buried shaft as Colin moaned against his lips. His body quivered under Hernán's and rippled along his rectum. Hernán suddenly needed to move, but the way Colin's arms and legs wrapped around him was so welcoming and secure he didn't want to disturb them.

Pleasure surged again alarmingly along his length and he was distressed to realize he was even closer to coming, just from being in to his balls. He sank his tongue deeper into Colin's mouth as he fought for self-control, trying to convey how he felt, the things he wasn't ready to say but was desperate for Colin to know. His admiration. His friendship.

His love.

Colin gasped and broke the kiss. His eyes squeezed shut and the grimace he made looked almost painful. "So good. Oh god, Nán, I'm sorry, it's too good, you're deep in me, I can't—"

And then his asshole pulsed around Hernán's cock as he began to spasm in Hernán's arms. Warm, sticky come splattered against their joined bellies and Colin cried out. The rhythmic pulse along his cock, the mineral smell of Colin's pleasure, carried him right off the edge too.

Hernán howled as his cock began to throb and shoot endlessly. The ecstasy was different than anything he'd ever felt, better than his hand or Colin's, and it reverberated in his teeth. He sobbed in joy and in relief.

The spasms began to ease and finally he stilled. The two of them stared at each other, wide-eyed and stunned, until Colin suddenly started to laugh. Hernán joined him a moment later, squirming around so the warm come between them slid and squelched in their navels. That made Colin laugh even harder. He squeezed Hernán with his arms and his thighs.

Hernán's mirth quieted enough for him to say, "Even I know it wasn't supposed to be over so quickly. I'm sorry."

Colin shook his head, but his eyes glinted and his mouth stretched in a huge smile. "Is it premature ejaculation if it happens to both of us?"

For some reason that made Hernán begin to laugh again. He was still hard despite the sense he should be embarrassed by his performance, and he couldn't resist thrusting playfully into Colin.

"Oh *now* you're ready to fuck me," Colin exclaimed. He dissolved into another fit of giggles. "Well, okay then."

"At this rate I figure I can do you ten times before breakfast," Hernán said, and he was gone too, pressing his face into Colin's neck as they both rocked with laughter.

"Oh my God, I love you," Colin said on a gust of breath, and then immediately froze. "Um. I mean. Shit."

Hernán raised his head and met Colin's eyes. The laughter was gone but he couldn't leave Colin with that panicked look in his eyes. He nuzzled their noses together. "Shh," he whispered. "It's all right. And I knew anyway."

Colin relaxed marginally in his arms and suddenly Hernán understood he had been wrong earlier. He *was* ready to say it.

He kissed Colin gently on the lips and then said softly, "Besides, I love you too."

Colin gasped. His hands shot up to Hernán's head and held him still. Eyes shimmering, he asked shakily, "You do?"

Hernán nodded and felt his throat tighten. Colin swam in his vision. "I love you. You're the best man I've ever known and I'm very happy we found each other."

Colin buried his face against Hernán's neck. His body quaked in Hernán's arms.

"Oh, don't cry, sweetheart," Hernán murmured. "Don't cry." Colin just shook his head as he tried to find his voice. Hernán held him until he remembered his dick was still encased inside a very full condom. "Hey, cariño. I think I'm supposed to take this thing off before I go soft."

They untangled themselves reluctantly, Colin reaching down between his legs to hold the edge of the condom as Hernán pulled free. It drooped with jism and he felt unreasonably proud at the impressed look in Colin's eye.

"Wow. That's a load and a half." Colin's voice still sounded shaky but he jumped out of bed to dispose of it in the bathroom. He carried back in two towels.

Shyly, Hernán said, "You know, if you're willing to give me another chance, I think I probably have the hang of it now."

Colin bent to kiss him. "You got me off doing nothing more than sliding into me. If you actually start fucking, I might die." He growled and tugged Hernán's lower lip in his teeth. "But I'm prepared to take that risk."

Chapter 19

COLIN WAS ALL but useless again at work later that day. Part of it was lack of sleep, but much more was being stupid in love. He gazed out his window at people passing on the streets, aware of a silly grin stretching his face and of a wonderful ache deep in his ass. He hadn't had anything more than a blowjob in nearly a year, and then there was Hernán.

Talk about diving in at the deep end.

A satisfying throb when he shifted in his Aeron chair made him blush as he remembered Hernán taking him the second time. Even, deep strokes like he was born to fuck had Colin writhing and calling out nonsense. He'd never been the type to yell and squirm wantonly during sex. *Maybe I just never had the right lover.* Shame at his behavior tangled with his joy.

Ridiculous, impossible plans spiraled through his head. He wanted Hernán to meet his family. Hell, he wanted to be with Hernán in Paris, and stroll down romantic streets arm in arm. Christmas was months away but maybe he could arrange a trip as a surprise?

Hernán said he loves me.

It didn't seem possible, yet it was everything he'd hoped for since the night he begged Hernán to accept his help as they walked through the Provincetown fog. Besides his useless crush on Brandon, there had been no one Colin felt that way about since Pranav went back to India. And no one, not a single man, had ever said he *loved* Colin.

HERNÁN SAT STIFFLY on the balcony next to Colin's bedroom, a cup of coffee clutched between his hands. He whooshed out a great exhalation. In some ways it felt so right to have gotten with Colin. Taking control, penetrating Colin instead of feeling himself tear, had been liberating and empowering and, frankly, fucking delicious. Even with his ridiculous failure to hold off coming long enough for one stroke, Colin hadn't seemed to mind.

The laughter they'd shared was one of his favorite parts of the night, er, morning.

And the *second* time. Well. Hernán was actually proud. The way Colin's eyes rolled into his head, the filthy things that normally sweet and polite man breathed into his ear as Hernán drove his full length into Colin's ass, the way Colin sobbed when he came… Oh yes, he might actually be good at the sex thing.

Now what, maricón? The hated voice crept into his head, making him nauseous. *Little princess, little fag. How long until you let that culero stick his prick up your ass? You've gotten a lot of good stuff out of him already, puto. Better grab more before he gets tired and throws your cheap ass out onto the streets. That's where you belong anyway, isn't it?*

A wave of nausea hit. Hernán struggled to unhear Abuela and to drown her out by focusing on the wonder of what had happened between Colin and him. Hernán had longed for someone of his own, who would see his soul and not just his face or body, and would say, "Yes. This man is mine."

He grew up knowing from his grandmother's words that was impossible. A man who wanted other men was dirty, shameful, weak, and certainly incapable of love. He learned that lesson when she punished him for what the deliveryman had done in his uncle's shop. Each rap across his knuckles was a painful reminder it was Hernán's fault, for enticing the man into his sin. When Lonnie claimed him, he understood he was being punished for his own pitiful desires.

Yet the dream never faded entirely. In a tiny, hidden corner of his heart, Hernán kept hoping there was man of honor who would put the lie to Abuela.

Was Colin really that man? Hernán rocked in his chair, agitated and restless as he argued with the voice. Colin seemed to love him; maybe he really thought he did. But they barely knew each other. It had only been a few weeks since they met. More likely it was just a crush on both of their parts. Colin might wake up when that Brandon guy returned, start sniffing around him again, and realize Hernán had nothing to offer him.

The whole afternoon passed that way, even when Hernán went for a workout in the basement of Colin's building. The gym there had good equipment, so he heaved dumbbells, pushed himself hard, ran six miles on a treadmill… Anything to drown out his noisy thoughts.

Rudy was the only one he could possibly talk to about his distress, but as much as he loved his cousin, he knew that wouldn't help. Rudy threw himself into relationships after the first night in bed, convinced each time he'd found his Prince Charming, crushed when the man turned out to be uninterested in anything more than sex, undaunted when it came time to try again.

Hernán could imagine Rudy's advice, and it would involve china patterns or getting tokens of Colin's affection. None of that was what Hernán wanted.

He wanted Colin.

He didn't know how to keep him.

Still at war with himself, he made the evening awkward. Colin showed up at six with flowers, and Hernán tried to be gracious. He saw the light in Colin's eyes dim, though, so he must have fucked up somehow. They made dinner together as usual, but Hernán drank too much. Colin chattered happily through cooking, touching Hernán every time he passed by, until Hernán turned sideways to avoid his hand. Hurt flared on Colin's face, and Hernán didn't know how to explain.

I'm not your possession sounded in his head, along with *I love you, please don't give up.* When it came time for their ritual of watching TV together, Hernán said, "I'm kind of tired. We didn't get much sleep last night so I think I'm just going up to bed."

The disappointed, resigned look in Colin's eyes was heartbreaking. "Sure, Hernán. Sleep well. I'll see you in the morning."

Hernán lay in his bed in the dark, unable to relax enough to close his eyes. His head swam unpleasantly from too much liquor before dinner. The cleaning service had changed the sheets, but he thought he could still smell Colin in the pillow.

Eventually Colin turned off the television below and climbed the stairs. He paused by Hernán's open door but Hernán pretended to be asleep until Colin moved on to his own room. His door clicked shut.

Hernán rolled to his side and punched the pillow in frustration. Why had he told Colin he loved him? He was so exposed, so foolish, to think he could have someone. Sleep was a long time coming.

He joined Colin for breakfast the next morning, pouring himself some coffee before he sat at the table where Colin made his way through a bowl of cereal.

"Good morning," Colin said awkwardly, and Hernán tried to respond with a grin. It probably looked more like a grimace.

Colin set down his spoon and leaned forward across the table. "Did I do something wrong, Hernán?" he asked seriously.

"No. Nothing." Hernán shook his head fiercely. *This is me fucking up.*

"I thought we were… I hoped…" Colin blushed and turned his eyes back to his bowl. "Never mind."

Shit, shit, shit. Hernán raged at himself. *Now I've made him think he's done something, like my craziness is his fault. Fix this!*

But he didn't know how to admit his torment. Colin would think he was insane and end anything between them before it even began. All he could do was distract Colin with a white lie.

He cleared his throat and Colin's head shot up. "It's just, it's been a lot. You know? Telling my story, wondering what the lawyers are going to do with it all. Maybe I'll have to go over it again and again. It's got me kind of worked up."

Colin blinked at him several times. "Oh. You're upset about the application process?"

Hernán nodded, pleased when relief began to show in Colin's eyes. Drawn away for the moment from their relationship, Colin talked for the next twenty minutes about how Hernán should feel proud he had survived, the lawyers would do a great job for him and try to minimize how many times he had to talk about it all, and so on.

Hernán was grateful but he felt like screaming, *I'm not strong. I'm not proud. I'm ashamed and I'm bad for you.*

He insisted on cleaning up their breakfast dishes while Colin finished getting ready for work. A few minutes later, Colin came back downstairs, looking handsome in a gray wool blazer seemingly tailored to his height and lean build. He came over to where Hernán stood in the kitchen and opened his arms with a hopeful look on his face.

Hernán hesitated just a moment before stepping into the warmth and security Colin gave unselfishly. *Yes please,* he thought. *Take me out of my noisy head. Just hold me until I know what to do.*

Colin hugged him tightly until Hernán pulled away. "Don't be late for work," he said.

"It's Friday. Let's go out for dinner tonight," Colin said. "My treat. We've eaten in almost every night." Hernán bit his lip but jerked his head in a quick nod. Colin smiled and gave him a kiss before he left.

TO DISTRACT HIMSELF from his agitation over what the *fuck* he was doing to mess up Colin's life, Hernán settled down with the sample immigration papers Colin had brought home for him to study. He wrote in pencil on a blank form as the lawyer Sofia had requested. She'd have the final version prepared neatly, but having him draft the answers by hand was more efficient than going over each question together.

Spotting the form for the medical evaluation he would need, he recalled he was overdue to pick up the copy he'd left with the doctor where Colin had sent him. He picked up his phone to check whether it was ready. The doctor's receptionist placed him on hold briefly, and then came back on the line to ask if he could come by the office at two.

After another basement workout and lunch, Hernán was less sure than ever what to do about Colin. There was no question what he *wanted.* He wanted Colin to love him. He wanted to spend every night in Colin's bed and learn all the ways to please him. He wanted to hide away from every doubt in his head until they couldn't even find him. He wanted to silence Abuela's voice in his head forever.

But what did Colin need with a worthless turd like him?

The struggle continued in his mind as he waited in the doctor's office. Eventually a nurse showed him into an examining room, so much nicer than any he ever saw in San Marcos. A few minutes later, Dr. McCracken bustled in, a folder in one hand and a laptop in the other. His blond hair merged into gray at his temples. Under his white coat he wore a nice shirt with bright pink checks.

Seating himself on a rolling stool, the doctor opened his laptop, typed a few things, and then glanced down at the folder. Looking up at Hernán, he blinked owlishly and said, "Thank you for coming in again, Mr. Portillo."

"Please, just Hernán."

Dr. McCracken nodded. He cleared his throat, returning his gaze to the folder. Silence stretched.

The first tinge of alarm crept up Hernán's spine.

When the doctor spoke again, his voice was rough. "Hernán, you know we ran a wide battery of tests. We always do in a physical. Most of yours came back just fine." He hesitated again, and Hernán closed his eyes. He already knew. "The thing is, you've tested positive for exposure to HIV."

The world fell away beneath him.

Chapter 20

"DO YOU NEED a minute?" Dr. McCracken's soft voice sounded concerned. Hernán closed his eyes and sealed his lips against the scream he wanted to let out.

It was Lonnie's last victory. Had to be. It wasn't bad enough Lonnie had forced Hernán to submit to those terrible things. No, he had to keep on crushing and ruining Hernán's life forever after.

The doctor had asked him a question. Hernán shook his head tightly. "What do…?" He had to stop to bite the inside of his cheek fiercely. He would not break, not yet. "How long do I have?" he asked and it came out in a throaty rasp.

The doctor rolled toward him on his stool. He rested a hand on Hernán's knee and said, "It's not like that anymore. This is bad news, but it isn't a death sentence. With proper care and medication, you can live a full, complete life."

Proper care. There was no such thing in El Salvador. Everyone he'd ever heard of who contracted HIV died alone and miserable, shunned by family, shut away from the world.

You got what you deserved, didn't you, little maricón? The voice in his head was taunting and cruel. He wanted to shout back at her, *This isn't my fault.*

But it probably was. If he hadn't run from Cuernos. If he had fought harder to get away from Lonnie.

Then I'd be dead anyway.

You'll be dead soon enough.

Hernán gripped his hair in both hands and pulled, desperate not to give in to tears. Not in front of a stranger.

Dr. McCracken said, "There's a lot of information we should discuss but not yet. Let me give you a mild tranquilizer and when it kicks in, we can talk more. All right?"

Hernán nodded miserably. He'd take anything offered to make the voice leave him alone.

"Is there someone I can call to come be with you?"

"Colin Felton." It was out before Hernán even thought, and as soon as he said it he was desperate for it to happen. He needed Colin there to tell him what to do.

"Certainly," Dr. McCracken said. "A nurse will come in a moment with something for you to take, and I'll talk to Colin myself. You stay here until he arrives. Yes?"

Hernán nodded, and the doctor patted his knee and left. A nurse entered a moment later to offer him a small plastic cup with a single pill in it. He swallowed it with some water she brought as well, and laid on the examining table.

His heartbeat gradually slowed to something approaching normal as the sedative kicked in. Staring up at the ceiling of the room, he tried very hard to silence the recriminations in his head and avoid the flood of memories. *The room in the crumbling house, Lonnie coming for him, arms of the coyotes holding him down, the tearing pain as Lonnie forced himself inside…*

When the sedative wrapped him in enough gauze, he could shut off the noise. He rolled onto his side, his back to the door, knees at his chest. Tears trickled across his nose and down his cheek.

After an indeterminate period of numbness, the examining room door opened behind him. "Hernán?" he heard Colin ask softly.

Hernán couldn't look at him. They had been so close to something Hernán wanted all his life, and it was gone before it even really began. What could Colin do with him now? He'd be kind, Hernán had no doubt, but nothing more. At the right time, he'd find a way to ease Hernán out of his life.

Maybe he should just go ahead and return to San Marcos, make it simpler for everyone…

Colin climbed onto the table with him and lay down, his arm wrapping tightly around Hernán's quivering body. "Dr. McCracken asked me to come but he didn't tell me why." He kissed the back of Hernán's head. "What is it, Nán? What's happened?"

It was easier to answer if he didn't have to look at Colin. He didn't want to say it at all, but with the sedative and Colin's arm around him, he thought he could get it out.

"I've tested positive for HIV."

Colin inhaled sharply and Hernán lost his last shred of control. He began to sob. Wet, messy, gasps of pain surged out of him and his body shook.

Colin tugged on him until he rolled over, holding him as Hernán buried his face in Colin's white shirt and poured out his misery. Stroking his hair, Colin kissed his brow as Hernán cried. At some point the door opened and he heard Dr. McCracken ask, "How is he?"

Colin answered softly, "I think we need a little more time, Chris. I'll come look for you when we're ready." The door closed again.

Eventually Hernán had no more tears. He lay silent and exhausted against Colin, soaking up what comfort he could before Colin realized he was contaminated and sent him away.

"Are you ready to sit up?" Colin asked and he nodded. They shifted around until their butts were on the paper covering the exam table and their backs rested against the wall, shoulders and legs touching. Colin held Hernán's hand tightly in his.

"I'm sorry," Hernán muttered.

"For what?"

"The other morning. I didn't know, I swear. I would never have put you in danger like that—"

"Hush," Colin chided softly. "We were completely safe, and of course you didn't know."

"I should have, though." He wiped his eyes with his free hand and then said, "I'll get out of your apartment as soon as I can."

"What are you talking about?" Hernán heard the frown in Colin's voice.

"You don't need this in your life. You've done so much for me. I'm sorry it was all wasted."

Colin hopped up off the table so he faced Hernán. He cupped Hernán's cheeks in his hands and forced him to look up.

"What is this, Hernán? What are you saying?"

"I'll probably just go back to El Salvador. I have some family there still who might help a little."

Colin hissed in pain. "You can't be serious." He forced Hernán to his feet and threw his arms around his back. "You aren't going anywhere. I know how poor the health care is in El Salvador for HIV/AIDS. No way are you putting yourself at risk that way."

The ferocity in Colin's voice threatened to bring tears again. Hoarsely, Hernán said, "Drugs are expensive. I won't be able to afford treatment in the States."

"Oh for…" Colin fumed and stepped back. He paced the tiny room. When he turned again to Hernán, his face was red. His voice when he spoke was strident. "What part of 'I love you' didn't you hear?"

Hernán looked at the floor. Colin crossed the narrow room to him and grasped his chin. Nostrils flaring, eyes flashing with blue fire, Colin was in full-on warrior mode.

"I'll say it again in case you didn't hear me or didn't believe me. I love you, Hernán. I don't care we've only known each other a few weeks. I don't care you don't have permission to stay here. Yet," he emphasized. "I don't care that you're proud and independent and don't want to accept help from me. You will *accept* help because I have it to give. You'll get treatment and asylum and any other damn thing you need because I. Love. You."

Hernán wanted to quail before Colin's anger, though it wasn't precisely directed *at* him. This Colin was a stranger to him, though in some ways it was nothing more than he'd glimpsed at the restaurant in Provincetown, that day when the warrior first appeared.

Still, pride stiffened his spine. "You didn't know I was sick. That changes everything. I know you're kind and noble but nobody should have to deal with this."

"You have an infection. That's it," Colin all but shouted, throwing his hands in the air. "You aren't sick, and if it's handled well you'll never get sick."

Hernán blinked. He tried to sort through those words, but they didn't make sense. "Of course I'm sick. I have AIDS."

"Hernán, you have HIV. It isn't the same thing."

"It is in my country. Everyone I've ever heard about died."

"Well, I'm telling you it's a manageable condition."

The door opened just then and Dr. McCracken stepped in. "While I agree with you, Colin, could you please keep your voice down? You're alarming my other patients."

Colin whipped around. He and Hernán said at the same time, "Sorry."

"This room is small for three people. Come with me to my office and we'll talk there."

Hernán and Colin followed Dr. McCracken down a hallway to a neat office with a nice view. The doctor closed the door behind them, gestured at two upholstered chairs facing his ornate desk and then seated himself. "Hernán, are you all right with Colin being present for our conversation?"

Colin stiffened but Hernán reached across the gap between their chairs and rested a hand on his arm. "Yes. I want him here." He had no idea where any of this was going but he knew Colin would fight like the devil if he tried to kick him out.

"Good. The single most important thing you need is a support network. I've known Colin for several years, and I doubt you'd find a better friend to help you get adjusted to this."

Without looking, Hernán could tell Colin was blushing and preening at the same time. "Don't gloat," he said out of the corner of his mouth. "I heard you and I'm trying to listen."

"Then let me repeat what I, and everyone in my office, heard Colin tell you. You have an infection that is manageable. I have many HIV-positive patients who have been asymptomatic for years, even decades. In all other respects you're completely healthy. You obviously take care of yourself and you'll want to continue."

Dr. McCracken made a few more notes on his laptop, muttering to himself as he typed. "We need to draw some more blood to check your CD4 count and your viral load. We also test for a particular gene to make sure you can tolerate one of the medicines incorporated into the regimen we use."

"What is the regimen?" Colin asked, and the doctor focused on them again.

"Nowadays we use a single pill containing four different antiretroviral agents. Hernán, you'll only have to take it once a day but it's very important you take it faithfully. Intermittent use could lead to resistance to the drugs. Understood?"

Hernán nodded. A single pill? It didn't seem possible after the rumors he'd heard in El Salvador. "How much does it cost?" he croaked out.

Colin said, "Don't worry about that—" at the same time Dr. McCracken said, "It can cost thirty to forty thousand dollars per year."

Hernán gasped. That was more than twice what he could earn,

even forgetting about food, housing, clothes…

Colin clutched his hand and said, "We'll talk about the cost later. Chris, what are you testing for? Can he start the pill today?"

"As I said, we need to make sure Hernán's virus isn't resistant to any of the available drugs by running a Genotype test. If it is resistant, there are other regimens. We also need to check kidney function."

Colin inhaled sharply and shot a look at Hernán. The scars on his side throbbed with his awareness. The stabbing…

"If you're thinking about the kidney wound, don't worry," Dr. McCracken said. "From what you told me when we met the first time, the damage you suffered won't have impaired your kidney functions. What we're looking for is different, something like diabetes, and you've told me there's no history of that in your family."

"What about side effects?" Colin asked. Hernán hadn't even thought to wonder, but the doctor shrugged.

"You might have some nausea for a few days. That's pretty much it. You have to remember the drugs are the latest results of thirty years of research. We've learned so much. As long as you're able to take the antiretrovirals and stick to the regimen, we'll likely be able to get your viral load down to undetectable levels in a matter of weeks.

"Now, after all that, I expect you need time to absorb and process everything. We'll just have Nina draw blood and then I'm sending you home with some materials to read. Be careful about the internet. There's as much wrong information out there as right. Come back in three or four days and we'll look at the results and start on the regimen. We can go over any questions you have when you return. Anything else for me right now? No? Wait for Nina in the examining room please, and then talk to Frank at the desk about your next appointment."

Colin looked as if he wanted to ask a question but he didn't. Hernán stood with a shaky breath. The words *thirty to forty thousand dollars* reverberated in his head. *Later*, he told himself.

He shook hands and said, "Thank you, doctor."

"Please call me Chris. I suspect we'll see a lot of each other in the near future."

Hernán nodded and followed Colin to the reception area. He was feeling numb from the information overload, the remains of the tranquilizer and Colin yelling at him. He remained wrapped in sadness, grief and worry, but what surprised him most was, somewhere in the morass, he also felt a faint stirring of optimism.

WHILE HERNÁN TALKED to the receptionist, Colin pulled out his phone to call the office. He told his assistant, "I'm not coming back in today. Will you let Maryanne know?" A pause to listen, and then he snorted. "Of course I'm being a coward. I've taken a lot of time off lately without notice." Another pause. "Let her know I'll make it up on the weekend and I'll be ready for the Hill visits. Nothing else is pressing right now anyway."

He disconnected, knowing full well he'd get at least one snarky text from Maryanne before the day was over. Of course he was being irresponsible, but Hernán needed him. That took precedence.

They both pulled on their autumn-weight jackets and left the office. Colin glanced at his phone; it was nearly five o'clock. "Do you feel like having a drink somewhere? Or an early dinner? We were planning to go out tonight anyway." Hernán bit his lower lip and looked up at him from under his lashes. "What?"

"I can't believe how calm you are about this," Hernán said finally. "It seemed like the end of the world for me, but you just take it in stride."

Colin gripped his elbows and tugged him out of the stream of pedestrians. He leaned in slightly so as not to be overheard. "Listen to me, Hernán. I'm not taking this lightly. I can imagine this must devastate you. But I also know a lot of people living with HIV. Maybe you haven't been around that enough, and you've only seen the ravages of the disease. But what I've seen gives me hope. Until you wrap your mind around it, I'll hope enough for both of us."

"I love you," Hernán blurted out, and then looked down at the sidewalk. "That isn't fair for me to say."

Colin pulled him into a hug and sighed. "Oh Nán. You can say it to me every hour upon the hour and I'll never get tired of hearing it. I just hope you mean it."

Hernán leaned back. "Why do you say that?"

Because you were so distant yesterday, after the best night of my life. Because you didn't want to look at me, or touch me, or share a bed. Colin looked around, aware of the number of people. "Look, let's grab a drink in this bar I know, and then we'll decide later about dinner."

He led Hernán to a nearby hotel with a nice cocktail lounge he'd visited many times with congressional staffers and others he was trying to lobby. Hernán looked nervous as Colin guided him through the marbled hotel entrance and into the wood-paneled lounge.

A pianist in one corner played softly. A few patrons sat at the bar, while men and women in suits occupied several clusters of leather club chairs, having a drink as they performed the usual professional dance. Colin found two chairs facing each other across a cocktail table, a little distance away from any others.

Ivan, a flirty and handsome young waiter with Slavic features who had served Colin many times before when he brought in guests, hustled over moments later. "Mr. Felton. It's nice to see you again," Ivan said with his Eastern European accent prominent. Colin suspected the accent was deliberate to make him seem more exotic.

"What can I get you gentlemen?" Ivan flicked a glance at Hernán, and then took a slower second look. His eyes rounded.

Colin was hardly surprised. No matter how big the tips he left, Ivan still ignored the plain-looking Colin for the stunningly handsome Hernán. He was about to answer when Hernán growled at Ivan, "My *boyfriend* will have a Grey Goose and tonic, with lime. An IPA for me." He glared until Ivan hustled away, and when he looked back, Colin fought a smile. "What?"

Colin shook his head. "No one has ever ordered a drink for me before. I think I like it." He leaned forward and took Hernán's hand. "I also liked you warning off the waiter."

Hernán's face colored. "I didn't like the way he was looking at you. All possessive, like he..." Hernán glanced at their joined hands and abruptly dropped Colin's. "Oh. Did you and the waiter... Do you see each other?"

"I've never gone out with Ivan, no." Colin couldn't help the smug tone he heard edge his own voice as he added, "Besides, the guy I'm seeing is *so* much hotter than Ivan could ever hope to be."

Hernán blushed and reached again for Colin's hand, and then stopped abruptly. He looked around the room, wide-eyed, to see if anyone had noticed. "I'm sorry. I wasn't thinking—"

"Everyone who matters knows I'm gay, Nán. I've never seen a reason to hide it."

"That's amazing to me," Hernán said with a sigh. "I've hidden all my life." He closed his eyes and looked as if he heard someone speaking, but then he shook his head. He leaned forward again and his voice when he spoke was low and tormented. "It's been tearing me up, Colin. I feel so much for you, but I've always been told it's wrong."

Light dawned, and his understanding of the awkward evening and morning shifted around. "Is that why you were so cold to me?" Hernán flushed in confirmation. "I figured it was more than worrying about your application. I thought you regretted what we'd done."

"No, not regrets. Just, I'm sorry—" Hernán began, but Colin cut him off.

"No, *I'm* sorry. I tried like hell to control myself but I see now I've pushed you too much." Worry flared up in Colin, tangled with shame. "Did you feel like you had to kiss me or...the other stuff? Because I was helping you?" He winced in anticipation of the answer.

Hernán said earnestly, "Everything I did with you was because I wanted to." Colin breathed easier but it was Hernán's turn to wince. "I wanted it and I put you at risk. I'm a swine, like my grandmother always said."

Colin wanted to yell at Hernán's grandmother or to just hug him, but Ivan returned with their cocktails. Oblivious to the tension, he set glasses before them on paper napkins. With an eye on Hernán, he intoned in a drawl he probably meant to be sultry, "Here we are, gentlemen. Now, can I get you anything to snack on? Would you like to see the bar menu?"

"No," Hernán said through gritted teeth. "Thank you. This will be fine." He waited until Ivan had sashayed away before picking up his beer and taking a big gulp.

Colin sipped at his cocktail. He rehearsed in his head what he wanted to say before putting down his glass and leaning forward to take Hernán's free hand. Hernán tensed at the move, and then seemed consciously to relax. "Please listen to me, Nán. Nothing we did put me at risk and I really want you to get that out of your head. If you're willing, I want to do it again and again and again."

Alarm shot across Hernán's face and he started to protest but Colin talked right over him. "We'll use condoms and I'll go on this preventive medication they have now. PrEP, I think it's called. We can ask Chris about other ways to stay safe because I know it matters to you. And I appreciate your concern for me. If you want to stick to touching and kissing, well, okay. I'd regret it because you show tremendous promise as a world-class top."

Colin paused until he saw a small smile and glint of pride appear on Hernán's face. "But you *never* have to do anything with me that makes you uncomfortable. The only thing you could do to hurt me is to walk away from this." Hernán's eyes took on a sheen, and his own burned.

"Will you do me a favor?" Colin continued, his throat tight. "Let's forget all the heavy shit for tonight. We've spent a lot of time together, but we haven't been on a real date. I'd like to have a quiet drink with you here and flirt. I want to take you for a really great, expensive, indulgent dinner and not hear a word of protest from you about the cost. I want to go home with you afterward and sleep in the same bed."

He smiled and went on. "You don't have to put out, seeing as it's our first date, but I really hated sleeping alone last night, knowing you were just down the hall.

"So. How does that all sound?"

Hernán blinked rapidly and seemed unable to speak for a moment. Finally he answered, his voice thick with emotion. "It sounds wonderful. I hated sleeping without you too."

Colin released Hernán's hand and settled back into his club chair with his vodka tonic. He took a sip, and waited until Hernán did the same.

He had no illusions things would suddenly be easier in the morning. HIV was manageable but still serious. Immigration status, figuring out how to make a relationship work, getting Hernán to accept his help—it was going to be a challenge. Add in the fact that eventually he would have to introduce his family, and hope the experience didn't send Hernán running for the hills.

All of that might be tough, but Colin wasn't afraid in the least. He wasn't going anywhere.

He winked and said, "So, Nán. I never asked—what's your astrological sign?"

Chapter 21

THEY DIDN'T HAVE sex that night. When they climbed the steps to bed, though, Colin proffered his hand. Hernán took it to follow him to his room.

Colin stripped his clothes quickly and had a moment of indecision. Normally he slept in a shirt and loose pants, but he wanted to feel Hernán's skin against his. Gambling that if he climbed into bed naked Hernán would do the same, he was relieved when Hernán dropped his clothes on a chair and joined Colin under the sheets, also nude.

They slid close together. When they were face to face, Colin gave the sweetest kiss he could manage. He tried to say everything in one simple, chaste brush of lips. Hernán smiled back at him and followed it with a "good night" before he rolled over to switch off his lamp and then shift to rest against Colin.

Colin put his glasses on the nightstand, turned off his lamp as well, and spooned himself along Hernán's back. The warmth of the smooth body aligned with his own threatened to give him an erection, but the day's tension, lack of sleep the night before, and cocktails with dinner put him under.

A shout dragged him abruptly awake. Hernán thrashed in the sheets and kicked out, getting Colin in the shin.

"Nán," he said hoarsely and hesitated. Hernán moaned and twisted, shoving his hands forward while his head whipped side to side. Colin got himself out of striking range and stretched a long arm to shake Hernán's shoulder. "Hernán. Wake up," he said more loudly.

Hernán threw himself to a sitting position, panting. His eyes glistened in the near-darkness as he swiveled his head back and forth.

"It's okay. You're safe," Colin said. Hernán turned to him, blinking, mouth open. "You're safe," he said again.

Hernán sighed heavily and sank back down against his pillow. "I woke you up," he said with gravel in his throat. "I'm sorry. Did I hit you?"

"It's fine. Do you want to talk about it?"

Hernán shook his head, glancing at Colin. "I really don't know what it was about. Lonnie, the house..." He huffed in frustration. "I used to get these nightmares when I first lived with Rudy, but they faded away. Maybe it's talking about him again that stirred the bad dreams. It doesn't matter."

"It does matter." Colin hesitated. He wanted to ask again about seeing a therapist, but Hernán had resisted from the first time Colin mentioned it. The middle of the night, on top of Hernán's bad news, wasn't the right time to push it. But Hernán needed to talk to someone. He resolved to find a way to bring it up in daylight hours.

Hernán's eyes were wide, picking up the little light in the room so they glinted as he lay on his back. After a moment, he began to roll out of the bed as he said, "I should go to my room so you can get some sleep."

Colin reached for his arm and tugged him back down. "Please stay. For me."

Hernán hesitated, nodded and settled down on his side. Colin rolled to face the same direction and fit his back against Hernán's front. He all but held his breath until Hernán entwined his arm with Colin's and kissed the back of his head.

Soon he heard Hernán's breathing slow and even out, and the arm holding him slackened as he drifted off.

Sleep was harder for Colin to find. He was trying to be everything Hernán needed, and that seemed to work for their living situation and for the immigration process. With the latest blow, though, he couldn't help wondering if he were strong enough. His mother no doubt would say he'd done his best and he should let go before he got hurt.

But Colin wouldn't give up on Hernán.

He tested his feelings, examining a parade of thoughts to see what reaction they provoked, looking for the weak spot he knew had to be there.

I've had sex with someone who's HIV-positive.

No, no tremor of fear there. He meant what he said to Hernán, that he was confident about how safe they'd been. Colin and everyone he knew had grown up with condoms and safe sex talks. Nothing he and Hernán had done was risky.

We'll have to be careful as long as this relationship lasts.

A niggle of concern arose from that thought. He'd heard of PrEP but didn't know much about the drug protocol, its side effects, long term consequences or any of that. Some disappointment appeared to weigh on his mind as well. Colin had long fantasized about barebacking but he'd never indulged that desire because he'd have to be in a relationship with someone he trusted enough to take such a step. Condomless sex was likely off the table forever with Hernán.

Although...what if Colin were the top? That shouldn't be risky. He shook his head; with what Hernán had suffered, he'd probably never be comfortable letting Colin inside him. That was a selfish set of worries in any case. Hernán was dealing with much more immediate and visceral fears. That should be their priority, not expanding their sexual relationship.

What if he leaves me and goes back to El Salvador? Or is denied legal immigration?

Those questions brought a quiver of fear, tinged with sadness. Even though they said they loved each other, the truth was they hadn't spent enough time together yet for Colin to trust love would be sufficient. So all he could do was hope they had long enough to forge the kind of bonds they would need to survive whatever was coming their way.

Hernán might get sick.

That thought produced an earthquake in his brain. Colin had never lost a close friend to AIDS but he had known a few people who died from it. In his charmed life it had been a vague issue of concern, but it hadn't truly touched him. His knowledge of HIV and AIDS was passive, absorbed from random news stories and anecdotes on the internet. He was sure he'd been hearing that ever-evolving drug trials had reduced infection to a manageable condition, as he'd said to Hernán, but suddenly he realized how few facts he knew.

Did the antiretrovirals work for everyone? Did it matter how long someone had been infected before they started on a drug cocktail? Hernán would fight when Colin tried to pay. Were there programs or grants Hernán could rely on to supply the needed drugs, or at least let him feel that Colin wasn't bearing the entire cost?

And suppose the drugs didn't work. If Hernán got sick one day, was Colin strong enough to help him through it?

Stop, he ordered himself when his chest tightened. *The common thread of everything I'm thinking is that I don't have information. Until I get that, I'm only borrowing trouble.*

Surprisingly, the moment of self-awareness calmed him quickly. Gathering information meant a project. Organization. He could break his questions down into categories, find resources—Chris McCracken or HIV support groups—to get them answered, and then make sure Hernán did what he needed to take care of himself.

No, what *they* needed to do to protect *themselves*. As long as Hernán would have him, Colin would try to be the warrior Hernán claimed he could see.

HERNÁN BEGAN SLEEPING in Colin's bed every night. Colin respected his wishes not to have sex until they returned to Chris' office to have a serious discussion about the parameters to keep Colin safe and uninfected.

Sunday, Colin left him alone for a few hours while he went to play basketball with some friends. He invited Hernán, but didn't push when it was clear he needed some time alone. An hour later, though, Hernán caught himself looking out a window as despair inched its way up his spine.

He imagined he could feel something wrong in his blood. He started to envision the virus as a black speck, dividing and multiplying, polluting his blood, consuming his organs… Alarmed, he grabbed his shoes and went for a long run on the basement treadmill until the rhythm of his pounding feet drove the image out of his head.

After his run and a shower, Colin had not yet returned. When the bad thoughts tried to creep back into his head, Hernán immersed himself in studying the HIV materials Chris gave him, and then worked on his immigration papers. Both activities kept his brain busy enough to hold dread at bay.

Then Colin came home from his game, and he was no longer alone.

Climbing into bed again with Colin after talking and watching TV grew increasingly natural, except for Hernán's guilt over sex. Colin woke every morning with an erection. The first two times, he rolled away and tried to hide it before heading for a long shower. Hernán stayed in bed, knowing Colin was probably masturbating alone out of respect for his fears.

On Monday morning, when Colin moved to carry his stiff cock and tight balls into the shower, Hernán decided to act.

"Wait," he said, his hand on Colin's arm and butterflies in his stomach. Colin settled back onto the bed, eyes intent and cheeks red as he kept a leg bent in order to hide his predicament. The tips of Hernán's ears burned as well. "I hate when you leave me to jack off alone. Just because I'm not ready to, uh, fuck again yet doesn't mean there isn't stuff I'm comfortable with. Stuff we can do together."

"Oh?" Colin blinked, and then licked his lips. "Like what?" he asked cautiously.

Hernán slid closer, threw back the sheets and blankets, and pressed down on Colin's bent leg until it lay flat. In the morning light that filtered into the room, his lean, naked body shone. His beautiful prick reared up over his belly, pale with a rosy-purple head.

Colin's tousled hair, sleepy eyes and self-conscious smile made Hernán's heart trip and his semi-hard cock flex. He maneuvered their legs together and let his length fall against Colin's hip as he wrapped his hand around Colin's erection.

"Would it feel good if I stroked you?" Hernán asked, looking up from under his lashes. Colin bit his lip and nodded, eyes intent. Resting his head on Colin's chest, Hernán began lazy movements up and down the silken skin of Colin's dick. He teased it, the way he liked to do to his own, running just fingertips lightly up and down the hard length. Clear liquid appeared at the slit and he resisted the urge to taste it, safe though that would surely be. Instead, he rotated his palm in small circles on the head, smearing precome around and earning him a hiss.

"You're wicked, Nán," Colin said in a throaty voice.

Hernán brushed a kiss against Colin's chest and took firm hold of his erection again. He moved more deliberately, squeezing slightly as he approached the head, relaxing his grip as he pulled the skin back toward the root. Colin was circumcised, which fascinated him. He wanted to press his tongue flat against the pretty, unsheathed head and swab it until Colin came in his mouth.

No. Not until we clear it with Chris.

The second-best option was to make Colin feel so good with his hands that he forgot how little Hernán was able to give. He rearranged their bodies until he sat on his heels between Colin's thighs. With his left hand he kept stroking Colin's hard cock. With his right, he fondled Colin's balls and ran the pads of two fingers over the skin below, before dipping down to circle against his hole.

Colin sighed contentedly and spread his legs, inviting Hernán to drive him higher. Hernán resisted the urge to breach Colin with his fingers but he was pleased with the noises he drew out. The prick in his hand turned a deeper shade of purple as he stroked it and brought Colin closer and closer. The temptation to put it in his mouth became almost irresistible.

Colin panted and rocked his hips against Hernán's fingers at his opening. Head pressed back to the pillow, he almost sobbed, "I want you inside me again. Aah..." He flicked a glance toward the drawer of his bedside table, and his cheeks pinked.

Colin clearly wanted to ask for something but was too embarrassed. Hand sliding steadily on Colin's shaft, slick with the clear juice that leaked down the head from its slit, Hernán inclined his head toward the drawer. He asked, "Is there perhaps a toy in there you'd like me to push inside your ass?"

Colin's blush deepened to a pretty shade of red as he nodded sharply. Hernán leaned over his prone boyfriend to claim a kiss, his right hand taking over the cock between their bodies while his left pulled open the drawer. He gave a quick glance and made a sound of surprise. Colin groaned and looked away, his face fast approaching scarlet.

"That's so hot," Hernán breathed as he reached into the assortment of dildos and other toys. Plugs. A thick red band big enough to use as a cock ring. Living with Rudy had been an education, but still he wasn't sure about the application of everything in Colin's drawer. He thought he'd like to learn though.

Colin peeked back at him. "It doesn't freak you out?"

Hernán shook his head slowly. "All these shapes and sizes, Colin. You have to show me how to use them. For this morning, though, I think..." His hand hovered over the array before he pulled out a blue silicone cock. It was probably seven inches long, slightly shorter and more slender than Hernán's erect dick. "This will do."

He spotted a bottle of lube and grabbed that as well. Releasing Colin's flesh, he examined the toy. "Do you like this one?" he asked as he coated it with lubricant in a twisting motion to make sure it was slippery. Colin nodded and twisted his lower lip. He was still red but not as alarmingly so.

Hernán nudged him with a knee. "Please don't be embarrassed. With this I can fuck you and make you feel good. I want you coming with me, not alone in the shower."

He felt Colin's gaze as he ran the dildo over his own chest, nudging at each nipple with the flared head, sliding it over his pecs. "It feels nice on my skin," he said in a low voice, lifting his eyes to watch Colin's reaction. "Cool. Silky. Do you think it will feel nice as I press it into your ass?"

Colin's eyes never left Hernán's as he nodded. He bent his knees more and slipped further down the bed so he was exposed. Only the faintest blush remained as his eyes grew hot and needy. Hoarsely, he said, "It won't be as good as your dick. But yes, it'll feel nice."

Hernán swiped his lubed fingers over Colin's tight ring of muscle before placing the head of the dildo there. "Pretend it's me," he whispered, and pressed it forward with a slight twisting motion. Colin's ass yielded to accept the toy.

"Oh, that's so sexy. This blue cock is disappearing inside your hungry hole." He flicked a teasing glance up at Colin. "That's about two inches. Is it enough?"

Colin moaned and shook his head, squirming against the invading dildo. "More. I need it, Nán. I need you." His voice was husky and desperate.

Hernán took Colin's shaft in his free hand and slid down its length at the same speed he worked the silicone version inside. The noises of pleasure coming from Colin had Hernán so hard that he might himself shoot a load from the sound alone.

When the wide base of the blue cock was flush with Colin's body, Hernán paused to say, "You've got it all now, cariño." He pulled it steadily back until the ridged head pulled on the edges of Colin's hole. He moved it in small circles, and then plunged back in. Colin gasped and arched his back, squeezing his eyes shut, nearly undone.

Hernán released his throbbing cock and waited until Colin settled down a little. "Oh no. You don't get to finish so quickly. Here. Show me how you like to do yourself with these toys."

Colin looked shocked all over again but he didn't refuse. Heat grew in his eyes and his jaw slackened as he stretched one long arm down between his raised legs to grasp Hernán's wrist.

Pulling on it, he drew the dildo out several inches, and then reversed course to shove the thing back inside roughly. He repeated the motion with increasing speed, eyes locked with Hernán's, chest heaving as he fucked himself hard using the blue surrogate for Hernán's cock.

Soon he squinted again in a look of almost-pain Hernán recognized meant he was about to come. Hernán stilled the toy, watching the anguished expression on Colin's face as his orgasm retreated again. Colin panted and sagged down, boneless. He licked his lips and growled at Hernán, "You're a cruel man."

Hernán asked innocently, "Should I let you come? Or may I keep playing with my toys?" He twisted the dildo in Colin's ass and the silky skin of his erection, earning a hiss.

"I don't think I can take much more," Colin said through gritted teeth. "Too good."

"Then let's get you over the edge." Hernán stroked Colin's prick more firmly, at the same tempo he used with the dildo. Colin's legs trembled and he panted, fucking up into Hernán's grasp as his cock flushed a darker purple. Hernán reamed his ass with the toy until suddenly Colin gasped. At that, Hernán pressed it as far inside Colin as it would go.

"Aaah fuck," Colin choked out, squeezing his eyes shut and hunching over as a geyser of come erupted from his cock, over Hernán's fist, to splatter his chest, chin and sheets. Hernán held the dildo in place while he milked Colin's prick to squeeze out every drop of semen.

Finally Colin shuddered and covered the hand on his cock with his own. "Too sensitive," he gasped, and Hernán chuckled softly. With a slack mouth and eyes that glimmered in the morning light, Colin watched Hernán carefully withdraw the dildo and set it aside.

"That was so hot. I need to come," Hernán rasped out and lay back on the bed. His hand went immediately to his own prick, wet and slick already because he'd leaked as he worked over Colin. He skinned back the hood and pulled it down tight, and then slid up until the foreskin closed completely before stroking again.

"What can I do for you?" Colin asked breathlessly, his eyes focused on Hernán's prick.

"Hold my balls. Yes, like that. And watch me. I like your eyes on me. See how hard you make me?" Hernán gasped and shook, moments away from his own orgasm. "I haven't come since I fucked you. I need it too. Look at how much you excite me. ¡Mierda!" and then he came hard, spurt after spurt coating his belly and his hand in white.

He sagged back, one hand on his twitching cock, the other thrown over his eyes. "Oh Colin. Sweetheart."

Colin rolled off the bed and returned in a moment with wet washcloths. They wiped themselves as clean as they could, though only a shower would get rid of all the lube and lingering stickiness. Colin flopped down and put his head across Hernán's chest. The room smelled pleasantly of semen.

"I don't think I've ever shot that much," Colin said. "My God. You had me on the edge over and over." He quivered and then said in a strangled voice, "I never even thought about using toys with someone else."

"You like them, huh?"

Colin nodded. "I do. Part of it is just that I don't get a lot of sex. But yeah, I've always thought dildos were exciting. I can't believe you fucked me with one. What you must think of me."

"Couldn't you tell I loved it by how hard I came right after you?"

Colin buried his face against Hernán's chest. "I know. It's just...so *wanton*, somehow. To have you do things to me like that. Things I've only done alone in a dark room."

"Oh, mi corazón, I want to do more. I want you to show me every single toy in there and tell me what you think about when you use it."

"I can do that, if you're patient with me. But as much as I like them, it's no substitute for the real thing." He rested his hand on Hernán's spent dick. "When you were working me over with Bluebeard, I pretended it was your cock fucking me."

"Bluebeard? You name your dildos?"

"Oh God. Why do I open my mouth?" Colin groaned and burrowed more deeply into Hernán. "I think I'll just die of embarrassment here. Don't mind me."

"Not until you tell me what you call the gigantic one I saw in your drawer. It must be, what, eleven or twelve inches long and thick as a can of Coke." Colin muttered something into Hernán's armpit. "What?"

"I call him Paul. For Paul Bunyan."

"It's going to be fun having Paul skewer my boyfriend," Hernán teased. "I want to share you with your silicone friends."

Colin inhaled sharply. "About that. We haven't talked about sharing or really about anything relationship-wise. You haven't had sex before and I'm not exactly the hottest guy out there. Everywhere you go, these super-handsome men watch you. Maybe you shouldn't have to limit yourself to just me."

Hernán tugged up Colin's chin and frowned. "I don't want to have sex with anyone but you. Do *you* want to have other people? I know I don't have much experience but I'm trying to learn—"

"Oh my God, no! I don't want anyone else at all. It's just that I'd like to have at least some of your attention, even if that means you want to get with other guys sometimes."

"Colin. Cariño." Hernán pulled him up into a hug. "Stop putting yourself down, because I think you're sexy and handsome. I can't believe I have to say it but look at this mess you've brought home. I'm here illegally, I've been raped, I've got all these trust issues and now, on top of that, I have HIV. You shouldn't put up with me for one minute, and I don't know what you see in me that you love. How can you imagine I'd treat this casually? That I'd want anyone but you?"

He kissed Colin hard, trying to express himself physically since his words seemed feeble. Colin finally pulled away long enough to rest a hand on Hernán's cheek and say earnestly, "You're the best thing that's ever happened to me."

Hernán kissed Colin's palm and said, "And you are my friend and my lover. You're passionate and funny. You love *Doctor Who* and you love sex toys. There's so much you keep locked away inside but still you let me see it. I want everyone else to see it too. To know *my* Colin. I'm screwing things up but I'm trying, I really am. Don't give up on me. Please."

Colin's eyes were shiny. "You haven't screwed anything up and I'll never give up on you. But the same has to go for you, okay? If I do something wrong and make you mad, you can't walk away without telling me. Give me a chance to fix it."

"Deal," Hernán murmured. "Mi amor."

"Mi amor," Colin agreed.

Chapter 22

THE FOLLOW-UP VISIT with Chris McCracken on Tuesday eased many of Hernán's concerns. Blood tests showed his viral load was low, and that he should have no problem with the antiretrovirals. Chris passed Hernán his prescription.

Colin took his hand. Knowing what was coming, Hernán felt his ears burn. Colin's cheeks pinked up, too, but he managed to say, "Chris, can we talk about sex now?"

Chris' eyes twinkled but he kept his face serious as he nodded. "Of course. Even with good numbers like yours, Hernán, it makes sense to take precautions for now."

"For now?" Hernán asked, puzzled.

"Once the antiretrovirals have a chance to work, it's likely your viral load will become undetectable. Once that happens, the chance of you being able to transmit the virus becomes almost nil."

"Almost," Hernán stated back flatly.

"Well, I can't responsibly say that it's zero. As far as safe practices, I'd keep using condoms for now if you have anal intercourse. Oral transmission is extremely unlikely."

Colin blushed as he asked, "You mean if I, uh, receive orally or anally, I assume?"

"Right. There's no risk at all if Hernán swallows your semen. I'd also say there's no measurable risk if you penetrate Hernán without a condom, barring something like an open cut on your penis."

Hernán was sure his eyes bugged at the frank discussion. He'd never been around people able to discuss sex so casually. He understood what Chris was telling them, but he couldn't help worrying that Colin would still be at risk.

To Colin, he said, "I'm not sure I'm comfortable with that. Even if the chances are practically zero, I don't know if the risk to you is worth it."

"What about PrEP?" Colin asked the doctor. "Is there a downside if I go on preventive treatment?"

"It can cause kidney problems in a few percent of people, so we need to monitor that periodically. Otherwise it is a pretty benign drug. I'll give you a prescription if you want. Give it a week and then you should be effectively immune.

"I remind everyone, though. Truvada will prevent the transmission of HIV but not other sexually transmitted diseases. If you're monogamous that shouldn't matter. If you're with other partners, use condoms."

Colin gripped Hernán's hand tightly and smiled at him. "That won't be an issue."

They left the doctor's office and went to a nearby pharmacy. Hernán came to a halt outside the doors, the paper in his hand trembling.

He knew he needed to fill the prescription, but he didn't know how much it was going to cost. No insurance, and he had less than a thousand dollars left after having sent money to Rudy. There was simply no way he could afford a full month's supply of the medication. Perhaps the pharmacy would let him get a partial prescription, and he could come back when he had more money—

Colin put a hand on his arm, startling Hernán from his reverie. He looked up into earnest, concerned blue eyes.

Softly, Colin said, "I'm not trying to show off or impress you about money. You get that, right?" Hernán nodded. "I just feel like you should understand something." He leaned close to whisper a very large number in Hernán's ear, and Hernán's jaw dropped. When he pulled back, their eyes locked.

"That's how much is in my trust fund. I know. It's ridiculous. I take control of the whole fund when I turn thirty. In the meantime, I get the interest and dividends from all that money in quarterly checks. Even that's far more than I need to live on. I could never spend so much on myself in a lifetime, so I do a lot of other stuff with it. I support a number of charities, and I give scholarships when I meet someone at the center who I believe deserves a boost. If I want to spend some to keep my boyfriend healthy, is that so bad?"

Hernán blinked nervously and released a sigh. "Of course not."

"I know it's weird, angel. It's just who I am, and how I grew up—

with a lot of money. But I'm not Nimble. I'm not trying to control you or confuse you or buy you. And please don't suggest you're taking advantage of me. Honestly, I've encountered people all my life who think I'm an easy mark, so I know you're nothing like that. Tell me how I can help you get comfortable with letting me pay for your medication."

Hernán looked down. Colin barely heard him whisper, "It's just...hard. To accept help. To *need* help."

"I promise, I'll help you look for ways to reduce the costs going forward. There's an AIDS Drug Assistance Program, though I'm not sure whether you'll qualify until you're granted asylum. I'll check that for you. Today, though, please let me pay."

Hernán hugged him. His voice was thick when he said, "Thank you."

DAVID JAMES HAD returned from his honeymoon, and Sofia contacted them to schedule a second meeting about Hernán's case. She said to Colin, "I've figured out how to have you in the meetings without waiving attorney-client privilege. I'll explain when we get together."

Wednesday afternoon, Sofia and David greeted them in a conference room. Hernán hadn't met David in Provincetown so they shook hands before settling down around the conference table.

David said, "I'd like to address something right away." His gaze took in both Hernán and Colin. "My husband Brandon is Colin's best friend. I assure both of you that anything we discuss in the context of your representation will be strictly confidential. I don't tell Brandon about my cases except in the most generic terms, and he doesn't ask. But if it makes either of you uncomfortable, I can find one of my partners to guide Sofia, and I'll drop out. I won't take any offense, I assure you."

Colin glanced at Hernán, expectantly. Hernán shrugged and answered for both of them. "I have no concerns with you keeping my case, David."

With that, Sofia addressed them. "Let's discuss privilege first. Colin, you have significant expertise in asylum and similar immigration issues, I believe."

Colin nodded. "Well, yes. As a matter of fact, I'm leading a team now to lobby specifically about asylum issues. I've spent a lot of time recently understanding the development of various interpretations of legal terms used in applying the standard."

"You also have in-depth knowledge of the situation for LGBTI individuals in various Latin American countries," David commented. "When you and I handled that project with Joe a few months ago, you were a tremendous resource."

"Thank you, but what does that have to do with privilege?" Colin asked.

Sofia said eagerly, "We—the lawyers—would like to retain you as a consultant on Hernán's case. Your knowledge base will be directly relevant. We might even need to call you as an expert witness, depending on how matters develop. As a consultant to Hernán's attorneys, we can include you in strategy discussions about his case without blowing the privilege."

"Huh," Colin mused. "That's clever. Of course I'll donate my time since you're doing the project pro bono."

"Excellent. We'll prepare a simple engagement letter for you to document your role. In the meantime," Sofia said with a grin, "consider yourself on the clock. Let's get started.

"Hernán, we've reviewed the legal options open to you. You've told us your parents and your brother don't have green cards themselves, so they aren't able to sponsor you. Your uncle and your cousin are permanent residents, but unfortunately the law doesn't make them eligible to sponsor you either. You don't have an advanced college degree or professional skills to qualify for an employment-based visa.

"Therefore, we believe your best option is to seek asylum. You'd be filing what's called an affirmative asylum application. In essence, you're going to the U.S. Citizenship and Immigration Service and asking for permission to stay in the country. If the application is granted, you can remain indefinitely, and you're also able to seek permission to travel outside the States and return. After one year, you can get a green card, and then five years on, you can apply for citizenship."

"And I could work?" Hernán asked.

"Yes," Sofia said. "In fact, if we don't get a decision within 180 days after we file your application, you're entitled to a work permit while it's pending."

David leaned forward to rest his elbows on the table and met Hernán's gaze. "You need to know that this strategy isn't risk-free. If the asylum officer denies your application, you'd be referred for removal proceedings. The deportation process isn't automatic, though. We'd go before an immigration judge on the grounds for asylum and get another bite at the apple, so to speak."

"We can't give guarantees, but you do have a strong case," Sofia said. "The initial stalking and intimidation Cuernos del Diablo tried was sexual in nature. Your experience with them and your fear of retribution comes specifically from you being targeted because you're gay. With all that, you have a well-founded fear of persecution based on your sexual orientation. I'll need to do some research to gather evidence on why you couldn't expect help from the authorities."

Colin spoke up. "As it happens, I've been studying U.S. State Department reports on country conditions throughout Central America for that lobbying effort I mentioned. Abuse or abandonment of LGBTI people in El Salvador is pretty well-documented. I've been through some shocking reports of public officials and even police who engaged in violence and discrimination against gays, lesbians and intersex people. When LGBTI individuals tried to seek help, they were ridiculed or strip-searched, and asked demeaning questions. I can send you the reports this afternoon."

"Perfect," Sofia said. "That and any similar materials you have will speed my work on portions of the application."

Hernán looked at Colin for guidance. Softly, Colin said, "I think you should do it, Hernán, but ultimately it's your choice to make."

True, but what was the alternative? He could spend his life in fear of immigration enforcement officers finding him. Let assholes like Gerald Nimble control and manipulate him through terror. Or...he could take the lifeline Colin had found for him. Nothing worth having was free of risk.

"Let's do that," Hernán said. "Seek asylum."

Colin's relieved smile warmed his belly.

"Excellent," Sofia said. "Were you able to work on the forms I gave you?"

Hernán pulled papers out of a folder he'd brought and passed them to Sofia. He stared at the tabletop and said, "There's, uh, something else. Something new you should know about."

Colin took his hand. Sofia and David waited patiently while Hernán found his voice. "I went to a doctor to get the evaluation you said I would need. I found out, uh..."

Blood rushed in his ears from his suddenly-pounding heart, and the room seemed to blur. He couldn't say the words. David was a stranger, and he'd only met Sofia once. Would they think he got infected in San Marcos? Did they think there were others before Lonnie? He stared at the conference table surface.

"Hernán found out that he's HIV-positive," Colin said, leaning forward in his chair. "At the time he was discharged from the hospital after his stabbing, he tested healthy. He thinks he must have contracted it when Lonnie Heath raped him, because he never had sex with anyone at all before that." He blushed. "Or after, until the time he was tested."

Sofia put her hands to her mouth. "Oh, Hernán. That must be devastating."

David asked, "Are you getting treatment? I understand remarkably effective drugs are available if it's caught quickly. From what Sofia told me, the infection would have happened about seven or eight months ago, right?"

Hernán nodded, unable to speak. He risked a look around the table, to see if anyone was pushing back, or away from him. No one had moved.

Colin continued, "We've been to see Chris McCracken." To Hernán, he explained, "Chris is a good friend of David's. It was a strange coincidence, to discover we'd been going to the same doctor."

"Not really," David said with a smile. "He's one of the few openly gay doctors around, and that's important to both of us. Also we only live a few blocks apart, so Chris is kind of our gayborhood doctor anyway."

Colin gave David a smirk. "I concede the point, counselor."

"Anyway, Chris is excellent." David addressed that to Hernán. "He has a practice specialty for people living with HIV. I can't imagine someone better qualified to help you stay healthy."

Sofia made some notes on her legal pad and shook her head. "It's really unfair. You tried to get safe and then this happens. It's small comfort, I'm sure, but your HIV status should be one more reason we can argue for asylum. Colin, do you have any materials regarding HIV/AIDS treatment in El Salvador?"

Colin nodded and made a note to himself. "Yes. I've been reading that, statistically, HIV treatment has improved dramatically in Central

America in recent years. In practical terms, though, sex workers, transgender women, and gay men get infected disproportionately. Those groups also face the highest barriers to getting treatment and to reducing the rate of new infection. Some of the reports blame the lack of public information and access to medical resources, stigma, and fear of reprisal or of ostracism."

He glanced sideways at Colin, suddenly feeling his heart constrict in fear. The statistics and reports made it sound so distant, but it was his life being discussed.

Colin didn't see the look and kept talking to Sofia and David. "There's a law to prevent discrimination on the basis of HIV/AIDS-status," he said, "but the law is rarely enforced. Discrimination actually remains widespread. I'll get together some more materials for you on that, Sofia."

Hernan shuddered. Quietly he added, "The people I've heard of get pushed out of sight. There was a family that lived near my grandmother's house. The son got AIDS and they kept him locked up. They'd use separate plates, sheets, towels—everything. He didn't last long." *That could be me, if I have to go back.*

Colin finally glanced at Hernán and his eyes widened. Sliding his chair closer, he grasped Hernán's trembling hand. "Nothing like that is going to happen to you. I swear," he said fiercely.

Hernán kept his eyes locked on Colin's and squeezed the hand holding his as he tried to draw deep breaths. Slowly he found his center again. Maybe it was a relief after all, to have his infection in the open, to have it talked about.

He croaked, "I've started a drug protocol and...we're dealing with all those other things." Sofia seemed to miss it but David gave a small, sharp nod of understanding. His racing heart gradually regained its steady rhythm. "It's still a lot, but I'm trying to get my head around it."

They talked through the details of the asylum application for an hour, until David excused himself to attend another meeting. "Sorry, gentlemen, but I'm still catching up from being away for three weeks. Colin, I know Brandon is excited to see you. Perhaps you'd like to come to dinner tomorrow evening?" His eyes included Hernán. "Both of you."

"Let's do that," Colin said enthusiastically, but then glanced quickly at Hernán. "I'm sorry. Is that all right with you?"

Hernán tensed and relaxed at the same time. He appreciated that David seemed to understand and accept that Hernán and Colin were together, but he couldn't help a small pang of fear. With all the shit that he brought to Colin's door, being around Brandon might remind Colin of earlier love.

No. It wasn't the time to indulge his insecurities. "Can we bring anything?" he asked.

"Just yourselves. Seven-thirty?" They nodded and David left.

Sofia had taken a few minutes to organize her notes into a checklist of the tasks they had to accomplish in order to move the application forward. "Medical records from El Salvador of the stabbing, an affidavit from your sister or your grandmother about the event, an affidavit from your cousin Rudy about getting you released from the smugglers..."

She paused to study her list. "Yes, I think that's it. I'll take the forms you filled out and have the paperwork typed up. Hernán, you'll take care of contacting people for the records and statements we need. Do you have any questions for me?"

Hernán stood to shake her hand as he asked, "Just one. What's the timetable for all this? I've written to the hospital already, but it may take a while to get in touch with my sister. She moved in with our aunt who doesn't have a telephone."

"We have to get the application on file no later than one year after your arrival in the States," Sofia explained. "The sooner the better, though, just in case ICE happens to pick you up. If you already have an asylum application pending, they're unlikely to start removal proceedings."

The words terrified Hernán all over again. For months in Provincetown he lived with a persistent fear of being caught, but since he'd been with Colin all of that seemed like a distant dream, like someone else's worries. He tried to keep his face neutral when he nodded.

Colin peered at him, and took his hand. "Don't worry, Nán. There's no reason for immigration agents to be looking for you."

Hernán gripped his hand back and gave a tight smile, but inside he still felt cold.

Walking out of the building, hand in hand, Colin said, "It looks like the whole process is in good shape. Do you think you're ready to begin at the Immigration Initiative?"

Hernán nodded slowly. In the anxiety of telling his story, he couldn't have handled teaching strangers—Colin had been absolutely right about that. Add in the fact of his diagnosis and he would have been a disaster.

But with the prospect of a new life taking shape, he could finally repay a little of Colin's generosity. Colin's work was important to him, Hernán knew, and he liked the idea of sharing in that passion. As well, the money Colin had insisted he accept in advance had begun to weigh heavily on him, like an unpaid debt on his soul.

Yes, he was ready.

"Can I start tomorrow?" he asked, thrilled when Colin lit up like the morning sun.

HERNÁN MADE HIS way back to the condo after the meeting. Nerves jangled at the thought of stepping in front of a classroom of students, but excitement was there too. He would use the afternoon to make progress on the documents needed for the asylum application, and then he'd be ready to begin his new work with Colin.

Once in the apartment, he reviewed his task list from Sofia and decided to start with a call to Tío. They talked for a few minutes about what Hernán was doing in DC, but in vague terms. Hernán wasn't ready to risk telling his uncle about himself or his relationship with Colin. He asked Tío to pass along a message to Brijith, to contact him when she was able.

Next he called Rudy about the affidavit he needed. They talked often, but guilt gnawed at the edge of Hernán's mind. He'd revealed little about what was happening between him and Colin, perhaps afraid that talking of it would break the spell. He hadn't even explained how he came up with the money he'd sent to Rudy.

And he hadn't mentioned his diagnosis, because every time he said the words made it more real. Even with his optimistic doctor and supportive boyfriend, sometimes the reality of his diagnosis curdled in his belly, or wrenched him awake at night. He couldn't forget the people he'd heard about in El Salvador, abandoned to the ravages of AIDS.

Would that be him, some day?

Rudy was his best friend, and Lord knew he told Hernán everything about his life in smutty detail. He owed it to Rudy to speak up about what Colin was doing for him. *Like paying for my medicine and giving me a place to live, and telling me he loves me.*

When Rudy picked up the phone and they'd exchanged superficial news, Hernán steeled himself. "Primo, I didn't want to do this over the phone but I've got some stuff I need to tell you." He swallowed hard against a wave of panic and nausea. "It, uh...for my immigration papers. I had to get examined by a doctor." Hernán made himself form the words.

"Rudy, I've got HIV."

The weight of Rudy's silence was palpable. When he spoke, his voice sounded thick with tears. "Oh, Nán. I'm so sorry. It was that bastard Lonnie, wasn't it? I wish I'd been able to get you away from him before this happened but I didn't know—"

"There was nothing more you could have done. I'm learning a lot about HIV, though. It's better here than in El Salvador. There are treatment programs to keep me from ever getting sick."

Rudy sounded doubtful. "That must be really expensive. The drugs, I mean. There are AIDS support groups here in P-town and I went out with this one guy who was positive. He told me that even with insurance, he spends a thousand dollars a month to keep up with the medication."

"Colin's checking into some government programs that subsidize medication even for undocumented people. And, uh, until then...Colin's paying for my treatment."

Dead silence from Rudy. Finally he spoke in a flat tone. "Colin is paying for your medicine, on top of giving you a place to live and working on your immigration papers. This is starting to sound like me with Gerald."

"No! Rudy, he isn't like that. Colin's just got this big heart, and money isn't a problem for him."

"It wasn't a problem for Gerald either. Until he got tired of me."

What could Hernán say? *Colin won't get tired of me. Colin would never treat me the way Gerald treated Rudy.* How did he know?

Because he loved Colin. And he believed Colin, that he loved Hernán too.

In a small voice, he said, "I haven't been telling you everything, Rudy. I'm sorry." He explained about how their relationship had developed, how they were adapting to the HIV diagnosis, the way Colin treated him.

When Rudy spoke again, the concern of a close cousin warred with the delight of a perpetual romantic. "Nán, I'm really happy for you. I hope this works out. It's just...well, you're always the one to warn me not to get my hopes up too fast. And I hate to admit it but you've always been right. It's strange to hear you talking like this."

"I don't know what to say except Colin loves me. I just... I trust him."

"Okay." Rudy paused again; when he spoke his tone was deliberately light. "Hernán in love. You need to get this man of yours to fly you back to Provincetown so I can see this miracle in person. I want to be your maid of honor when you get married. Hell, I want to be your wedding planner!"

They laughed at absurdities for a while until Rudy had to go to work. Before he signed off, in the most sincere voice Hernán had ever heard from him, Rudy said, "Be careful. I want you to be happy and I think you have better luck than me in picking a good man. But if anything goes wrong, you don't have my calluses either. You'd have a hard time getting over a broken heart."

"I know," Hernán said softly. "I'm starting to see that 'careful' doesn't really come into it though. Safe sex we can do. Safe love? What does that even look like?"

"If I knew I'd tell you. Love you, primo."

Chapter 23

COLIN TOOK HERNÁN to the Immigration Initiative's offices with him the next morning. He walked gingerly because Hernán had done a number on him the night before.

Hernán raised his head from Colin's glistening cock, one hand still wrapped around the base. "How's that?" he asked, and smiled at Colin's groan. "It feels good in my mouth. And the taste! I had no idea why everyone always raved about blowjobs but I love doing this to you."

Colin tried to raise his head from the pillow but failed. "Ah, chupame. Suck me, please. I was almost there."

"Nuh huh, bello. I've got other plans for you." Hernán rummaged in the drawer that contained secret desires. With a dirty grin, he began working Colin's ass with Bluebeard to pry him open. After a few minutes he switched out that toy for Jesse, a thicker, red dildo with small bumps down its eight-inch length.

Abashed at first, Colin soon relaxed as Hernán whispered filthy stories in his ear about the "man" between his legs. When Hernán pulled Paul Bunyan out of the drawer, he held Colin's gaze while he licked the huge thing up and down and tried to fit it into his mouth.

He couldn't take even the first inch so he murmured, "Have you really had this monster inside you?" Colin nodded nervously, his face warm, but Hernán ran it across his belly. "I can't wait to see Paul disappear inside you." He brought the toy to Colin's lips. "Work him up. Show me how much you want Paul inside you."

Mortification warred with arousal as Colin let Hernán run the giant dildo over his lips. He opened his mouth wider and took the head inside. "Such a good cocksucker," Hernán praised. "That's it. Make Paul wet. He wants to fuck you."

Colin closed his eyes and took the thing deeper. He could manage no more than a few inches but having Hernán feed him the silicone dick made his own ache. And then, Hernán slid down the bed to lube up the thing and press it to his hole...

Oh God, Colin was sprouting wood on the sidewalk. He shifted his gait until he was a few steps behind Hernán, hiding his arousal as best he could and grateful for the thigh-length coat he'd put on that morning. Hernán gave him a big smile over his shoulder, clearly aware of what Colin was doing.

"Did I go too hard on you last night?" Hernán asked innocently, though a devilish glint in his eye showed he already knew the answer.

Colin shook his head. "You did everything just right."

"Mmm. Surely there's room for improvement," he teased.

After a quick look to make sure no one was in hearing range, Colin hissed, "The only way it can get better is if you give me the real thing again."

When Hernán looked forward and didn't answer, Colin's heartbeat stuttered badly. He'd said the wrong thing, like an idiot. His semi-erection deflated and he hustled to take Hernán's hand and walk beside him. "I'm not pushing—"

"I know, corazón." Hernán cut him off with a smile, and Colin's heart rate slowed back to normal. "After last night, I think I might be ready to go further. If we're careful."

"You're trying to kill me, aren't you?" Colin groaned. "How am I going to get any work done today with that bouncing in my head?"

"Aw, I'm sorry," Hernán said smugly. "I thought two orgasms last night would've taken the edge off for you."

"You know damn well it didn't," Colin answered, pouting. "The more I get of you, the more I want. I'm greedy that way."

"My greedy blanquito. I don't know if I can compare with all your other men like Jesse and Paul."

"What bullshit. You know exactly what you do to me."

Hernán gave him a sideways look. "Yes, I do," he admitted. "You do it to me as well."

Colin squeezed his hand. Tightly.

They stopped for egg sandwiches and coffee at a diner on the street level of the building that housed the Immigration Initiative not-for-profit center. When Colin led the way out of the elevator and through a set of glass doors, he said to Hernán in an aside, "Don't get flustered by Maryanne. She may embarrass you a little but she'll really be trying to get under my skin."

He guided Hernán down the hall to Maryanne's office and rapped on the door frame. Her black hair glinted in the light streaming through her window. She stood up when she saw Colin had someone with him.

"Maryanne Rhee, I'd like you to meet Hernán Portillo. He's joining us today as a volunteer and he's agreed to give us about thirty hours a week."

Her practiced, welcoming smile quickly turned into something wicked and mischievous. As he'd feared, Maryanne remembered the name Hernán. Colin groaned inwardly.

She extended her small, plump hand with its bright red fingernail polish. "Hernán, it's a pleasure to have you." She flashed a twinkling look at Colin. "And how did you come to hear about us?"

"Colin mentioned that you need Spanish speakers, and I'm interested in teaching."

"That Colin. He's something else, isn't he?" Maryanne cooed, and Hernán nodded uncertainly. "Such a darling. And so handsome, don't you think?"

"Uh..."

"My gosh, he'll do anything. Even give the shirt off his back."

"I..."

Oh don't mind me, Hernán. I know he's taken. In fact, I seem to recall him mentioning that he was quite smitten—"

"I never said smitten," Colin interrupted. "Dammit. Yes, this is *that* Hernán."

She laughed brightly and the sound made Hernán visibly relax. "Well, it's nice to have you here no matter what persuasion Colin had to use. Sit, please. Let's chat."

She gestured to her visitor chairs and they spent the next twenty minutes talking about the center. Maryanne volunteered, "I got involved with immigration work because of the way I've been treated my whole life. I'm hapa. Mixed race, quite literally. My moms are Korean and Angolan. They wanted a baby that looked like them, so they used Eomma's egg—that's the Korean part—and found a black sperm donor for Meme."

She winked at Hernán. "I'm pretty sure they picked the donor out of a catalog instead of going all the way back to Angola. I have a baby brother, too. They reversed things for him and used Meme's egg and a Korean sperm donor."

Hernán was so red by that time Colin feared momentarily that he'd have a stroke. He reached for Hernán's hand, and got a grateful flash of wide eyes in return. Hernán cleared his throat and said, "That's, uh... Your mothers make a lovely mix of features in your face."

Maryanne slapped her desk lightly and rolled her eyes at Colin. "See? That's how you give a compliment." To Hernán, she said, "Numbnuts here ignored me and asked to see a picture of my brother."

"I did not," Colin protested in vain.

Maryanne went to work on Hernán in earnest then. Colin was in awe of the speed with which she made Hernán comfortable, drew him in, and then recruited him for a slate of volunteer activities more extensive than anything Colin had imagined.

They quickly settled on daily ESL classes for Spanish speakers, and then some ad hoc sessions to help people with job-hunting skills. In addition, Maryanne talked Hernán into signing up as a French translator. "We don't get many Nahuatl speakers," she told him, "but your Arabic might come in handy."

"I'm not very good at it yet," Hernán protested, but she waved it away.

"Whatever you can speak is more than anyone else on staff here. We've seen an increase in the number of Egyptians, Iraqis and Lebanese immigrating and needing help. Even rudimentary communication will go a long way to making them feel comfortable and welcome." Hernán nodded reluctantly.

When Maryanne apparently felt she'd extracted every drop of commitment possible, she released Hernán with an engaging smile. "You're going to be a tremendous help to us. I'm very excited to have you." She grinned toothily and said in a suggestive tone, "I'm sure Colin is excited to have you as well."

"That's it," Colin huffed. "I'm updating the sexual harassment file *and* sending out my résumé this afternoon."

"No, you're not. You love it here. But okay, enough teasing. For now." Maryanne laughed again. "Colin, will you introduce Hernán to Vonda so she can get everything set up?"

She rose and extended her hand to Hernán. "Seriously, welcome. My door is always open if you need anything."

Hernán looked dazed and wrung out already. He muttered something polite to Maryanne before Colin led him to the volunteer coordinator's cubicle.

"Vonda, this is Hernán Portillo," Colin told the young woman who tracked the various educational programs. He explained about what Hernán had agreed to do. Then he said to Hernán, "You're in good hands. My office is just down there." He pointed with his chin. "Come find me when you're ready for some lunch."

Settling down to his own work, Colin felt a surge of enthusiasm for the organization. Watching Maryanne at work on a volunteer or donor, and hearing the passion she had when she spoke about their efforts, reignited his own commitment. He hoped Hernán would grow to feel the same fire for their work. He'd never before had anyone to share it with.

Fantasies about what it might be like to have a man in his life who understood the important role the center played unspooled in his head. He started going through his emails, and snorted when a one-word message popped up from Maryanne:

Wow.

Colin typed back:

Hands off!

She ended the exchange with a smiley face.

Chuckling, he began to focus on the details for the upcoming Hill visits. Great progress had been made in expanding the applicability of asylum in recent years to include sexual orientation and gender identity. Many of those gains were under attack by the new administration and by xenophobic legislators who ran on a platform that equated immigration with crime and terrorism.

His team would be lobbying members of two Congressional committees against a bill recently introduced by a consortium from Arizona, Texas and Florida. Their bill would reduce the available paths to lawful immigration, including a severe curtailment of asylum.

His enthusiasm became eclipsed by his nerves. He trusted Maryanne but he couldn't agree he was the best person for the important assignment. Stomach in knots, he read through the draft agenda and the team background.

He knew all the steps required, the protocol for the Hill meetings, the "elevator speech" he needed to have ready for any member of Congress he could corner for a few minutes…but he didn't want to do it. He liked being in the background, where he could work with the lobbying teams on refining their message and stay behind as a resource.

Maryanne kept insisting that he take on a bigger role with the Initiative, though. She didn't understand his reluctance to take the lead, and he couldn't really explain it either. He just believed that he'd let everyone down, sooner or later. Colin sighed past his reluctance and returned to the matter at hand.

Around eleven his phone rang, and the name "Brandon" flashed up. They hadn't had much chance to talk since his friend returned from the honeymoon, just enough that Colin had gushed about Hernán and their growing closeness.

When Colin picked up, Brandon drawled, "We still need that conversation you wanted when I was in Paris. Should we meet for a drink tonight before dinner or somethin'?"

"No, I got past that crisis. Honestly, this thing with Hernán is evolving so naturally and quickly that I almost worry it's *too* easy."

"I hear ya. Just communicate a lot and make sure you're both on the same page. That's the best advice I'd have anyway." Brandon paused, and Colin could hear the smile in his voice when he spoke again. "You sound really happy. Hey, am I allowed to do the thing tonight where I grill your boyfriend about his intentions?"

"Don't you dare," Colin sputtered. "He'll be nervous enough."

"Okay, I guess I can leave it be for now. But you know it's my responsibility as your friend to put the fear of God into him if he hurts you. If not tonight, soon!"

"Shouldn't you go beat up a client for shirking their physical therapy exercises while you were gone?"

"Yes, as a matter of fact. We'll see you boys at seven-thirty."

A little after noon, Hernán peeked into his office. Colin was on the phone, but he waved toward his visitor chair. Hernán parked there until Colin was free. When he hung up, he leaned his elbows on the desk to lean toward Hernán. Excitedly, he demanded, "Tell me about your first morning."

"Sure, but can we bring lunch back here? I'm slotted to teach an

English class already this afternoon at two and I want to go over the materials. I thought we could buy something nearby and come back."

They returned to the diner to get food—a roast beef and Swiss sandwich for Colin and a Caesar salad with turkey for Hernán—before heading to Colin's office again. Hernán filled him in on the morning's introductory activities and confessed his nerves over the class he'd be handling that afternoon. Yet Hernán's eyes sparkled, and his cheeks grew flushed. He suddenly had a purpose and something to offer, and that awareness made him glow.

Hernán had never looked more compelling to Colin than when he described how he was planning to break the ice with his first group of students and then dive into the English lesson.

"The textbook you use here is great," Hernán said as he poked a plastic fork into his salad. "We used it in my school. It has dialogues to help the student feel confident in trying some basic conversation outside of class." He caught Colin's rapt gaze. "Do I have lettuce in my teeth?"

"No. It just thrills me to see how much you're enjoying this."

Hernán winked at him. "Let's see how I feel after my first class. They may boo me out of there."

"Are you kidding?" Colin snorted. "One look at you and we'll probably end up with fifty new students who want to be teacher's pet." Hernán's face shuttered for a moment. Colin got it. Being admired for his looks was something Hernán associated with unwanted attention and abuse.

He tried to change the subject quickly. "Do you think you'll be done in time that we can still go see David and Brandon for dinner? Brandon's looking forward to meeting you."

"I guess we didn't really meet, did we? I saw him sitting with you that time at Veranda but we never spoke. Rudy likes him."

"Oh, Brandon's great. He's really easy to talk to."

Hernán closed up his salad container and tossed it in the trash. "My class ends at four so I'll have some downtime to prepare for tomorrow's session before we go to dinner. When do we need to leave home?"

Home. Colin's heart skipped a beat and he looked away to hide his no-doubt goofy grin. "It's about a fifteen-minute walk. If we leave at seven we can stop to pick up a bottle of wine on the way."

"That should work. Come get me when you're ready to leave for the day, okay?" Hernán came around the desk and leaned toward Colin. He hovered with his lips inches from Colin's, and said softly, "Thank you for suggesting this. I didn't know how much I needed it but already I feel different. Charged up."

He closed the gap between them and gave Colin a deep kiss that promised more. When Colin opened his eyes again, Hernán was studying his face. "I really love you, cariño."

Colin's throat felt tight. "I love you too. Now go kick some ass, maestro!"

WALKING BACK TO the condo at the end of the day, he listened eagerly while Hernán talked about his first class. "I was so nervous but you were right. They settled down as soon as I started. We did that ice-breaking exercise I mentioned and it went really well. It's going to take some time to sort through who is at what level because some of them have a better grasp of English already. Maybe we could break things up into a beginning and advanced group?"

"That's possible," Colin said. "You should talk to Vonda about it. We haven't tried it before because of a lack of instructors, but if you're willing to commit the time—"

"I am," Hernán interrupted forcefully. "I didn't know for sure I was going to like teaching so much. After months of washing dishes in Provincetown, I feel like I have a direction again. Like the education I started in El Salvador really prepared me for something."

Hernán had just changed his clothes for dinner and joined Colin in the living room when Hernán's cell phone rang. He glanced at the display and said in surprise, "It's Sofia." He answered the call in speaker mode. "Hola, Sofia. Buenos días."

"Hola, Hernán. Listen, I have some news for you and I couldn't wait any longer. I've got something to tell you. Something I hope you'll be happy about."

Hernán crooked his head, a puzzled grin stretching his mouth. "What?" he asked.

Sofia sounded nervous. "I hope you won't think I overstepped. I was very careful, though. Very explicit to the investigator I used about no contact."

"Just tell me," Hernán said with a small chuckle.

"I found Albert and Andrea. They're in the States and they're fine."

Hernán's mouth dropped open and he gasped. His eyes glistened with sudden tears, as his lower lip trembled.

Sofia continued. "Yes, I'm sure. I hired an investigator the firm uses sometimes. He found them in Midland, Texas. They moved there almost as soon as the children came over the border. I have an address and phone number for you."

She read off the information but Hernán was trembling so much he couldn't write anything down. Colin grabbed some paper and a pen and had Sofia repeat the information.

Hernán burst out, "Can I—?" He choked and had to start over. Tears running down his cheeks, he said in a thick voice, "Can I call them?"

Sofia replied, "As I said, the investigator made no contact, but I don't see why not. You aren't mad at me?"

"No, of course not," Hernán choked out. "I'm going to call right now."

"Let me know how it goes," she said and disconnected.

Hernán's hands shook badly as he tried to peer from the paper to his phone.

"Here, let me," Colin said. He took the phone and dialed the number he'd written. "It's ringing," he said softly, and placed the phone back in Hernán's trembling hands before standing to leave Hernán in privacy.

Hernán shot out a hand to pull Colin back down on to the sofa next to him. His eyes flared when the call connected. Colin heard a woman's voice say, "Hello?"

"Is this…?" Hernán cleared his throat and tried again. "Is this Miranda López? My name is Hernán. Do you remember who I am?"

From the excited, loud voice, Colin knew that she did. Hernán put the phone on speaker, and then set it on the coffee table. He took Colin's hand in both of his as Miranda called out in the background, <<Albert, Andrea. Come, quickly.>>

The sound of running feet and a boy asking, <<What is it, mamá?>> made Hernán almost sob. Eyes fixed on Colin's, he said shakily, "That's Albert."

Miranda seemed to have put her phone on speaker as well. <<Babies, do you know who is on this phone?>> The children exclaimed and fussed, asking who who who?

Hernán spoke. <<Andrea. Albert. Do you remember me?>>

A hushed, shocked silence broke into loud, joyful cries. A girl's voice asked, "Hernán, is it you?"

"Yes," he said, nodding though the children couldn't see him. Colin brushed tears from Hernán's cheeks. "Are you well, niños? I'm so happy to hear your voices."

Albert and Andrea chattered and interrupted each other, filling the space between DC and Texas with their happy voices.

"...And there was a *snake*, Hernán, right when we came out of the car," Albert said.

"No, the snake was when we were coming out of the basement," Andrea corrected.

World War III almost erupted as they squabbled. Hernán spoke over their argument. "I'm glad the snake didn't get you, no matter where you were. Are you in school?"

The diversion worked beautifully, as the children told him about their classes and their teachers. After ten minutes, Miranda came back on the line. "I'm sorry to end this, but my husband is due home from work soon and I have to finish dinner."

"Of course, Miranda," Hernán said. He hesitated, and then asked in a shaky voice "Were...were they all right when they got to you? Did the drugs harm them?"

"They slept a long time and they were very hungry. But nothing else. The children talk about you and Isela all the time. Thank you for keeping them safe."

"Would it be all right if I call again sometime? Or can I write?"

"Claro. I'm so happy you found us."

They ended with a plan to speak again in a week. When Hernán disconnected, he threw his arms around Colin to sob onto his shoulder.

"Sometimes they were in my nightmares. Giving them the pills so the handlers wouldn't force them—that was the worst thing I've ever done in my life. I've dreamed for months that they died from the drugs, and their ghosts blamed me for betraying them."

"But you didn't betray them. It was their mother's decision and you made it as easy as you could on them. Now they're okay," Colin murmured into his hair. "Albert and Andrea are safe. It's time to forgive yourself."

Hernán nodded and squeezed harder. "I'll try."

Chapter 24

TO EASE HERNÁN down from the emotional storm the telephone call had wrought, they walked quietly on the short journey to David and Brandon's row house on Fifteenth Street. A look of relief gradually suffused Hernán's gaze while they walked, and he kept Colin's hand tight in his own.

When they arrived at the house, Hernán ran wide eyes up the three-story brick façade, and made a soft noise of awe. David opened the door at their knock. He gave Colin a one-armed hug and held out a hand to Hernán.

"Great to see you. Come on in."

As David accepted the bottle of wine they'd brought, Brandon came down the hallway to greet them. He wore cargo shorts, and had eschewed the leg-shaped covering for his prosthesis. The silvery shaft extending from just below his knee sported stickers of a lightning bolt, The Flash, and Sonic the Hedgehog.

Colin belatedly realized that Hernán must've only seen his friend sitting down at Veranda that day, because he didn't seem to know where to look.

In his warm Texan tones, Brandon said, "Hi Hernán. We didn't really meet in Provincetown but I've heard a lot about you."

Hernán shook his hand, straining not to look down. "Colin has told me a lot about you too," he said in a strangled voice.

Brandon crooked his head and gave a grin. "I guess he didn't mention my leg."

Colin shrugged. "I suppose I didn't. Honestly, I rarely think about it anymore."

Brandon laughed. "Neither do I, 'cept when I have to go through airport security."

David closed the door behind them and gestured for everyone to go into the living room. "Don't let Brandon fool you. He had a great time freaking out the TSA guys. He stood there at the scanner and said, 'Oh wait. Forgot something.' And then he just yanked his leg off right there. I thought the woman behind him in line was going to faint."

Brandon put his arms around David's waist. "I offered to let her hold it and everythin'. You turned purple when I asked that hunky guard to carry me through the scanner. He was plenty big enough. He could have done it!"

David bent to kiss the top of Brandon's head. There was nearly a half-foot difference in their heights but Colin thought they looked like a perfect fit. "You're lucky he didn't throw you over his shoulder like a sack of potatoes," David said with a laugh.

Colin hoped the joking helped Hernán to relax. He should have mentioned the situation, but it'd been a year since Brandon lost his leg. It rarely crossed his mind anymore. Once in a while Brandon would mention his frustration that the police had never been able to find the driver who hit him on his bike one September morning. Other than that, he seemed comfortable with his situation and rarely showed even a flash of bitterness.

Brandon said to Colin, "Hey, I signed up for a marathon in Virginia in November. Will you come cheer me on?"

"You can run a marathon?" Hernán exclaimed, and then immediately blushed. "I'm so sorry. I don't mean to be rude."

Brandon grinned at him. "Don't worry about it. Believe me, it took a long time for me to get used to the leg too."

Hernán was almost scarlet as he looked between Colin and Brandon. "I've just never met anyone with an artificial leg."

"You want to look at it?" Brandon asked and extended his prosthesis as he held on to David. "It's a lot lighter than you'd think, but really strong." Hernán seemed very nervous but he crouched to take a closer look. "See where the cup meets my stump? I just pop in and out of that."

"Don't do it, Brandon," David warned, a stern look in his eye.

"What?" Brandon asked, all innocence. "I just want Hernán to see how cool the thing is." With a shit-eating grin, he pulled it off and balanced against his husband on his natural leg while offering the device to Hernán. Eyes wide, Hernán accepted the prosthesis.

"It's really light, isn't it?" Brandon prompted.

Hernán licked his lip nervously. He hefted it in his hands and agreed. "It is." He looked over the apparatus. "Do you have to buy special shoes?"

"Nah, regular ones. The foot on there is made to the same measurements as my other foot so I just buy normal pairs."

"Of course I'll come to your marathon," Colin interjected. He glanced at David. "Are you running too?"

"I might do the ten-K. I don't think I have the stamina to pull off twenty-six miles."

"You carried me up six flights of stairs at that hotel in Paris, cowboy" Brandon said with a chuckle. "You've still got some life left in you." To Hernán, he said, "We didn't realize the hotel we picked in Montmartre was so historic that it didn't have an elevator. After a day of sightseein' I was wiped. Couldn't keep my gait to handle the stairs on my leg. So David carried me on up!"

David smiled fondly at his husband. "Just carrying you over a threshold would have been so normal and boring."

The glow on Brandon's face pleased Colin. His crush truly over, he was nothing but grateful that Brandon and David had each other.

He couldn't help a glance at Hernán. Would they one day have the same rapport he found so appealing in his friends? It was hard not to let his excitement carry him away. He'd already shared more with Hernán than with any man he'd ever dated before, and he couldn't wait to see where life took them.

With the awkwardness over Brandon's leg resolved, Colin saw that Hernán was able to join in conversation more naturally. They sat in the living room around a marble tray of cheese, prosciutto and slices of baguette. Hernán confessed he spent more time on a treadmill than running because the DC streets still made him sort of nervous.

David immediately invited Hernán to join them on one of their training runs. "We could swing by your condo one morning and take you down to the Mall," he offered. "Colin, you come too."

"I'm not really a runner," Colin tried, but Brandon just laughed.

"Bullshit, buddy. You run up a storm during kickball season. Come on, give it a shot. You might like it."

Reluctantly, Colin agreed to try with them, though he had his doubts he'd enjoy it. Kickball was fun. Running for the sake of running seemed like work.

Dinner was relaxed. Conversation, lubricated by David's excellent wine selection, ranged far and wide. Brandon and David talked about the places they'd gone on their honeymoon. Colin had visited Europe often with his family so he knew many of the same iconic museums and landmarks. He downplayed the experiences, though, to make himself sound like a tourist rather than the guest of wealthy families, celebrities and even nobility who knew his father.

He started to worry they were excluding Hernán, but his boyfriend surprised him.

"I'd love to go to Paris," Hernán said eagerly into a natural pause in the conversation. "I studied French as well as English in school. I loved the cultural lessons about Paris, almost as much as the ones about New York."

"Hernán speaks fluent French, along with his Spanish, English, Nahuatl and Arabic," Colin preened, proud to the point of bursting.

"I'm not at all fluent in Arabic," Hernán muttered.

"You must have been a good student," Brandon said. "I always had trouble sittin' still in school. Barely got my therapy degree."

"I really loved college," Hernán confessed. With a glance at Colin, he ducked his head and said, "I'd like to go back and get a degree someday."

"That's great," Colin said, at the same time Brandon asked, "You didn't get to finish?"

"No. I dropped out," Hernán said. Tentatively, he added, "I was stabbed in El Salvador, and I didn't go back to college after that." Seeing Brandon's stricken expression, it was clear David had told him nothing of Hernán's situation. Hernán volunteered more of his life, including the reason he'd gone to David for legal help. He even mentioned vaguely his journey to cross the border.

Brandon shook his head sadly when Hernán finished. "Those Cuernos dudes sound like bad news. I've seen talk about them in the papers. Do you really think they'd come after you in the States?"

Hernán shrugged and winced. "My uncle thinks they would, to prove a point or to keep up their reputation. How can I really know?"

David brought them back to happier topics, observing, "It sounds like you're a gifted linguist, Hernán. Have you thought about enrolling in a degree program for that? Lots of businesses and government agencies are desperate to hire people with strong language skills, particularly Arabic."

"Huh." Hernán tilted his head and looked at Colin. "I suppose I could look more into that, if I get papers."

"Even before," Colin said. "Most schools will let you enroll regardless of immigration status. You can't get certain benefits like government student loans, but some places reduce tuition in that case."

"Well, the new job I'm doing at your nonprofit is enough for now. But yes. I think I'd like to go back to school some time. Once I'm more comfortable at the center and in my classes, maybe I'll research academic programs."

OVER DINNER, COLIN had to resist the temptation to fist-bump the air. Hernán got along with David and Brandon like they'd always been friends. Brandon's antics with his leg and Hernán's willingness to disclose his past broke the ice so thoroughly broken that it might as well be snow. It was a perfect night, reminding Colin of those few months in his college days when Pranav had gathered friends in Colin's apartment.

Colin ignored a frisson that things would end the same way. No one would take Hernán from him, if he could possibly prevent it.

Walking home afterward, Hernán took his hand. "I feel like I'm in a wonderful dream. This day teaching, talking to Albert and Andrea, dinner with gay men who are married and in love—you can't imagine how far this is from my life in El Salvador."

Colin squeezed his hand. "And you can't imagine how different this is from my life before I knew you. I hung out with Brandon, sure, and sometimes David. But I never felt so much a part of things as I do with you." He looked around happily at the houses and buildings as they walked, part of the pulse of the city.

"Brandon really doesn't know about who you are? I mean, about your family?" Hernán asked.

Colin shook his head slowly. "No, I don't think so. Brandon's been to my condo and flown on my plane, but he seems to assume I'm just kind of successful. He's pretty transparent, so if he's ever googled my family, I think I'd sense it."

"You've told me a few stories about your brother and sister, but not why you keep it all secret from your friends."

"I'm not sure *I* know," Colin admitted. "From my earliest memories, I was embarrassed about who we were. It was fun, though, a lot of the time. I can't deny that. My parents have a house on Nantucket and we spent almost all summer there every year. I had everything I wanted, but it never seemed...important. I didn't want to work in the family's insurance business like my dad and Katherine. I'm not the life of the party like my brother Griff. If I didn't look like my folks, I might have thought I was adopted."

Hernán frowned at him. "You know, what I'm hearing you say is that you didn't fit in with them, and you feel guilty about that."

Colin considered. He nodded. "Yeah, that feels about right, actually."

"No, it's wrong," Hernán said firmly. "They didn't fit in with *you*, I think. They make money, you make other people's lives better. They have a bunch of material things and enjoy them. You value people." He suddenly turned his head away. "Okay, I'm out of line. It's just that I get worked up when it sounds like they might not appreciate you. But that isn't fair because I don't know your family."

"Would you like to?" Colin asked. Hernán glanced at him, puzzled. "My mother has been asking me to come up for a visit. Maybe you'd go with me, next weekend? I'd like them to meet you."

The sidewalk drew Hernán's attention. He muttered, "I don't know." They walked in silence for another block, and then Hernán shot a furtive glance at Colin. "I'm so..."

"What? You're so smart, handsome, kind, driven? Don't be egotistical." Colin grinned widely to make sure Hernán knew he was teasing.

Hernán barked a laugh. "Funny. I was going to say, 'so in love with their son' but now I've changed my mind."

Colin tightened his grip on Hernán's hand and said seriously, "Don't joke about that."

Hernán blushed. "Sorry. What we have is too important to make fun about. But look at me, Colin. Are you sure you're comfortable bringing me to meet your family? I'm a poor, undocumented immigrant."

Colin gaped. "Have I made you think they wouldn't approve of you?" he exclaimed. "Dammit. I drank too much wine. I don't know if I'm supposed to defend my family or reassure you."

Hernán turned red and looked ahead, over the busy DC streets. "I... If your parents said I wasn't right for you, it would be hard to fight them. I understand that."

The tremor in Hernán's voice acted like ice water on Colin, and changed his perception of the simmering tension about a visit. It had nothing to do with Colin's family, and everything to do with Hernán's fears and doubts. The poison his grandmother had injected into his veins made him believe no man would ever really love him.

And maybe he's right to doubt me. Maybe he can sense the ways I failed before, so he knows how risky it is to rely on me.

Colin could think of only one way to put both their hearts at ease. He tugged Hernán to a stop and begged, "Please, angelito. Come meet my family. Let me prove you have nothing to fear."

Hernán put a hand on Colin's cheek. His dark eyes shimmered in the light of the street lamps, but he nodded. "Of course. We'll go next weekend."

THE NEXT FEW days seemed to fly by. Colin listened and provided feedback when Hernán planned out his classes. The time they spent in Colin's office or at the dinner table, talking about lesson plans or ideas to convey tricky idioms, made up some of the happiest hours of Colin's life.

Hernán's enthusiasm for his students and his pride at doing something useful brought out a confidence in him that held Colin spellbound. When he recalled the Hernán who saved him from Provincetown Harbor, with his head down and long hair hiding his face, he couldn't believe it was the same man.

Maryanne teased Colin unmercifully about his puppy dog eyes tracking Hernán through the office, but she was delighted to have Hernán's time and energy as well.

Hernán still resisted seeing a therapist, but Colin hadn't been awoken by Hernán's nightmares since he'd spoken with Albert and Andrea. No doubt there were landmines waiting to be tripped, but Colin proceeded as carefully as he could. In bed he waited for Hernán's lead.

Outside the bedroom, the easy comfort they found in one another seemed to be changing Colin. He was more assertive at work, more decisive about their lobbying strategy and his other projects.

When Maryanne commented approvingly, he spent the next hour in his office considering his behavior. Yes, even he could see the changes, and the reason came to him: he wanted Hernán to be as proud of him as he was of Hernán.

Over the weekend, they went shopping for clothes for Hernán. Temperatures had begun to drop, with the evenings growing almost cold, and the belongings he'd amassed in Provincetown weren't well suited to fall in DC. Colin tried to buy him a new wardrobe, but Hernán refused.

"You pay me a lot for my work at the center, Colin. You won't take money for rent or for food anymore, so I have plenty now. I can pay."

Colin sighed. "I know. It's just I'd rather you save your money for college or something more important than clothes."

Hernán chuckled. "Warm clothes seem pretty important on a chilly day like this."

"Okay," Colin grumbled. "Will you compromise on one thing?" Hernán looked suspicious, but gestured for Colin to continue. "You buy all the practical clothes you need for the fall, but please let me buy you a good suit. I know you won't need it every day, but maybe you'll go on a job interview at some point. Or you'll let me take you to the theater in New York. Or—"

Hernán cut him off firmly. "I'll buy the suit, but you can help me pick it out. It has to be reasonably priced, though. *My* kind of reasonable, not yours."

The guilt Colin felt for pushing a suit on Hernán ended the moment he saw his boyfriend step out of the changing room in a slim-cut, gray pinstriped jacket and trousers. Even before the clothes had been fitted, they clung to Hernán's frame, accentuating his broad shoulders and narrow hips. With his thick dark hair and beard, smoldering eyes and a body that looked poured into his suit, Hernán belonged on the catwalk, not in a classroom. When he saw Colin's open-mouthed awe, he blushed shyly but looked pleased.

Fortunately the clothes could be tailored in time for their trip to New Jersey. Colin had half an idea to take Hernán from Saddle River right to New York City for a night, where they could maybe take in a play.

With each day that passed, Colin grew increasingly certain that Hernán was the man he'd longed for all his life. And he thought—he *hoped*—that Hernán felt the same about him. Colin shouldn't bombard Hernán with the gifts and trips of his own fantasies, but controlling the impulse was difficult.

If a suit was a negotiation, how would Hernán react when he saw how Colin's parents lived?

Chapter 25

AFTER A NICE weekend together, Monday brought a shock to start Colin's day. No sooner had he booted up his computer than Maryanne bustled into his office.

"Sabeen Hassani sent me an email. She says she can't handle the lobbying trip and she wants out."

"Fuck," Colin said, rolling backward in his chair in disappointment. His new-found confidence quavered at the blow. "I thought I had her on-board. I'm sorry, Maryanne. I told you someone else could have done a better—"

"Stop, Colin. It's a setback, not a failure. Get her to come in, or go see her. Try to make her change her mind."

Colin nodded, turned to his computer and sent Sabeen a request to talk more. She finally agreed to come in the afternoon.

Hernán poked his head into Colin's office a little before twelve. "Cariño, do you want to get some lunch?"

Colin looked up at him and shook his head. He heard the frustration in his own voice as he said, "I can't. I'm going over Sabeen's material again to try to figure out how to either change her mind or still get in front of Senator Gerragos."

Hernán sat in his visitor chair. "She dropped out? Well, you were afraid of that." He looked at his hands. "Hey, uh, can I help? Maybe she'd be more confident if she could work with you in her own language."

Colin looked at him, puzzled. Then he got Hernán's meaning. "Oh! Good idea. Is your Arabic enough, do you think?"

Hernán shrugged. "I don't believe I could translate complicated ideas, but I know enough to handle every-day conversation. Let's give it a try."

"She's due in around three. Is your class over by then?" Hernán nodded, and Colin closed his manila folder. "It's a plan. Maybe I've got time for lunch after all."

Shortly after three, Hernán joined Colin and Sabeen in a conference room. Sabeen appeared to be in her mid-thirties, with dark eyes and brows. Her hijab was turquoise in color. Hernán introduced himself in halting Arabic, and she gave him a smile and a greeting in return.

Colin explained that Hernán would try to translate if anything was unclear to Sabeen. They spent the next hour together. A few times, when Hernán hesitated or stammered, Sabeen lowered her head and shyly helped him seek a word or phrase in Arabic.

With Hernán's help, Colin explained how important her story was to their mission, and impressed the fact she would only be talking to a few people at a time.

"It isn't a big public gathering?" she asked through Hernán. "Like those meetings at the United Nations I see on television?"

"No," Colin assured her. "It would be four or five people at most, plus our group. You would only have to talk to them for a little while, to tell them your story and answer a few questions maybe."

"Ah. I didn't understand before," she said. They discussed the project some more, with Colin impressing upon Sabeen that the legislation they were working to defeat would make it harder for people like her to find safety in the United States.

Finally she nodded. "All right. You have persuaded me. I will do it."

Colin gave a relieved sigh, and threw a big smile to Hernán. "Great. Let's go over your story again. You know we want you to tell it in English, but with Hernán's help we can try to make sure everything is clear. Then we can practice some questions you might get."

<<Will you be there with us?>> Sabeen asked Hernán in Arabic.

When he translated, Colin nodded thoughtfully. "That's a good idea, so we're ready if there are any questions we didn't anticipate. If you're willing, I'll clear it with Maryanne."

"Of course," Hernán answered immediately. "Just let me know exactly when so I can make adjustments or get coverage for my ESL classes."

After Sabeen had practiced, she left with a list of possible questions and answers in English and Arabic to study. Colin immediately took

Hernán into Maryanne's office to explain their plan.

She was delighted. "See, Hernán? I told you even some Arabic would be useful. And good job, Colin, on changing her mind."

"It was really Hernán—" he began, but Hernán cut him off.

"Your words convinced her, Colin. I just translated for you."

"I knew you could do this," Maryanne said smugly to Colin. "You're going to kick ass up on the Hill this week."

THE MORNING OF the visit to Capitol Hill was also when David and Brandon arranged to take Hernán and Colin running with them. Colin would have begged off but he knew Hernán was still uncertain around new people. A run would help distract Colin from worries about his lobbying mission as well, so he rose at the ungodly hour of six a.m. to put on shorts, a long-sleeved, wicking shirt and his running shoes.

They met in front of Colin's building. When David and Brandon jogged around the corner and came to a stop, neither of them had even broken a sweat. Their enthusiastic greeting made Colin mutter, "Save me from morning people."

Brandon punched him in the arm. "We'll keep the run reasonable. Promise. David 'n I figured two miles for your first time would get the blood pumpin'. Y'all will be back for coffee before you know it."

They set off toward the Mall at an easy pace. Brandon ran next to Hernán while David stayed near Colin, a half-block behind. Ten minutes into the run, Colin gasped, "Go on, David. Leave me and save yourself!"

David chuckled. "You're doing fine, Colin. I like to run but Brandon is a lot faster even with the prosthesis. Hernán is keeping up with him and that takes some pressure off us."

"What do you think of Hernán's chance for getting asylum?" Colin managed to ask.

"A lot of it can depend on which immigration officer hears the matter," David admitted in a conversational tone, as if they were standing around a water cooler instead of destroying their bodies on a hell-run. "I'm sorry to say there are a few homophobes in there who resist granting asylum when the application is based on sexual orientation. Don't worry about it much, though. As I said, there's a second bite at the apple before an immigration judge if we get one of the bad officers."

Soon after, they completed a loop back to the condo building. Hernán looked flushed and excited. Colin wanted to die, but happily watched Brandon cajole Hernán into trying a longer run.

"You handled this easily. You could probably do a marathon with no more trainin'."

Hernán grinned. "Well, I doubt it, but I would like to run on the streets and paths more. It's so much more interesting than the basement of our building." He glanced hopefully at Colin.

"Oh no," Colin exclaimed. "Leave me out of your masochism. I said I'd try it but this isn't for me. Kickball any day!"

Laughing, Brandon and David made plans for Hernán to join them again the next morning. They ran off to keep training while Colin and Hernán visited a nearby Starbucks for coffee.

As Hernán added sugar to his drink, he bumped his shoulder into Colin's. "Running wasn't really so bad, was it?"

"It wasn't terrible but I'm not a convert."

"You aren't wiped out, though, are you?" Hernán asked, lifting an eyebrow.

Colin's heart began to flutter. His mouth went dry but he answered, "Not wiped. Why? What are you thinking?"

Hernán sipped his coffee and gave Colin a wink. "Well," he drawled. "We're up earlier than usual. The blood is pumping. We don't have to be at the center for a few hours yet. Maybe…"

Colin swallowed hard. "You'd better not be teasing me, Nán." He could feel himself chubbing up already. The thin liner in his running shorts would do absolutely nothing to hide the erection threatening to grow.

"I'm not. Based on what Chris said, and how long you've been taking, uh…" He trailed off to look around the coffee shop. No one was near. "Anyway, I had a really dirty dream about you last night. I want to see if it feels as good awake."

They stepped out of the coffee shop and began walking toward the condo building. By that time of morning, pedestrian traffic began to fill the sidewalk with go-getters hustling to work. Colin rested a hand on Hernán's waist and whispered fiercely, "You are downright wicked. You have to walk in front of me now. These shorts show exactly how much I like where your mind is—"

"Colin!" Despite the morning traffic noises, the voice that called his name sounded familiar. Colin turned, dropping his hand from Hernán and already tensing.

Ethan Schinderman hurried up the sidewalk toward him. Colin hadn't seen him since their kickball season ended in July. Ethan had been heavy as long as Colin knew him, but he'd apparently lost a significant amount of weight in the past months. The suit Ethan wore seemed to droop around him. His face was gaunt.

"Ethan," Colin said cautiously. "I'm surprised to see you here."

Ethan came to a stop and peered up at Colin. His bushy brown hair was partially tamed, but he wore the same thick glasses that tended to slip down his nose. Dark smudges under his eyes showed through the lenses.

Whatever was going on with Ethan's appearance didn't seem to affect his smug tone. "I changed jobs two months ago. Lambda Law Fund was a dead end for me. I work at the George Washington University law school now, in one of the legal clinics."

"That's great," Colin said politely. "I remember you weren't happy at the Law Fund."

Ethan's gaze swept over Colin in his athletic clothes, passing over Hernán initially. Then his attention snapped back. Colin saw his eyes widen.

With one finger Ethan pushed his glasses back into place. "Well," he said breathily. "Is this your latest recruit to the team?"

Colin ignored the question. "This is Ethan Schinderman," he said to Hernán, his tone as remote as he'd use in a professional meeting. "We play kickball on a league together sometimes."

Ethan gave a slow, sly grin. "Hernán, you say. I love your name."

"Thank you," Hernán answered cautiously. "It's nice to meet you."

"So, have you played kickball before?" Ethan asked. "You look like you'd be a natural."

"Uh, kickball?" Hernán said to Colin, uncertainty in his voice. "Is it like football? I mean soccer?"

Ethan didn't let up. "Oh, there's a great gay soccer league. I mean, assuming you're gay…" His voice trailed off, though his lip curled slightly at one side. Hernán flushed, giving answer enough. "I play volleyball, too, in the spring. Colin never got involved with that team, though. If you're interested I'd be happy to introduce you to the group I play with."

Colin interjected, "I'm sorry to run, Ethan, but we've got to get ready to head up to the Hill."

"Oh? What are you lobbying for today?" Ethan asked.

Colin answered, "The usual immigration issues" at the same time Hernán volunteered, "Asylum." He stopped immediately when he realized he'd spoken over Colin, and blushed.

"Immigration," Colin said again, hoping Ethan would drop it.

Ethan's eyes took on a calculating look. When they'd been friends, Colin usually ignored it as nothing more than a sign of mischief. He'd come to recognize—too late—that the look was a warning he should heed. It meant Ethan sensed something going on he wanted to unravel, either to satisfy his own curiosity or, more often, to stir up shit.

"Hernán, are you an asylum seeker?" Ethan asked.

"This isn't appropriate to discuss," Colin interjected awkwardly before Hernán could answer. "We really have to go. Good to see you again, Ethan. Best of luck with the new job."

Ethan wouldn't take the hint. His lips curled slightly. "You know, Colin, you've avoided me since we stopped dating."

Hernán's eyebrows went up.

Shit, Colin thought. *I should have expected this.* Aloud, he said, "Come on, Ethan. We went out one time more than a year ago. That's hardly dating."

The comment was for Hernán's benefit, but Ethan flared his nostrils. He flicked a glance back and forth between Colin's burning face and Hernán's pale one.

Ethan's smile stretched wider. "So sad, Hernán," he said. "We all used to be so close. Colin. Me. Tom. Scott. Brandon." Ethan rattled off names of teammates, but his eyes glinted at Hernán's flinch. He'd scored a hit with Brandon's name. "Then Brandon got involved with someone, Johnny and Scott broke up, and Colin…" He threw a glance Colin's way. "Well, he pined for Brandon for such a long time."

Hernán's remaining color drained.

Colin tried to keep his tone civil. "Ethan, you're perfectly aware Brandon and I are just friends. He's happily married to David now." It was a little bitchy of him to say, because of the torch Ethan had carried.

Not to be outdone, Ethan nodded. "I heard. That must have been tough, Colin. I know the two of you dated."

Double shit. He hadn't seen a reason to discuss that with Hernán.

Did he mention it, the first night in Provincetown when he was drunk? He couldn't recall. In any case, Ethan made it sound like a big deal and Hernán would probably wonder why Colin kept it from him. Through clenched teeth, he said, "We went out just a few times. Really more as friends than anything."

He frowned. "But how did you know about it?"

Ethan shrugged, his eyes on Hernán. He clearly scented blood. "Hernán, you should have seen our friend Brandon. Just gorgeous, with the sweetest Texan accent you ever heard."

Colin opened his mouth to bark at Ethan, but Hernán spoke first. "Actually I know Brandon. We had dinner with him and David recently. Very nice couple." He stuck his hands casually into the pockets of his running shorts. "Colin, should we be heading home to get ready for work?"

Ethan deflated, and Colin permitted himself a silent cheer for the way Hernán handled him. "Yes, you're right. Ethan, take care." He put a hand on Hernán's back to usher him away toward their building.

He risked a quick glance back at Ethan, only to see him lowering his cell phone and slipping it into his coat pocket.

HERNÁN LED THE way back to their apartment. Once inside, Colin stopped him with a hand on his arm. "Hey, about the shit Ethan said—"

"Don't worry about it. I could tell he was just trying for a reaction." Hernán shrugged. "So he likes my boyfriend. I can deal with some competition."

Colin laughed. "Believe me, there's no competition there." He sobered slightly and said earnestly. "Or with Brandon. You know that, right?"

Hernán smiled slyly. "Yes, I believe you. But just in case *you* have any doubts, I'd be happy to re-enact my dream…?"

Colin all but dragged him up to the bedroom, both laughing all the way. As Hernán pulled off his running shirt, he sniffed his pits. "Should we take a shower?"

"Nuh huh," Colin said as he frantically removed his shoes and socks. "I love the way you smell when you've been working out."

He dropped his shorts and shirt before joining Hernán in the middle of the bed. Their bodies were a little ripe but it just turned Colin on even more. His cock jutted forward, hard as a bone. It slid tantalizingly over the smooth skin of Hernán's hip as he rolled his lover over and on top of him.

Arms wrapped around each other, bodies fitted together, they kissed like the first time. Colin broke away to ask, "Can I suck you, Hernán? Do you feel okay about that?"

Hernán nodded and then gave a small smile. "I'll show you how my dream started." He swung his body around so that his beautifully thick cock was near Colin's mouth and his lips were inches away from Colin's erection. He grasped the base with one hand and took Colin's sac in the other. "I still may not be very good at this, but I've been thinking about it a lot since the first time we tried."

"Oh my God," Colin moaned, shivering as Hernán took him into his mouth. He was a little uncertain with Colin's dick, a little awkward with teeth and lips, but in no time he seemed to have solved the important problems. He figured out that Colin loved it when he swiped the tip of his tongue just beneath the head. He couldn't take more than a few inches into his mouth, but he worked the rest with his fist and sucked as much cock as he could.

At an especially loud groan, Hernán raised his head. "Sounds like I'm onto something here."

He went down again. The wet swirl of Hernán's tongue over the head of his dick went right up Colin's spine to make him open his mouth and suck Hernán in deeply. The precome leaking from its folds or foreskin tasted salty and sweet, and he dug his tongue in to lap up more.

The circuit closed as each man sucked the other, pleasure zipping between Colin's dick and his mouth. The heft of a meaty cock against his tongue, burrowing toward his throat, turned Colin on so much that he grasped Hernán's ass cheeks with both hands to pull him in even deeper. He choked slightly, pulled back, and dove forward again until the head pressed into his throat.

He desperately wanted to feel Hernán lose control and shoot in his mouth. The PrEP he was on and his own research convinced him he had nothing to fear from swallowing Hernán's seed.

Hernán's lips and tongue were too good. In less than a minute Colin put a hand on his head to still him. "I'm going to come if we don't stop." Hernán held his eyes as he gave one more long, depraved lick from the base of Colin's cock to its head.

"I want that," he said wickedly. "I'm going to taste you and drink you down. But not quite yet." Hernán reached into the bedside drawer to pull out Bluebeard and the bottle of lube. "This was part of my dream too."

He popped open the lube and drizzled some on the dildo and on his fingers. He swallowed Colin down again as his fingers stroked over Colin's hole. He pushed two fingers inside, making Colin tremble before he pulled off his cock with a gasp.

Colin locked eyes with him as he pulled Hernán's dick toward him again and resumed his oral assault. The sweet juices leaking into his mouth made him ravenous for more. The half-lidded dark gaze of his lover inspired him, and he silently asked permission as his fingertips crept closer to Hernán's crease. Hernán inhaled sharply, but nodded. Colin did nothing more than brush over Hernán's opening, teasing the surface even as he drew Hernán's dick into his throat.

When he closed his eyes to concentrate on bringing Hernán pleasure, he felt the cool head of the dildo against his asshole. Hernán's mouth was on his dick again as he slid Bluebeard inside, torturing Colin with his lips and his tongue and the toy.

Colin moaned around the dick in his mouth as the chilly, slick silicone entered his body. Hernán knew how he liked it, what he could take, how fast… In seconds, Hernán was fucking him hard with the dildo while he sucked with greater abandon, excitement helping him to take Colin deeper down his throat. The pressure in his ass, the wet warmth around his dick, the glorious cock in his mouth and the fiery blaze of Hernán's body pressed against his sent Colin quickly to the top.

Hernán, too apparently, because he stopped sucking Colin to say hoarsely, "I'm about to come. You should stop." Colin shook his head as well as he could with a stuffed throat, and stroked more determinedly with his fingers along Hernán's backside. Hernán groaned and took Colin back into his mouth, licking and sucking frantically on the top few inches as he mauled Colin's ass with Bluebeard.

Soon he spasmed and gave a muffled cry. Colin's taste buds watered at the spurts of creamy, salty, mineral fluid blasting into his mouth. It sent him spiraling over the edge as he came. Hernán stilled the dildo and swallowed what Colin gave him.

They both sagged onto the bed. Hernán carefully pulled the toy from Colin's ass, but Colin refused to release the dick in his mouth. He kept nursing gently as Hernán softened, letting him down slowly from his orgasm until Hernán put a hand on the side of his face. He withdrew his dick gently and turned his body around so they were face to face. His eyes were wet, though whether from tears or from the cock that had been buried in his throat, Colin couldn't tell.

Lips swollen and red, he met Colin in a blistering kiss. He let Colin use his tongue to probe and taste, and then he did the same. Colin's ass throbbed pleasantly from the dildo and his cock tingled with aftershocks as the kiss went on and on.

Eventually Hernán broke away long enough to glance at a clock. He grimaced but said, "We should start getting ready soon."

Colin sagged bonelessly. "I know you're right, but I really wish we could stay right here."

Hernán gave him a concerned look. "I don't know how I feel about coming in your mouth like that."

"Did it feel good for you?" Colin asked, and Hernán nodded. "I loved it. You taste wonderful. Between the Truvada and your low viral load, it's really fine."

Despite Hernán's concern, he returned a shy smile. "You taste great too. Your dick got so hard when I fucked you with Bluebeard while I was sucking. It made me feel powerful."

"Was it really okay, what I did with my fingers?" Colin asked, suddenly aware that he had risked triggering some reaction in Hernán.

"It was. There was a moment when I got a little scared, but I just said to myself, 'It's Colin.' Then I was fine."

"Maybe… Before we get any more adventurous, I think we should talk about things. I mean, what you're okay with, what makes you nervous, how I'd know if you're uncomfortable with something. You know?"

"That makes sense." Hernán kissed him. "But not now. Your mission awaits."

AS THEY FINISHED their showers and were dressing, Hernán unzipped the black cloth bag containing his new suit. "It was so lucky that the alterations were ready in time," Hernán said, excited as he tugged on the elegant pants. Colin stood behind Hernán, facing a mirror over his shoulder and helping him to knot his necktie. Hernán leaned back against Colin as he took over to pull the triangle of material snug.

Colin held up the suit jacket for Hernán to slip on, and then rested a hand on his shoulder. "You're gorgeous, Nán," he whispered to his boyfriend facing him in the mirror. "Better than Andrés Montiel on *Club de Cuervos.*"

Hernán laughed. "I've created a monster. You're addicted to the show, aren't you?"

"Guilty," Colin admitted as he donned his own dress shirt and tie.

He turned to face Hernán and shook out the nervousness in his hands. "This is it. All the planning, and now I'm leading a group up to Capitol Hill."

Hernán put his hands on Colin's face. "You'll do great, corazón. You know every word of what you need to say, and the team trusts you completely. You're going to kick so much ass they'll be wiping it off the interior of the capitol dome for days."

Colin exhaled heavily. "I'm glad you're going to be there with me. And not just for Sabeen."

"I love you. I believe in you. And after you crush it today, I'm going to show you how my dream ended."

Chapter 26

SIX HOURS LATER, Colin and Hernán collapsed onto chairs in Maryanne's office. She squealed. "It went great, didn't it? I can tell from your faces."

Colin loosened his tie and nodded. "Everything went smoothly. The whole team was ready, and everybody had their shit down cold. Sabeen needed Hernán's help on a few questions from this one prick of an aide to Senator Gerragos, but she kept calm. I was so proud of them."

Hernán swatted him lightly on the arm. "Don't be so modest. You were the one who set the tone and controlled each meeting. I had no idea what to expect, but you were amazing to watch in action. I was so proud."

Colin blushed fiercely as Maryanne cackled. "See? I knew you'd be fantastic once we got you out of your office," she gloated. "Now go through it for me step by step."

Hernán excused himself to check on his class materials for the next morning, while Colin launched into a detailed discussion of the mission. Even down the hall from Maryanne's office, he could hear the excitement and confidence in Colin's tone as they discussed each senator and congressperson on the agenda.

The debriefing went on and on, to Hernán's amusement. He brought his teaching guide into Maryanne's office and sat on a small sofa in the corner as they went over every nuance of every question from the staff members and aides.

Colin's hands flew around as he praised each team member's performance, slammed a bigoted congresswoman for her remarks about terrorism, and described how one senator agreed to take a fresh look at his support for the immigration bill in light of the stories he'd heard that day.

They finally adjourned from the office to have dinner together, Maryanne and Colin still deep in their post-mortem. The excitement in Colin's voice, the sparkle in his eyes, and the fire Hernán could see in him were alluring. Watching his impassioned boyfriend began to affect Hernán. He shifted to keep his half-erection from becoming too noticeable in his new suit pants.

When their entrees were served, their conversation came to a pause while they began to eat. Hernán jumped into the silence. "Colin, have you ever thought about running for office yourself?"

Colin froze with a fork halfway to his mouth, eyes round. Maryanne took the question seriously, and leaned in.

"That's actually a great idea, Colin. You're passionate, personable, smart, connected. Think of what you might eventually be able to achieve on immigration issues from inside Congress."

"That's ridiculous," Colin murmured, lowering his fork and staring at the plate. "I'm nobody special."

"Oh cariño," Hernán protested. "That's just not true. You're incredibly special."

"I'm not saying you should form an exploratory committee tomorrow," Maryanne added. "But think about it for a while. Let the idea percolate. Use that brain of yours to examine the path various people took into office."

Colin looked back and forth between the two of them, shyness and fear warring in his eyes. "You're not making fun of me, are you?" he asked softly.

Maryanne made a sound of protest, and Hernán took his hand. He said firmly, "I'd never make fun of you. You're my warrior, Colin. You have so much to give. Just think about what giants you'd like to slay next."

Colin nervously changed the subject, bringing the conversation back to the lobbying visit. Even that topic ran dry by the time dessert arrived, and Maryanne asked Hernán questions about himself. As much as he liked her company, though, he didn't feel ready to tell the woman in charge of his unofficial place of employment too many personal details. They chatted about life in El Salvador, but Hernán stayed far away from any mention of Cuernos or his immigration status.

Colin grabbed the check when the meal ended. It made Hernán uncomfortable as always, but Maryanne just shrugged as she pulled on her coat. "He always does that, Hernán. I gave up fighting over checks a year ago."

"I wish you'd learn that lesson," Colin murmured to Hernán with a smile. Hernán looked pointedly at the suit jacket he was pulling on at the moment, and Colin laughed. "Okay, you're making progress."

"I want you to take tomorrow off, Colin," Maryanne said before they parted. "You worked so hard on that lobbying visit you deserve it." To Hernán, she said with a faux-frown, "Not you, though. Your ESL classes are in high demand."

"You get that he's a volunteer, right?" Colin asked. "Besides, I'm taking him to meet my parents this weekend."

"Oh shit," Maryanne breathed. "I met your mother that time she came to DC and hosted our fundraiser. Scary as fuck!"

"Stop it," Colin laughed. "You're just trying to freak Hernán out."

"Is it working?" she asked Hernán with a wink.

"Yes, but I'm still going to New Jersey tomorrow afternoon," he said, slipping a hand into Colin's. "My ESL classes are at ten and one tomorrow. I'll be there."

BACK IN THEIR apartment, Colin hung up their coats and then pulled Hernán into a kiss. "Thank you again," he said in a low voice. "I was scared as shit that I'd fuck up this whole Hill visit. Having you there with me meant the world."

The taste of wine on Colin's tongue made Hernán's cock stir again. "You would have been just fine without me. But if I can help you in any way, I want to do it," Hernán said. He pulled Colin closer, pressing their bodies together to make sure Colin could feel his growing arousal. "Now, warrior, I think we're due a conversation of our own."

They both changed out of their suits and into loose pants and T-shirts, and then settled on the bed in Colin's room.

Hernán started, thoughtful despite his eagerness. He knew what he wanted that night, but Colin was right to be cautious. "What you said this morning, about talking before we try new stuff. It makes sense."

He paused, staring down the bed at his toes. "I haven't run into any situation with you that upsets me or scares me. I did get nervous for a moment when you touched my ass today. All I had to do was remind myself it was you, and everything was fine."

Colin said slowly, "I remember when we kissed that first time, and

I wasn't careful enough. I scared you that night, when you felt me get excited."

"Well, true," Hernán agreed. He twisted his lower lip as he recalled his panic at the feel of Colin's erection pressing into his side. "I realize it wasn't that long ago, but in some ways it feels like it's been months."

Their eyes met again. "I know you so much better now. I know I can trust you. More than that, I know how happy you make me. I always had an idea that sex was this big secret thing. Shameful, furtive, embarrassing. It helps that you've showed me it's the most natural thing in the world. It's just so much fun!"

Colin smiled and kissed him. "It is, with you. Honestly, sex has never been like this for me before. Maybe I was too needy or insecure or inexperienced. I don't know. But when we're together, I can give in to my fantasies or do crazy things and just be in the moment. Even laughing with you makes it all so much sexier. When I hear you laugh, I know you're enjoying it and not afraid."

"Even when I'm not laughing, you have to know that I love everything we do together. Right?"

Colin nodded. "I believe you. Sometimes when I'm holding you or looking into your eyes, I get so emotional I couldn't laugh if a clown ran through the room."

"Please tell me you don't fantasize about a clown threesome," Hernán said with a wide grin. "I'd do it if you really wanted, but I think Jesse and Paul would get jealous."

Colin chuckled, nuzzling the side of Hernán's head with his nose. "No threesome. Gotcha."

Hernán turned serious. His dream from the night before, their shared pleasure before work, his hunger for Colin as they sat through dinner all pooled in his belly. The heat he felt inside and the rush of blood in his ears told him that it was time.

He said in a low voice, "There is something I want, though. Before you say anything, I've thought it through. I think I'm ready for this, and if I'm wrong, I know you'll stop."

Colin's mouth had dropped into an O of surprise already, and Hernán nodded. "I want to feel you inside me."

Colin made a low, throaty sound as he slowly ran a hand down Hernán's neck and over his T-shirt. The flush of desire creeping up his throat told Hernán that Colin had thought about it too, and wanted him.

"That's what happened next in my dream," Hernán whispered. "You made love to me. Will you do that for me, Colin? Will you love me?"

COLIN'S DICK PULSED in time with his racing heart. Would he love Hernán? With every fiber of his body. The laughter was gone, and Colin felt the weight of responsibility. Hernán trusted him with the most intimate act two men could share. It had been *forced* on him before with violence, yet he wanted to share himself with Colin. In love.

The pressure Colin felt did nothing to douse his passion. As Hernán tugged off his shirt and pants, he felt himself leaking already. He stripped quickly and then lay back, arms open for Hernán to come to him.

The bed dipped under Hernán's weight as he crawled across the comforter toward Colin and lay on top of him. His muscled, sculpted body lowered to meet Colin's chest, firing his blood. Hernán kept his eyes open as he moved in for a kiss. Colin brushed a lock of hair off his forehead, and then put his hand around the back of Hernán's head to tug him down.

Hernán was wrapped in his arms, his smooth skin gliding against Colin's as they embraced. His thick cock pressed between their bodies, slick and leaking every bit as much as Colin's. Their lips brushed, the tip of Hernán's tongue stroked, and then Colin was lost to desire.

Still, he had to check again. "You're sure, Nán? You know I have everything I need already. You don't have to—"

"I want you inside me," Hernán interrupted. "I've been thinking about it a lot, and my dream last night..." He shivered. "I *need* it, Colin. Um, there's one thing."

"Yes?"

"It's, uh, your choice. Whether we use anything. A condom." Hernán blushed adorably.

Colin's dick surged to full hardness and flexed automatically as the thought of being bare inside a man for the first time in his life hit Colin right in the balls. He almost came from the idea alone. How was he going to hold off long enough to make love to Hernán the way he deserved?

Colin heard the excitement in his own voice when he responded. "Then I choose not to. With everything Chris told us, I'm not worried at all. Are you okay with that?"

Hernán nodded, his eyes burning. Despite his nervousness, he seemed to want it raw as much as Colin did. "That's what I think about," he whispered. "You sliding up inside me, filling me when you come."

Colin shuddered and grabbed the base of his dick tightly, squeezing to hold off his orgasm. His voice trembled as he said, "Roll over and lie back now. If you want me to stop at any point, just say so. Okay?"

Although Hernán had asked to be penetrated, his jaw went tight as he repositioned himself. Still, he nodded agreement at Colin's words and braced his feet apart to raise his knees. He wanted Colin, but he seemed slightly afraid at the same time.

Colin needed to be worthy of the trust placed in him. The best way he could repay it was make Hernán wild before he entered. He retrieved the bottle of lube from his drawer, and then spontaneously reached back in to grab his slenderest dildo. Dropping the toy within easy reach, he popped the cap on the bottle to pour liquid onto his fingers.

After tossing the bottle aside, he slid up along Hernán's body for a kiss while his long arm reached down. Slick fingers stroked between Hernán's legs. Hernán moaned softly against his mouth when Colin glided fingers across Hernán's smooth balls, down between his legs, and into the crevice between his cheeks.

He found the tight ring and rubbed in small, light circles around the rim until he sensed it relax underneath his touch. Pressing his tongue firmly into Hernán's mouth, he worked his middle finger into Hernán's ass. The velvet texture and heat inside sucked him in. Within moments, he began carefully fucking in and out. His long arms allowed him to keep kissing Hernán, even as his finger probed and searched for… There it was.

Hernán gasped when Colin found his prostate and stroked over it. His cock released a dollop of clear fluid between their bodies that Colin longed to lap up, except he was fully occupied already. They kept kissing, the heat of it rising to molten levels when Colin slipped in a second finger and renewed the prostate massage.

Hernán thrust against the invading hand as he gripped Colin by the hair and pulled his head back. Nostrils flaring, pupils blown wide, he gazed up at Colin in wonder. "More. I can take more."

Colin freed himself long enough to pick up the narrow silicone cock. Yellow and pink, its colors twisted like a candy-cane up to its lightly-flared head.

Hernán growled low when he saw it. "Who's this one? I don't believe we've used him before."

Colin winked. "Meet Ronald. He kind of reminds me of a clown."

"Oh no, is this the threesome after all?" Hernán chuckled as he reached to tug on Colin's cock, his strokes eased by the precome leaking copiously from its slit.

Colin rested the head of Ronald against Hernán's opening and wrapped his slippery hand around Hernán's thick erection. He slid up and then back down, tugging Hernán's foreskin tight at the same time he pressed Ronald inside.

"Aaaah," Hernán groaned, his back arching to thrust his dick up into Colin's hands. "So strange. So good." Colin twisted the toy around as he worked in a few more inches, all the while stroking Hernán's cock.

In moments, Hernán's hand shot out to still Colin's. "Too close." Colin withdrew Ronald and tossed it aside, and then shifted around again to position himself between raised knees. There was Hernán's hole, exposed and hairless, shiny with lube and a little puffy.

Hernán grabbed himself and squeezed Colin's sides with his thighs. "Come here, lindo. I have to feel you inside. Right now."

Colin's cock jutted up hard and red, glistening at the tip from his excitement. He poured more lube into his hand and made a show of sliding his palm over and around his erection, hissing when his fingers trailed over the corona. Hernán's eyes, heavy-lidded in lust, watched his dick hungrily. Colin swiped more lube over his hole and tested whether it was open enough.

"No more," Hernán said in a voice that sounded drugged. "You. I need you." He reached to pull Colin down, cradling him. Colin raised Hernán's legs to rest over his shoulders, and the head of his dick brushed against Hernán's asshole.

They kissed again as Colin slowly penetrated him. Hernán's body yielded while Colin sank in millimeter by millimeter. He sucked in a shuddering breath as Hernán engulfed his cock, drawing him down a tight, caressing, warm tunnel.

Colin was thunderstruck by sensation. He was bare inside his lover. The enormous, monumental fact of Hernán sharing himself so completely made him want to cry his joy aloud.

"Aah," Hernán hissed slightly as Colin slid deeper. He pulled back just enough to meet Colin's eyes, lips slightly parted.

"There we are," Colin said on a sigh as his pubic bone met Hernán's ass. "I'm all the way inside you."

Hernán nodded and his eyes shimmered. "Inside me," he echoed. "Inside…here." He freed an arm to tap on his chest, above his heart. Colin grasped that hand and kissed his fingertips. He pressed further inside, and then withdrew slightly. As he sank in again, he said, "I love you so much, Hernán." His own eyes began to burn. Hernán blurred before him. "Does it feel good?"

Hernán nodded. He tried to speak but seemed unable. Colin thrust again, picking up the speed, lengthening his strokes. Hernán tried again and rasped, "It feels better than good. Amazing. I love you."

The passion and lust between them built as Colin repositioned their bodies. Dropping Hernán's legs to hold in his crooked elbows, he raised himself to fuck at a new angle. He could tell he was hitting Hernán's prostate with the head of his cock from the glazed look in Hernán's eye and the huffs he made at each thrust.

Colin freed one hand to wrap around Hernán's wet and slippery cock, glazed with the precome that Colin's fuck forced out of it. Shifting again, he plunged deeply inside, holding there as Hernán squeezed the walls of his rectum around Colin's dick.

"Almost there," Colin choked out as he began to piston in and out of Hernán, faster and faster.

Hernán gripped Colin's biceps. "Come inside me," he gritted out. "Pure sweet come. I need it." He all but screamed then, as his own cock started to pulse between their bodies. Hot cream flooded their bellies, trapped between them by Colin's grinding hips.

The wonderful smell of Hernán's seed, the slick warmth between them, and the tight sheath pulsing around his spike of a cock sent Colin soaring over the cliff too. He poured himself into Hernán, gasping and cursing as what felt like a year's worth of come emptied his balls.

Pleasure kept Colin's cock hard and twitching when he collapsed. He claimed Hernán's mouth again as he fell forward with a cry, sweeping his tongue over Hernán's lips and stroking the roof of his mouth.

Hernán tightened his grip around Colin's back and rolled his hips up even more, as if to keep Colin inside. He squeezed his eyes tightly shut and Colin raised his head, full of concern. Hernán began to tremble beneath him.

"¿Mi ángel?" Colin asked softly. He tried to pull out but Hernán clutched him more tightly. He clenched his ass again and again, milking Colin's buried cock. Suddenly Hernán burst into tears.

"Oh no. Oh Hernán, I'm sorry. What did I do?" Colin begged.

Hernán shook his head back and forth desperately. "Nothing wrong," he choked out. "It feels so good. Colin, I love you."

Colin had no idea what to do except let Hernán cling to him. He kissed at the tears leaking from tightly closed eyelids, and nuzzled Hernán's ear. Despite Hernán's best efforts, his spent cock slipped out of Hernán's ass. He rearranged their bodies so they lay pressed together.

Hernán sobbed into his shoulder while Colin stroked his hair. "I'm sorry for crying," he gasped. "Nothing is wrong, I swear. Just…overwhelmed."

"Me too, Nán. I didn't know it could be like that."

Hernán nodded his buried head. The sobs quieted and stopped, and he gradually relaxed and softened in Colin's embrace.

When he opened his eyes finally, Colin kissed the tears from his eyelashes. "¿Angelito?" he asked again, tentatively.

Hernán quivered. "I'm fine. Promise."

"Do you want to talk about it?"

"It was just so good. Everything we've done together is wonderful, but this was so… I don't even know. *More.*"

Colin nodded. "For me too." He hesitated, but he needed to know. "What you said, about pure sweet come." Hernán tried to bury his head again but Colin stopped him with a finger on his chin. "Please. Tell me."

A long moment stretched before Hernán murmured his answer. "I've felt so dirty ever since I got the diagnosis. This black thing is growing inside me. And I've been worried I'm not giving enough back to you. Pleasure, I mean."

"Hernán—"

He put a finger to Colin's lips to cut him off. "When you didn't even hesitate about entering me, it was like this switch went off. You want me, even with this in my blood. Not just a pretty boy. Not a body. Me."

"I do," Colin said earnestly. "Just you. Always you."

Hernán nodded. "While you were inside me, I felt so right. What you give me isn't money or shelter or medicine or a job. You give me *you*. All that stuff just comes along with it. When I got that..." He hid again. "It's going to sound so childish."

"I need to hear it. Please, Hernán."

"Everything you do is love. You light up my body when you touch me. It's as if you're erasing the bad things that happened to me. No, not erasing, *Replacing*. I wanted your come, Colin. I wanted your essence to drown out the poison Lonnie left behind. I could *see* it when you came—this light pouring into me."

"That doesn't sound childish. That's beautiful." He kissed Hernán's lips. "You're so beautiful."

"I think you are too. My Colin."

Colin nodded because his throat was tight. "Yours," he got out.

Chapter 27

FRIDAY MORNING COLIN stretched in bed. He'd woken briefly when Hernán rose to run with Brandon and David. The spot next to him was still empty when he stirred again, but the shower was on. Minutes later, Hernán came into the bedroom, drying himself vigorously.

Colin held out his arms. "Come back to me."

Hernán laughed as he ran the towel over his legs. The vision of his tight body, gleaming from the shower and backlit by the bathroom lights, went straight to Colin's dick. He threw off the covers to expose himself and to get Hernán interested.

"Stop that," Hernán laughed. "You may have the day off but I have an ESL class scheduled for ten."

"That isn't for...," Colin glanced at the bedside clock. "Another two hours."

Hernán sat on the edge of the bed, leaned down and kissed Colin soundly. He twined his fingers through Colin's hair and pressed their foreheads together. "I'm a little sore from your 'inauguration' last night," he murmured with a smile.

"So good," Colin said with a shiver. "But even with that off the menu, you've taught me a lot of other wicked things. Like when you pushed Bluebeard inside me in the morning while you—"

"Stop!" Hernán demanded with a wink. "Your wiles won't work on me today, villain. I have students to teach. I didn't get to finish preparing my lesson yesterday." He stroked Colin's hard cock twice with a twisting motion that elicited a gasp. "Save this for me. Are we still going to New Jersey?"

"Absolutely," Colin said. "Well, let me check the weather to make sure it's good for flying. But unless a storm has popped up, we'll head out as soon as you wrap things today."

Hernán gnawed on his lip. "Do you think your parents will like me?"

"I think they're going to love you. We'll have a great time, I promise. Remind me when your last class ends?"

"I should finish by two."

"Perfect. I'll pick you up at the center and we'll head right to the airport. Just throw together a few clothes for the weekend before you go."

Hernán leaned in for another kiss, his naked skin gliding over Colin's bare chest. "Will I be sleeping in your room or in a guest room?"

"Oh, in my old room with me," Colin assured him. "My parents have known I'm gay forever. It isn't a big deal for them."

"That must be amazing," Hernán said, his face softening. "Other than Rudy, nobody in my family would accept it. Our family always knew about Rudy, of course, and made life hard for him. His father, my uncle Elías, didn't like it but at least he got Rudy out of San Marcos. I don't think even my uncle Juan would accept it about me, and he's the one I'm closest to except my sister."

He thought about that. "Well, Brijith might understand. But growing up, nobody even mentioned the possibility I was gay, except for my grandmother when she got mad at me."

Colin's blood boiled whenever he thought of Hernán's grandmother but he held his tongue. Instead, he said, "Be prepared for sleeping in a room decorated in Vintage Nerd."

Hernán grinned down at him. "Have you ever had sex in that bed?" Colin shook his head, and Hernán whispered, "Then be sure to pack one of your friends and some condoms. From what Chris said, you've been on PrEP long enough now. I think I'm ready to make love to you again, if you want that."

Colin groaned. "You're trying to kill me, aren't you? I'll be sitting around all morning thinking about you inside me and I won't get shit done."

"Pobrecito," Hernán said with a small laugh. "I think you'll make it."

He finished getting ready for work and Colin lay there, watching him. A peculiar, bubbly feeling tickled his chest as he tracked Hernán doing his morning routine. Watching him apply deodorant, brush his teeth, dry his hair… It was all prosaic, yet gave Colin a sense of well-being he'd never experienced in his adult life.

Hernán retrieved clothes from the guest room but carried them back in to get dressed. "When we return from New Jersey," Colin said, "why don't you move your clothes in here? There's plenty of room in the drawers and closet."

Hernán glanced at him shyly. "Are you sure? Then I'd like that."

The bubbly feeling in Colin's chest expanded.

He got up to make them both some breakfast, and sent Hernán off with a kiss. Since he had a few hours to kill before they departed, Colin checked the weather to make sure conditions remained favorable for flying. The reports were so good, in fact, that he decided to fly up under visual flight rules, or VFR.

I wonder if Hernán would ever want to learn to fly, he mused. It would be wonderful to have someone share his hobby. That idea made him think of his grandfather, which brought his thoughts around to his parents.

He called his mother, since their last talk had been a week or two earlier.

"Colin, dear," his mother said brightly when she answered. "How are you, darling?"

"I'm great, Mom. We had a really good lobbying trip to Capitol Hill yesterday. Did you get my message about coming to the house for a long weekend."

"Yes, and I'm so excited to see you. I assume you're flying yourself? I'll send Watkins to pick you up if you know about when you'll land. Your father is home this weekend and we haven't seen you in months. Katherine is coming over this evening as well to see you, but Alhaadi took the children camping. I asked Rosie to prepare a lovely dinner for us. And you're staying until Monday?"

"Yes, until Monday. We'll probably land about four o'clock." Colin hesitated; he hadn't told her about Hernán yet. "Um, Mom? I didn't mention this in my message, but I won't be alone. I'm bringing someone with me to meet you."

"Oh, are you seeing someone now? You've never brought a man home before."

"Yes. It, uh, he's really special." Colin frowned, nervous to be talking to Mom about Hernán. "To me anyway. And he likes me. I think."

Mom laughed softly, kindly. "Darling, don't fret so. I can hear your mind churning through the phone."

Colin whooshed out a gust of air. "You're right. I don't know why I do that."

"Well, tell me about him."

"His name is Hernán Portillo." Colin edited the story, mentioning only that Hernán was originally from El Salvador, they'd met in Provincetown and Hernán was doing volunteer work at the center. The rest of it—Hernán's immigration status, the fact that he was living with Colin—could wait.

"He sounds charming. Your father and I can't wait to meet Hernán."

"I think you'll like him. I kind of wish Katherine wasn't coming to dinner tonight. I don't want to freak him out, and I think meeting you will be plenty."

"Colin Richard Felton. Are you embarrassed by your family?"

He squirmed. "Of course not. It's just, the house is already a lot to take in. He comes from a poor family. He knows we have money, but I think it's theoretical for him."

He could hear Mom's smile in her voice. "I suppose your father and I should move down to one of the guest cottages. We could pass ourselves off as the caretakers. Rosie can slip dinner in through the back door."

He pretended to take her joke seriously. "Well, if you wear some jeans with holes and a flannel shirt, you might be able to pull that off. Does Dad have any overalls?"

"Silly boy," she laughed. "If this Hernán feels about you the way you obviously feel about him, he won't get sidetracked by the house. And your father and I are perfectly capable of being charming hosts without namedropping every two minutes. I'll ask Katherine to hold off on the third degree until at least the dessert course."

They chatted for a few more minutes, and Colin was glad they were making the trip. He really missed his parents, and he had an immature need for them to see the handsome man he'd won for himself.

He checked in with Hernán by text mid-morning.

How was your first class?

> *Great. Real progress. Vonda asked me to translate for a new client between ESL classes so I won't have time for lunch. Can you bring me something to eat?*

Will do. I'll be downstairs at 2

Colin got himself ready to go. He stowed Bluebeard in his bag along with some lube and several condoms. Blushing, he added the rubber bulb for his portable enema kit. If Hernán was truly ready, Colin wanted to be prepared as soon and as often as possible after they got settled at the house.

With time left to kill, he opened a book to take his mind off his excitement, but the apartment felt empty without Hernán there as well. Even when they were in different rooms, Colin was always happily aware he wasn't alone. He'd never realized before Hernán moved in how lonely Washington was.

At one-thirty, he loaded his small Tumi suitcase and flight bag into the Audi, along with Hernán's knapsack. By the time he reached the immigration center's building, Hernán waited on the sidewalk.

Climbing in, Hernán leaned over to kiss Colin. "Maryanne told me to let the class go a few minutes early," he explained. "I think she's excited about us going to see your parents and she told me she was just kidding last night about your mother."

They ate the sandwiches Colin had picked up at a deli as they drove to his airport. Hernán stood back to watch as Colin maneuvered his plane out, and then stowed his Audi inside his hangar before locking the sliding doors again. As he moved around the plane to get it ready to go, Hernán asked, "Is there anything I can do to help you?"

Colin grinned. "Sure, if you're interested. I can teach you some of the readiness checks." He showed Hernán how he got down on hands and knees under each wing and pressed the metal spike on top of his fuel cup into the nearest of five sumps.

"I'm checking to see if there's any water in the tank. If so, it would sink to the bottom because water is heavier than aviation fuel." He held the blue liquid collected in the cup up to the light. "And this is all fine." After repeating the check twice more, he opened the cap on the right wing.

Peering inside with Hernán next to him, he said, "See how the fuel level is close to the top? I have gauges in the cockpit as well but we always confirm visually that the tanks are full." Carefully, he poured in the small amount of liquid he'd drained from the sumps, and then replaced the cap.

Under Colin's careful eye, Hernán did the checks on the left wing, and then walked with Colin around the plane to inspect it visibly. "We're making sure no antenna is bent and the skin hasn't taken damage," he explained.

When they'd finished all the checks, Colin finally clapped his hands together and enthused, "All good to go!"

Hernán grinned. "I love how excited you are about flying."

"And I love that you're willing to go up with me. I've got friends and family who won't set foot in my plane." That sounded like they didn't trust him as the pilot, so Colin hastened to add, "They think it's too small to be safe."

Hernán gave him a lopsided grin. "To be honest, it is a little scary but I have faith."

"In aerodynamics?"

"In you," Hernán said simply.

Well, that shut Colin up entirely. The bubbly feeling he'd had all morning threatened to spill over. His voice sounded hoarse to him as he said, "When I have precious cargo like you, I'm extra careful."

He made sure Hernán was properly situated in the passenger seat before buckling himself in. After another few minutes they were airborne. Hernán's expression was joyful, and he seemed far more relaxed than on that first flight from Provincetown.

In between making radio calls, Colin explained various instruments and panels on his plane. Hernán asked a lot of question about the displays, obviously grasping their uses and importance.

Cautiously, Colin took the opening. "Do you think you might enjoy flying lessons?"

Hernán crooked his head as he thought about that. "I'm not sure. I'm kind of happy being ferried around in the sky by my boyfriend. Why? Would you like me to take lessons?"

"Only if it's something you get interested in. It's a lot of time to put in even to get your license. Usually between seventy-five and a hundred flying hours, plus you have to study written materials and pass a test. If you then want to get an instrument rating, that takes a lot longer."

"I get the feeling you haven't had a lot of people to share aviation with," Hernán said.

"True, at least since my grandfather died. My dad was never interested in learning. Neither were my brother and sister. My mom actually did take a few lessons, but she decided it wasn't for her."

"I'll think about it," Hernán said after a pause.

The hour-long flight went by quickly until he had to concentrate for landing. He put down at Teterboro, a private airport in New Jersey close to Manhattan and the nearest one to his parents' house in Saddle River.

When they had taxied to a stop, opened the gull-wing doors of the plane, and emerged, Hernán's face went blank. A man in a black suit waited for them next to a limousine. Colin said sheepishly, "Mom sent the driver to pick us up. Sorry I didn't warn you."

Hernán fidgeted as Watkins greeted "Mister Colin" and unloaded their bags from the plane's cargo hold to put in the trunk of the limo. Colin tugged Hernán toward the open door and into the back seat. When they were settled, Watkins closed the door behind Hernán before taking the wheel.

He whispered to Colin, "Did you grow up with a driver?"

Colin took his hand. "Yes. I hated it then. Watkins drove my brother, sister and me to and from our boarding school. It used to embarrass me, frankly. Most of my friends showed up in ordinary cars. Katherine always loved it though."

"Katherine is older than you, right? You don't talk a lot about her. Will she be there this weekend?"

"Yes, she's coming for dinner. Her husband and two kids are camping somewhere. Though what Alhaadi considers camping, I can't guess. It's probably a luxury cabin in the woods with a pool."

"Do you and Katherine get along well?"

"We're very different people without a lot in common. She loves business and started working with Dad as soon as she could. I was never even tempted."

"How about your brother, uh, Griffin?"

"We see each other more often. He didn't want to work with Dad but he's got almost as much business acumen as Katherine. He started a line of organic soaps and shampoos for people with sensitive skin. It's doing really well. A few big stores in DC carry his products so I see him when he comes for meetings."

Hernán's nerves practically showed through his skin. "Your lives are so different from anything I ever knew in El Salvador. What if your family doesn't like me?"

Colin kissed his knuckles. "Please don't worry about that. Look, I know how lucky I am. There's money and comfort and all that. But I don't think I was ever really happy until you came into my life. My parents are going to see that right away, and they'll love you for that alone."

Hernán blushed and hid his head on Colin's shoulder. Colin debated closing the privacy panel, but he didn't think Hernán would be comfortable shutting out Watkins. He contented himself with tightening his arm around Hernán.

The drive didn't take long, and the industrial parts of New Jersey quickly gave way to vistas of horse farms and large houses. Hernán watched out the window, rapt. The car wove its way into a tree-lined and manicured neighborhood, with large houses partially obscured by hedges or carefully planted evergreens.

Colin took a deep breath as Watkins turned into his parents' driveway and took them up to the front entrance rather than along the side of the house to the courtyard. The look on Hernán's face was some combination of awe and terror.

"¡Dios mío!" he whispered, looking at Colin round-eyed and slack-jawed. "It's a castle."

Hernán had a point. The honey-colored stone and gray slate roof had been inspired by French chateaux. The looming windows, dormers, brick chimneys, and huge oak front door were designed to be impressive. Fortunately, from the front, it wasn't obvious just how big the house really was. The tightly manicured hedges, clipped into serpentine shapes, at least helped to soften the appearance, Colin thought.

He winced. "Yeah, it's a little much." Hernán just shook his head.

The front door opened and Mom stepped out. Colin almost laughed, because she wore blue jeans and a flannel shirt. He'd never seen her in anything so dressed down in his life. Her blonde bob framed patrician features and icy blue eyes, the whole effect warmed by her smile.

Watkins opened the door and Colin slid out quickly to greet his mother. Bending to kiss her cheek as they hugged, he whispered,

"Thank you. I didn't think you own anything that isn't couture."

Mom brushed her thumb over the smudge of lipstick she'd left on his cheek. "Darling, these jeans are Chanel."

"Of course they are." He turned, one arm around Mom's waist, to hold out a hand for Hernán. "Margaret Felton, this is Hernán Portillo. My boyfriend."

Hernán stepped closer, clearly tense. He held out a hand and said, "I'm very happy to meet you. Thank you for letting me stay at your home." His eyes seemed drawn upward to the façade.

Margaret held onto his hand. "This was all Jim's idea. My husband. He went to Disneyland as a boy and all his life wanted to give a daughter Cinderella's castle. So when Katherine was born, he built it! I had to make him take the towers and drawbridge out of the architect's rendering though."

Hernán chuckled, his shoulders relaxing slightly. "All it needs is that fairy flying over it and sprinkling pixie dust."

"Hey, I'm standing right here, but I forgot my pixie dust," Colin protested with a wink for Mom.

"I think there's some in your room, dear," she said. "Hernán, would you like a tour?"

He looked over his shoulder at the car. "Our bags—?"

"Watkins will take them to Colin's room. Come along." She looped an arm through Hernán's and led the way into the house, Colin following with fingers crossed.

HERNÁN FELT LIKE he was walking through a museum or a movie set. At least, a place that someone like him shouldn't touch. The interior of the house seemed even more grand than the outside.

Margaret was kind, welcoming and elegant. She kept up a running conversation as she showed him through huge rooms with vaulted ceilings and rich, upholstered furniture. He barely noticed her questions or the answers he gave as he craned his head over gorgeous paintings and other works of art.

The dining room table looked like it could seat twenty or more. The living room featured a grand piano and two fireplaces. A smaller parlor—the size of Colin's entire apartment, it seemed—had French doors opening to a courtyard. Beyond that he could see a pool. And was that a tennis court?

Margaret ended the tour of the first floor in the kitchen. She gestured to a sturdy stool pulled next to a marble-topped island. "Boys, please have a seat. Let me get you something to drink while I check with Rosie about dinner."

Hernán sat next to Colin, who rested his elbow on the marble and his cheek on his hand. "It's all too much, isn't it?" Colin asked.

Hernán shook his head in a daze. "It's beautiful. There's just...so much of it."

Margaret stood near the kitchen range—easily ten yards away—and talked to a woman in a white uniform and apron. Then she returned to lean against the other side of the island. "Rosie will be over with your drinks in a moment. What do you think, Hernán? Should we take a break from the tour and let Colin show you his room? Oh, thank you," she said to the uniformed woman, who appeared next to her with two glasses of juice.

"Mister Colin, I hope you still like grapefruit juice."

"I do, thanks. Rosie, this is Hernán."

She bobbed her head politely at him. "Very nice to meet you, sir. If you need any food or drinks, please don't hesitate to ask." She left them to return to her stove, from which wonderful smells filled the room.

Margaret glanced at her watch, a delicate gold thing at odds with her outfit. Hernán suddenly understood she'd dressed to make him comfortable, and the thought made him squirm, embarrassed.

"Your father will be home around six, Colin. Why don't you show Hernán upstairs or rest, and we'll have cocktails in the parlor at six-thirty. Katherine said she'd come by around seven, so we'll sit to dinner after that. All right, dear? Is there anything you need, Hernán?"

He swallowed hard and stood up, glass of juice clenched in his hand. "No, thank you, Mrs. Felton. This is all so lovely."

"Call me Margaret, dear. Run along and we'll visit more soon. I want to hear more about these language classes you're giving at Colin's little nonprofit."

Hernán blinked, unsure how to react. He didn't realize he'd told her about the language classes, but then remembered the skillful way she'd asked questions as she led him through the tour. But she'd called the Immigration Initiative "Colin's little nonprofit." That seemed dismissive, but he bit his tongue and nodded his head.

Colin led him out of the kitchen, down a long hallway, and up a wide, spiral staircase with wrought-iron railings. On the second floor, they passed an open door revealing a wood-paneled room filled with bookcases and chairs. "The library," Colin said, and then at the next door, added, "This is mine."

The door was open so he gestured for Hernán to proceed him in. The room seemed huge, with walls painted a peculiar shade of a deeply saturated blue that somehow made it feel cozy. A high window with floor-to-ceiling damask curtains looked over the courtyard and swimming pool.

A king-size four-poster bed sat next to the window. Two chairs and a sofa created a seating area next to a fireplace, in which a nice blaze was going. Closets lined one wall, and another door opened to what appeared to be a bathroom.

Only gradually did Hernán see through the wealthy trappings to find Colin's personality in the room. *Star Wars* figures posed in a glass case. A wall cabinet contained swords, and another was full of masks Hernán recognized as being from all over Latin America. The bedspread was blue and black, with a white square in the center. It contained embroidered words that began, "Police Telephone, Free for Use of Public."

He knew that phrase. Racking his brain, he realized from where—*Doctor Who*. He looked up again at the walls and gaped.

"You painted it TARDIS blue!"

Colin blushed. "Yeah, well…I told you this was Vintage Nerd. I should probably let Mom update my room, but I dunno." He looked around, hands in his pockets. "I still kind of like it."

Hernán said, "It suits you, even now."

"Hey, are you interested in masks?" Colin said, leading Hernán to the cabinet.

COLIN HAD HOPED they'd have sex when they got to his room, but Hernán seemed uncomfortable and overwhelmed by the house. Instead of playing in the sheets, Hernán had Colin dig out some of his favorite games. They spent an hour laughing together through a session of the original *Star Wars* board game. "I remember this as being a lot more fun," Colin pouted as he lost.

After the game, they sprawled on Colin's bed, Hernán's head on his chest, and talked. When it was time to dress for dinner, he showed

Hernán his marbled bathroom.

Hernán stepped out of his clothes and paused, looking at his bare feet resting on the floor. "It's warm," he said flatly.

"Oh good," Colin said. "A maid thought to turn on the radiant heat in the floor. The marble gets chilly otherwise. Towel racks are heated, too."

"Of course they are," Hernán said, shaking his head. "I didn't know people actually live like this."

"Oh shit, if this bothers you, then you're really going to hate the rest of the house. On the lower level, there's a huge wine room for Dad, a home theater, a game room my nephews and niece have claimed entirely, an indoor putting green…"

"Shut up," Hernán said with a laugh. "You're teasing me."

"Hand to God. I'll show you after dinner."

AT SIX-THIRTY, COLIN led Hernán back downstairs and to the parlor. "We can see the rest of the place later, if you want. That is, if you're still speaking to me after dinner with my parents and Katherine."

In the parlor, Mom had changed to a more typical outfit, a soft blue sweater and tailored wool slacks. His father stood by the bar in one corner, pouring a sherry for his wife and a scotch for himself.

He was as tall as Colin, sturdy and well-groomed, with blue-gray eyes. His thick, iron-colored hair was styled in the same way he'd worn it for decades, and his red cashmere sweater over a white shirt was the trademark "casual look" the publicists had created for him.

He glanced up when Colin and Hernán entered. "Son, good to see you. Can I make you travelers a drink?"

Colin brought Hernán over and introduced them. "Jim Felton, this is Hernán." They shook, and Colin said, "I'll take a vodka tonic, if you're pouring."

"Of course," Dad said, reaching for the Grey Goose. "Hernán? The same?" Hernán nodded.

Taking their drinks over to one pair of facing sofas, Colin sank back into the cushions while Hernán stayed perched on the edge, as if about to bolt.

Mom said to Dad, "Jim, Hernán speaks five languages."

Hernán muttered, "I'm only fluent in four."

"Only four," Dad chuckled. "That's remarkable. What do you do,

Hernán?"

Colin jumped in. "Hernán's working with me at the Initiative for now. He gives language classes and does some translation. He saved my neck this week." With that, he launched into a description of the lobbying visit. He described the way Hernán had gotten Sabeen comfortable, the great job all his team members did, and how great Maryanne's leadership had been.

Hernán looked at him, puzzled. Colin wasn't sure why.

Before he could ask, Dad said, "I'm glad you've stuck with the nonprofit, Colin. Usually you'd have given up by now." Colin felt his face begin to burn. To Hernán, Dad chortled slightly, "Colin tried all kinds of things as a kid, but nothing really kept his attention. He didn't want to play sports, or join activities. He didn't even want to go to Yale or work in the family business. I really worried he'd never find something to hold his attention."

"Dear," Mom said, resting a hand on Dad's arm. "You know Colin loves his aviation. He's always been committed to that." She asked, "Hernán, how do you like going up with my son?"

Hernán sipped his drink and wet his lips. "I like it. Colin has so much passion for flying that I feel completely safe with him."

Jim smiled. "Passion isn't a word we usually use for Colin. Is it, Son? But yes, Hernán. My father flew in World War II and kept it up ever after. He took Colin flying as soon as Margaret would let him. Colin, remember when he wanted you to join the Air Force?"

"I still think I would have liked it," Colin said quietly into his cocktail.

"Oh no," Mom laughed lightly. "I can't imagine any of my children living in barracks or whatever they have in the military. You like your comforts! Bad enough when you ended up with that little apartment in Berkley. Dear, do you remember how small that place was?" she asked her husband.

"I don't know why you wouldn't just let us buy you a nice house out there. It would have been a good investment, too, the way real estate has continued to soar."

Colin was spared the need to answer when his sister arrived. Katherine looked more like their father than their mother. Only thirty-one, she carried herself with gravity Colin associated with much older people. She wore slacks and a blouse with a few pieces of African jewelry Colin recalled her Kenyan husband giving her over the years.

He rose and kissed her cheek before introducing Hernán. Dad fetched her a glass of white wine and she sat on the sofa between Mom and Dad. Before she could start in with quizzing Hernán in that aggressive manner she had, Colin decided to divert her attention.

"I hear Alhaadi is off camping with the brood," he said. "Where did they go?"

The ploy worked. Katherine loved to talk about her children, and quite willingly described the "camp" her husband had taken them to, which sounded as far from camping as Colin could imagine. He didn't need to say much, though, which was a plus.

Hernán was very quiet as well, watching the interactions between Mom, Dad and Katherine while occasionally shooting a puzzled glance toward Colin.

They sat down to dinner in the breakfast room, where the round table certainly seemed more welcoming than the enormous affair in the dining room. It would also be less overwhelming to Hernán. He caught Mom's eye and mouthed his thanks; she winked at him.

After Mom and Katherine were seated, Colin held a chair for Hernán next to his own. Rosie came in almost immediately with a soup to begin the meal.

Halfway through the fish course, Dad said, "Colin, I meant to tell you. Do you remember Michael Salvio, the head of our government affairs department? Well, he recently moved on to take a position with the U.S Trade Representative. That leaves us with an opening."

Katherine spoke up, "You'd be good at that, Colin. Even the experience you got at your little charity will help, since you already know your way around Capitol Hill."

Colin flushed and stared at his Dover sole. "I'm happy with the Immigration Initiative. You know that."

Mom gave a pretty laugh. "Well, of course you are, darling. But is that really what you see yourself doing with the rest of your life? You're almost thirty, love. When are you going to be ready to take a real job?"

"He has a real job."

Colin's head jerked up, surprised at Hernán's words and at the edge he heard.

"Colin is influencing Congressional policy on immigration," Hernán continued. "I was lucky enough to see him in action. He's very good."

Dad huffed a pleased noise. "Of course he is. But that's just it, Son. You have experience and skills that would be very useful to the company. I'd like you to come work with the family, with Katherine and me. You could have even more impact."

Katherine leaned forward. "Colin, you must know we face regulatory issues at the federal and state level. We're in a constant battle over premiums, reserves, coverage decisions, protection from frivolous lawsuits. We need someone like you, who knows the players in Congress and how to capitalize on our connections. Imagine lobbying the Senate for litigation reform, for example. Instead of helping a few people at a time, you'd be able to help us save our members tens of millions of dollars."

Hernán made a noise. When Colin looked at him, he saw flushed cheeks and a glint in his eye. Desperate to avoid a conflict between his boyfriend and his family, he decided to make himself a target.

"I'll think about the job. But hey, this is crazy. Maryanne and Hernán here suggested *I* think about running for office."

Mom sipped her glass of wine. "Can you imagine? You grumbled at all the fundraisers we've hosted and attended, all the handshaking and speechmaking." She shook her head. "You'd hate that lifestyle. Too funny."

Hernán tilted his head, frowning. "I don't understand why it's funny. Maybe I don't fully appreciate American politics, but Colin seems like exactly the kind of person who should be governing. He's brilliant, passionate and very knowledgeable. Colin could have a direct impact on the issues he cares about."

Katherine rolled her eyes at both of them. "Oh Hernán, you must not really know my brother yet. He'd drop out of the race two days in. Colin always gives up on everything when it gets difficult."

Colin flushed and looked at his plate, cheeks burning. *Shut up, shut up*, he pleaded silently. Of course he agreed with Katherine, but saying it in front of Hernán stung. The shame flared bright, and he realized it wasn't a new feeling.

Dad smirked as well. "How many different sports did we try? And musical instruments? Katherine, remember when he wanted to play the tuba?"

Too conscious of Hernán at his side, he panicked over what his lover would think of the growing litany of failures. Shocking himself, he blurted out, "You yanked me from every single thing I ever wanted to do, Dad. How would I know if I could learn to be good at anything?"

Mom protested, "Dear, we never forbade you from trying anything you wanted."

"Yes, I could try anything *once*. Then you'd pat my head and tell me it didn't matter and I should try something else, something I might actually be good at. Gramps was the only one who ever believed in me."

"Colin Richard Felton," Mom exclaimed. "You know that isn't true."

"Do I? It hasn't stopped to this day. All this mocking of my job at the Initiative, telling me it's time to grow up. How is that any different?" Colin jumped up. "Excuse me," he said, tossing his napkin on the table and hurrying away.

As he left the room, he heard Hernán say to his family, "Colin gives people hope and help and a chance to start over. He saves lives with what he does at the Initiative. Have you ever saved anything more than a dollar?" Then he scraped back his chair and hurried to catch up with Colin, grasping his hand before they reached the hallway together.

HERNÁN FOLLOWED COLIN through the massive house, his heart pounding with anger. The way the family treated Colin was shameful. He could see the love too, but Jim hung on every word Katherine said while dismissing or belittling Colin. Margaret seemed tolerant of Colin's life, but distractedly. It was all just subtle enough that he hadn't wanted to open his mouth and stir a family quarrel about which he might be entirely wrong.

From the look on Colin's face, he wasn't wrong.

Colin led them to the second-floor library and closed the door behind them. Hernán sat in one of the wingback chairs as Colin paced.

"I'm sorry you had to see that, Hernán. It normally isn't that bad. Pushing me to take that job at the company, teasing me about my failures—sure, they do that kind of thing, but tonight…" He stopped in front of a wooden bar cart and poured himself a finger of amber liquor. "Do you want one?" He asked Hernán, who shook his head.

"Colin, I'm sorry I spoke rudely to your family. I owe you and them an apology."

Colin crossed the room to sit next to Hernán. "You don't owe anyone an apology." He took a swallow of his drink, grimaced, and then continued. "Reminds me of the night I got drunk in P-town. Why am I drinking this?"

"Because you're mad, and it's there." Hernán reached across the gap and took the glass from Colin's loose fingers. He took a sniff and made a face. "I don't like bourbon either."

"Am I mad? I guess so."

"I'm proud you spoke up to them. I guess that isn't something you do very often."

"You're right. I don't." Colin sighed. "Usually it's easier to let them talk, keep the focus on Katherine and off of me. I don't know why I did speak up, today." He winced and studied his shoes. "Shit, that's not true. I didn't want you to see me through their eyes."

Hernán slid off his chair and to Colin's feet. He rested his arms across Colin's lap. "There's not a thing they said that could make me think less of you. Or that I believe, actually. They don't know how much you've accomplished, so how could their opinion move me?"

Colin's eyes on his swirled with emotion. He reached down to run his fingers through Hernán's hair. Quietly, he said, "I wish I were the man you seem to see. The warrior."

"You are," Hernán said firmly, like he would say the sun rose in the East.

Chapter 28

THEY SAT LIKE that in the library for a long while, Colin's eyes locked with Hernán's. *The way he defended me to them... No one's ever done that.* Finally, aware of the passing time, he exhaled roughly.

"I'd better go apologize. We always had a family rule about not going to bed angry." His phone trilled in his pocket, and he said, "That's probably Mom, wondering where in the house we're hiding out." He decided to ignore it in favor of a few more minutes of quiet with Hernán, but in seconds it trilled again. Then Hernán's chimed in his pants pocket.

Sharing a frown, they each got out their phones. Colin had to pull on his glasses to read the text message. Hernán looked down at his screen, and almost immediately his face turned pale.

The message was from David James:

Sofia just saw the attached in online version of The Washington Post.

Below the text was an image, apparently from that newspaper. It took Colin a moment to recognize himself in profile, a hand intimately spread against Hernán's back. Hernán's handsome face appeared clearly in the photo. They both wore their running clothes, and Colin's mind flashed to the day before. They had turned to walk away, and as Colin had glanced back, Ethan was just putting away his phone.

He didn't!

He clicked through the link to open the article David forwarded, from a gossip column called The Reliable Source. With the photo was a short block of copy:

> *Socialite and activist Colin Felton, son of financial powerhouse Jim Felton, is squiring around this hot and handsome hunk of a Latin lover. Word is that Hernán (last name unknown—so far!) is*

seeking asylum. With looks like those, we're sure plenty of people would line up to give Hernán a place to stay!

Colin looked up to find Hernán staring at him, aghast. Heat rushed through his body at the despair he saw in Hernán's eyes.

"I'm sorry," he said immediately, sweat dampening the nape of his neck. "I know how this looks but it's just nasty gossip. I don't usually get much of this since I stay out of the limelight. Griffin gets hit with it all the time."

Hernán shook his head slowly. "It isn't that." He swallowed hard and looked at his phone's screen again. "That's my name and my picture. And it puts me in Washington. With you." His strangled voice and sick expression finally made sense.

With horror in his tone, Hernán added one word. "Cuernos."

AS QUICKLY AS he could, Colin dialed David's number. He could see the dread in Hernán's face, and that almost superstitious fear instilled by his uncle and by growing up in El Salvador, where Cuernos was a lethal, daily presence.

"Hello?" he heard David's urgent baritone.

"It's Colin. I'm in New Jersey with Hernán. We just saw your message."

"I have no idea where the story came from, Colin. You know neither I nor Sofia would say anything about Hernán's legal situation—"

"I know," he cut David off. "I think it was Ethan. We ran into him on the street yesterday and Hernán mentioned I was heading to the Hill to lobby about asylum. Ethan made a lucky guess." Beside him, Hernán moaned. Still on his knees, he leaned forward with his face in his hands, and Colin rubbed circles on his back.

"That little shit," David fumed.

"I know. We can deal with him later. Hernán's afraid that members of Cuernos may see the picture and put together where he's hiding."

"I get that," David said. "I wish I could say it was unlikely, but with the reach of the internet it's possible this could spread. Hold on." The line was silent for a moment, and then David spoke again. "I've conferenced in Sofia. We need to either kill the story or get ahead of any fallout."

Sofia said, "I just saw it on Twitter. With Hernán's looks and the reference to Colin's father, people are retweeting it like crazy. I had no idea you were one of those Feltons."

"Shit," Colin sighed. His phone began to chime with incoming messages, but he refused to look. "Any ideas? I'm kind of in shock here."

David spoke up. "One of my partners at the law firm is good friends with the managing editor at the *Post*. With Hernán's permission, I'd like to call her, explain the situation and ask her to make an appeal to pull the article because of the risk to Hernán." Colin muttered the plan quietly to Hernán, and he nodded.

"Go ahead, David. It won't stop what's being retweeted but maybe it will keep the story from growing."

Sofia chimed in. "I'm worried this might draw ICE attention earlier than we'd hoped. I was pretty close to wrapping up Hernán's asylum application anyway but I think we should expedite that and get it on file as soon as possible. I'll head back to the office now and see if I can get a draft ready for you by morning, David."

"Thanks, Sofia. I'm sorry to ruin your weekend but I agree we should do that. Colin, you said you're in New Jersey?"

"Yes. We came up to visit my parents."

"I don't want to sound paranoid, but that's probably good. On the off chance that someone in Cuernos sees the article, you're not hard to locate in DC."

"You look intimate in the photo," Sofia agreed. "And they name you. It wouldn't be a stretch to see Hernán means something to you and track you down for information."

Colin sucked in a breath. "Holy shit. I never even thought of that."

Hernán seemed to pick up the gist of the conversation. His eyes shimmered. "I'm sorry. I've brought my darkness to you. It's what I was always afraid of."

"No, Hernán. Stop," Colin ordered. "Don't think that way. We'll figure this out together and we'll be fine."

"You don't know that," Hernán moaned. "In my country Cuernos are everywhere. I've seen the news articles. They're here in the States as well. We'll never be safe."

David could apparently hear Hernán's words. "Look, Colin, I don't want either of you to take any risks. Until things are more clear, you should stay out of DC."

Colin thought rapidly. "We could remain in Saddle River indefinitely, I suppose. No, shit, the paper used Dad's name too. It would probably be easy to locate us here. Oh fuck! I have to warn them." The magnitude of what Ethan had potentially unleashed began to hit finally. Hernán had seen it right away, but Colin was only putting the pieces together.

Authoritatively, David said, "We have enough to get started on damage control. Colin, you talk to your family. Sofia will work on the application. I'm going to see what I can do about the story. Let's regroup in an hour and see where we are."

Hernán looked so miserable as the call disconnected that Colin slipped to the floor next to him and pulled him close. Hernán trembled in his arms.

After a few moments, he made Hernán rise to sit in one of the library chairs. His own phone pinged relentlessly with messages and notifications. Nothing like that onslaught had ever happened to Colin. "Do you want to stay here, or come with me to talk to my parents?"

"May I stay here? I'm already ashamed of what I said to them earlier, and with this horror I've created..."

Colin kissed him firmly. "Angelito, you have nothing to be sorry about. All you did earlier was defend me, and you didn't stir up this trouble. Ethan did. But okay. You stay here and I'll come get you in a little while."

He left the library door open and went in search of his parents. Descending the main staircase, he met Dad coming up, cell phone in his hand.

"My public relations people saw as soon as the article hit the web. What the hell is going on, Son?"

"Can we talk downstairs?"

Dad guided them toward a small sitting room on the first floor. He called down the hall, "Margaret? I found him. Come join us if you want."

"Where's Katherine?" Colin asked.

"She went home after that scene. What you said—"

"Can it wait, Dad? I know I owe you an apology but we need to talk about this news item. There may be danger."

Mom stepped into the sitting room just then and sank gracefully onto an upholstered settee, confusion and concern mixed in her face.

She tugged her husband's hand until he sat next to her, and then gestured for Colin to speak.

Colin took a deep breath. "The news item is accurate. I just never expected it to come out this way. Hernán is living with me in DC while he seeks asylum."

"That means he's in the country illegally, I suppose. What have you gotten yourself into?" The disapproval in Dad's gruff voice mixed with concern for his son and doubt that Colin knew what he was doing. It was the same thing he'd heard for years.

"This isn't the time, Dad," Colin said firmly. "We have reason to believe Hernán may be in physical danger as a result of this article. His lawyer is working to suppress it but given the story is already on Twitter I doubt we have much chance of that."

He explained as succinctly as he could about how Cuernos had stalked and nearly killed Hernán, how the police officer who tried to help had been murdered, how Hernán's uncle had told him he was in danger and should get out of El Salvador.

"Look, this all just blew up today so I have no idea whether Hernán's fear is valid or overblown. Given what's reported about Cuernos, I think it's dangerous to dismiss his fears. It'll be easy for the people who may, emphasis on *may*, be after Hernán to track him to my condo in Washington. If they're sufficiently motivated, I can imagine them tracking you both down here. Maybe even Katherine and Griff."

"Jesus, Son." His father exhaled heavily when Colin finished. "Okay, I agree. This isn't the time. I'll alert my private security firm to make sure everyone is under guard." He looked at his wife in silent communion, and then back at Colin. His voice when he spoke was lower and full of concern. "What about you though? Are you safe?"

That was the father he loved, ready to use every tool at his disposal to keep his family protected and comfortable. It was why they lived in a fairy-tale castle with every whim granted. Jim Felton wanted them all to be happy, even when he didn't know what to think about his middle child.

It had seemed cloying when Colin was young, but he knew his father had his back. That meant the world.

"We were planning to return to DC Monday morning," he answered, "but that doesn't seem like a good idea anymore. I also don't like the idea of staying here, but I don't have a better plan."

"What about the house in Nantucket?" Mom asked. "It's somewhat hard to get to, especially off season."

Colin thought about it. "I don't know. You've had the house so long and we've all been photographed for various events. A simple Google search would probably turn that up."

"I wonder if we're overreacting," Dad said. "Let me talk to my security guys to get their input."

"We need to make sure the team keeps a very low profile though," Colin said. "You're right, Hernán is in the country illegally. We think we have excellent grounds to get him asylum, but in the meantime we want to stay off the ICE radar if we possibly can. I'm worried we'll get a security group that wants to go overboard by posting men at everybody's door and harassing people. That could end up drawing even more attention."

"Oh boy," Dad said with a sigh. "Okay. I'll make sure the detail head knows we want them to watch discreetly and from a distance only." There was a pause, and then his father asked in a softer tone. "Is this worth it, Son? Is this Hernán fellow who you choose?"

Colin's voice was thick as he answered, "Yes, Dad. He is. Maybe you don't see it after the dinner table—"

Mom cut him off. "Actually, that's why I do see it. Perhaps we've made mistakes as parents, and we can talk about that calmly when this matter is resolved. At dinner, however, I saw a shy man out of his depth, who nonetheless jumped to defend and praise you when he felt you were wronged." She smiled. "Your eyes shine when you look at him, and his do as well. He loves you very much, and he'll fight if he thinks you've been attacked. What mother wouldn't want someone like that for her son?"

Colin's throat grew tight, and he blinked back tears.

Dad only made it worse. "I like Hernán too. You go on back and take care of him. I imagine he's pretty scared right about now."

"Thank you," he whispered. With a kiss on his mother's cheek and a hand on his father's shoulder, he left and returned to the library.

HERNÁN HADN'T MOVED from the chair where Colin deposited him. Colin filled him in about the security precautions his father would begin to put in place right away.

Hernán moaned. "I'm so sorry, Colin. I hoped I'd never put you in danger this way."

Colin dropped to his haunches and took one of Hernán's cold and trembling hands. "We don't know for sure we're in danger, mi ángel. We're just being smart and taking precautions. It's one of the hazards of being wealthy. When I was a kid we actually had drills on what to do if one of us was kidnapped." He kissed Hernán's fingers. "My parents have always been overprotective and right now that's a good thing. They have resources you wouldn't believe." He forced a chuckle and almost made it convincing. "Since you and I are together now, you get the full Felton treatment as well."

His phone rang again. When David's name appeared on the display, he answered on speaker.

"Okay," David began. "I came down to meet Sofia. We're here together in my office. I've made the request about pulling the article but it will take some time yet to hear back. Even if it's pulled, we're all over social media."

Sofia spoke up. "Between the mention of Colin's father and Hernán in running shorts, the story is going viral. What I'm seeing is everything from comments on Hernán's looks, to Colin's looks, to comparisons to Prince William marrying Kate Middleton. There's some ugly homophobic and racist stuff too, though not much. Is there a risk people who know your family will comment and leak word out where you are?"

Colin sighed. "I don't think so. The staff have all been around a long time, I think. I'd say they're pretty loyal."

"Staff?" David asked.

"I mean people who work for my dad. At his company," Colin rushed to cover his error, but realized the barn door flapped in the wind, horses long gone, since he'd been so publicly identified as Jim Felton's son. He sighed.

"Anyway, my brother Griffin has had a few run-ins with the paps before. I don't recall that any leak was ever traced back to staff. My father is lining up security for the whole family right now. He even suggested Hernán and I hide out at their place in Nantucket. I don't think that makes sense, though. Too easy to link me to the house, and a lot of people know me there."

David snapped his fingers. "Nantucket is out, but what about Provincetown? You could stay in my house. Did you fly your plane up to New Jersey?"

Colin looked at Hernán, who had turned ashen and whispered, "Provincetown. I didn't even think about it. Rudy might be in danger."

Colin said, "Why don't you step into our bedroom and give him a call, just to warn him?" Hernán pulled out his phone and closed the door to the library behind himself.

Continuing his own call, he said, "P-town does seem like a good choice. I don't have obvious connections there. It's reasonably remote. The weather tomorrow is supposed to be clear so I could get there VFR."

Sofia asked, "What does that mean?"

"It means I'd be flying under visual flight rules, so I don't have to file a flight plan. If anyone knows the tail number of my plane and I have a plan on file, they can do a simple internet search and see where I'm heading."

"So Provincetown it is," David said. "I'll ask Jane or Sara to meet you at the airport tomorrow when you have a sense of when you'll be landing, and one of them can give you a key."

Hernán returned to the room and said, "Rudy is in Boston overnight but he knows to be careful."

Colin gestured for Hernán to join him again, and pulled him close. "Good. We'll see him soon in Provincetown."

Sofia spoke up. "I think we'll have a draft of your immigration papers ready for you to review by tomorrow evening, Hernán."

"I leave a laptop and basic office equipment in the P-town house," David added. "Jane can give you the password and what you need to access and print the documents."

There didn't seem to be anything else they could address together, so they ended the call with commitments to text at any significant development.

Colin escorted a nervous Hernán back to the first floor to tell his parents about the plan to head to Provincetown in the morning. They were still in the sitting room; Dad hung up just as Colin brought Hernán in.

"Okay," Dad said, sounding tense but in control. "The security firm is sending a team to watch the house right away, one to Katherine's and Griff's places, and another to your condo in DC. They know to be unobtrusive and they'll give me a call as soon as they're in position. Watkins will get you to the airport tomorrow. I've texted you the detail head's cell number so you can talk to him about arranging security on the Cape."

Hernán said, "Mr. and Mrs. Felton, I want to apologize for the trouble I've caused, as well as for my rudeness at dinner."

Mom stood and folded her hands. "Please, no apology is necessary. All you did was support my son when you felt we were being unfair." She glanced at her husband and back as she said, "I actually must thank you, for pointing out blunt truths. Sometimes a newcomer sees dynamics that we've always taken for granted. You've given us a lot to consider."

Mom's gaze took in Colin as well. Her comments weren't exactly warm, but Colin felt her sincerity. Only time would tell if his outburst and Hernán's comments had gotten through to his parents.

Chapter 29

LATER, BACK IN Colin's bedroom, Hernán paced around like a jungle cat in a cage. His eyes flickered from surface to surface and he couldn't seem to figure out where to rest his hands. When he saw Colin watching him, he winced.

"I don't know what to do, Colin," he confessed. "I've brought this evil to your door, and I can't make it better."

"You didn't cause this. Ethan did, when he sent that picture to the paper." The urge to scream at Ethan nearly overwhelmed Colin, but it would only tell Ethan he'd scored a blow. "Look, I'll call the security guy about P-town, and then there's really nothing more for us to do tonight. Why don't you change and get comfortable? I'll do the same in a minute. We'll watch some TV, have a snack sent up if you want, and get to bed. Okay?"

Hernán chewed his lip but finally gave a sharp nod. Twenty minutes later, after Colin had talked to a man from the security company, they settled onto the sofa in Colin's room together.

Television wasn't working to distract Hernán, and fooling around didn't seem likely. His restlessness began to weigh, and it frustrated Colin that he couldn't help him relax.

Colin used his iPad to check the weather for the following morning and prepare for an early flight. When that was done, and with nothing further to distract him, his anger at Ethan began to grow. How could someone who ever called himself Colin's friend do something like that? Even if Ethan didn't know the magnitude of what he'd put at risk, there was no question he'd been aiming to hurt.

Was the nastiness directed more at Colin or at Hernán? That was difficult to say. Colin had no reason to believe Ethan carried a torch for him, after their one abortive date something like a year and a half earlier. Maybe it was intended to induce Colin's family to step in and break them up, as a way to free Hernán for a pass from Ethan? That was equally absurd. He turned it over and over in his mind, his rage mounting, but he could find no reason for Ethan's action beyond spite.

In the quiet house, he also began to wonder how much of their panic was legitimate. He and the others had jumped to address Hernán's fear, but was it spiraling out of control? For fuck's sake, they had security watching his *condo*.

That was probably why, when Hernán said, "I'm going crazy in this room," Colin snapped back.

"Nán, we're all doing the best we can." He heard the frustration in his own voice.

So did Hernán. His eyes narrowed. "I know that, Colin. But all your father's men can't protect every possible person Cuernos could go after."

Colin threw up his hands as his frustration found a new target. "Despite the name, they aren't really devils. They're just hoodlums. Yes, there's a lot of them. Yes, they can be dangerous like a rabid dog. But they aren't some vast underground army, Hernán. You're one person that a few gangbangers attacked in El Salvador. Why are you so sure they would want to hunt you down in the States?"

A wounded look appeared in Hernán's eyes. "They killed that police officer after I identified two of them, and they said they were coming after me. How can I know how far they'll go? Wait," Hernán added heatedly. "You don't believe me. You say you want to help me, but that's because you don't think there's any real danger."

Colin wondered abstractedly if he were right. Was he only going along to play on Hernán's insecurities?

He rejected the idea. He might suspect Hernán's fears were slightly irrational, but no way was he trying to manipulate Hernán. He barked back, "That isn't true. I've done everything I possibly can to help you work toward getting asylum."

Hernán's voice rose, and a flush came to his cheeks. "Why, if you don't believe me? Why go through all of this shit?"

"Because I want you, Hernán. I want you in my life and I want you to be safe from deportation."

Hernán sneered. "You want to own me, you mean. Maybe you're more like Gerald Nimble than you can admit. House me, clothe me, give me an allowance, give me a job to do. It sounds just like what

Gerald did with Rudy, until he got tired of him and kicked him out."

Colin sucked in a strained breath. "That isn't fair. And it isn't true. I've done everything I know how to give you independence. I don't ever want you to feel like you have to stay with me, or to feel trapped."

"Yet here I am, in a fancy cage in New Jersey because of your friend and your rich father and—"

"Stop it, Hernán," Colin pleaded. "Yes, Ethan did this, but leave my father out of it. He's only trying to help us."

Hernán lapsed into Spanish as he stalked around the room. <<Protect you, maybe. Who am I? An undocumented immigrant with no money. Someone to take pity on, to feel sorry for because I was stabbed and raped. Who are you? A rich boy with no real responsibilities and nothing to fear in this world.>>

Colin's anger collapsed into stunned pain. "What?" he stammered. "Do you really believe all that?"

Hernán stopped his pacing and whirled. His mouth was open to speak until he looked in Colin's face. The color in his cheeks drained away, leaving him chalky. He dropped to his knees before Colin. "I'm sorry. I'm so sorry. I just lashed out. I know none of this is your fault."

Colin blinked at him. He finally croaked out, "I understand your fears. If I've done something to make you feel trapped, please talk to me about it. I swear I don't mean to do that. But it hurt, what you said."

Hernán dropped his forehead on Colin's knees. "I don't really think that you're controlling me. I'm just so scared."

Tentatively, Colin lifted a hand to stroke Hernán's black hair. Part of him wanted to brush away the fight and the ugly words as spurred by stress.

Part of him worried that was what Hernán truly believed, deep down.

And if it was, what kind of future could they have together?

THE NIGHT WAS long. Hernán was too tense over the argument with Colin, too fearful his new life was about to crash around him, to rest. Where had all that ugliness come from? Of *course* Colin and his family were doing everything they could. And maybe he *was* overreacting. Maybe it was just his ego that made him believe Cuernos would come after him, thousands of miles away from El Salvador.

The things he'd blurted out in anger, though… Those were things he wasn't consciously aware he still feared. He thought he'd overcome his concerns that Colin was like Gerald and would throw him away if things got messy.

Apparently not.

He could tell from Colin's stillness that he was awake too, but he didn't know what to do about it. He wanted to be held, but not after the way he'd lashed out. He wanted to wrap Colin in his arms to keep him safe, yet send him away before Cuernos tracked him down. No harm could come to his sweet, naïve man.

Eventually he must have fallen into a doze, because he woke with a start when Colin's cell chirped. Confused and still half-asleep, he registered light showing around the edges of the drawn curtains in the bedroom. The clock on the nightstand read six-fifteen.

"Hello?" Colin said into his phone. He sat up in bed. When he caught Hernán's eye, he mouthed, "It's security."

Colin listened intently for a few moments, eyebrows furrowing. In a strained voice, he said, "I understand. Thanks. We're set to leave around seven this morning. The driver will take us to Teterboro to get my plane."

When Colin disconnected, he turned to Hernán, the concern in his face alarming. "That was the detail chief. He heard from the people who are watching the DC condo. They reported two other men also watching the building. At one point these men used the intercom but apparently got no answer. Then, early this morning, they tried to follow a couple into the building. The front desk receptionist made a scene and they backed off. They didn't leave the area though. One of the security guys walked around the block as an excuse to get a closer look."

Colin paused. "He said the men both had a tattoo on their faces. Horns."

Hernán's blood ran cold. "Cuernos del Diablo," he said, and Colin nodded.

He pushed himself up in bed to rest his back against the headboard, aware he'd broken out in a cold sweat. His knees seemed to be trembling. He didn't know if the room had gotten loud or if he was deafened by the rush of blood in his ears. *Cuernos*. They really had come looking for him.

Colin shifted closer to take Hernán's trembling hands. "I think you were right, Hernán. I'm sorry if I didn't take your concerns seriously."

Hernán shook his head slowly. "No, what I said last night wasn't true. It's just…" The despair creeping through his bones echoed in his voice. But he couldn't give in to it. His fears had already made him hurt the very man trying to help him. He had to be stronger, for both their sakes.

Colin started to get up from the bed, but he put a hand out to stop him. "Cariño, I'm not sure anymore going to Provincetown together is a good idea. You should get away from me. I'll go somewhere far so Cuernos comes after me and leaves you alone."

Colin dropped back down and pulled Hernán to him. Chin on the top of Hernán's head, he said fiercely, "I'm not going anywhere without you. What brought this on?"

Hernán wanted to let Colin hold him forever. He felt loved in Colin's arms. All the selfish things he'd ever wanted were right there. Instead, he pulled away. Brushing his eyes, fighting the tightness in his throat that threatened to become a sob, he said intently, "They came to your fucking home, Colin. I did that to you. I put you in danger. If someone hurt you, I couldn't live with myself. It's better if you get away from me now."

Colin shook his head slowly. "Oh Nán. That just isn't going to happen." He peered into Hernán's eyes and gave a small, rueful smile. "You'd have to make me believe that you don't love me before I'd leave, and you aren't that good an actor."

"I want you to go because I *do* love you," Hernán pleaded.

"I get that. The answer is no. So now what?"

Hernán stared at Colin, his frustration and fear battling in his gut. He wanted to say terrible things to drive Colin away, even if it would break both of their hearts. He wanted to put Colin in a box and lock him away where Cuernos could never find him. He wanted Colin to save himself.

But none of that would work. Colin was right—Hernán couldn't intentionally hurt him.

The minutes ticked by before he surrendered. He tried to sound resolved. "Okay, we stick to the plan. There's no indication anyone has tracked us to New Jersey, right? Let's get up, get dressed, and fly to P-town. We'll lie low there and figure out the next move while we wrap up my asylum application."

Colin rose from the bed and tugged until Hernán stood as well.

"Good. I know we haven't solved anything yet, but we're taking steps. Right?"

Hernán nodded and said, "We should let everyone know, about the Cuernos members in DC. I'll call Rudy while you call David. And then let's get cleaned up and out of here." Hernán said it brazenly, his determination to pretend to be a warrior becoming easier with each word. A steely glint echoed in Colin's eye, easing more of Hernán's worries.

As scared as he was, it wasn't like San Marcos. He wasn't alone.

Colin phoned his security contact when they were ready to leave. "Got it," he said, and then turned to Hernán. "Apparently there are press folks milling around Teterboro. Maybe it's for us, maybe someone famous. Security wants me to have Watkins load the bags plane-side, and us to stay inside the limo until we're ready to go. Then we'll climb into the plane quickly before anyone takes note."

Hernán felt a shiver down his spine. How had his life brought him to such desperation he needed a security guard? The reality of the situation shook his fleeting bravery.

Breathing out his fears and anxieties on a sigh, Hernán picked up his bag and took Colin's hand. With a lightness he didn't feel, he asked, "Does this flight to Provincetown serve breakfast?"

Colin managed a grin for him. "As a matter of fact, it does. Watkins will have coffee and bagels for us to take on the plane."

THE ESCAPE FROM New Jersey went smoothly. Just twenty minutes after Colin hugged his mother and father goodbye—and they in turn hugged Hernán—he watched from the back of the car as Watkins loaded their bags into Colin's plane.

On the cell, the detail head was saying to Colin, "My colleagues are on their way out from Boston. They should arrive in Provincetown not long after you get in. I'll text you their contact information so you can get in touch directly."

Seated in the cockpit, Colin carefully but quickly completed his preflight inspection, and then called Jane and Sara to give an estimated time of arrival. Shortly after, they were underway. Due to prevailing winds, Colin explained, they departed to the south.

The small plane climbed out of Teterboro and began a bank that would bring it around to head northeast. The Hudson River and

Manhattan glistened out Hernán's window. Early morning sun shone in a bright blue fall sky, casting shadows of the skyscrapers across Central Park and the Upper West Side. He put his fingers on the glass, eating up the New York landmarks and monuments with his eyes.

"This view is amazing," he whispered.

"We'll come back to see it from the ground together, one day soon," Colin vowed through his headset.

They ate their bagels as they soared over Long Island Sound and crossed into Connecticut. Colin explained their flight plan to Hernán using his iPad. It was clearly a gambit to distract Hernán but he went along with it.

The app fascinated him, with aviation maps he could expand and contract with his fingertips. Hernán made a game out of it, calling out landmarks and points of interest he found on the screen to see if Colin could locate them in real life.

They flew over Block Island, and then eventually fabled places like Newport, Rhode Island. Colin brought the plane low enough that the shape of huge mansions along the water showed clearly in the morning light.

"We'll have to go see those too, sometime," Colin said. "The cottages from the Gilded Age are astonishing."

"They look smaller than your parents' house," Hernán said with a smile, praying all the while there would indeed be time for them to do things like that.

Not long after, they flew over Narragansett Bay, and on into Massachusetts airspace. Then Cape Cod Bay opened before them. Its sapphire-blue waters, touched with whitecaps, brought Hernán's heart into his throat.

"It's so beautiful," he said.

"Look there." Colin pointed to the sweep of land along the horizon to the right of the plane's track. "That's all Cape Cod, wrapping around. And up ahead..." he gestured, "you can see the Pilgrim Monument. That's Provincetown."

Colin brought the plane lower and lower as he prepared for landing, until Hernán could see the details of fishing boats trawling across the waves of the bay. A spiral of seagulls glinting in the morning sun caught his eye. He gasped when a whale breached the waves before submerging again with a flip of its broad tail.

"Did you see that?" he said excitedly to Colin. "It was a minke whale. Rudy talked me into a whale watching cruise this summer, and we saw pods of them then."

"Maybe it's a good omen."

Into his radio, Colin said, "Provincetown traffic, Seven Alpha Victor, three miles out on long final to runway seven."

The plane continued its descent, gliding toward a sandy beach and a runway that cut through the dunes. Hernán couldn't help tensing as Colin brought the plane in, flying a few feet above the ground until he gently, gently touched down. The slightest squeal of rubber, the slightest lurch, and the plane slowed. It turned off of the runway in order to taxi to the parking area.

"Provincetown traffic, Seven Alpha Victor, clear of the active runway seven," Colin radioed. He turned to Hernán. "You looked nervous. Did I scare you?"

"Oh no," Hernán said quickly. "It's just that sensation of waiting to connect with the earth again that made me feel funny."

"I hear you," Colin said. "The winds are calm so we had an easy landing."

"Well, I'd still give Air Felton a perfect review on Yelp."

Colin brought the plane to an area where three others sat parked. Several large Ts had been painted on the ground, with coils of white rope at each point. Deftly, he positioned the plane over one of the Ts and shut everything down.

Hernán helped Colin secure the plane. Together they ran the coils of rope through three wing eyelets, installed foam plugs in the cowling, and locked the doors. Beyond a gate leading from the tarmac, Jane waited for them next to a tan Lexus. Her white hair glinted in the strong morning sunshine. She pulled Hernán into a hug, and then kissed Colin's cheek.

"It's good to see you both again," Jane said. "David didn't tell me what was up but he said you need to lay low here for a while. Did you have breakfast?"

They assured her they had as they climbed into her car, Colin in the passenger seat and Hernán in the back. Jane drove out of the parking lot and into town along Race Point Road. "I'll take you right to the house then. Are you able to tell me what's up? Maybe I can help."

Hernán glanced at Colin before he responded, but he trusted Jane and Sara implicitly. They'd been nothing but kind to him and Rudy all summer. He said, "This has to stay between us and Sara, but I think I'm being hunted by members of the Cuernos del Diablo gang."

"Oh no," Jane said worriedly. Her eyes met Hernán's in the rear-view mirror. "I've read such awful things about them. Why would they be after you?"

"I'm not completely sure," Hernán admitted. "I was stabbed when I was in El Salvador, and I spoke to the police at the time. It may be that some of them think I'll come back to testify against them."

Colin spoke up. "Did you see that gossip item on us that went viral? Well, after that, two men apparently tried to get into my condo building. They had the Cuernos gang symbol tattooed on their faces."

Jane nodded slowly. "Is that why you came to stay in David and Brandon's house? You're unlikely to be followed here?"

"Exactly," Colin said. "My family has a place in Nantucket but I haven't spent much time in P-town. There's less reason to think anyone would look for us here."

"You know, I met your parents once. Your mother chaired a gala a few years back," Jane said. "I didn't realize you were related to Margaret when we met before. Anyway, it's a good time to be here. The tourists are pretty much gone, though we still get a smattering on a nice weekend. Many of the part-time owners come out for Thanksgiving, but that's weeks away. Hopefully this will all be resolved before then."

Hernán looked out the window. The truth was, he had no idea how the mess would get resolved. He and Colin couldn't hide indefinitely. Colin had a life and a job he cared about. Family. Friends. It wasn't like they could just run and run, a step ahead of Cuernos.

"Sara picked up some groceries for you last night, after David called," Jane was saying. "Many of the restaurants have closed down for the season already." She looked in the mirror again at Hernán. "Come to think of it, I haven't seen Rudy around. Did he go off-Cape for the winter?"

Hernán shook his head. "No. Well, at least not yet. He told me he's been over to Boston to look for work, but he hasn't given up his place here."

Jane turned the SUV off Commercial and headed up Pleasant Street before pulling into a gravel drive next to a yellow house. Hernán had walked by that captain's cottage many times. Its front garden in the summer was charming and inviting. Tall grasses surrounded a flag patio, on which stood a teak dining table and chairs. The butter-yellow of the house repeated in the picket fence that surrounded the property, while a shake-shingle roof gave a romantic feel to the cottage.

Colin had obviously been there before, but Hernán looked over the house in wonder. He'd often thought about the homes he passed as he walked through town, and imagined what they were like inside. Other than Jane and Sara's house and the ones he cleaned, he hadn't actually been inside very many.

Entering the cottage on Pleasant Street was a fantasy fulfilled in some ways. Wide plank floors, a ceiling with exposed wooden beams, a living room with a fireplace... Hernán followed Jane through with his head on a swivel to take in everything. It was all so different from the interior of a Salvadoran house. After the grandeur of the Feltons' castle, it was also cozy and comforting.

Colin said to Jane, "Why don't you give Hernán a tour? I'll take our bags upstairs. Do you know where David wants us to sleep?"

"He said you should take the master," Jane replied. "David and Brandon aren't planning to be up until Thanksgiving and he wants you to be comfortable. A cleaning service comes in to change the beds and all, so just settle in and relax."

Hernán watched Colin disappear up the staircase, and then followed Jane through the dining room and to the kitchen. She showed him a bathroom with shower, down a hall that led to a rear door opening on a patio. Evergreens surrounded a hot tub and created a private nook sheltered from street view.

"I think Colin probably knows how to use that if you want to get in," Jane commented. "I love getting in a hot tub on a clear, cold starry night and running back inside to a warm fire." She put an arm around Hernán's shoulder. "The last time I saw you two I thought you were just friends. It looks like something a little more has happened. Am I right?"

Hernán blushed and nodded. "Yes, we're together now. Colin is wonderful to me. I've never met anyone like him before." He blinked at her. "I didn't think you knew I was gay, though. I never admitted it to anyone but Rudy."

Jane smiled back kindly. "It's in the eyes. I could see who you looked at. I figured you'd talk about it if you wanted to." She laughed.

"But now I owe my wife twenty dollars. Sara bet me there was something developing between the two of you."

Colin joined them in the kitchen. "All squared away. I'll show you the upstairs if you want, Hernán."

Jane glanced at her watch. "I have to get going. I'm showing a few houses to a nice doctor and his boyfriend today." She pulled a piece of paper from her pocket and set it on the counter. "These are the numbers for my cell and for Sara's, and the password for the wifi. Let us know if you need anything. Sara wants you to come over for dinner tonight if that's all right with you."

After sharing a glance with Colin, Hernán nodded.

"Wonderful. Six o'clock, don't bring anything. Oh, Colin, Brandon wants you to give him a call."

Colin sighed. "I figured that was coming. Okay, I'll check in later."

Left alone, Colin took Hernán's hand and guided him upstairs to show the three bedrooms and full bath. Their bags sat on the bed in the largest room. Through a window on one wall, Hernán glimpsed the harbor.

"I feel a little funny using David and Brandon's bed," Colin said, "but it is the best room."

Hernán looked around the space. "It's really cozy," he said. "I like it."

Colin's phone trilled in his pocket. He read the message, and then said, "The new security detail is on its way." He typed a response. "There. I sent them the address. We should probably call David to check in."

Returning to the kitchen, they used the speaker function on Colin's phone to talk to the lawyers. David reported the Post was killing the story about Colin and Hernán, though it was probably too late to do much good.

Sofia said, "I just got comments back from David on the draft of your papers, Hernán. I'll get these turned around this morning and I should have them for your review early this afternoon."

"Thank you," Hernán said fervently. "I hate how this is taking up so much time for you both."

David said, "Please, don't worry about that. We're here for you."

Hernán sighed gratefully. "I can't tell you how good that feels. I'm grateful I'm not alone in this."

Colin squeezed his shoulder.

Chapter 30

HERNÁN EXPLORED THE cottage more while trying not to listen in on Colin's conversation with Brandon.

"I just didn't want anyone to treat me differently, Brandon. That's why I never talked about it. I guess Ethan must have figured it out though… I know, and I'm sorry… Yes, we'll talk more when things calm down."

Colin disconnected with a sigh. "He thinks I lied to him, by keeping such a big part of my life hidden," he said miserably to Hernán. "I didn't mean to, but I see his point."

Hernán put a hand on his shoulder. "He's your friend and he'll forgive you. Your family ultimately won't make a difference to him."

Colin nodded.

Since neither man had slept well the night before, and there was nothing they could accomplish just then, they decided to nap. The short rest helped, and Hernán woke to find Colin pressed along his back, his arm over Hernán's waist. The warmth and weight of his boyfriend stirred feelings of safety and love that muted, at least for a time, the fear he'd suffered since word of the gossip item hit. Was it really less than a day ago?

When the security team arrived an hour later, they introduced themselves as Nick and Melody. Nick was African-American, with a shaved head and broad shoulders. He stood probably just under six feet, and seemed whipcord thin under his black ribbed sweater. Melody was Caucasian, not tall—perhaps five and a half feet—but her frank gaze and loose stance signaled she was not to be fucked with. She wore her dark blonde hair pulled back into a tight ponytail, and had on a body-hugging jacket with slim black pants.

Colin showed Nick and Melody to the two guest rooms on the second floor and left them to get situated. Downstairs in the living room a little later, Hernán saw Melody moving around outside, eyes running over the front of the house. He guessed she was checking on ways in and out of the cottage.

Nick joined them and sat on the edge of a long leather ottoman. "Okay, guys. We've had a briefing from New York about the publicity item and your concerns. I'd like Mel and me to remain pretty low-key so we don't attract attention that could lead to the press finding you here," he said. "Suits would stand out, given how quiet the town seems to be this time of year. If you agree, we'll just wear casual clothes. When you go for a walk or out to eat, one of us will accompany you at a reasonable distance. We'll be close enough we can get to you if anything happens, far enough away that it won't be obvious you have security."

Hernán had no experience with any of the arrangements Nick described. Since Colin seemed satisfied with the plan, he nodded his agreement too.

"Good," Nick said. "We'll stay out of your way as much as possible for the duration."

Colin asked, "How long do you think that might be?"

Nick shrugged. "You have to tell us. How long do you expect you'll need security?"

Colin shared a look with Hernán. "I'm not sure yet," he said reluctantly. "This all just blew up yesterday. We haven't had time to think far enough ahead to come up with a solution."

"We're here for you if you want to discuss any ideas. In the meantime, Mel is scoping out surveillance locations. I'll work upstairs."

"Thanks, Nick," Colin said. "We feel better with you here."

Nick gave a thumbs-up and left the room.

Alone again with Colin, Hernán said, "I have no idea how to get out of this mess. I know we can't stay here or hide forever."

Colin looked troubled, but he nodded agreement. "This is a stopgap, sure. It gives us time to get your application wrapped up and on file. Once that happens, I understand the risk from removal by ICE at least will go down. Maybe then we can go to the police about a longer-term fix. Let's raise that with David and Sofia on the next call."

Hernán had no better ideas. They self-consciously settled on the couch, aware of strangers moving around in the house, to watch a TV mounted over the fireplace.

Still restless an hour later, the beautiful autumnal afternoon beckoned them outside. With Melody following at a short distance, they strolled down Pleasant Street together and turned onto Commercial. After a stop at Joe's Coffee, they continued their walk toward the center of town.

Through gaps in the buildings, Hernán could spy the calm waters of Provincetown Harbor. From conversations overheard in September, he suspected nearly all the boats were gone to winter storage or warmer climates. In any event, what he could see of the harbor looked empty.

They passed only a few people. Many of the bars and restaurants had signs up thanking everyone for a good summer season and promising to open again in April or May. Blank windows and hand-lettered "closed" signs created an air that he and Colin had been left behind.

After the vibrant and busy summer Hernán had spent living and working there, what remained seemed like an empty theater. The play had ended, the crowds were gone, and the lights had come up on an empty stage.

"Nantucket gets like this too," Colin said as they walked. "Maybe not as dramatic, but there's a big shift when the season ends and the crowds go home."

"It's very melancholy, isn't it?" Hernán asked. "There are so many people crowding Commercial all summer that sometimes you can't move. And now, poof, we can walk down the middle of the street. But I'd rather have the crowds back."

They walked as far as MacMillan Wharf and out to the end of it. Fishing boats still lined the pier but the pleasure crafts were mostly gone. Cormorants carpeted a narrow breakwater, before which a lone, green fishing boat bobbed in its protection.

They finished their coffees, leaning shoulder to shoulder, lost in thought.

When they finally turned to walk up the wharf, Melody was pretending to take photos of the harbor with her phone. They ignored her, as instructed, and drifted back to the house.

Later, they sat with the two guards around the kitchen island. Colin had persuaded Hernán during their walk that complete disclosure was their best bet for soliciting advice, so he told the security team about some of what he'd been through, including his immigration status. They bandied about how to determine whether Hernán was at risk and what to do about it, but no clear ideas emerged.

Sofia texted that she'd emailed the draft asylum papers to Colin's email account. He opened David's laptop, connected it to the printer and made a copy for Hernán to review. After offering to make tea, he left Hernán at a small desk to work through the document.

Hernán expected that reading his own story would be difficult, but Sofia's framing of it gave the emotional distance needed to focus on its accuracy and completeness. She'd adopted a theme that Hernán had suffered a lifetime of abuse for being gay, in a country where homosexuality continued to be anathema. He'd had no one to turn to when Cuernos targeted him as a gay man—not family, nor church, nor police. She had captured it all. The terrifying encounter as a child, the punishing response by his caregiver, the torment by Cuernos, and the nightmare of the journey with the other pollos.

Sofia left out the graphic details of the time he was trapped with Lonnie in the border town, mentioning only that "I was raped during the journey, and I have since learned that I contracted HIV as a result." She also omitted all but oblique references to Albert, Andrea and Isela.

The narrative concluded with the words, "Eventually, family members lawfully in the United States paid the ransom necessary to get me over the border."

It was only when Hernán lifted his pen to make some edits that he realized how badly his hands shook. The most fleeting references to Lonnie still made him sweat, and a cold shiver ran down his spine. The name brought back the vile feeling of his helplessness, his impalement. Hernán could see again the predatory, possessive stare Lonnie would throw at him across the dining room. He saw the coyotes coming through the dormitory for him…

"Are you all right?"

Nick's voice in his ear made Hernán jump. He looked around wildly. "What? Oh. Nick. Sorry about that."

"No worries," the guard said gruffly. "You looked upset."

Hernán flushed and stared at the document before him. He'd intended to edit but his pen pressed so heavily into the pages on top that it had torn them. In an unsteady voice, he said, "Some memories hit me hard."

Nick nodded and backed off, but a few moments later Colin came in from the kitchen. He crouched by Hernán's chair.

"Do you want to talk about anything?" he asked gently.

Hernán looked down at him, dazzled all over again by the compassion he saw in Colin's eyes. His instinct was to conceal his emotions, but Colin deserved more. "It's the part about Lonnie. Even seeing his name makes me feel…I don't know. Weak. Afraid."

"But you aren't, Nán. You survived him."

"It left scars inside," Hernán whispered. "My disease and my fear."

"Badges of honor," Colin insisted. "It was terrible but you won in the end. You're fighting back with the compassion you show at the immigration center."

Hernán managed a small smile. "How do you find the good in every situation? I wish I could do that."

Colin returned a chuckle. "It's easy. I'm in love."

Hernán ran a hand through his hair and blinked back tears. He nodded, unable to speak.

Colin continued, "Do you want help with the revisions, or to talk through any part?"

Shaking his head, Hernán said, "No. Sofia did a great job. I can't think of anything important she left out of the narrative. All I've done is add a few details I remembered as I read through her summary."

"What about the portion with the legal argument, about why you deserve asylum?"

"I haven't read that section yet." Shyly, Hernán said, "Can we read it through together? I'd appreciate your perspective."

"Of course." Colin looked so pleased Hernán berated himself for not asking immediately. "Let's sit at the kitchen island to go over it."

It was nice, there in the kitchen. Bright sunshine poured in through a bank of windows and a skylight. They read through each page of Sofia's argument, jotting notes or questions here and there. The argument seemed compelling. She wove together facts from Hernán's story with materials Colin had provided to demonstrate El Salvador's general intolerance for LGBTI and HIV-infected people and its unwillingness to protect victims or prosecute offenders. To those strands, she applied the legal standard for CIS to grant Hernán asylum.

By the end of the three-page brief, Hernán wanted to cheer. Just reading it all gave him the first real spark of hope he'd known. It might actually work. He might actually be able to stay in the country legally.

With Colin.

"It's really good," Colin said. "Sofia always does great work for the clients we send to the law firm way, but this is a step above. We should use David's scanner on these pages to get our comments to her." He blushed. "Do you know how? We have assistants at the center, so I've never learned."

"How would you survive in the TARDIS, cariño?" Hernán teased gently. "But yes, I think I can do it. Would you like some more tea? I was thinking it would be nice to sit on the patio in the sunshine for a little while."

"I'll make it while you scan."

Hernán took away the documents and heard Colin ask Melody and Nick if they'd like some tea as well. Both agreed, so after Hernán had scanned and emailed comments back to Sofia, the four of them sat at the table on the front patio.

The security team radiated readiness to act if anything happened, even as the warm afternoon sun relaxed Hernán in a way he hadn't expected. The sense of being protected—not just by the guards but by Colin, Sofia and David, and even Colin's parents—brought Hernán unexpected insight.

This must be why Colin is so bright and trusting. He's always had this.

Suddenly Melody sat up straight in her chair. The apparent languor of a woman drinking tea vanished to reveal a trained soldier. Nick also stiffened before Hernán and Colin even had time to understand what had triggered their response.

"Nán!" they heard, and quick footsteps.

Melody leapt from her chair and actually cleared the picket fence before Hernán could call out, "It's my cousin."

A strangled sound came from the other side of the mounded grasses. When Hernán and Colin made it to the fence to look into the street, Melody had Rudy on his knees, one arm bent behind his back. Rudy looked terrified.

"It's okay, Mel," Colin called. "This is Rudy. Hernán's cousin."

She nodded, helped Rudy up and apologized brusquely. Rudy looked from her to Nick and then finally at Hernán, wide-eyed. "What's going on?"

"Come in to the yard, Rudy," Hernán said. "We'll explain."

Seated again on the patio, they told Rudy about the security arrangements Colin's father had initiated.

Rudy still seemed stunned, though his gaze returned frequently to Nick. "I just got off the bus a few minutes ago and ran here. I'm so glad to see you, Hernán. And you too, Colin. I saw the tweet. Oh my god, Nán, you looked fabulous in that picture. Did you read the comments? I counted at least fifty marriage proposals, and twice as many indecent propositions."

Hernán felt his cheeks burn. "No, I didn't read any of them."

"I did," Nick volunteered. "Wanted to see if there were any direct threats to focus upon. We didn't find anything specific, and nothing that connected you to New Jersey or to Provincetown."

"Well, that's good news," Rudy purred at Nick. "You're so helpful."

Nick seemed nervous at the attention, and Melody looked like she was choking back a laugh. She said, "I'm going to do a perimeter check, Nick. I'll do a tight loop and then a broader one."

Hernán brought Rudy up to speed on what they'd been doing.

"It sounds like you don't know how long you'll stay in Provincetown," Rudy observed. "Well, at least I can keep you company."

"No luck with a job in Boston?" Hernán asked.

Rudy sighed dramatically. "No. I think I went to fifteen different restaurants and bars yesterday and this morning. Unless I want to bus tables or wash dishes—no offense, Nán, but that would suck—nobody wants to hire me. I need to let my landlord know soon if I'm keeping the apartment through the winter. I don't have any work here, but I don't want to let the place go until I get set up in Boston."

"I'm sorry. I'm sure something will turn up for you," Hernán said. He looked at Colin. "I didn't mention before that Rudy is having trouble finding a job. Could he come to DC with us to look there?"

"Of course," Colin said enthusiastically. "We have plenty of room, Rudy. You're welcome to stay with us while you job-hunt, for as long as you need."

Rudy squealed in excitement as Hernán pulled Colin close for a kiss. "Thank you, corazón," he breathed into Colin's ear. "You're the kindest man I've ever met."

Even Nick looked cautiously pleased for Rudy, but he said to Colin, "I guess we still don't know how long you'll want to stay here before you return to DC."

That comment sucked away the enjoyment. Colin glanced at Hernán, and then shook his head. "Not yet. We'll figure something out though. Rudy, I think you should go ahead and give notice at your apartment. Surely this will be resolved before you need to move out."

"Oh Colin, I'm going to love you as an in-law," Rudy sighed. Looking at Hernán, he made a long face. "Why couldn't I have been the one to pull mister man here out of the harbor?"

Chapter 31

THE NEXT FEW days passed for Colin in a spiral of emotions. His concern and worry gave way to contentment at time spent with Hernán, and that turned into a fierce protectiveness bringing him back to concern.

Despite the circumstances, he enjoyed being part of small gatherings of people. They saw Jane and Sara for dinner the first night, and lunch the following day. Rudy joined them for dinner out at one of the few restaurants still open, while Nick and Melody occupied a nearby table.

After the first night full of tension and doubt, Hernán also seemed calmer in the morning. When they heard Nick leave for a run while Melody moved around downstairs, he pulled Colin closer to make love. Their kisses were more subdued than before the gossip item. They were more mindful of their moans than in the privacy of the apartment. Still, when Hernán hovered over Colin, his arms holding up Colin's thighs, sheathed cock carefully sliding inside, the love Colin saw in his face stunned him.

"Hernán," he whispered.

Hernán cupped the back of Colin's head with one hand as he lowered himself for a kiss. He rolled his hips, lobbing his thick cock deep inside Colin before beginning to thrust.

As the pace built, the fat head of Hernán's cock dragged repeatedly across Colin's prostate, making him clench his jaw to keep from shouting. He shoved back against Hernán, hands on Hernán's ass to urge him on to a soul-shaking fuck.

The headboard squeaked but Colin ignored a flash of worry Melody would know what they were doing. At that moment, modesty was gone. All he could think about was the firm muscle, glowing eyes, flushed cheeks, and glorious smile of the man pounding him into the mattress.

He barely had time to grab his own dick between their bodies, slick from sweat and precome, before Hernán changed his angle and slid his cockhead directly against Colin's gland. Fountains of come erupted from his dick.

Hernán claimed his mouth, drinking in Colin's shouts. Then he shifted again to slide in and back with long strokes, faster and faster, until his body, too, stiffened. His muscles strained and glimmered in the morning light as he fought to draw out the moment as long as possible. Finally he plunged to the hilt inside Colin, crying his passion into Colin's mouth as he filled the condom.

Collapsing onto Colin's sweaty and sticky body, Hernán huffed quietly in his ear. "Do you think there's any chance Mel didn't hear?"

"None whatsoever," Colin whispered back. He refused to feel ashamed.

The passionate start to the day led to an intimate breakfast. Within an hour, though, lassitude and even boredom took over as they milled around the quiet house. No messages from the lawyers, no news from his father... Colin felt like a fly trapped in amber.

When Hernán said he'd like to go for a run, Melody accompanied him while Nick stuck around to watch Colin.

ANOTHER DAY PASSED, and Sofia sent them the final versions of the asylum papers by email. Hernán had collected the supporting statement from Rudy and the hospital records he needed to prove his stabbing, but he hadn't been able to reach his sister in San Marcos. Sofia filed the papers that were ready and told Hernán they could supplement the record if needed.

"Now we wait," David said. "It usually takes several months, even as much as a year, before we get a hearing date."

Colin glanced at Hernán, who seemed alarmed at the delay. "It's fine, Nán. If you want to move on from the center, remember you can work if you don't get a hearing in six months. You can start school. You can do anything you want."

Hernán rested his head on Colin's shoulder.

ON THE FOURTH morning in Provincetown, Hernán sat at Colin's shoulder when his video call with Maryanne connected. Colin used Skype to keep in touch and continue to do work for the Immigration Initiative. They had quite a bit of follow-up to the lobbying visits to attend to, including sending thank-you letters and providing additional information and position papers.

Maryanne's image said, "Oh, hi Hernán. Your classes really miss you. Nancy is taking them through the materials but you have a real connection with the students."

"I miss them too, Maryanne. Hopefully we'll find a solution soon and I'll be back." They hadn't told Maryanne much more, but she'd seen the tweet about the two of them. Colin opted to leave it at that, and let her believe nothing more than a desire to avoid paparazzi motivated their absence.

At the end of the call, she said casually, "Oh, I almost forgot. Colin, a Latino man showed up at the center to ask for you. He refused to leave a name or say what he wanted."

"It might be nothing," Colin said to Hernán after the call ended.

"Or it might be Cuernos."

BY THE FIFTH day, Colin's father reported no trouble had come to his parents or siblings. "We've had some press inquiries and a few photographers hanging around, but that's it," Dad said. "I've talked to my security group, and we're going back to our standard levels of protection. You keep your team as long as you need to, though."

"Thanks, Dad," Colin said. "We're trying to figure out what to do, but it's like proving a negative. How do we know if the threat has gone away unless we resume our lives, and then what do we do if we're wrong?"

"You've impressed me with your dedication to this, Son," Dad said. "You're in a difficult situation but I haven't seen the slightest doubt from you. There was a time you would have given up already. Your mother and I have talked about it all recently, after what you and Hernán said. Maybe it was our fault you didn't finish things. What worked for Katherine and Griffin didn't work with you. We should have seen that was our failing, not yours."

Colin's eyes watered. "It really did feel sometimes like you and Mom didn't believe in me. I was too harsh, though, and I'm sorry. But going through this has made me realize something. If I didn't stand up for myself or those I cared about before, it was because I didn't want it badly enough. Now I have Hernán, I think there's nothing I wouldn't do to keep him safe. If I could put Hernán on an island away from the entire world, I'd do it. That makes me understand the way you and Mom were with me better. I probably never said it, but thank you for loving me so much."

His father seemed flustered, and his voice was husky. "You're welcome. And your Hernán was right, by the way. There's nothing funny about my stubborn, independent son deciding he can do good by running for Congress."

Colin's cheeks burned. "I didn't say I was going to do it—" but Dad cut him off.

"I like the sound of *Senator* Felton, by the way. Or not. Whatever you choose to do with your life, your mother and I are proud of you." He cleared his throat, and signed off.

ON THURSDAY, THE sixth day, Hernán's phone rang. He looked down and said, "It's Sofia." Connecting the call, he said, "Hi. What's new?" He listened for a few moments, his brow furrowing as the lawyer talked. Finally he said, "Okay, I think I understand. I'll let everyone know but you're right. It's probably nothing."

He hung up and said to Colin and Melody, "It's a little weird. Sofia called the CIS field office to make sure my application was properly on file and to check if there was any word of a possible hearing date. The woman she talked to checked the computer and said it was odd, the files had been accessed by a different office. Apparently the clerk shouldn't have said anything because she wouldn't answer more questions. Sofia asked her to report it to her supervisors, just because it seemed unusual."

Melody frowned. "Is it possible ICE had already started to look at you, Hernán? Perhaps as a result of the gossip item?"

Colin nodded slowly. "That makes sense. We were worried about the risk of deportation. It's one of the reasons we rushed to get the application on file."

They discussed it a little longer, but could come up with no new interpretation.

By Friday, even Colin had started to go running with Hernán and the security team. He had to do something active and hoped the exercise would help him generate some strategy.

Almost immediately he lagged behind. Nick slowed to keep pace with him while Hernán and Melody ran a half-block ahead, up the middle of a deserted Commercial Street.

In a conversational tone Colin couldn't have managed then, Nick spoke up. "On open-ended assignments like this, Mel and I usually rotate in other team members for the weekend to give us a chance to see our families. Do you have any concerns about that?"

"No," Colin wheezed. "Sorry, it didn't even occur to me."

Nick chuckled. "No worries, but my wife has plans for me to clean out the garage this weekend."

Rudy would be disappointed to learn Nick was married to a woman, Colin thought. "When do you leave?" he managed to ask as they tackled a slight hill on Commercial Street.

"I'll get someone out this afternoon to replace me, and come back on Sunday if nothing changes. Mel will stay until I return and then head to Boston for two days. That way we keep continuity. Hey, let's move over to the side."

Colin heard the sounds of an approaching car from behind them. Nick maneuvered him to the curb and put a hand on his shoulder to stop him from running. Placing himself between Colin and the street, Nick angled his body toward the oncoming car. Colin noticed Mel doing the same thing with Hernán ahead.

A blue Mercedes S55 moved smoothly along the road, driven by a Caucasian man who appeared to be middle-aged. Colin relaxed marginally at the sight, as did Nick. The face he could see through the car window looked familiar, but he couldn't quite place it. The Mercedes passed Colin and had almost reached Hernán, similarly standing behind Melody, when it hit him.

Gerald Nimble.

There was no time to tell Hernán to hide his face. Through the rear window of the car, Colin saw Gerald glance at Hernán, and then do a double-take. A moment later, the car sped up.

"Oh shit," he breathed, and Nick looked at him quickly. His hand immediately dropped to the holster he wore under his running clothes. "No, nothing like that," Colin said. "It was just someone I didn't think we'd run into here in the off season."

They jogged to catch up with Hernán and Melody. "Nán, did you see?" Colin asked.

Hernán nodded. "Gerald. I'm pretty sure he recognized me."

Melody asked, "Should we be concerned? Is he tied to the Cuernos people?"

Hernán shook his head. "No, it isn't connected. He's just this asshole who we had a bad experience with a few weeks ago."

Colin grunted his agreement. "I wish he hadn't seen us, but it doesn't really affect the reason we're here."

NICK'S TEMPORARY REPLACEMENT, a heavily-muscled and curly-haired Latino named Jaime, arrived early in the evening. While Jaime received his instructions and briefing, Hernán whispered to Colin, "Rudy's going to flirt with this guy even more than Nick."

Jaime looked around the main floor of the house to get his bearings, and observed tersely, "Not crazy about all the ways in and out of the ground floor."

Nick shrugged. "We keep the two doors onto the rear patio locked, and from the living room we have good sight-lines across the entire floor."

Shortly after the briefing, Nick drove away and Melody escorted Jaime up to the room where he would sleep.

ON SATURDAY AFTERNOON, Rudy came by the cottage again. When Melody let him in, he flopped dramatically on a love seat in the living room, the back of one hand held to his forehead.

Hernán chuckled. "A little hung-over today, primo?"

"Sí, pero estoy aquí por tu novio."

"And just why are you here for my boyfriend?" Hernán asked, eyebrow arched.

"I said I'd show him the art museum. Do you want to come with us?" Rudy asked.

"I think I'd rather go for a run." He turned to look at Jaime. "Is that all right? If you go watch Colin, and Mel takes me running?"

The big guard nodded and Rudy's face lit up. "I'll feel so much better with you there," Rudy cooed. "You look like you could take on four Cuernos single-handed."

Jaime blushed slightly but was saved from answering when Colin came downstairs. "Hi Rudy. Ready to go?" Colin bent to kiss Hernán's cheek, and then let Rudy lead the way. Jaime followed a few steps behind.

Melody came into the room and asked Hernán, "You ready for our run?" He grabbed his shoes, laced them up, and waited outside until Melody had secured the house again. They took off in the direction of Herring Cove beach.

COLIN LAUGHED WITH Rudy for the entire twenty-minute walk to the museum. Rudy was full of stories, about Hernán as a child, about the waiters from Bulgaria who worked in P-town for the summers, about love affairs that crashed and burned.

"What happened with the guy from Vermont?" Colin asked. "Hernán told me about him. Sounded like you were kind of hooked on him."

Rudy sighed dramatically. "Oh, I was. He came back to see me a few weekends later and oh *my* were we good together. Then he invited me to visit him at his college. We went to a faculty event the first night I was there. I tried to be demure and ladylike. No, I really did, Colin! But *someone* was playing the piano, and I simply had to perform my tribute to Adele. Anyway, I thought we were all having a good time but my professor was *not* amused. So that ended tragically, like all the others." He winked. "The piano player came to see me the following weekend, though."

Colin made appropriate noises and said he would have loved to see Rudy's routine. Walking up the path to enter the art museum while they chatted, the door opened and Gerald Nimble stepped out, eyes on the ground. He hadn't yet noticed them.

"And speaking of tragic endings," Rudy said loudly.

Gerald's head snapped up. Colin watched multiple emotions surge across his face as he registered Rudy standing with Colin, flanked closely by a large man. What might have been a spark of longing as he looked at Rudy quickly turned cautious. A cold sneer twisted his features when his eyes landed again on Colin.

"Don't tell me you've moved on from Hernán already," Gerald drawled. "What an interesting item that was in the *Post*. So, you spirited Hernán away to Washington, and now you've brought him back. Is that to trade him in? I do understand Rudy's charms to the unwary."

Colin felt his ire grow, but he ordered himself to say nothing.

Rudy had less restraint. He tossed his hair dramatically out of his eyes and leveled his gaze on Gerald. "Well, if it isn't my ex. How awkward," Rudy snapped. "Bought yourself any new boy toys lately? Blackmailed anyone else into your little sex games?"

Gerald snarled, "Watch your mouth, Rudy. We have a contract." Rudy snorted, and Gerald glared at him. "I don't have to blackmail anyone into bed."

"Oh, yes? Like Hernán *wanted* to go to your house," Rudy said dismissively.

"There was no blackmail involved. I just told him what I wanted—"

"And threatened to have him fired if he didn't comply," Colin said savagely. *So much for staying out of it.* "I was there, Nimble, at Veranda. I heard what you said to him."

Gerald's gaze flickered between Colin and Rudy. A touch of uncertainty vanished in a burst of malice. More wheels turned behind his gray eyes, and he growled. "Ah, Jim *Felton's* son. Jim's a director on the board of the fund. That's why I was…"

He shook his head pityingly at Colin. "Couldn't fight your own battles, could you? Had to call on daddy and his friends?" That struck Colin right in the gut, and Gerald showed a little tooth in his grimace. "I suppose it's what comes to me for not doing the right thing in the first place," he said.

"What, learning no means no, and staying away from people who find you repulsive?" Rudy asked sarcastically.

Colin saw a flash of pain cross Gerald's face. "I suppose you mean you found me repulsive all those years, when you were taking my money and eating my food?" The tone was smug and dismissive, at odds with the wound showing in Gerald's eyes.

Rudy flared up indignantly. "I never asked for anything. You just threw things at me. I was stupid enough to think I meant something to you and that you *wanted* to give me gifts. Until you sent me away to bring in someone younger."

"Don't deny it, you were bored with me," Gerald hissed.

"Bored with your snotty friends and you showing off your money."

Jaime broke in, his deep voice cutting through Rudy's high-pitched squawk of outrage. "Mr. Felton, sir, we should go inside."

Colin nodded but before he could move, Gerald sneered at Rudy. "What I mean about doing the right thing is calling Immigration."

"What did you do?" Rudy demanded, his voice reaching even higher decibels.

"Just what I said. I called ICE in Boston this morning to alert them to an undocumented immigrant hiding in Provincetown." Glaring up at Jaime, Gerald added, "He's apparently here to cause trouble, given the thugs he brought with him."

Colin clenched his fists to keep from throwing a punch. He'd never hit a person in his life but Lord, he wanted to lay Gerald out.

"You malicious piece of shit," he said in a low, dangerous voice. "Is it any wonder no one will be with you unless you force them or buy them? Well, you're too late to cause trouble that way at least. Hernán's application for asylum is on file already."

Rudy gasped suddenly and grabbed Colin's arm. "What Hernán said last night, from when his lawyer called."

"What do you mean?" Colin asked, frowning.

"She said someone at CIS or maybe ICE accessed Hernán's records improperly. What if it has to do with Cuernos?"

"I don't follow," Colin said, but Gerald interrupted before Rudy could answer.

"The Cuernos del Diablo gang? What could they possibly have to do with this situation?" he demanded with a snort.

"It's the reason Hernán came to this country in the first place," Rudy said, glaring at Gerald. "He was running for his life because Cuernos targeted him in El Salvador."

"Because he's gay? I knew it," Gerald gloated.

Colin almost let his fist fly but Rudy beat him to it. Grabbing Gerald's jacket in his hands, he shoved him back against the door of the museum.

Almost in tears, Rudy said, "How could I have ever felt anything for you? You are such a pig. Yes, Hernán is gay. He was nearly killed *because* he was gay and then you tried to force him to have sex with you. How are you any better than a rapist? I don't care what our contract says or what you do to me. If anything happens to Hernán because of your evil bullshit I will let everyone know about the clothes in the trunk and the role-play. Do you understand me, pendejo?"

He shoved Gerald to the side and flung open the doors of the museum. "Come on, Colin. I need some class after stepping into the gutter with this pinche idiota."

Colin followed warily after Rudy, aware of Jaime looming behind him. He turned slightly to see Jaime bend and whisper something in Gerald's ear. Gerald turned pale and scurried off down the path to Commercial Street.

Inside the museum, Rudy had stepped to the right of the door and leaned his back against the wall, his eyes glassy and his chest heaving. Colin put a hand on his arm.

"That was perfect, Rudy. I wanted to punch him, but what you said was better."

Rudy tried to blink away tears but his eyes filled. "I used to think I loved Gerald," he whispered. "I'm so stupid."

"No, just hopeful. You'll find the man deserving of your love one day." Colin pulled him into a hug. "Hernán's going to be so proud of you, and I am too."

Chapter 32

When Hernán got back from his run with Melody, the others had not yet returned from the museum. He took a shower and set about organizing food for dinner. Colin and Rudy walked into the kitchen about an hour later, faces closed and stormy. Colin glanced guiltily at Jaime.

Gruffly, Jaime said, "He needs to know about the call. And you should tell the lawyers."

Colin sighed and had Hernán sit on a stool at the kitchen counter. He described the run-in with Gerald, what the man had done. With a glint in his eye, he added what Rudy said to Gerald. Rudy blushed and looked at the kitchen floor.

Hernán stared up at Colin, aghast. Heart racing, he had trouble catching his breath suddenly. He'd worked so hard to keep his secrets, but even Gerald knew them now. He'd tried to stay far under the radar, yet Gerald had told ICE exactly where he was. Enforcement officers might be coming for him already.

Despite what Sofia and David said, his asylum application was just that—an application. He didn't know if it would be enough to save him from deportation, or if the right people would even listen.

"I should have just slept with Gerald," he whispered, swaying slightly on his stool. Rudy cried out his protest and Colin scooped up his hands.

"No, mi ángel. It would have fixed nothing. Gerald might never have stopped demanding sex, and you could still have been caught by ICE at any time. Now at least we're prepared. We've taken as many steps as we can to protect you."

The earnestness and sincerity in Colin's eyes couldn't keep Hernán from trembling. "You don't know if it's enough. You *can't* know. I might be sent back to El Salvador."

Colin looked over his shoulder. "Can you give us a minute?" he begged.

Melody nodded and led Jaime and Rudy into the living room, though she kept a clear path open to them in the kitchen.

Colin put a finger and thumb on Hernán's chin and tugged to get his attention. He leaned closer. "Listen to me, Hernán. I swear, no one will take you away from me. If the worst happens and ICE tries to deport you, we'll leave the country together. I don't care where we live. Or I'll marry you so we can stay here." He flushed horribly. "That isn't... That's not how I want to propose to you. But I'll move heaven and earth to keep you safe and with me for as long as you want to be with me."

Hernán's eyes filled. His throat ached terribly. What Colin suggested was so huge he couldn't process it. Colin had everything in the States—his job, his family, his life. How could Hernán let him move to El Salvador?

And *marriage.* The idea was terrifying and exhilarating at the same time. They'd known each other for such a short time. Yes, he'd thought about it. He could even imagine it happening, when they were ready. Marriage was huge and sacred and should bind them together for nothing less than love. How could he let Colin marry him for something as selfish as a green card?

Yet how could he let Colin go, if the ruling went against them?

Fighting back his tears, Hernán said in a gravelly tone, "I know you'll do everything you can to help me. That means so much—" He had to stop when sobs threatened to take his voice. He shook his head abruptly. "Okay. I'm borrowing trouble. We have a plan and I need to have faith. Let's tell Sofia what's happened and see what she thinks."

They called her on Colin's phone in speaker mode and asked her to patch in David. When all four were connected, Colin repeated what Gerald had done. He finished and there was a silence.

David spoke first, sadness in his voice. "You know, Gerald used to be my friend. I can't believe what he's turned in to." He sighed heavily. "Another time. Listen, Hernán, this is why we rushed the papers through. The asylum argument is strong. As long as the application is pending, there should be no risk of you being deported, even if you're picked up by Immigration officers. It's important you tell anyone who does try to arrest you that you've sought asylum. Keep the case number with you at all times, and provide it to everyone and anyone."

Sofia said, "I'm texting it to both of you now, along with every phone number for David and for me. If anything goes wrong, try to reach one of us. Since you aren't a citizen, Hernán, you don't necessarily have a Constitutional right to consult a lawyer, but keep asking."

They talked longer, with Colin, David and Sofia basically trying to calm Hernán's nerves. Rudy joined them in the kitchen, for once standing quietly with his hand on Hernán's shoulder, offering strength. Their earnestness and support gradually worked through the brittle shell that had sprung up around Hernán when he first heard what Gerald had done.

You aren't alone, he repeated to himself over and over. *You aren't alone.*

In a somber mood, Colin and Rudy prepared food while Hernán sat at the island, watching. The camaraderie of the days before was gone, replaced by tension and fear. Rudy left for his apartment soon after they finished eating, and Colin tried to entice Hernán into an episode of *Doctor Who*.

He couldn't focus on the plot—something about the Daleks and Winston Churchill—but he appreciated Colin's warmth next to him on the sofa. Melody and Jaime periodically took turns walking around the neighborhood to make sure nothing unusual had developed.

Colin and Hernán went to bed early, holding each other in the king-size bed, looking through the window at a full moon over Provincetown.

HERNÁN SLEPT BADLY, too full of tension to relax. Every creak in the antique cottage snapped him to alertness. By the time he started to drift off, exhausted, one of the guards went down the noisy stairs and out the front, probably heading for a run. Colin stirred when the front door closed. Though they lay pressed together, neither was in a state to pursue anything erotic.

Eventually, Colin whispered, "Sorry, angelito. Gotta pee." Once he slid out of bed and headed for the bathroom, Hernán decided he might as well get up too.

They made coffee and breakfast, and then Colin settled in to do some work for the center. Hernán tried to read, but even that took more focus than he could muster. He looked out the window onto Pleasant Street instead.

The sky was gray and pendulous, with thick clouds threatening rain. A strong wind stirred the trees he could see, stripping the last of the leaves to send them skittering up the street. He shivered.

Melody passed through the living room just then, and paused to turn on the gas fireplace. Hernán smiled at her wanly. "Would you like some tea?" she asked. "I was about to make some for myself." Hernán nodded and followed her to the kitchen. They talked about random things in a low voice so as not to disturb Colin.

Jaime returned from a run, his cheeks red and chill pouring off his body. "It's cold out there today," he grunted. "Pretty typical for the Cape, but I'm not ready for winter yet."

"Do you want to go running?" Melody asked Hernán.

"Thanks, but I'm not up for it this morning."

"You're worried about the call to ICE," she said.

Hernán nodded. "I've never felt so exposed before. The one thing every undocumented person knows is to stay out of sight and off the radar. Between the gossip item, the asylum application, and Gerald turning me in to ICE, I feel like I'm standing in a spotlight."

Melody ran a hand briskly up and down his arm and patted his shoulder. "You'll be fine, Hernán. We've worked for Colin's family before and I know they'll never leave you hanging. As for the rest, it sounds like you have some good lawyers on your side."

He couldn't help asking, "Does it bother you? That I'm in this country illegally?"

Melody cocked her head. "No, it doesn't," she said firmly. "I grew up in the restaurant business because my mom had a small diner in Springfield. I knew a lot of the people we hired were undocumented. Just like everywhere, a few were jerks but most were great people. I heard stories about what conditions could be like in other countries. I suppose it made me appreciate even more I was lucky enough to be born in the U.S. I didn't earn my citizenship, not like some of the people my mom hired. It's why I joined the Army, actually.

"I remember this one lady, Marta. After she got her green card she studied the materials for the citizenship test at every break. I was there, when she got sworn in as a U.S. citizen. She was so proud because she worked for it."

Jaime looked uncomfortable. Hernán would have let it go, but Melody said to him, a little aggressively, "How about you? You don't like the immigration thing?"

His gaze flickered between Melody and Hernán. "Look, it's none of my business. We're here to do a job and keep Hernán and Colin safe. I'm going to do so to the best of my abilities."

His attention finally settled on Hernán. "It isn't personal. You seem like a great guy and I understand why you came to the States. But it's still a crime. My mother came legally from Colombia. There are paths to get here the right way, and I think people should follow them. If you stick to the rules, you don't have to be afraid of ICE or getting rounded up or anything." He flushed and said again, "It isn't personal."

"Well, I did ask," Hernán said, bristling. "But it hurts you think that. Maybe your mother and you never knew what it's like to be desperate, or have forgotten. I was terrified I'd be murdered if I stayed in El Salvador. I thought if I could get away from Cuernos, I'd be safe. America is the only other place I had family. What should I have done? Sat in front of an embassy and hope Cuernos didn't find me first? In a perfect world, I would have waited to see if permission came through. That just wasn't my life."

Melody gave Jaime a sharp look. "That's why we're here. To protect you and Colin."

The day dragged. Rain came in waves, drumming loudly on the skylights for a time before tapering off again. A chilly draft crept through the house from somewhere Hernán couldn't find. The weight in his heart grew heavier and heavier. He felt something bad coming.

What scared him most was the thought of trouble coming for Colin. If ICE did show up, Colin would try to protect him—there was no doubt in his mind. But that path led to legal issues for Colin too.

If I were braver, I'd go to Boston and turn myself in. See if what David and Sofia did is enough to keep me here. If not, I'd go back to El Salvador and face the consequences. Anything other than putting Colin at risk.

A little after four o'clock, Melody's phone rang. "It's Nick," she said, and put the phone to her ear. Hernán saw her face pale. Melody gestured at Colin, Hernán and Jaime to come near and put the phone on speaker. "Nick, would you say it again? Everyone's listening."

Nick's voice through the phone sounded tense. "Boss called. We have a report of a car heading in to Provincetown. Apparently six men were crowded in. It may be nothing. They might just be on their way to stay for the week. Given the circumstances, though, we need to be ready."

Colin said, "Where did this report come from?"

"Someone named Gerald Nimble," Nick answered. "He didn't know where to find you, Colin, so all he could do was contact your family about the car he saw. I guess he knew how to get in touch with your dad. Then Mr. Felton called my boss."

Colin stared at Hernán, his mouth wide open. "Gerald *Nimble*? You're sure of the name?"

"Yes," Nick answered. "I didn't talk directly to him, but I'm sure that's what my boss said."

"Thanks, Nick. We'll keep an eye out and let you know if anything changes." Melody hung up and faced Jaime. "What do you think?"

He shrugged, though his face was tight. "It could be completely unrelated to us, I suppose. There are plenty of reasons for a group of men to come to Provincetown. The fact it's on a Sunday in October when the weather is bad, though, makes me nervous."

"Should we call the police?" Colin asked, wide-eyed.

"What would we say?" Melody asked. "We don't have any idea where this car was headed, and nothing concrete to show they're a threat anyway." She flicked her eyes then, and Jaime followed her upstairs.

In the small house, Hernán distinctly heard the sound of a magazine clicking into place on a gun. When the guards came back down, each had a second holster visible. They all tried to act normal, but every attempt at conversation died away.

Twilight came early to Provincetown. It wasn't even five when they had to turn on all the lamps. Jaime looked larger somehow as he glanced around the shadowed living room and out the window facing Pleasant Street.

To Melody, he said, "I'm not happy with all the light we're putting out. This seems to be the only house on the street occupied and lit up. Let's say someone is driving around and looking for Hernán. We're almost a beacon."

Melody agreed. She moved around the room, flicking off most of the lamps and the outside lights. The sense of oppression grew in the dimness.

"Colin, Hernán," she said. "I'd like for you to go upstairs and stay there for the evening. That will minimize the risk of crossfire if anything happens."

Colin's forehead looked sweaty, and his hands clenched tightly. He wordlessly obeyed Melody's suggestion. Hernán nodded as well, though his legs and arms felt like they would cramp if he moved. He couldn't draw a full breath.

His foot was on the first tread when the front door to the house exploded inward. Simultaneously, he heard a crash and slam of what sounded like the back door being kicked in.

Five men poured into the living room. Melody moved quickly to pull her gun but one of the men hit her arm with a tire iron. Bone crunched. Melody cried out as she dropped the gun, but she went to a crouch and knocked the man's legs away with a sweeping kick.

Jaime had one man's arms around his neck as he punched savagely at a second. The two guards moved like machines but the room was cramped. They couldn't get enough space to fight back properly.

Melody tossed a guy's head into the mantle and he sprawled out on the floor, moaning. A man with a knife lunged at Jaime. He grabbed the knife hand and outstretched arm to flip the attacker onto his back. A lamp smashed to the ground. Another invader swooped up the fallen tire iron and came at him before Jaime could reach his weapon.

Hernán looked around wildly for some way to help. Melody and Jaime didn't need them, but he felt useless and cowardly on the landing. In another few moments, it looked like Melody and Jaime would have everyone down.

That was when he heard Colin gasp and the sound of a pistol being cocked inches away.

He whirled as Colin was yanked off the landing and to his knees on the floor of the dining room. A pistol that seemed huge huge *HUGE* pointed at Colin's head. Hernán cried out and his eyes flew to the man holding the gun. His racing heart all but stopped.

It was Lonnie Heath.

The monster from his nightmares, the darkness haunting him, stood there with a gun pointed at Colin. Hernán heard a wail, a keening fill the room, and it took him seconds to realize the noise came from him.

Lonnie called loudly, "I have the rich kid, motherfuckers. Stop fighting or I pull the fuckin' trigger right now."

The struggle in the living room stopped instantly. Lonnie grabbed Colin by the hair. Holding the pistol against his temple, he dragged Colin around and into the living room.

Hernán couldn't move. His legs had turned to stone, and he panted so rapidly the dining room swam. *No. Don't do this,* he ordered himself. *Colin needs me.*

The thought brought focus to his fear. *Lonnie has Colin.* He took a shaky breath, trying to listen over the pounding in his ears, and stepped toward the living room as well.

Melody was on her knees over a fallen man with a tattoo of devil horns on his face. One of her arms hung awkwardly but she'd clearly been in the middle of beating the shit out of the guy. Two men lay stunned or unconscious on the floor. Jaime had crossed his arms to protect his body against two others, who had him backed into a corner where they'd been hitting him with a tire iron and a piece of wood. Both Jaime and Mel had frozen in place at Lonnie's threat.

The sight of Colin on his knees, with death pressed to his temple, was the most horrible thing Hernán had ever witnessed. "Lonnie," he croaked. "What are you doing here?"

Colin's head jerked at the name, but Lonnie tightened the hold on his hair. He looked back and gestured with his head for Hernán to come around in front of him. The three remaining Cuernos roughly pushed Melody and Jaime there as well. One retrieved his fallen knife and held it ready to cut either guard.

Lonnie smiled darkly at Hernán. He said, "There you are. I owe you, boy, for what you did."

"What I did?" Hernán asked incredulously.

"You didn't know your place. You belonged on your knees in front of me, takin' my cock any way I wanted to give it to you. Instead you whined like a little bitch and got the bosses involved. Two weeks after you left they kicked my ass out and put that cocksucker Carlos in charge."

"I didn't do anything," Hernán protested.

"Pretty boy ran," Lonnie sneered. "I weren't done with you yet."

Colin struggled and cried out as Lonnie yanked his head back. He put the muzzle of the gun at Colin's cheek and snarled, "Stay still, rich boy, or I'll knock your goddamn teeth out." Colin froze. To one of the three standing men, Lonnie said, "Bring in the culero. We're done with him."

The man left through the front door and returned a few moments later, his fist scrunched in the back of Rudy's jacket as he pushed him into the house. His torn coat, bloody lip and black eye told the story. The man pushed him hard.

Rudy sprawled on his hands and knees. He sobbed as he looked up at Hernán. "I didn't tell them anything, Nán. They grabbed me and hit me and asked where you were. They said they were going to—"

"We still might," Lonnie leered. "Pretty, but not as pretty as Hernán. It might be fun anyway. Right, guys?" he said to the men standing around. "Just drivin' along through the streets, lookin', and what do we see? A chica, just prancing along. What are the chances of two fag Salvadorans in the same town? We just drove around while my boys here had some fun, and then we saw the lights. Took a look." He aimed a kick at Rudy's ribs, drawing a ragged moan.

"Stop, please," Hernán begged. "What do you want?"

"I'm taking you with me, puto," Lonnie said grimly. "I want my favorite cocksucker back where he can do what he does best. Those languages you speak are gonna be real useful."

"You're taking me back to Mexico?" Hernán gasped.

"I'm through with that shit-ass place at the border," Lonnie snarled. "The jefes ran me off? Fine. I got my own setup now in Honduras. My own crew. My boys 'n me, we're makin' a name for ourselves. And you're gonna help us with settin' up new routes using that language shit or whatever."

"You aren't with... Cuernos del Diablo didn't send you after me?" Hernán asked. Maybe it didn't matter, but he needed to know.

"Why would Cuernos give a shit about you?" Lonnie scoffed. "Never heard a word about them looking for you. But me and the boys here, we figure Cuernos is gonna go down sooner or later. Too big, too messy, too much attention. They got fingers in pies you wouldn't believe. So my boys here decided they were done with Cuernos and are gonna work with me instead."

"Who came to the condo in Washington then?" Hernán gasped.

"Sent two of my best—" he gestured at the men guarding Jaime, their tattoos plain, "—to look for you in DC but you didn't show. When that tweet shit went viral, I knew you were just what the doc ordered. We'd grab the rich boy's piece of ass, make some headlines as we head out of the country, get our rep started. I'd get a translator and a hole to fuck in the process."

"How did you find us in Provincetown?" Colin asked raggedly. Lonnie jerked his hair back and forth, making Colin yell.

"Please stop," Hernán begged. "Don't hurt him."

"Miguel, there," Lonnie said, jerking his chin at one of the still men on the floor. "Cuernos got him workin' inside with the ICE cabrones. He got access to computer files, word about raids before they happen, all that shit. He put some kind of fuckin' app or whatever in the system so we knew when anything about you popped up. Yesterday it told us someone called the tip line to report exactly where you was holed up."

Gerald's call. Of course.

Hernán made himself focus on what Lonnie let slip. "You want me, not Colin," he choked out.

Lonnie leaned down to look into Colin's face, holding his head tilted by his hair. "Yeah," he drawled. "Shame though. He got good cocksuckin' lips too. But that shit's too big for now. We take rich boy here, the wrath of God comes down."

He straightened and looked scornfully at Hernán again. "But you? Ain't nobody comin' after you when we haul your ass back."

"I will," Colin said savagely. "If you try to take Hernán away, my father will use every resource at his command and hunt you down."

"That right?" Lonnie said thoughtfully. "Well, maybe we'd be better off with no witnesses to put him on the trail. What do you think, fucktard?" he drawled at Hernán. "Should I put a bullet in rich boy's face so no one tells his daddy to come lookin' for you?"

What do I do? His hated grandmother's voice rang in his head, saying *What else is gonna happen to a little fag?* Rudy sobbed on the floor. Melody looked murderous but her arm was broken. She had no chance with Lonnie holding Colin hostage. Jaime looked like he was calculating something; Hernán could see his muscles tense. If Jaime moved, Lonnie might shoot Colin.

"Stop! All of you," Hernán yelled. "I'll come with you. I won't fight."

"Hernán, no—!" Colin cried.

"I have to. Lonnie, leave them alone and I'll come with you quietly.

Colin, tell him you won't look for us. Swear it," Hernán begged.

"I wouldn't believe him if he did swear," Lonnie said with a cruel laugh. He crouched again and hissed into Colin's ear. "But I tell you this, asshole. If I see you or your guards or if anybody tries to take away my personal little puto, I'll put a bullet through his head. Think about it before you try some kind of rescue."

He stood and shoved Colin forward so he landed on his knees next to Rudy. Then he grabbed Hernán and pulled him closer. <<Watch them until we're out of here,>> he barked to his men. <<I'll bring the car around.>>

<<What about them?>> one of the thugs said, gesturing at the unconscious men.

<<Get them up. We'll deal later.>>

Lonnie walked backward, dragging Hernán along, gun outstretched at the people in the room. He stepped through the front door and down the two steps to the path, and then yanked Hernán after him.

"Down," a voice barked, as a black boot crunched into Lonnie's gun hand, kicking his arm skyward. The pistol went off as Lonnie yelled.

Hernán recognized the voice as Nick's. He hit the wet ground, staying low as the two men struggled. Lonnie swung wildly with the pistol, trying to hit Nick with it or to get far enough back to pull off a shot.

Inside, sounds of fighting erupted. Lonnie jerked himself free and kicked at Nick simultaneously, sending him stumbling backward. He raised the pistol but Colin hurtled through the front door, bellowing in fury and wildly swinging the tire iron. The iron caught Lonnie on his back. He shouted in pain and stumbled, but didn't fall.

Whipping his arm around, he knocked Colin to the ground. He aimed his pistol, this time at Colin, and Hernán didn't even think. He swung his legs around like Melody had done, sweeping Lonnie off his feet. The pistol roared harmlessly at the night sky. Lonnie tumbled back and fell heavily, his head cracking on the flagstones. He was utterly still.

Colin scrambled to Hernán's side where he lay on the sidewalk. The sounds of fighting inside had stopped. "Are you all right?" Colin demanded. "Did he shoot you or Nick?"

"I'm fine," Nick said, striding over to kick the gun far away from Lonnie's outstretched hand.

"I'm okay," Hernán said at the same time. Colin buried his face in Hernán's shoulder, hugging him so hard Hernán choked. "Sweetheart, I can't breathe."

Colin relaxed his grip but he didn't let go. "I was so scared for you," he said in a wet voice. Hernán felt tears drip down his cheek as Colin sobbed in his arms.

"I was scared for you too," he whispered. "My warrior. You were so brave."

Melody appeared in the splintered doorframe. "We've got everyone inside under control. Jaime is calling the police." Her arm hung awkwardly. "I'm going to need medical attention."

"This asshole too," Nick said, tossing his head in Lonnie's direction. "He's alive but he got knocked out when Hernán floored him." He grinned at the men wrapped in each other's arms. "We should offer a job to the dynamic duo here. Nice job, guys. Wish I'd gotten in that kick."

Hernán called out, "Be careful with Lonnie's blood. He's got HIV."

Nick nodded, accepting his word. "We'll alert the EMTs when they show."

"You weren't due back for hours," Melody said to Nick. "It's lucky you came early."

"After I told you about the warning from Gerald Nimble, I hauled ass down Route Six to get here. Then I came across a car parked illegally, just as Commercial turns onto Pleasant. I called the police then, but this is a small town. The only officers on duty were miles away dealing with something. I got out of my car and came on foot. Once I saw what was going on, I waited for a chance. Figured they'd have to go for their car and I might be able to get the drop."

Rudy pushed his way past Melody and dropped to his knees next to Colin and Hernán. He wrung his hands in his lap, as if afraid to touch them. His face scrunched miserably, causing his lip to begin bleeding again. "I kept telling them I didn't know you or where you were, but they hit me and hit me. They said…they said they were going to take turns if I didn't tell them." His voice turned to steel. "But I didn't."

Hernán wriggled free from Colin to pull his cousin in for a rough hug.

Rudy's voice was muffled against Hernán's shirt when he asked disbelievingly, "Did I hear Nick say *Gerald* tried to help?"

Nick answered. "Yes. I got more of the story while I was on the road. Nimble told Mr. Felton he knew there was potential trouble and he was sorry for his part in it."

"It's something," Colin said. "Maybe you got through to him at the museum."

They huddled together on the path until the sounds of a siren approached, and rotating blue lights lit up Pleasant Street.

Epilogue

February…

HERNÁN'S HANDS SHOOK as he read through the single sheet of paper. He looked up at Sofia, afraid to believe. Her smile was joyful and blinding.

"Does this really mean…?" he tried to ask, and she nodded.

"Granted, yes. You've got asylum, Hernán."

He hugged Sofia fiercely, not caring if he wrinkled her neat suit. David beamed behind her, so Hernán released Sofia to grab him too. His face felt wet and he knew he was crying.

David hugged him back quickly, and said, "It's odd but we're lucky in a way, that Lonnie Heath came after you. The publicity persuaded USCIS to give you a hearing faster than normal, and it even supported your claim of being targeted for your sexual orientation."

Hearing from Lonnie that Cuernos wasn't pursuing him in the States had lifted an unbearable weight from Hernán's soul. The lightness and freedom that followed carried him up to skies as clear as he could see from Colin's plane.

There'd been some concern by the police and ICE that Cuernos members in the States would interfere with the prosecution of Lonnie and his gang, all U.S. citizens. Since they'd gone rogue, though, apparently Cuernos took no interest. Lonnie Heath was in federal prison in Kansas.

"Thank you. Both of you," Hernán said roughly. "You put so much work into this. Into *me*."

Sofia rubbed his back as he read the paper aloud again: "It has been determined you are eligible for asylum in the United States."

"Do you want to phone Colin?" Sofia asked.

Hernán shook his head as he swiped a thumb under his eyes. "I'd like to tell him in person." He glanced at his watch. "He should be at the center."

"I'll drop you off," David offered. "We go right by there on the way to the office."

Hernán climbed into the back seat of David's BMW sedan, and Sofia sat in the passenger seat. She rotated slightly to talk to him as David navigated his way from Virginia into DC. "Now that you have permission to be here legally we can get you a work permit. Come by the office next week and we'll get the paperwork squared away. And I think you want to talk about whether there are any options to help your sister come from El Salvador?"

Hernán agreed absently. He couldn't take his eyes off the paper in his hand. Everything was wrapped up in a single document—His health. His future and the possibility of returning to college. His safety from Cuernos.

His love.

His eyes burned again as he tried out ways in his head to tell Colin. *Hey, guess who's no longer undocumented?* Or, *Hi sweetheart. Just thought I'd let you know I can work legally now so you don't have to keep me afloat.* No. How about *Thank you, Colin. You changed my life when you brought me to Washington.* Better but still not right.

David pulled to the curb outside the center's building. Hernán leaned forward between the two seats. "I want to celebrate. Can you both come to Mata Hari this evening around seven? And Brandon too, please."

Colin and Brandon had talked more after they'd returned from Provincetown. Brandon was hurt Colin had lied to him by omission, but their friendship seemed to be mending slowly. Still, Hernán took any chance to get them into the same room.

After the lawyers agreed to the party, Hernán climbed out. He raised a hand in farewell as the car pulled away, and then retrieved his cell to call Rudy.

"Hi Nán," his cousin said brightly. "Can't talk long. I'm unloading inventory." Away from the mouthpiece, Rudy said, "Mal, can you put the fresh Flying Dog keg in place?" A voice grumbled assent in the background. Returning to Hernán, Rudy asked, "What's up?"

"I'll tell you later but I want to ask, can you reserve one of the side rooms in the bar for a private event this evening?"

"Sure," Rudy said. "It should be a quiet night so I don't see any problem with closing one of them off. You won't tell me now?"

"Tonight."

Rudy signed off to get back to work.

Hernán was so happy for him. Once Lonnie and the rest of his rogue crew had been hauled away by the police in November, they'd said goodbye to Melody, Nick and Jaime. The next day, Colin flew Hernán and Rudy back to Washington to resume their lives.

After a few weeks of Rudy job-searching, David mentioned a local gay bar named Mata Hari needed a new manager. Rudy applied, David and Brandon vouched for his character and his skill set, and the owner gave Rudy the job.

He'd taken to running the gay piano bar like a pro. "Well, I should know what to do," he'd giggled to Hernán. "Lord knows I've spent enough time in bars looking for a man. I think I can figure out how to keep this place going smoothly!"

By January, Rudy had found an apartment in Virginia for himself and moved out of the condo.

"You know you're welcome to stay," Colin said.

Rudy wrapped an arm around his shoulder. "Oh, I know. You're both adorable and sweet and all. The problem is, my earplugs aren't doing a good enough job. Until I find myself a man of my own, I don't think I can keep listening to the two of you going at it."

"What about Jaime?" Hernán asked teasingly. "He's been down twice from Boston to visit."

Rudy's eyes sparkled. "I do like the big, mysterious types. But we're just having fun. Normally I'd be all up in the fantasy of a bodyguard as my soul mate. But if I've learned anything from you, primo, it's to hold out until I find real love."

"Hi Hernán." The voice of one of his ESL students brought him out of his reverie.

"Esteban," he said, clouting the man on his shoulder. They entered the building together and rode the elevator up, chatting about the class.

"Are you teaching today?" Esteban asked but Hernán shook his head.

"I took the day off. I'll be back tomorrow though, and the rest of the week."

"Good," Esteban said grimly. "Nancy is fine but your lessons make more sense to me."

Pride filled Hernán's chest as he said goodbye and made his way to Colin's office. His boyfriend faced his computer but rotated around in his chair as Hernán entered.

"Hola, mi ángel," Colin said brightly, his blue eyes glinting up at Hernán through his glasses. "Did you have a good session with Dr. Fleming?"

Hernán had almost forgotten he'd told Colin he was going to see his therapist. She'd helped him get Abuela's voice out of his head and come to terms with the many things that had befallen him. Mostly, she'd guided him to understand that he deserved love.

Closing the office door behind him, he leaned against it. "I may have told you a little fib." Colin raised an eyebrow but said nothing. "I didn't really have an appointment with Dr. Fleming. I went with David and Sofia to pick up my ruling."

He held out the piece of paper but with the smile stretching across his face, Colin didn't need to read. He jumped out of his chair and gathered Hernán into his arms.

"Oh, Nán. That's wonderful. Asylum?"

Hernán nodded. "Yes. Sofia said we can file for my work authorization next week."

"It's the best news I've ever heard. We have to celebrate."

"My thoughts too. I already called Rudy to get a private room at Mata Hari tonight, and invited David, Brandon and Sofia. We should invite a few more people. Maryanne for sure."

"She'll be so happy. Let's go ask her."

Hernán didn't let Colin loose. "I set this up for seven o'clock." Colin nodded, puzzled. "And it's only two in the afternoon. So I was hoping we might get some private celebrating in before the party."

Light dawned in Colin's eyes. He grinned wickedly. "I'll tell Maryanne I'm taking the rest of the day off."

FIFTEEN MINUTES LATER, they entered the apartment. As soon as Colin set his keys down, Hernán pulled him close for a passionate kiss. Colin melted into his embrace, sagging in Hernán's arms. Their lips moved against each other's, confidently, lovingly.

Hernán knew every inch of Colin's body, even through his clothes. He couldn't wait to peel them off, to expose Colin's pale skin and smooth chest. To stroke his fingertips down Colin's neck and across his nipples. To go to his knees and take firm hold of Colin's beautiful dick. To bring its wet and salty tip to his mouth while Colin's eyes burned down at him.

His own hard cock pressed achingly against his trousers, and Colin's erection burned against his hip. Hernán paused the kiss reluctantly. Colin flushed already, his eyes glazed with lust and love, making Hernán's heart beat wildly in his chest.

"Mi amor," he whispered. "Thank you."

"You did it all," Colin whispered back. "You and Sofia. I just helped a little."

Hernán shook his head. "It's so much more than just help. You didn't give up on me in Provincetown when I was an ass and pushed you away. You didn't give up on me when I couldn't touch you without flinching. You let me take everything at my own pace, and waited patiently for me to come to you. You found wonderful lawyers who believed in me and got me asylum. You cared for me when I got the news about my HIV. You gave me shelter and helped me find a purpose. You fought for me when it put your own life at risk. I love you so much."

Colin's eyes gleamed and that time he kissed Hernán, his lips salty with tears. He tugged Hernán to go up the stairs with him to their room. They stretched on their bed, still partially dressed, kissing and rubbing their bodies together, driving themselves higher and higher.

"I need you, Nán," Colin finally gasped. They stood to help each other undress. Hernán straightened from removing his briefs to see Colin gazing at him in wonder. He put his hands on Hernán's bare, muscled shoulders and slowly, reverently, ran them firmly down his body.

"So beautiful," Colin whispered. They stepped close together again, Hernán's hands curling around the small of Colin's back. Their cocks pressed together between their bellies, bodies aligned like they were made to fit.

Hernán caught Colin's eyes. "When everything happened back at the end of October and we were running, you said something that came too early." Colin immediately flushed; he remembered. Hernán's heart began to thump against his chest as he continued.

"It's been almost six months since I found you in the harbor,

Colin. To some people, that isn't a lot of time, but I was waiting for you all my life. I didn't know what you looked like or where you were, but I knew you were there. I missed so much of your life, and I don't want to miss another minute."

The trembling he could feel in Colin's arms, the pride and love in his face, filled Hernán's heart to bursting. He already knew the answer, but he wanted very much to ask the question.

Hernán licked his lips, and then said softly, reverently, "Colin Felton, will you marry me?"

Colin put a hand around Hernán's neck and pulled forward until their foreheads touched. Voice low, eyes threatening to spill over, he said, "You saw things in me I didn't know were there. You shook my family out of the habits of decades to make them really look at me. You call me a warrior, but if I am it's what you brought out. If I ever run for public office, I couldn't do it without you by my side. You are my friend, and my love. You are my very soul. Yes, I would be proud to marry you."

He whooped then and swung them around in a circle, Hernán laughing in his arms.

Every step of Hernán's journey from San Marcos to Provincetown and then to Washington had carried him, all unknowing, to the man he'd dreamt of. He buried his face in Colin's shoulder, overcome.

Colin nuzzled his ear, and then said, "We're going to fly Albert and Andrea and their family in for the wedding. They should be there." He kissed the corner of Hernán's mouth. "And Isela, if we can find a way. Brijith. Your tío, if he'll come. Anyone you want." His eyes were wet and Hernán stretched to kiss the tears away from his lashes. Surprisingly, Colin chuckled softly.

"What?" Hernán prompted.

"My mother is going to go crazy over this. She'll want to throw the biggest summer wedding anyone in Nantucket has ever seen."

"Oh Lord, Rudy is going to be right in there with her, egging her on. It's lucky they all got along at Christmas."

"Would you mind, if she goes over the top? Because I'm warning you, she'll be booking the band the minute after we tell her."

Hernán chuckled. "I'd marry you in the smallest government office or in the biggest church you can find. There's only one thing I care about, and that's being able to say, 'I'd like you to meet my husband

Colin.'"

"And I'd like to introduce you to the bravest man I know, my husband Hernán." Colin said it with a smile, though his eyes brimmed with tears.

"My *husband,*" he repeated in an awed whisper. "We met when he threw himself into Provincetown Harbor to save me. He saved me at work too, when I was convinced of my limitations. He saved my family when my parents didn't even see how much pain they inflicted."

"I think we saved each other," Hernán said fervently. "We were both lost in different ways, cariño. I was drowning in fear, you in loneliness, and we didn't even know it. Then you offered me your hand for no better reason than to help a stranger. Your light cleaned away the shadows. You never pushed, only waited for me to find my way. How you could ever doubt yourself confounds me, because I've never met a stronger man.

"This country gave me asylum, Colin, but you are my heart's true home."

The End

Thank you for reading *Asylum*. I hope you enjoyed it!

Subscribe to my newsletter at *robertwinterauthor.com* for giveaways, my latest book news, LGBT romance recs and deals, and more! I won't spam or share your email address.

If you did enjoy the book, **please consider writing a review** on Amazon or other sites that discuss MM romance. I appreciate any feedback, no matter how long or short. It's a great way to let other romance fans know what you thought about this book. Being an independent author means that every review really does make a huge difference, and I'd be grateful if you take a minute to share your opinion with others.

Acknowledgments

I am deeply grateful to Dr. Christopher McMackin and Dr. Andrew C Jorgensen, who answered my questions about the current status of HIV treatment. Many thanks as well to Niels Frenzen of the USC Gould School of Law for information about the state of immigration law and the obstacles faced by those seeking asylum. Finally, I want to thank the sensitivity readers who helped make *Asylum*—hopefully—a better book. All errors are mine.

Readers love *September* by Robert Winter

2017 Rainbow Award Finalist, Best Gay Book

"September is a book filled with hurt and comfort, moving on and finding love, and living your best life."
—Joyfully Jay

"The emotional pull in this story is unbelievable. … The writing was captivating and the characters were remarkable."
—Love Bytes

"[Winter'] writing and storytelling ability are both beautifully brilliant, with characters that are full of emotion, and their plight and struggles real."
—Alpha Book Club

Reader Praise for *Every Breath You Take* by Robert Winter

2017 Rainbow Award winner for Best Gay Suspense Novel

"[T]he tension that Winter creates and builds combines perfectly with the other areas of the story, always leaving the reader with an apprehension about the next move of the perpetrator. For me, Every Breath You Take and Robert Winter deserve a full five-star rating!"
—Joyfully Jay

"The juxtaposition of the killer's stalking and escalating madness with the growing friendship and attraction between Thomas and Zachary … kept me biting my nails right up until the end."
—Scattered Thoughts and Rogue Words

"This story starts out on a murderous note, with the prologue leaving me absolutely needing to know how its dark events were going to figure in the lives of the main characters."
—It's About the Book

Excitement for *Lying Eyes* by Robert Winter

Five stars
"Every book gets better… This is an easy recommendation, even more so if you're a romantic mystery and/or suspense maven."
—Hearts on Fire

"Robert Winter is now an auto-buy author for me. Spectacular writing!!!"
—Amazon reviewer

"There are pulse-racing action scenes to go along with the intrigue and building romance, and an ending that goes above and beyond to supply gratification to the reader, as well as to the characters."
—It's About the Book

"4.5 stars!!"
—Bayou Book Junkies

"Robert Winter has definitely made it onto my favorite author list. This is his third book, and they just keep getting better!"
—Scattered Thoughts and Rogue Words

Vampire Claus by Robert Winter

"Wow wow wow, Winter stuns again with his brilliant writing. … I simply can't resist Robert Winter's writing. I've read everything he's published so far and have enjoyed every single story. From age-gap to mystery/suspense to PNR, he covers tropes like they were in his personal sandbox to play with.?
—Goodreads reviewer

"Robert Winter's stories are always creative and completely unique, and he has outdone himself with *Vampire Claus*. This novelette is complex and a bit dark, and Winter weaves an intriguing tale with a positive and hopeful message. These are characters I definitely hope to see more of in the future."
—Goodreads reviewer

"I loved this story. It was so good. A paranormal story with demons and vampires and Christmas. An odd combination, but Robert Winter makes it all very normal. It is captivatingly charming, nail-biting scary, and enchantingly sweet."
—Amazon reviewer

About the Author

Robert Winter is a Rainbow Award-winning author who lives and writes in Provincetown. He is a recovering lawyer who prefers writing about hot men in love much more than drafting a legal brief. He left behind the (allegedly) glamorous world of an international law firm to sit in his home office and dream up ways to torment his characters until they realize they are perfect for each other.

When he isn't writing, Robert likes to cook Indian food and explore new restaurants. He splits his attention between Andy, his partner of seventeen years, and Ling the Adventure Cat, who likes to fly in airplanes and explore the backyard jungle as long as the temperature and humidity are just right.

Contact Robert at the following links:

Website:
www.robertwinterauthor.com

Facebook:
facebook.com/robert.winter.921230

Goodreads:
goodreads.com/author/show/16068736.Robert_Winter

Twitter:
twitter.com/@RWinterAuthor

Email:
RobertWinterAuthor@comcast.net

Photo by Brad Fowler,
Song of Myself Photography

Made in the USA
Lexington, KY
29 July 2018